WELCOME TO PLANET LARA, BOOK ONE

"There are ... stipulations on your inheritance, Ms. Clarke."

Lara J. Clarke is used to getting her own way. Motherless at ten and raised by her oft-absent eco-warrior/philanthropist grandfather, she lives the high life afforded by her seemingly bottomless trust fund—swanky downtown Vancouver loft, apartments and villas around the world just a chartered flight away, a passport overflowing with stamps from the chicest hot spots, a closet bursting with catwalk couture, and a spoiled B-list actor boyfriend whose interest in Lara is tied to her exclusive L'Inconnu wallet.

That is, until Grandfather Archibald sheds his mortal coil in a very public manner, and Lara's privileged life is set adrift—and headed for a collision course with the gorgeous, private Thalia Island off the coast of British Columbia. According to the will, Lara will step into the role of Project Administrator, wherein she has one year to fulfill her late grandfather's dream of a self-sustaining, eco-friendly, family-centered utopia.

The stakes are real: fail, and lose access to the family fortune —forever.

Convinced Thalia Island will be an extension of the heiress lifestyle she's long led, Lara is surprised to find her new coworkers—and neighbors—aren't as pliable as the underlings of her former life. Even with the hunky lead engineer Finan Rowleigh showing her the ropes, Lara quickly learns just how unprepared she is to trade her Louboutins for steel-toed Timberlands.

When a series of calamities reveals a sinister element undermining the security of the island and her residents, Lara and Finan must reach beyond their job descriptions to protect Archibald's precious utopia from those who would do her harm.

And while keeping her late grandfather's flame alight, Lara finds her own flame burning hot for a charming, kind man who wants nothing from her but her heart.

WELCOME TO Planet Lara

ELIZA GORDON

S·G·A
BOOKS

ADVANCE PRAISE FOR

"I absolutely loved *Welcome to Planet Lara*! It made me feel all the feels ... what a crazy ride! Eliza, once again, brings her characters to life with humour, heart and realness. **I loved every minute of it and did not want it to end**! Cannot wait to find out what Eliza has in store for Lara."

— BRANDEE BUBLÉ, children's author (*O'Shae the Octopus* and *Jayde the Jaybird*)

"Smart, hilarious, and completely unpredictable, **Welcome to Planet Lara** is your next must-read. West Coast Canada **Schitt's Creek** meets **grown-up** *Nancy Drew* for a riches-to-rags adventure filled with murder, romance, mystery, and a heroine you love to hate—until the moment you realize you just love her."

— SUZY KRAUSE, author of *Sorry I Missed You* and *Valencia & Valentine*

"Eliza Gordon delivers a unique premise, delicious romance and plenty of intrigue. I loved it and can't wait for more from Planet Lara!"

— SAMANTHA YOUNG, *New York Times* and *USA Today* bestselling author

"I love it, and **I CAN'T WAIT TO READ THE NEXT ONE**. The concept is amazing, and the eco-message is so timely and very dear to my heart. [Eliza] has tackled so much, and done it with her usual spunk and zest."

— STEPHANIA SCHWARTZ, author and editor

"Welcome to Planet Lara has the perfect mix of a great read that keeps you hooked and intrigued until the very last page. After all, you never truly know what really happens beneath the surface of a person, or a place."

— KATRIN B.

"Eliza Gordon's 'Welcome to Planet Lara' is a wonderful book! I found myself reading late into the night and sneaking time during the day to finish it. I miss the characters already Lara's spirited energy and vulnerabilities draw us in and keep us rooting for her ... I can't wait to see what happens next with Lara and her peeps in the next book, 'Planet Lara Tempest.'"

— KRISTEN F.

"What a wild ride—and it's not over yet! ... If you've read Eliza Gordon before, you know she delivers on heart and humor (looking at you, Hollie Porter *wink*), but *Welcome to Planet Lara* adds in suspense, mystery, OMG, and dun-dun-dunnnn moments, along with some extra spice (eyebrow waggle)."

— KATIE D.

"Love all Eliza's books! She spins a tale that makes you unable to stop turning the pages and hopeful it will never end. *Welcome To Planet Lara* stays true to these well established facts!"

— SUSAN H.

"I really enjoy Eliza Gordon's writing. Her characters are witty, real, complex. I love their internal dialogue, and how they interact with each other. Welcome to Planet Lara has all of this!"

— STEPH B.

"Every time I hear that a new Eliza Gordon book is coming out, I get excited. You're guaranteed a funny and heartwarming book. And this book was no different."

— MIRANDA H.

"All you have to do in life is be passionate and enthusiastic, and you will have a wonderful life."

STEVE IRWIN

"You don't have to drive an electric car or live off the grid to make a difference. Start small. Do what you can. And when you stumble, get up and try again."

DR. ARCHIBALD MAGNUS CLARKE I

"Extinction is the rule. Survival is the exception."

CARL SAGAN

First edition April 2021

Cover art and design by Bailey Designs Books

Ebook ISBN-13 (ePub): 978-1-989908-02-0
Paperback ISBN-13: 978-1-989908-03-7
Hardcover ISBN: 978-1-989908-04-4

www.sgabooks.com
www.elizagordon.com | www.jennsommersby.com

To Ann
A true warrior

ALSO BY ELIZA GORDON

Dear Dwayne, With Love

I Love You, Luke Piewalker

The Revelation Cove Series:

Must Love Otters (Book One)

Hollie Porter Builds a Raft (Book Two)

Love Just Clicks (Standalone, Book Three)

AUTHOR NOTE

Welcome to Planet Lara was written during the COVID-19 pandemic of 2020. The book does not address the pathogen, its myriad international responses, or the politics associated with such. If it's going to bother you to read a book that does not include social distancing, mask wearing, canceled public events, shuttered businesses and schools, and vaccine protocols, don't read on.

And please, *please*—don't eviscerate authors in the reviews for not wanting to include this very new tragedy in our stories. An informal, rolling poll of readers and fellow writers over the last year has made it pretty clear that no one wants to read about COVID *quite* yet. Maybe by 2022, I'll include it in storylines. But probably not.

There is a casual, could-be-COVID mention in Act II, but yeah … COVID-free book, fellow humans. Wash your hands. Thank a healthcare worker and the kid at the store who restocks the toilet paper. And now, more than ever, be kind.

xo,
  Eliza

AUTHOR NOTE NO. 2

Those of you who are already Eliza Gordon fans, a few morsels for thought:

1. This is **not** a romantic comedy. In the words of one early reader, "Welcome to a sexier, more mysterious and thrilling Eliza Gordon novel. Welcome to Planet Lara." This series has a little of everything—funny moments, sure, but also family drama, intrigue, small-town life, dangerous secrets, a little mystery, some steamy romance … and an awesome dog. Of course.

2. This book **ends in a mild cliffhanger.** Don't freak out—book two, *Planet Lara: Tempest*, is written and will be released later this summer. Book three is underway at the time of this writing!

3. There is an actual **love scene** in this book. I know! I blushed all the way through writing it! It's probably a three out of five on the steam meter, and I don't use any graphic language. I tried to follow in the hallowed footsteps of the romance authors I most admire and make my scenes romantic, loving, consensual, and delicious. It's a departure from the fade-to-black in other Eliza books, but I think the characters deserved more. I hope you agree.

ONE

DEARLY BELOVED

I don't know why they have pickles on this table. My mom hates pickles. *Hated*. Past tense. I heard Rupert correct my grandfather when he mentioned my mother the other day—they were talking in Grandfather's huge office lined with bookshelves and Louis XV Savonnerie carpets and giant windows the housekeepers complain about cleaning when they don't know anyone's listening, and Rupert referred to my mother in past tense. I wasn't supposed to hear their conversation—that's why the outside door was closed. When it's closed, I'm not allowed in. But I'm very good at hearing things I'm not supposed to hear because, like that kid in my class who always smells like wet dog says, I'm so scrawny, he could stuff me into his rolling backpack and throw me into the ocean and no one would ever miss me.

I'd like to think that someone would miss me. Only now that we're speaking of my mother in past tense, I guess that's one less person who would wonder if I'm floating out to sea, trapped in a rolling backpack covered in dog hair. Also, I'd like to think my English teacher, Mrs. Buck, would be proud of me for understanding the difference between present and past tense, even if her nylons on her beefy thighs scrape together when she walks between our desks and the sound makes me shiver.

Like I was saying, I'm scrawny, so two days ago, I snuck into my grandfather's office and tucked myself into the antique liquor cabinet —he doesn't drink so the cabinet is empty and the perfect place for me to hide when I don't want his bossy housekeeper to find me because her job is to vacuum and change sheets and make Grandfather's special food but now she keeps trying to hug me and pet my hair and her boobs squish my face and I can't breathe, so she thinks I'm crying about my dead mom, my mom who's only alive in the past tense now, but I'm not crying about my dead mom. I haven't cried yet. I think that makes me the worst kid ever.

Yeah—I mean, *yes*, since Rupert won't allow me to say *yeah*—so I was in the cabinet and I heard Rupert say we needed to refer to my mother, Cordelia Josephine Clarke, in the past tense. "It will be easier for Lara if we don't give her hope that her mother will be returning." Rupert—I call him Number Two, like that character in *Austin Powers*, a movie I wasn't supposed to watch but did anyway because one of the housekeepers invited me to her daughter Madi's ninth-birthday sleepover because she felt bad for me that I never get to go to sleepovers. So I went, and Madi is basically my best friend now, but the housekeeper and her husband drink a lot of wine that comes in a box and they play their country music really loud. The biggest difference from the Number Two in the movie and Rupert Bishop is that Rupert doesn't have an eye patch and he hardly *ever* laughs or smiles and even if he *does* smile, he's like a hundred feet tall so I can't even see up to his unsmiling face most of the time.

"They didn't find a body, Rupert. They found the wrecked plane, but no Cordelia. What if she made it? What if someone in that godawful jungle has her?"

Through the slats in the square cupboard door, I saw Number Two shake his head and look down at his shiny brown loafers. One of these days, I'm going to take a black marker and color the tops of his shoes so he can't shine them anymore. I'm also going to cut off those stupid tassels and use them as fishing lures.

"Sir, this is the best course. Do not cancel the memorial. Plant the tree, give Lara some closure. Let her move on. She's only ten. Still young enough to have a satisfactory life wherein her memories will fade, even in the face of this tragedy. It's not as though she's spent a lot of time with her mother anyway."

My grandfather's face hardened for a minute, that look he gives when he's about to blow his top, his chin jutting and eyes narrowed.

"Pardon me, sir. I overstepped." Rupert folded his hands behind his back. He's not wrong, though. My mother hasn't been around for a long time. She works a lot, or so she says. When she's home, it's all fun, fun, fun, like she's trying to make up for the next time she leaves a note on my nightstand covered with Xs and Os and smiley faces and promises of trips to zoos and museums and amusement parks and my favorite ice cream shop when she gets home.

Rupert told me once that my mother's first love was her airplane. And even though she named it Lara, after me, I have always known that Lara the plane was more important to my mom than Lara the human kid.

My grandfather, unlike me, has cried a lot since the men in black suits showed up a week ago and asked for a place to talk privately. Rupert's comment has made my grandfather cry again. Maybe I will forget coloring his shoes and just drop them all—his entire collection of fancy, tasseled loafers—into the pond in the back with the koi.

Cordelia was my grandfather's only daughter. His only child, actually.

I am his only granddaughter.

Archibald Magnus Clarke the First, and only, was almost an old man when Cordelia was born. Her mother left her behind, just like Cordelia left me behind.

I haven't cried yet. Maybe I will later.

But there are pickles on this big stupid table, and Cordelia hated pickles. And everyone in the room—all these faces I've never seen before—are looking at me like they're expecting me to burst into tears at any moment.

Instead, I pick up the plate of pickles of all varieties and whistle once with my fingers tucked into my lips like Madi taught me. Once I'm sure I've got the room's undivided attention, I launch the plate overhand, anticipating the satisfaction that will come when the glass hits the de Gournay papered wall and shatters into a thousand pieces and stinky pickle juice seeps across the bamboo floor and into the fibers of the eighteenth-century Persian rug we're not supposed to wear our shoes on.

Except at the same moment, this tall, lanky kid steps into the plate's trajectory and the heavy crystal hits him instead with a dull *crack!*

Everyone in the spacious, light-filled room gasps. The kid, stunned, looks in my direction, big brown eyes wide, not quite sure what just happened. And then blood spills down the side of his head and he slumps to the floor into the pile of pickles and juice, followed by grown-ups freaking out and the big-boobed housekeeper barking orders at some other member of the house staff to get the first-aid kit and then Rupert's bony but well-manicured hand is around my arm and he's pulling me out of the solarium and forcing me down onto the soft, carpeted steps in the main foyer.

"What on earth possessed you to do that, young lady?"

I look up at him and am surprised when tears sting my eyeballs. I didn't mean to hit that kid.

"My mother hates pickles. If any of you guys even knew her, you'd know she hates pickles."

Past tense, Lara. Your mother hated *pickles.*

Rupert kneels, his joints cracking even though he's not even that old.

A commotion behind us draws our attention. Two parents huddle around the tall boy who is again on his feet. They pause just long enough for me to look at the kid, a bloody cloth pressed against the left side of his head and face.

"Sorry," I whisper.

He nods once, and they leave.

Then I start crying, and I don't stop for a year.

TWO

CUT THE RIBBON ALREADY

The cacophony pouring from the hastily constructed, oversized gazebo is the opposite of music. Maybe no one explained to Grandfather what marching bands are best at: marching. Instead, forty-odd adolescents, sweating under the hot lights in their full blue-and-white regalia, must rush out their *Born to Run* and *Uptown Funk* before they're pushed off the stage, to be replaced with the real reason all these people are crowded into this shoreline park in their finest attire, their Jimmy Choos sinking into the sand, in front of a modest structure that promises the future is just inside its double glass doors.

A giant pair of silver scissors, cast from recycled car parts, sits on an equally giant velvet, bamboo-stuffed pillow atop a 3D-printed, biodegradable table made of cornstarch and wildflower seeds that will be left out in the inevitable spring rain to melt and blossom once the ceremony ends. The bold red ribbon stretched across the structure facade trembles at its proximity to the sharpened blades.

A trumpet misfires. The audio system roars with feedback. The impressive crowd groans and flinches. Dainty, bejeweled hands not holding champagne flutes cover delicate ears against the assault.

Thankfully, the song ends. Lukewarm applause plays the marching band off the gazebo, their noise replaced by the ambient serenade of whale song and falling rain pumped through the surround-sound speakers. It makes me need to pee.

"Canapé? It's fresh, smoked wild Pacific salmon on artisan rye and topped with dill, all ingredients grown in one of Dr. Clarke's self-sustaining vertical farms."

"He grew the fish in one of his skyscrapers?"

The redheaded server looks confused. This information wasn't included in the script his boss fed him before sending him out with a tray.

"I think the salmon came from the ocean?" His Adam's apple bobs nervously. I should feel bad. Probably just a college kid trying to make tuition for next semester. Some people have to do that. He has no idea who I am. Or maybe he does, and that's why he's sweating.

"Allergic to salmon," I lie. "But I will take more bubbly." He nods and hurries away, forgetting to hand out his canapés to the buffed-and-polished deep pockets around me.

"Do not treat the staff like they're below you, Lara. You never know how quickly life can change. You might need the charity of others someday."

Grandfather's voice in my head worsens the martini headache that's already trying to push my eyeballs out of their sockets. I wish Canapé Boy would hurry up with that champagne.

I'm supposed to be backstage with Grandfather's entourage to wave at his adoring crowd and field the accolades that his years of scientific achievement and dedication to the environment and sustainability have birthed. Just waiting for Rupert's hail, at which time I will slide in behind the crowd. I tried to decline—Dr. Archibald M. Clarke I is a big boy. He doesn't need me standing up there with him faking a smile while his offering plate is passed around. But Grandfather did say he thinks this will be his last public shindig, so I will obey, like a good little cyclone is supposed to.

My phone buzzes in my black clutch. It could be Connor texting to find me in the throng, although he wasn't sure if he'd be wrapped in time to make it. Too bad. The Pacific Ocean looks beautiful from this very expensive patch of real estate. We could sneak off and get sand in our undies and hope that someone records it.

It's not Connor.

Please join us. Rupert, a.k.a. Number Two, Grandfather's steward, valet, assistant, his right-hand man in all things. Tall, pinched, British, and annoying.

Yes, sir.

He doesn't respond. Rupert tolerates me only because he is paid to do so. The feeling is mutual.

I weave through the crowd, eyes seeing through everyone so no one stops me to ask for anything. Someone is always asking the Clarkes for *something*. And as I'm here solo tonight—my assistant, Olivia, had some other engagement, and Connor, well, who knows—I have no one to run interference.

The sky purples as the sun dips a toe behind the horizon. While it's unseasonably warm for April in Vancouver, the breeze coming off the water will soon see bare-shouldered partygoers pulling on wraps and accepting tuxedo jackets from their dates.

Canapé Boy passes with a tray of champagne, and I slow my momentum to lighten his load by two flutes. The pampered, overdone blond next to me tries, and fails, to furrow her brow. "Do you need both of those?" she asks. She looks like she French-kissed a beehive.

I drink the first glass in one long pull, and then the second, never taking my eyes off her.

"Aaaahhhhh, Moët. Refreshing," I say, handing the emptied glasses back to the sweating server.

"Bitch," she growls.

I eye her augmented cleavage, one brow hiked dismissively. "Did you know the world's oceans will have more plastic than fish by 2050?" I move on.

With the last body out of my way, I manage the four metal stairs, minding the hem of my dangerously short dress and hoping my calves look gorgeous in these Louboutin stilettos, to squeeze in behind the heavy green, rough-cotton drapery surrounding the stage. Grandfather stands in the center of his small crowd, like the nucleus of a comet, the source of all this light. I don't like many people, but I adore my grandfather. And he knows it.

7

"Rupert," I say, pushing in beside him.

"My Lara Jo is here," Grandfather says, handing Rupert his custom, hand-carved cane so he can wrap his arms around me. The only hint that Archibald Clarke is ninety-four comes from his bent spine—and it's only bent because he took a spill on his solar-powered bike in Toulouse on his eighty-eighth birthday, and the spine doc couldn't do any better than the fusion that gave him the slight hunch. His brain is still sharp as a razor, his eyes as clear as a Caribbean lagoon.

Though there is the little issue of the dodgy pacemaker …

"Hey, old man, how are you tonight?"

He kisses the back of my hand and pinches my cheek. Same thing he's done every day of my life. We remain with hands clasped—even though his is smaller and thinner than years past, I still feel safest when Archibald Clarke anchors me to shore—as Rupert and the stage manager whisper and nod about getting the next phase underway.

Number Two nods at us both, pats Grandfather's shoulder, and steps out into the spotlight. The applause rolls over the audience, growing louder, punctuated with whoops and hollers.

"Showtime," I mutter to Grandfather. He winks, winds my arm through his, and retakes his cane from one of the stage assistants. His face is a mask of friendly calm, and although I am used to eyes on me, this sort of occasion does make me nervous. I'm sure someone will find something to pick apart about my outfit or hair in time for WickedStepsister's press deadline.

Rupert, center stage, unhooks and grasps the microphone like he's going to bust into some Michael Bublé. I'm surprised Bublé isn't here. He lives, like, a half hour away, the only person in the city who might be more famous and beloved than my grandfather.

With a raised, long-fingered hand most suited to piano scales and reprimands, Rupert calms the gathering. A few of his female admirers catcall from the area closest to the stage, followed by laughs. Joke's on them. Rupert doesn't have time for love and other nonsense, "and if I did, it wouldn't involve vagina."

His words, not mine, and only after an evening of Macallan "borrowed" from my teetotaler grandfather's collection of gifts he's never touched. It was one of three occasions in my life I remember Number Two behaving in a manner more akin to a real-live human than obedient robot.

"Welcome, everyone, to this glorious evening of celebration," he starts. For approximately a million minutes, he extols the many virtues of my grandfather's esteemed scientific career, his dedication to the people of Earth, his passion for sustainability, even when people have laughed him out of boardrooms for his crazy ideas, how he was Elon Musk before Elon was even a twinkle in his mother's perfectly lined eye.

"But no one is laughing now, now that we stand on the brink of an unprecedented era, on the precipice of an irreversible tipping point. In answer, Dr. Clarke has gifted us with an invigorating new way to live sustainably and in harmony with Mother Nature and our fellow earthly cohabitants. Searching the stars for new homes is a fool's errand, not when we have a beautiful home right here, crying for our help."

I roll my eyes at Rupert's melodrama and instantly regret it as a renewed surge of pain pings inside my dehydrated skull. I again promise myself I will never drink another martini as long as I live.

"You remember what I told you?" Grandfather leans over and asks under his minty breath.

"About what?"

"Everything." He winks again. I kiss his cheek. I don't know what he's talking about, but I don't have time to ask for clarification.

"And now, without further ado, I would be so very honored if you would join me in welcoming everyone's favorite eco-warrior, the son of Gaia herself, Dr. Archibald Magnus Clarke!"

More applause, more whoops. As we walk to center stage, I spy a woman in the front row with tears streaming down her face.

Archibald M. Clarke is happy to take the tall stool Rupert slides behind him. I help him onto it, holding his cane. Under the lights, he looks tired—I know he's been working around the clock to maintain his myriad projects and make sure they're all ready to be managed by his crack crew of experts once he "abandons this mortal coil." He's tried to rope me into helping, but I won't hear of him leaving me, so no, Grandfather, leave me out of it and get back to work.

His speech continues on where Rupert's left off. I stand next to him, his hand still clasped in mine, my obedient, grateful Clarke smile in place as he introduces me to his "friends." I nod at the appropriate times, even if I'm mostly just scanning for the nearest champagne fountain. The crowd slurps up Grandfather's words like that fresh, wild Pacific salmon still making its rounds.

"Enough about me," Grandfather finally says, the onlookers oohing and aahing and clapping again. "Let us cut this ribbon and welcome our generous visitors to the presentation center for the Nature Tower, Vancouver's first eco-cooperative, self-sustaining, family-friendly, mixed-use high-rise community!"

The Nature Tower. One of many ongoing Archibald Clarke projects —I cannot possibly keep them all straight, despite long discussions over our last-Sunday-of-the-month family dinners. And by family, I mean Grandfather, me, and Number Two. That's it. We're all that's left of the Clarke clan, a dynasty started in Europe via textile manufacturing and railways during the early days of the Industrial Revolution and moved to America in the late 1800s to finance inventors and thinkers. The Clarkes are excellent with business, not so excellent with reproduction to secure the family's lineage. Too busy thinking to make babies.

And Rupert isn't even a blood relative. He's just been with Archibald for so long, he's become a remora, suction-cupped to my grandfather's flank as they navigate the tempestuous waters of science and discovery.

Either way, I'm usually three sheets to the wind by the time they get heated about the number of hipsters and free-range chickens their high-rises will house.

Rupert steps in with the giant, shiny shears as my grandfather finally releases my sweaty hand. Archibald takes the scissors; the red ribbon before us has stilled. It has accepted its fate.

We begin the count. "Three! Two! One—"

The scissors plunk noisily to the stage floor, followed immediately by my grandfather keeling face-first onto the red-carpet-covered plywood.

Everyone freezes, me included, the only sound the subtle recording of keening whales and steady rain floating from the speakers.

Followed in short order by shouts and yells that aren't quite screams but probably could be. I drop to Grandfather's side, turn him over, grab his hand, and pat his cheeks. "Open your eyes, Archie. Let me see you in there," I demand.

He obliges, his blue eyes bright as the sunrise. "Take this," he says, pointing to the sole piece of jewelry I've ever seen him wear. "My little cyclone." He struggles to remove his thick white-gold-and-stone ring as the crowd crushes closer to the stage to see what the hell has just happened.

"Grandfather, keep your ring on. We're going to get you some help."

"I love you," he says, and then his hands flop to his chest and his eyes fixate on something overhead, the light draining from them like an incandescent bulb whose filament has just flamed out.

"Grandfather ... Archie!" I yell, patting his face harder, shaking his shoulders. "Wake up! Please wake up!"

Panicked assistants converge from offstage. Rupert pushes me aside to make way for the audience member who has rushed up the gazebo stairs and is initiating CPR ...

I lean back on my haunches in my too-short evening dress and watch Rupert and this stranger bounce on my grandfather's rib cage to attempt to restart the heart I know has finally given up. Memories of my mother's wake flood into my head, what later became known as The Pickle Incident. Whatever happened to that kid ... one of the few things I've done that I actually feel guilty about.

I wish I had something to throw right now.

"Lara, move!" Rupert barks as Grandfather is hoisted onto a stretcher. I hop back, numb, legs tingling from crouching, as my last remaining relative is carried behind that heavy green curtain, away from public view. He's surrounded by so many people, I only catch a brief glimpse of his smiling but bluish face, glazed eyes staring into nothingness.

Another assistant appears next to me, her hand on my arm, her headset making her look like an alien or maybe an astronaut. "Ms. Clarke, Ms. Clarke, do you want to go in the ambulance?"

I look at her, see her mouth moving, but I'm underwater.

The red ribbon dances before us, happily untouched by those menacing, giant silver scissors now left forgotten on the stage.

Inches from the pointy toe of my shoe sits Grandfather's ring. I bend to pick it up.

Slide it on my middle finger. The dark red stone stares up at me, confused.

It's still warm.

THREE

MUSHROOM SAUCE

The earth has her mouth wide open, awaiting the arrival of Archibald Magnus Clarke I. And unlike the ribbon-cutting ceremony of ten days ago, today's weather is more like a normal spring day in our fair coastal city.

Number Two offers his arm as we follow the pallbearers up the graveled path and through the lush, forested area on the back of my grandfather's rolling estate. In true Archibald M. Clarke fashion, his final wishes eschewed the idea of a traditional cemetery, places he called "abominations of the modern age, the ground poisoned by the toxic chemicals from chemically embalmed corpses and overpriced boxes made of lethal varnishes, all in the name of vanity." Even the idea of cremation got his ire up: one human body burned to ash emits about 250 pounds of carbon dioxide into the air.

Yes, good old Archie had some Opinions with a capital O.

Today, he's in a plain wooden box, the wood harvested from a dead tree on this very property, untreated and held together with wooden screws and biscuit joints. My grandfather himself is dressed head to toe in a mushroom burial suit wherein the mushroom spores will eventually eat him and absorb the toxins released by his decomposing body, thereby soaking all his juicy juices into the soil and nourishing the green lawn and forest around him. Like Grandpa Soup for all the flourishing flora.

The idea of mushrooms, soup or otherwise, turns my stomach. The no-martini rule I swore to myself the night of the ribbon cutting lasted approximately four hours. Hey, my grandfather dropped dead in front of me and five hundred of his closest friends. I'm grieving. Martinis are good listeners.

"You're green," Number Two says.

"You wouldn't happen to have a flask on you?"

He tightens his clench on my arm and shifts the umbrella against a gust. *Guess that's a no.*

"Today of all days, Lara," he scolds. "You couldn't remain sober, even for this?"

"I am sober."

Rupert is enough taller than I am, even in my heels, I don't bother tilting my head to see the disappointment on his face.

Someone calls my name from behind. "Wait up!"

"He does know this is a funeral, not a game of dodgeball," Rupert says. He never hides his disdain for Connor Mayson. Instead, he releases my arm and walks ahead, taking the umbrella with him.

"Hey, babe, yeah, sorry. I forgot the gate code." Connor Mayson is a legend in his own mind. A model since thirteen—the earliest age deemed safe enough for Accutane to clean up the skin overlying that perfect bone structure—he transitioned into acting a few years ago when the modeling gigs started going to younger, fresher faces. He enjoys a bit of celebrity locally and never shies away from groupies of his one hit TV show, *Super George*, about an accountant who gets caught in a terrible storm and wakes up with X-Men-like powers, but between you and me, the show is terrible. Connor is hot, but he can't act his way out of a paper bag.

And, as usual, he has his umbrella. "Do you *know* how much I pay to keep my hair looking like this?" is his most common refrain. Right after bragging about how much he paid for the umbrella at some swanky umbrella store downtown. And by *he* paid, he means *I* paid. Connor pays for nothing if he can help it.

"Is your grandfather in that box? He's, like, super rich, and they're burying him in that? Looks like someone nailed it together from an old Costco pallet."

"No nails."

"What?"

"Never mind." I don't have the energy to explain the part about steel nails leaching into the soil as they disintegrate. Or something. Grandfather talked at length about his plans for his eternal sleep. I don't think my bloodstream was entirely free of Grey Goose that day.

The night of the fundraiser, I rode in the ambulance with my dead grandfather, holding his ever-cooling hand during the short ride through downtown Vancouver, lights and sirens clearing our path. As soon as the ER doctor pronounced Archibald Magnus Clarke I assuredly deceased, I wandered out of the hospital exit, into the nearest bar.

Rupert had to pick me up at closing, pay the tab because I somehow lost my clutch, chastising and scolding me all the way to my loft.

He doesn't know the conversation I had with Grandfather earlier that week, the one where I was actually sober, the one that involved him revealing he'd stopped taking his heart medication weeks ago, the one where he knew his time was coming—and he was ready for it. Rupert doesn't need to know that I spent my last wonderful moments with Grandfather without an audience or a giant red ribbon. I'd like to think that good old Archie was having a hearty laugh (pun intended) while all those posh society types whispered, aghast, behind their 98 percent post-consumer recycled paper cocktail napkins while the well-intended frantically tried to coax his ticker back to life.

Connor's voice is still annoying my ears as we reach the gaping maw. He shuts up when he sees the pallbearers, men hired from the funeral home who had to sign a formidable stack of nondisclosure agreements and were not allowed to bring phones to the burial site. They ease Grandfather onto the green straps that will lower him into the arms of his original and favorite lover.

About ten feet away, a man dressed in black with a colorful stole emerges from the cover of the trees. My throat instantly tightens with emotion. My grandfather was not a religious man, but he was very spiritual. The man approaching with the kind eyes and soft smile is Father Brooks—I don't know if he's an ordained minister or a priest or what—but he and my grandfather have been very close for the last twenty-five years, their debates about God versus Gaia versus Carl Sagan and his *Cosmos* often turning loud and always running late into the night, at least until Grandfather would pull out a nice bottle of sparkling water for himself and an expensive red for Father Brooks. That would calm things down.

When I was a young teenager, I wondered if perhaps Father Brooks was my grandfather's boyfriend … I wished he were, so my grandfather wouldn't be alone in his golden years, but no. Just two very good friends who knew each other better than the wrinkles on their own faces.

Father Brooks, surprisingly, I like very much.

"Lara," he says as he stops in front of me. That's it. The tears tumble down my face. Father Brooks hugs me and then offers a clean, starched white handkerchief from inside his black suit coat. I dab at the mascara threatening to streak my flawless foundation as Brooks solemnly greets Rupert.

"Hi, I'm Connor, Lara's boyfriend." He reaches out and pumps the father's hand like he's about to buy a used car. I jab Connor in the side.

Father Brooks returns his attention to me. "I'll say a little about your granddad, and then if you have anything you want to add, I'm sure he'd love to hear it."

I nod. I'm not saying anything in front of these men. Sure, if it were just me and Father Brooks having a chat with my dead grandfather, maybe. But it's not. And showing any sign of weakness in front of Number Two or Connor is unwise. Even the tears are a risk.

We take our spots next to the hole in the ground. The pallbearers have made themselves scarce, though still within our sight line. This is good. If one of them dared to pull out any sort of recording device or snap a photo, I'd finally get to use the MMA moves I've been learning from my brutally overpriced trainer.

The wind picks up Father Brooks's wispy, white hair for a beat before it floats back against his pink scalp. He takes a deep breath, relaxes his shoulders, and launches softly into his eulogy. He reminisces about funny moments between him and my grandfather over the years, how they met at a fundraiser for upgrading the turbines of California's wind farms back in the '90s, held by a Canadian clean-energy innovator; he speaks slowly and reverently about those hard years after my mother died and Archie was left as the sole caretaker for a distraught, precocious ten-year-old; and he details the pride my grandfather felt when he realized his dream of building Thalia Island, the private, eco-friendly utopia off the BC coast that has become the perfect marriage between nature and community.

"And although he was hard on you, Lara, he loved you. With every ounce of his heart."

I nod and look at my grandfather's rough casket through blurred eyes, twisting his ring around my middle finger. It's too big, but I haven't taken it off since the night he died. And I don't care about the tears now. In an uncharacteristic moment of tenderness, Number Two squeezes my shoulder.

With a few final words, Father Brooks beckons the pallbearers back to lower Grandfather all the way into the ground so we can each toss a handful of soil as a final wish for his safe journey to wherever he's going next.

"Babe …" Connor's whisper intrudes. "I gotta go. I have an audition downtown in an hour—for a pit-wipe commercial—and I need to change out of this monkey suit into something less morbid."

I stare at him, jaw clenched. He quickly kisses the side of my mouth and jogs away. My cheeks superheat—I cannot believe my so-called boyfriend just bailed on my only relative's funeral to go to an audition for deodorant.

Rupert clears his throat, lips pursed, and hikes an eyebrow with such disgust, I'm afraid it will get stuck there. "Honestly, Lara …"

"Shut it."

Father Brooks nods once at me—my cue to scoop up some soft, rich earth and drop it on my grandfather's mushroomy bed. Rupert follows suit, kneeling with his head down for a full minute, sniffing back his own tears, before releasing his final goodbye. Father Brooks whispers his thanks to the pallbearers and then leads our procession of two back down the gravel path toward Clarke Manor.

Out of the corner of my eye, I swear I see something move in the trees.

I pause, the rain hitting my face as Rupert continues on with the umbrella.

"Lara?" he pauses and asks.

I squint and scan the wooded area, fists clenched, the cortisol readying for battle. *If that's the fucking paparazzi, I will feed them their cameras.*

Nothing moves. The rain picks up.

"I thought I saw someone."

Rupert wraps an arm around my shoulders. "No one would get past Humboldt."

"He'd probably slobber them to death," I say, my heart slowing at the thought of that ridiculous dog. Big bark, no bite, more saliva than a garden slug. "Shit, what are we going to do with him now?"

"We can talk about it later," Rupert says, dropping his arm, as if he's just expended his daily kindness quota. "Will you be staying for dinner?"

"On a liquid diet, remember?"

He grunts and shakes his head once. There we go. The disappointment is back. That's more like it.

We've reached the portico outside the double side doors that lead into the mudroom and fitness wing of the ultramodern, carbon-neutral mansion. Rupert closes his umbrella and keys in the code to open the door, but instead of following the two men inside, I offer my hand to Father Brooks.

"Thank you for being here for him. I know he appreciated it."

"I wouldn't have missed it for the world. He was my best friend," Father Brooks says, his eyes watery.

I nod, visualizing myself as an ice queen so the tears are chased back to where they belong. "He was lucky to have your companionship all these years."

"I'll phone you day after tomorrow to finalize the meeting with your grandfather's lawyers, for the will," Rupert says. He bobs his head once and then disappears into the house. Humboldt barks from somewhere deep within. A relief—I won't be attacked by an affectionate bullmastiff with no respect for boundaries. My assistant just had this skirt dry-cleaned from the last time it was slimed.

"Take care, Father Brooks." I offer a tight smile and then go to move around him and toward my waiting car. His gentle hand on my arm stops me.

"You are not alone, Lara, even if it might seem like it."

"Thank you, but it does, in fact, seem like it." I reach on tiptoes and plant a quick kiss against his soft, jowly cheek, and hurry away before he has a chance to offer any more heartbreaking truths.

FOUR

FUN TIME WITH LAWYERS

I've been in lawyers' offices before. This one is no different. Dark paneling, shelves of law books, the western wall nothing but glass overlooking downtown and beyond, the line where the ocean sneaks in to kiss Vancouver's shore. The table is so big, it's laughable. I can't even imagine how many attorneys work in this firm to require a table this excessive. It's probably not even sourced from sustainable teak. How could Grandfather trust such a place with the handling of his estate? At least it looks clean with its near-blinding, polished shine.

The cup of tea sitting before me steams on its saucer. I hate Earl Grey—my stomach is already a bit unsteady and sloshy—but the pretty young assistant didn't have ginger or peppermint, so I get what I get, especially since my own assistant, Olivia, seems to have fallen off the grid. She was supposed to arrange a car and be here for this—that *is* what I pay her for, after all, but apparently, she is "sick" and "doesn't want to spread her germs."

I'm not heartless, but the last time Olivia was "sick," it was from a bad reaction to Botox. She couldn't smile for three weeks, but I don't need her to smile to manage my affairs.

Finally, the door opens and Rupert sashays in, a black, cactus-leather portfolio tucked under one arm. He's followed in short order by two other people, a man and a woman, both dressed in professional navy suits with white shirts and only minimal splashes of color, both at least in their forties. Add some dark glasses and they could be second string for the Matrix agents.

Rupert slides into the high-backed, wheeled chair to my left and offers a tight smile of hello.

"Ms. Clarke, thank you for being here today," the woman says as she sits at the head of the table. "I'm Heather Smithe and this is my colleague, Arthur Leyton. First, let me express our deepest condolences for the loss of your grandfather. He was truly an incredible man who did so much for everyone he knew, and I'm confident his legacy will live on through you."

I nod, barely able to swallow. *I'm not really legacy material, Ms. Smithe, but thanks.*

"As you know, we are here today to read your Grandfather's last will and testament, as well as discuss the finer points of his legacy plan as it pertains to you and Mr. Bishop." She bobs her head politely toward Rupert. I've called him Number Two for so long, I forgot he even had a last name. "If, at any point, you have questions, do feel free to stop and ask. Also—" Heather Smithe stops talking, makes eye contact with the young, tea-bearing assistant from earlier who has quietly reappeared, and with only a single gesture from her boss, the young woman hustles over and opens a drawer in an imposing side cupboard that matches the monstrous conference table. From it she withdraws a legal pad and pen and quickly deposits both in front of me. "In case you would like to take notes, Ms. Clarke."

The young assistant slinks away again. Five bucks says that in order to work here, you must pass a test to prove how quietly you can move through a gauntlet of legal journals and overfull coffee cups.

Heather Smithe and Arthur Leyton tag-team to explain my grandfather's many accomplishments, as well as the money he smartly invested over the duration of his life. As a result, his estate is worth a substantial sum—substantial, as in equivalent to the GDP of Iceland—which is ironic since he often touted Iceland as a superb example of a country harnessing its natural resources (volcanoes) responsibly and sustainably.

"As you know, Dr. Clarke had a number of projects in development at the time of his death, and work will continue on these projects as supported by Clarke Innovations and the Archibald M. Clarke Foundation, overseen by his board of directors, which includes myself, Mr. Bishop, and four other members handpicked by your grandfather over the last decade. It's a solid team dedicated to maintaining the integrity of Dr. Clarke's lifelong vision."

My eyelids feel heavy. I wish I could speed this along and get to the part where they tell me what Grandfather left me with so I can get a drink in this building's swanky penthouse bar. Instead, I pick up my pen and doodle circles and poorly rendered sunflowers to make it look like I'm taking notes. Anything to distract me from the reality that Grandfather is dead and mushroom spores are eating what's left of him at this very moment.

"With regard to Thalia Island, your grandfather's wish to welcome residents and continue forward with this groundbreaking experiment is still on track." Heather Smithe stops speaking long enough to take a drink from her own teacup and then exchange glances with Arthur Leyton and Rupert. She clears her throat. "Your portion of Archibald's estate is a worthy sum, of course. You were among his favorite people, as you know, and you are his sole surviving heir." Heather smiles. She has lipstick on her teeth.

She opens yet another folder and slides a paper across the table to me. I pick it up, my eyes swimming in the legalese as I scan for a dollar amount. I know this makes me sound like an asshole, but Grandfather likes his jokes—it was one thing he and I shared, the back-and-forth of trying to outdo one another—but I'm not in the mood for a chuckle right now. I just need to know what my life is going to look like now that he's gone.

"I'm sorry, can you translate this for me?"

Heather Smithe clears her throat again. She'd better not be coming down with something she'll share with me. Connor and I have Paris plans coming up. "Your portion of the inheritance includes interest in several of his ecological funds and initiatives, as well as majority ownership of Thalia Island."

I sit up a little straighter. "Okayyyy ... that's odd, since I've never been there." I click the ballpoint of my pen closed and set it down on the legal pad. "I'm sorry for seeming crass, but what I really need to know is if he's left me with a stipend or monthly dollar amount—"

"Of course, he has," Rupert interrupts.

"There are, however, stipulations on your inheritance, Ms. Clarke," Arthur Leyton says, folding his hands on the shiny tabletop. He points at the document sitting in front of me. "In order for you to access the funds and privileges left behind by Archibald, you will be required to move to and oversee the operations on Thalia Island."

The only sound in the room is the subtle whirr of an overhead vent.

"I'm sorry—what does that mean? I have a loft, a home here in Vancouver, plus our place in Zurich, the house in Copenhagen, the estate outside of London. I can't just move to some random island."

Arthur Leyton scoops up the stack of papers in front of him and affixes his reading glasses to the end of his bulbous nose once again. "In your grandfather's own words: 'My granddaughter, Lara Josephine Clarke, will assume the role of Project Administrator for Thalia Island under the joint umbrella of the Archibald M. Clarke Foundation and Clarke Innovations, wherein her duties will include (but not be limited to) overseeing the administration of the town council (until such time as elections are suitable and appropriate), establishment of residents, assignation of community roles including emergency services, fiscal management, and promotion of approved small businesses within the town, monitoring and managing the island's unique ecological footprint and organic farming output in tandem with the skilled staff already living on the island at the time of my death, as well as the furthered commitment to making the utopia of Thalia Island an example of sustainability, community, and cooperative living for the rest of Canada, and the world.'

"'Lara will have the period of one year from the date of execution of my last will and testament to complete the tasks listed in Schedule

A (attached) and usher Thalia Island into her second year of successful operation. If Lara is unable to complete the tasks as delineated in Schedule A, she will be removed from her position and residence on Thalia Island and granted a yearly sum of $30,000 CAD to cover living necessities, in perpetuity, with all additional interests and investments redirected to the Archibald M. Clarke Foundation.'"

Arthur Leyton sets the pages back onto the table in front of him and removes his reading glasses before looking directly at me.

I scan their faces—all three of them—for evidence that this is a joke.

No one looks like they're about to burst into giggles. In fact, no one looks much like anything except deadly serious.

What.

The.

Fuck.

My arm sweeps the tabletop, sending the legal pad, pen, and now-cold tea spinning across the room where it all slams into the long teak side cabinet. The cup breaks, Earl Grey soaking into my stupid doodles and the carpet underneath.

I stand and straighten my skirt. "You are insane. All of you." I turn face-on to Rupert, who looks exhausted and thin in his tailored suit. "And *you*—you engineered this so you could scoop up this big pot of gold for yourself, didn't you, you conniving, posh bastard."

"Lara, please, sit down. No need for another of your outbursts," Rupert says.

"Are you *kidding* me right now?"

Rupert stands abruptly. "You have an opportunity here to prove to your grandfather that you're not the spoiled brat—with obvious anger issues—we've all come to know over the last decade."

"Ha!" I spin and stomp away from him, as well as I can stomp in four-inch Louboutins.

"Where are you going? The meeting isn't finished, Lara," Rupert commands.

Shit. My purse. I stomp back over to my abandoned spot at the table and grab my purse from my chair. "Meeting's finished for me. Enjoy all your damn money, you weasel."

I storm toward the mammoth door, past the wide-eyed assistant who has already scurried over like a Roomba to clean up my mess. I yank on the handle, bracing to pull it open. "This goddamn door is a fire hazard!" Once it's propped against my body, the noise from the outside offices pauses as everyone within earshot stops what they're doing to look at me.

I pivot to face the morons still at the conference room table, the ridiculously heavy door trying to push me out of the way as my slippery-bottomed shoes refuse to grab onto the carpet. "I'll get my own team of greasy lawyers and prove that you're all out of your minds. My grandfather would die all over again if he saw the shady, underhanded malfeasance going on in this third-rate shark shack in—"

The door wins. It pushes me out into the hallway and closes with a final heavy click. All the workers in their perfect little suits with their little phones against their stupid ears and the stupid papers in their hands and the fume-spewing copy machine lids open—they're all staring at me.

Just for the hell of it, I grab a potted plant off the top of one of the wooden filing cabinets and tuck it under my arm. "I'm taking this. You people can't be trusted to care for a plant, not after what you've done to my grandfather's estate. Deduct it from my thirty grand a year!"

FIVE

CHLOROPHYTUM COMOSUM

I power walk as quickly as my tight skirt will allow toward reception, the long, skinny leaves of my new plant bouncing frantically with every step. I'm glad when some other suckerfish opens the glass double doors for me to exit the office suite. I'm furious enough that I might break those too—and enjoy it.

This building has an elevator attendant. Like we're in some New York City high-rise. *As if.*

"Ma'am?" he asks.

"Do I LOOK like a ma'am to you?"

He even has the white gloves. "Miss?"

"Exactly," I say. The doors ding closed, but we don't move. He's waiting for me to give him a floor number. "The penthouse bar. Now."

"Um, ma—I mean, miss, the penthouse was bought and converted last year. It's a private residence now."

"Probably one of those snakes sitting at the conference table," I mumble.

"Pardon me?"

"Nothing," I growl. "Ground floor, then."

He pushes the L button. I'll go to The Lobby Lounge at the Fairmont. They never let me down.

He stares at me for a beat too long.

"Can I help you with something?"

"No, miss. I mean, will you be needing a cab or car service?"

"Of course," I say, my return stare pointed.

As soon as the car stops and the doors open, the attendant scurries across the lobby and mutters something to the huge Black dude sitting behind the security desk. He lifts an eyebrow at me but then stands, walks around the counter, and meets me just as Elevator Kid nods and hurries back to push the buttons in his box.

"A car?"

"Yes, ma'am, right this way." He emphasizes the *ma'am* as he holds out a hand to direct me toward the building's front doors.

The *click-click-click* of my heels echoes around the monolithic, sterile lobby.

It's raining again. A lone yellow taxi sits at the curb of the half-round driveway in front of the building. The security guard signals for it, and the taxi's roof light goes off. The driver slides to a halt in front of us; the security guard opens the door for me, but he doesn't make eye contact as I shimmy into the back seat. I *really* need Olivia to talk to my tailor about how tight these pencil skirts are.

"Hotel Fairmont Pacific Rim," I say. The door slams closed behind me. I give the guard a dirty look, but he's already walking away.

"That's close enough to walk. You sure you want a ride?"

I glare at the driver in his rearview mirror, not looking at the seat under me for fear of what germs are waiting to soak into my flesh.

"I'm just saying, it's a minimum charge—"

"I will give you fifty dollars right now to please just drive."

"Ten-four," he says, shifting his Prius into motion. The fact that he's even driving a Prius—yes, my grandfather had a lot to do with the expansion of hybrid vehicles used as taxis in Vancouver after the first one was put into service in 2000 by a smart-minded cabbie named Andrew Grant. My grandfather's fingerprints are everywhere. He did a lot of good for so many people. He loved this city, this country. He loved the whole planet, even though it's filled with bloodsucking syco-phants who didn't deserve him. He had a pure heart.

And that's why those people on the fifteenth floor are taking advantage of him by thieving me out of my birthright.

My rage reasserts itself in the five minutes it takes for the cabbie to deliver me to the hotel's front entrance. As promised, I hand him a red fifty-dollar bill and climb out without a backward glance.

The bar is right where I left it. When was I here last?

Who cares.

I hustle through the lobby and into the lounge, scooting onto a stool at the bar. I set my new plant on the counter next to me, and remembering the vicious martini headache that never seems to go away, I order a mojito. "Two, actually," I say.

"One for your plant?" The bartender, a cute young thing who probably can't even grow a respectable Stanley Cup Playoff beard, smiles.

"She's thirsty. Her former owners mistreated her." The bar top in front of me needs to be wiped down again before I will touch it. I tap a fingernail to the granite.

"It's clean," the bartender says.

"Wipe it anyway, please." He lifts his brows and grabs a white towel perfumed with eau de bleach, sweeps it across the counter, and then follows with paper napkins.

"Thank you."

He nods once and then busies himself with my drinks.

I pull out my phone, angry that Olivia hasn't gotten back to me today but not surprised to see the messages from Connor: *Are we rich? LOL …*

As if my family's money has anything to do with him.

I startle when the phone rings in my palm. I slide my thumb across it. He talks before I even say hello.

"Hey, babe! Where are you? I'm just finishing up—one sec, Lar," he says, the phone away from his mouth so he can talk to someone else. "Yeah, bye, Suze!" The sound of cheeks being kissed twice. *You're not even French, you idiot.* "See you guys next week!—Hey, sorry, babe. Class just ended. I'm so exhausted. You know how draining mono-logue workshops are."

Certainly as exhausting as a real job, like digging a ditch or curing cancer.

"Anyway, where are you? How'd your meeting go? Did you get my text?"

"I'm at the Fairmont."

"Which one?"

"Pacific Rim. Always the same one, Connor."

"Ooooooh la-la," he sings.

The bartender slides the mojitos in front of me and my plant and offers a polite smile. "Join me if you want." I hang up and drop my phone into my bag. At least if I get sauced before Connor gets here, we can check into a room and I can sleep through whatever new sexual position he wants to try this week.

My mojito goes down smooth and quick, just as I like it. "You don't mind," I say to my plant, grabbing her mojito. "You don't seem in the mood." I lied to the bartender, though. Her former owners *did* take good care of her. She's very healthy and green. "I hope I don't kill you."

My phone buzzes again in my purse. Hoping it's Olivia responding to the dozen messages I've sent—we're definitely going to have to talk about this situation because I can't pay her out of my yearly stipend—but upon further inspection, it's just Rupert. "No." I zip my bag closed. I order a third drink, and the bartender slides a menu in front of me too. He's trying to slow me down so he doesn't have to cut me off. I know how this works.

While I still can walk a straight line, I ask the young cutie to babysit my plant and excuse myself to the front counter where I arrange a suite. Then I don't have to worry about getting home, and the bartender will continue serving until I black out.

I flash my key card at him once I resume my position at the bar, which is still mostly empty other than some loud tourists across the lobby.

"Do they think that draping themselves in red maple leaves and T-shirts printed with moose will help them blend in?"

"Not with those accents," the bartender says, winking once.

He's actually kind of adorable with that mop of brownish-blond hair and the tattoos his long sleeves aren't quite covering. The mojitos are sanding down the edges of my earlier fury and letting my inhibitions out into the pasture, which is their absolute favorite place to hang out.

"*Chlorophytum comosum*," the bartender says.

"Gesundheit."

"Nooo, I mean the plant. It's a spider plant. Some people call it a St. Bernard's lily or an airplane plant."

"Definitely less threatening than spider plant." I squint to read his name tag. "Benny … what's a green thumb like you doing in a place like this?"

"Waiting for my big break?" He smiles again. It's wide and natural, not an overprocessed white like Connor and his small-screen friends. Benny regales me with tales of his intoxicating life in rural Calgary, how he disappointed his father by not taking over the family's canola farm after graduating from the University of Manitoba with a BSc in plant biotechnology, about his move out here after graduation to try to break into the burgeoning marijuana industry.

"Right. Weed is big business here," I say.

"Especially now that it's legal."

I hold my tongue before telling him about my grandfather's investment in industrial hemp initiatives. Instead Benny opens his mouth and an encyclopedic knowledge of the history of hemp falls out: it originated in China around 2800 BCE, is super durable, grows fast, is one of the strongest natural fibers in the world. Like he said, he's still waiting for his cherry job to open in the cannabis sector, so until then, he's serving cosmopolitans to Vancouver's elite.

"So, cannabis—not canola."

"Yep."

"And your dad is displeased."

"Yep." He chuckles.

"I'm well versed in the practice of disappointing family." I pour a healthy swallow into my mouth. "What do you know about organic farming?"

"If I answer that, it will reveal what a huge nerd I am."

"Probably." I crunch an ice cube. "But therein lies the irony. I've just inherited some minuscule island where a bunch of hippies live and grow their own food, and I'll be lucky if my new plant child survives the week."

"An island? Impressive."

"It's not."

"Want to talk about it?" he asks.

"No."

Benny smiles and wipes the surrounding counter. More bleach wafts by. I'm grateful.

"How do you like Vancouver?"

"This city is cold. Not the weather—the people. Tough to make friends."

"You sound like Olivia."

"Who's Olivia?"

"Never mind," I say, uninterested in talking about my homesick assistant who misses Toronto and never stops whining about it. "Maybe you should ride around in a pickup truck and wear a cowboy hat. Chew on a piece of hay or something. That will get the city girls fired up. Plenty of romance novels written about cowboys."

Benny laughs again. "I have never chewed a piece of hay in my life."

"Maybe you should try it. Besides, big and cold is better than a small and nosy. Under a hundred thousand people and everyone knows your business."

He shrugs.

"Tell me, Benny, and then make me another mojito: Do you farm folks really romp in haylofts where there are bugs and dirt and actual cow poop?"

He laughs loudly, startling a woman down the bar.

"I can't speak for my fellow Calgarians, but I, for one, have never romped in cow poop."

"But there is dirt. And bugs."

"You and your plant should probably stay in the city." Benny—

which doesn't sound like a cowboy name, or does it?—obliges with that fourth mojito, pausing his chitchat only to serve the other guests who trickle in. He's deep into a discussion about the multitude of insect pests that threaten healthy canola crops when a body wraps itself around me from behind and bites my earlobe. Benny's eyebrow hikes, and I push Connor away.

"God, gross. Keep your saliva to yourself," I say, my words not quite slurred yet.

"That's not what you said the other night," Connor purrs. Ick. He knows how I feel about PDA.

"Benny, this is Connor. He's an ac-*tor*."

"Hey, Benny," Connor says, reaching over the bar. "I'll have whatever she's having, though it smells like she might be a little ahead of me." He pinches my ass; I backhand him across the chest.

Benny's whole demeanor changes as he makes Connor a drink. "That'll be $18," he says.

"Oh, just throw it on Lara's tab."

"How chivalrous," I say. Benny offers a tight smirk and disappears with his bleach towel. I guess that's the end of the story of Benny the Cannabis Cowboy in the Cold Coastal City.

Connor sips at the mojito and shivers. "Damn, that's strong." He tries to spin me in on my white-leather bar stool to face him. "Sooo, babe, tell me how today went."

"It was a meeting. Like any other meeting."

"And?"

I finish my drink, nausea prickling at the edges of my stomach. I slide the menu in front of me and flop it open. "I need bread. Benny!"

"Babe, keep it down. Other people in here."

"Well, if you're lucky, maybe one of them'll come ask for your autograph," I say, even louder.

Benny reappears.

"What do you have with bread in it, Benny the Cannabis Cowboy?"

"I thought you were doing a carb-free thing, babe," Connor says, trying to slide the menu away. I yank it back and flip it open again, flashing Connor a warning look.

"I can bring you our chickpea hummus with flatbread, or the garlic panisse—"

"Wait! Sushi? You have sushi!"

Benny nods.

"I'll take the hummus and flatbread and the Raw Bar platter."

Connor chuckles. "That's a lot of food, babe."

I glare at him. "Stop talking, Connor Mayson. And stop calling me *babe*. Besides, I'm not the one who has to stay skinny for my film career." Returning my attention to Benny, I close the menu but don't give it back to him. "And after that, dessert."

"Whatever the lady wants," Benny says, stepping away to key in my order.

"You OK, Lara? You only eat like this when something's not right."

I sip the ice water that has magically appeared in front of me. "Everything's great. My mother is dead, my grandfather is dead, Number Two and the lawyers are trying to cheat me out of my inheritance—"

"Wait—what?"

"Mm-hmm. He gave me that stupid island and I'm supposed to, like, run it or something ..." Whoa, the mojito juice is definitely settling into the wrinkles in my brain now. "Anyway, if I don't do it or manage it or whatever they want, I'm booted out."

"Booted out ... you mean, cut off?"

"I don't know." I rest my head on my folded arms.

A hand shakes my shoulder. "Lara, babe ..." Connor's voice pisses me off. I throw my head back and reach across for his mojito. He watches me while I finish it.

"My feet hurt in these shoes," I say, kicking them off. Ahhhh, the metal footrest on the bar stool feels so good on my aching soles. Or is it my aching soul?

"Why are you laughing?"

"I just made a joke ... didn't you get it?" Did I even say it out loud?

"Lara ..."

"Never mind, *Connor*. You wouldn't get it anyway." I slide a finger under one of my new plant's long leaves. "Isn't she pretty? She needs a name."

"Who needs a name?"

"My new *plant*, Connor. She needs a proper name."

Before Connor replies, Benny returns with the first of the food I ordered. "Another mojito, Cowboy!"

Connor shakes his head no to the bartender.

"You are not my dad. I don't even *have* a dad. I can drink as many mojitos as I want, especially since I'm paying for them." I look back at Benny. "Mo-ji-to, or no tip-eee-to."

"You're staying in the hotel, right?" Benny bites his lip.

"Yes, indeed. I done showed you my key card, pardner." I laugh to myself again. Now I sound like those loudmouthed tourists who were in here earlier.

Benny sighs but grabs the pestle and grinds the mint.

"See? At least someone knows how to do their job."

I shovel the hummus into my face as fast as I can, slapping at Connor's hand when he tries to take some of my flatbread.

"Lara, come on, talk to me. Explain what happened today."

"No." I keep chewing. And then I keep drinking, and then when the Raw Bar platter arrives, I share only because that is a lot of sushi, and listening to Connor whine about how hungry he is after his acting workshop is like fingernails on a chalkboard.

I'm just about to slide the last piece of wild sockeye nigiri into my mouth when Benny edges in front of me again. "Lara, it was lovely meeting you. I'm off shift now, so do you want me to charge this to your room?"

"Yes, darling Benny," I say, flopping a hand at him. "You working tomorrow? I'll stop by before I head out."

He smiles and pats the counter without answering. "You have a safe night, OK?"

"There goes Benny," I say, watching his rather fine backside hugged by his perfectly pressed black pants. "He's kind of hot."

"Uh, hello? Boyfriend sitting here."

My head weighs too much, but I turn it anyway. I've been here for a long time—the sun has dipped, cloaking the concrete jungle of downtown in grays and dark blues, and the hotel's inside lights have kicked on. "Do you only like me because you think I have money?"

Connor's mouth is halfway open, like the fish in the huge tank across the lobby.

"Do you?" I ask.

"Of course not."

"It is amazing to me that you have had a successful career as an actor, Connor Mayson, because you are the world's worst liar."

Connor's jaw clenches for a beat, and then he's off his chair, pulling his leather jacket back on. "That's enough. Let's get you upstairs and into a bath. I'll order room service and you can sleep this off."

"Yes, you'll order room service, but you won't pay for it," I bite back. "And I'm not going upstairs yet. I want to go shopping."

"Shopping? Right now?"

"I didn't plan on staying overnight. I need clothing." I gesture to my meeting-appropriate attire.

"We could be at your loft in, like, ten minutes. Why *are* we staying here?"

I fumble around with my purse and pull out a one-hundred-dollar note from my wallet. "Hey, bartender lady." I wave down the bar. The woman who's taken over for Benny isn't nearly as friendly looking. "Give this to the Cannabis Cowboy for me, will you?"

She takes the brown note, nods once, and goes back to helping the other people down the way who are giving me a dirty look. "What, you've never had a bad day before?"

Connor wraps his arm around my shoulders. "WAIT!" I slide my plant off the bar and hug her to me.

"Is that really yours?"

"Yes. I adopted her today. She's a spider plant."

"Whatever you say." He steers me out of the lounge.

"My shoes ... I need to put them back on. Hang on. Hold my plant —this is so hard—"

Connor takes the pot and helps me onto the back of a couch

huddled around an indoor firepit. He kneels and slides my shoes on one at a time. "You're like the prince and I'm like Cinderella and these are my glass slippers."

"Except you've never done a day of hard labor in your life," Connor mutters.

"I heard that." I push him off me but then realize I'm quite wobbly. "What time is it? I want to go to Misch. No—Boboli! Let's go to Boboli! Issey Miyake has this *gorgeous* chiffon twist top that I saw on their website—"

"On Granville? It's too late, Lara. They're already closed."

I snort. I could have Olivia call them and *make* them open for me ... "How far is Nordstrom from here? They don't have my designers, but I could get some basics to tide me over."

"Why don't we just go to your place—"

"Because I don't WANT to, Connor. Everything at my place reminds me that EVERYONE WHO LOVED ME IS DEAD."

The entire lobby stops moving and stares at me, including the guy playing the white baby grand piano. This is the second time today I've had everyone's undivided attention.

"OK, come on, let's go upstairs." Connor again tries to usher me along.

"Wait. I said I want to go shopping."

"It's almost eight, babe. Nordstrom probably closes at nine."

"So that means I have a whole hour to shop. And *be careful!* You're squishing my new daughter!" I yank the plant from him, spilling some of her dirt onto the pristine lobby floor.

Connor exhales heavily and then tucks my left arm into his so I don't fall over. Or maybe he just doesn't want me to yell again. I can just see the headline: *Drunken heiress, granddaughter of philanthropist Archibald M. Clarke, raising a ruckus at the Fairmont Pacific Rim with her Hollywood B-list actor beau ...*

"I am not a B-list actor," Connor says under his breath, smiling tightly as we pass other guests on our way to the front doors. His new veneers look good—I certainly paid enough for them.

"I really need to figure out when that stuff is inside my head and not outside my mouth." We step into the chilly spring evening, and I whistle through my fingers at one of the waiting taxis.

"Why do you have to do that right next to my ear?"

The cab pulls up—another Prius—and I steady myself against the car frame while Connor opens the back door. As soon as we're both in, plant tucked in my lap, I lean forward with my hand on the front passenger seat. "Nordstrom, please. I need to do some shopping."

The driver reaches into the dash console and pulls out a box of mints. "You're gonna need this before you get there."

I take them and help myself. "What a helpful cabbie. Make sure you tip him well, Connor Mayson."

The driver's face lights up as he turns and looks over at Connor on the seat next to me. "*The* Connor Mayson? You're the guy from *Super George?*"

"Perfect. You guys talk. I'm going to rest my eyes for a minute ..." I lean my head against the car door, not caring about the germs crawling onto me, while the driver fanboys all over Connor. It's actually kind of perfect—by the time we reach Nordstrom eight minutes later, Connor is all smiles instead of being a wet fart about my need to shop.

The driver won't let him pay the fare, but I pinch Connor's arm so he'll tip the guy.

I walk ahead, struggling to navigate the concrete stairs. It's better when Connor finally takes his position next to me. "You're like one of those silver canes old people use, the ones with the tennis balls on the feet so they don't slip, only you're human and not metal. And no balls." I laugh to myself again.

Connor holds open the door, and the perfumed air washes over me. I know exactly where I'm going—upstairs—and Connor trails behind like a good dog, my plant tucked under one arm. As we emerge from the escalator, I pause and look around, waiting for the personal shoppers to swoop in from wherever they hide.

They know who I am. Though I don't shop here often, when I do, a personal shopper *always* greets me. Olivia always sees to that. Speaking of Olivia, I think she might be looking for alternative employment after her little disappearing act today. Answering my calls and texts is basically her entire job description.

"I guess you're my personal shopper this evening," I say to Connor. "Maybe it will come in handy for a future role." He doesn't laugh, which is a shame because I find myself very funny.

Connor lifts his free arm so I can drape my choices over them. "I need pajamas, something for tomorrow, ooooh, and this is—oh my god, this floral is gorgeous. I don't usually go for florals, but this one …"

I'm a little too wobbly to attempt a fitting room tonight, plus honestly, where *is* everyone?

"Babe, they shut off the Muzak. That means the store is closing."

Before his sentence is even finished, the courtesy announcement rings through the store's speakers.

"Come on, let's pay and get you back to the hotel into a nice tub."

"Mm-hmm … you just want to see me naked."

"You look good naked," he says. "Take your plant for a sec." I do, and he piles the armload of my choices over the glass counter of the cash desk. A sheen of sweat coats his forehead and upper lip.

"Someone needs to hit the gym—you're worn out by shopping?" I laugh and then look around us. "Hello? Can we get some service over here?"

"Lara, stop. Here, you sit," Connor says, pushing me back toward the leather seats placed around a tasteful waiting area near the register. "Give me your wallet, I'll pay, and we can go."

"No way, mister. Not giving you my wallet." I push him aside. He huffs and plops into one of the chairs, yanking his phone from his pocket.

An impossibly skinny brunette appears from nowhere. "I am so sorry—I didn't know anyone was still over here."

"Well, I am."

The girl looks up at me. "Again, I am so sorry."

"Did anyone ever tell you that you look like Betty Boop?"

"I don't know who that is …"

"It's a compliment. She was a cartoon character from a million

38

years ago—my grandfather loved her, but he was very old. Anyway, she was gorgeous. All red lips and big eyes and great hair."

"Thank you," she says, her hands moving as she rings up my purchases and removes security tags.

I close my eyes again, lightly swaying to the rhythm of her beeping register. She tries to make small talk, but I don't answer—I'm thinking of the lipstick on Heather Smithe's teeth when she told me I'd be forced to either move to Thalia Island and run my grandfather's pretend world or live on $30,000 a year. Thirty thousand … are you kidding me?

"I'm sorry?" Betty Boop asks.

I open my eyes again. "Sorry. Nothing."

"Your total is … $1547.87."

I fumble with my purse again and drag out my wallet, slapping my Amex Centurion on the counter. She runs it while a second salesgirl, not as pretty, doesn't look like Betty Boop, wraps everything in tissue paper to tuck into the ribbon-handled paper shopping bags.

"Oops, that is declined," Betty says. "Do you maybe have another card?"

"It's a Black Amex. They don't get declined. Run it again."

She does. It declines again. I blow my breath out through my nostrils. "This is unacceptable." I flop open my wallet and pull out my JP Morgan Reserve Visa.

Also declined.

And then my Stratus Visa.

Again, declined.

It's at this point when the cold sweat coats me. "Something is wrong … oh my god, someone has stolen my identity. This is identity theft. This is why my cards have all been frozen!" My eyes burn. Am I going to cry? "Is there someone you can call?"

"Um, you can call the number on the back to see if your accounts have been locked due to theft, but it doesn't usually happen with multiple cards, and not usually cards of this caliber."

I narrow my eyes at Betty Boop. Her less cute sidekick has stopped wrapping my purchases. "What are you saying?"

"Nothing, ma'am. Just that usually when cards are declined—"

"I AM NOT A MA'AM! I AM BARELY THIRTY YEARS OLD!" My voice bounces off the ceiling and the glass fixtures, not even the shitty Muzak to drown it out.

"Lara, come on, let's go," Connor says, pawing at me again. I swipe out at him, my fist catching him in the face. He stumbles back, hunched over; when he looks up, his nose is bleeding.

"Ma'am, please! Calm down!" Betty Boop shrieks, and then all hell breaks loose.

I'm knocking over mannequins and I pick up the leather chair Connor was just sitting in, its arms still warm from his body, and I launch it into the full wall of mirrors reflecting the ugliness on my face right now. I swipe my arm across display tables and push over the stupid giant palms and I push in behind the counter and start shoving all of my purchases into the bags—

My head pounds and my ears hear nothing but roaring, like an angry ocean mixed with the screams of banshees. My eyes see nothing but red and white fury.

And then arms around me. Hard, mean arms, not like Connor's but someone bigger, stronger, someone way more official and not a pushover. I bite at the hand that gets too close to my face and the arm releases, but only for a second, and then … electricity.

I flail back but hit my head on something way harder than a human.

Lights out, Lara.

SIX

DECISIONS, DECISIONS

I try opening my eyes. Once is enough.

"Ah, you're alive. Good."

That voice. Enough of a trigger to remind me that wherever I am, it's not where I thought I would end up this evening.

"Lara, open your eyes." Number Two does not sound impressed.

"I need water." I move my right hand up, but it stops abruptly. I move it again, and it stops again. The metal clinking in my ears isn't from a bracelet, as I rarely wear those.

Handcuffs. A torrent of thoughts rolls through my head: Did Connor and I do something kinky tonight? Was I so blasted, I don't remember what we were up to after we went shopping? Did I finally say yes to one of his ridiculous role-play sex games?

I crack my lids, the light overhead way too blue and way too bright. "What's with the cuffs, Rupert? You really that afraid of me?"

He folds the magazine on his lap and plops it onto the cheap veneer cart behind him. Wait. This isn't the hotel. It's not my apartment either. "Why … are we at the hospital?"

"Indeed."

"Am I hurt?"

Rupert snorts.

"Are you laughing at me because I'm injured?" Both my eyes are open now, my heart pounding as I take in the surroundings. People beyond the blue waving curtains of our slice of real estate. Feet shushing by. Monitors beeping. Someone down the way yelling. Phones ringing.

"You're in the emergency department until you sober up. And also to check for concussion. You hit your head when the security guard tasered you."

"I thought … I thought Tasers were illegal in Canada."

"That's his problem, not yours. *Your* problems are different, and bigger, I'm afraid."

"Why am I not in a private room?" I lean back against the stiff, uncomfortable bed, trying not to panic. "I need to wash my hands. And my feet. Oh my god, my feet are dirty."

"You kicked off your shoes in your rage."

"Please, Rupert, can you get me some wipes? A towel? Can you please take off these cuffs?"

Rupert says nothing, does not move to get me wipes or a towel or remove the handcuffs.

"What time is it?" I stare at the ceiling tiles, trying to calm my breathing before I get myself in more trouble.

"Just after two."

"In the *morning*?"

"You've been out for a while."

"Where is my plant?" Panicked, I look at my right hand. Grandfather's ring is still on my middle finger. Thank all the gods. "Where's Connor?"

Rupert exhales his annoyance, which means Connor didn't stick around. "He wrote you a note." Rupert reaches into the breast pocket of his suit coat that hangs on the back of his vinyl chair. Always a suit, even when he has to come to the ER to rescue Archibald Clarke's miscreant granddaughter. He pulls out a folded paper and tries to hand it to me, but my movement is limited.

"Did they have to handcuff *both* sides? I'm not Charles Manson."

"No, but you *were* combative. Nurses don't appreciate being punched." Rupert lifts a brow and unfolds the page. "'Lara—tonight was crazy. Hope you feel better soon. Agent called with an audition tomorrow. Will call and let you know how it goes. XO, Connor.'"

I flop my head back against the bed again and instantly regret it. "When did he leave exactly?"

"When the police decided they were bringing you here." Rupert crumples the page and tosses it into the round bin behind him. "Why, Lara?"

"Why what?"

He shakes his head, disappointment sitting like gargoyles on his shoulders, their beady eyes fixed on me, their mocking tongues tasting the air. "Why *all of it?*"

The curtain parts and a very muscled, brown-skinned man with the most impressive beard I've ever seen walks in, thumbs on strong, hairy hands tucked into the thick belt holding up his black cargo pants. Rupert immediately rises to meet him, and they shake and share pleasant smiles. Then the man turns to me. "I'm Sergeant Wes Singh. If I take off these cuffs, do you promise to stay calm and keep your temper under control?"

I'm so embarrassed, I can only nod.

"Did I hurt anyone?" I whisper.

"Your boyfriend had a bloody nose, but he said it was just from allergies. And you slapped one of the nurses, but she's not pressing charges." The sergeant hikes an eyebrow as he leans over to unlock my left hand. *Wow. Connor lied to protect me? He probably lied because he needed to get his beauty sleep for his audition instead of dealing with police paperwork.*

Slowly, the scene at Nordstrom filters back, but it's fuzzy. Something about my cards being declined …

"You were drinking tonight, before you went on your shopping spree?"

I nod again. He moves around to the right side. Once both my hands are free, I rub at my wrists, noting a collection of small cuts and new bruises on my forearms and even my shins.

"What else do you remember about tonight?"

My eyes sting. "Not a lot."

Sergeant Singh gestures to the bed, as if asking if he can sit. It seems very … informal. Invasive, even. But I move my legs, and he hikes his utility belt, the mattress depressing under his weight.

"So, Lara, you broke some laws tonight. Did some serious damage in the department store. Do you remember that?"

I don't answer. I can't meet his eyes. And I really need to wash my hands and feet.

"Rupert and I go way back. And I knew your grandfather very well. In fact, he's the reason I joined the RCMP. He gave my mother a job when no one else would—he literally saved my family. And because of that, I feel like I need to do something to repay that favor, one deed at a time. Which is why I'm here, instead of the Vancouver PD beat cops who aren't always so amenable."

I look up at him. "Certainly Rupert can call our attorney and we can handle this. I made a mistake. I'll gladly pay for the damages, and it won't happen again."

Singh seems unmoved. "Rupert, you wanna take the wheel?"

Rupert positions himself so he's standing next to the burly cop, which accentuates how lean he's gotten over the last few months. "Here's the situation, Lara. You have two choices: You will take up your role as the administrator and overseer of Thalia Island in accordance with your grandfather's wishes as detailed during our meeting yesterday, or my friend Wes will call back the arresting officers and they will escort you to jail. You will be held until the bail hearing, likely in the morning but within twenty-four hours for sure. Whatever happens after that is your responsibility, as the Archibald M. Clarke Foundation is not liable for any legal entanglements incurred as a result of criminal behavior."

The prickly shakiness starts in my feet and by the time it reaches my head, I think I'm going to be sick. Singh reaches to the bedside rolling cart and hands me the flimsy cardboard vomit basin. Thankfully, I'm able to keep down whatever is in my gut, but I hang on to the basin just in case.

"Rupert, come on, I went shopping and my cards were all declined

—I'm the victim here! Someone has stolen my identity, and the cards weren't working. I told you, I will pay for whatever damages I caused—"

"Your cards weren't declined because of theft, Lara. And your temper tantrum is going to cost one-third of your yearly stipend. You will also have to move out of your loft as that $6000 monthly rent is now solidly out of your price range."

"Rent? We *own* that building."

"Clarke Innovations owns that building. *You*, however, do not."

Sergeant Singh stands. "Rupert, can I get you a tea or coffee? I think Lara needs a minute to consider her options."

"I don't want to keep you, Wes," Rupert says.

"I don't mind waiting another ten minutes or so." He smiles tightly and exits our curtained cubby, though he's replaced by a stern-looking nurse in triangle-print scrubs. She bobs her head once at Rupert, her short gray curls not budging with the movement.

"Feeling better? I see he took off the handcuffs, which means you're probably ready to behave," she says. I'm afraid to ask if she's the nurse I slapped, and she doesn't offer that information. She attaches the blood pressure sleeve and takes my temp with a forehead thermometer thing and then hands me a bottle of water plucked from the pocket on the front of her scrubs as well as a sample-size packet of Advil. "You're going to need that." She nods at Rupert again and disappears almost as quickly as she came in.

I turn to Number Two. "Please … there has to be some mistake. Those lawyers wrote that will—my grandfather would never have been so Draconian. He *loves* me."

Past tense, Lara.

"You're right. He did love you. And that's why he was the one who wrote the will, down to the last comma." Rupert scrapes his chair noisily over the scuffed floor and sits so I can see his face. At least I don't have to crane my neck to look at him as he ladles me in harsh truths. I unzip the foil packet and swallow the Advil dry.

"Archibald saw what you were becoming—an entitled layabout who mistreats people because everything has always been handed to her. You've never had to *work* for anything, Lara. He saw his own failings, especially in these last few years. His guilt and sadness over the loss of your mother, the absence of any real father figure—he was too lenient. He knew he had made a mistake in the way he'd raised you when he asked you to look after that kids' charity in East Vancouver, and you let everything fall apart."

I look down at the sweating water bottle staining the silk of my blouse. "I told him I was the wrong person to run that place," I mumble.

"Maybe you were. But you didn't even try, Lara. The Foundation made promises, and you didn't deliver. That was a huge disappointment, not to mention a PR nightmare."

"So sorry I made you look bad on social media."

Rupert sighs loudly again, running a hand down his tired face. "It's not about PR, Lara. It's about the people who were relying on the Foundation, on *you*, to help them. People who weren't born with your advantages."

"I never ASKED for any advantages. It's not my fault my mother ran off. It's not my fault my grandfather is who he is—I didn't get to *choose* my family, Rupert!"

He crosses his arms over his chest and leans back in his chair. He unbuttons the top of his shirt and loosens his dark blue tie, giving his Adam's apple more room to flex in disappointment. "You sound exactly like the spoiled brat who tore apart the department store this evening."

"I guess that's just who I am, then. Spoiled shitty little Lara who no one cares about, as long as she's not messing up anyone's busy schedule or making them look bad on Twitter."

Sergeant Singh reappears, a cup from a vending machine in one hand. "Everything OK? You promised you'd behave if I took off the cuffs."

Rupert suddenly stands and grabs his suit coat from the back of his chair. "I'm finished here. Lara has made her decision."

I have?

"Thanks for everything tonight, Wes." Rupert pats Singh on the chest once and then disappears through the curtain himself.

"Wait! No! Rupert, come back!"

He doesn't come back.

The nurse, however, does with my discharge papers, and Sergeant Singh tosses his cup into the small round bin to soak into the discarded note from my stupid boyfriend. Wes pushes the curtain aside, and two Vancouver Police officers walk in. A small blond female pulls her handcuffs from the little pouch on her belt, helps me off the bed, and asks for my hands behind my back.

"Lara Clarke, I am arresting you for the offences of causing disturbance ..."

"No, please. Please don't do this. If you let me make a call, I can get my lawyer down here. We can take care of everything right now, and you can get back out there to fight real crime for the good people of Vancouver. Honestly, I am *not* a criminal. I'm Lara Clarke! You know my grandfather, right? This was just a misunderstanding! Please? Think of the paperwork I will save you!"

The blond officer continues talking over me about my rights as she clamps a hand onto my elbow and pushes aside the hospital curtain.

"This can't be happening. Don't you know who I am?" I ask out loud, but no one listens.

I let my hair cloak my face as she and her partner walk me out to their squad car, but it doesn't matter.

The only person taking my picture tonight is the guy in booking who looks like Popeye.

SEVEN

ANDROMACHE RETURNS

It's three in the afternoon when I make it back to my loft—via cab, since neither Rupert nor Olivia showed up to bring me home. Why do I even have an assistant if she's not there when I need her?

When I reach my door, I find a letter taped to it, my name and a red OPEN IMMEDIATELY rubber-stamped across the envelope's front. I unlock and open the door … and freeze.

My furniture—all of it—is gone.

The only thing that remains is my ten-by-fourteen, hand-knotted Tufenkian artisan wool and silk rug the color of the Pacific Ocean on a summer day. I drop everything on the floor—purse, keys, phone, the urgent letter—and jog into my bedroom. Sure enough, the bed, TV and media cabinet, love seat, lamps, paintings, everything that isn't clothing, is gone. My entire wardrobe and shoes are in piles, like fashionable anthills if ants made hills out of Stella McCartney and Missoni and Valentino and Prada.

"How the hell did they do this so fast?" I say to myself. My best friend Rage reawakens in my chest, ready to call Number Two and ream him into next year for this game he's playing.

I storm out of my bedroom across the apartment to my phone. I slide my thumb across and dial Rupert, only to be met with the bone-jarring message that my phone is out of service and I can connect with customer service for further assistance.

He cut off my cell phone while I was in *jail*?

I try the landline. No dial tone.

How am I supposed to *call* anyone? How am I supposed to call Olivia to help me deal with this mess? Where is the housekeeper? I'm hungry, and Vera should *be* here making dinner by now.

I need a drink.

"A-ha!" The fridge is still here, maybe because they didn't have time to get it out of the apartment or maybe because it belongs with the building. I don't know, and I don't care. What I *do* care about is there is a bottle of Boërl & Kroff Brut in the back I've been saving for a special occasion, like when I'm thirsty, and I am very thirsty right now. Jail was gross and icky, and my feet are so dirty, I might cut them off, and as soon as I finish this bottle, I'm going to take the longest, hottest shower I've ever had in my entire life. My grandfather would be appalled about how much water I'm going to waste.

"I don't care if I have to sleep on a pile of my clothes tonight. I'm not going anywhere," I say, popping the cork and letting it fly across the huge, open-plan living space. Without the furniture and art and books, my apartment looks so much bigger. "And it ECHOES!" I yell. It doesn't really, but my voice bounces back at me once, making me feel less alone.

A few pulls of the champagne and my stomach settles. Instead of worrying about Rupert and his ridiculous little games, I toss my useless phone into some random basket his thieving minions left behind. I'm wearing disgusting cheap canvas-and-plastic, laceless sneakers from the jail, so I kick them off to burn later, trying not to think about the filth I'm tracking across my polished concrete floors. I then plod over and slump against the front door, reaching for the OPEN IMMEDIATELY letter.

I slide my finger under the sealed lip, hissing when I give myself a paper cut. I yank the letter free and flatten it with the hand that isn't holding the champagne bottle.

It's an eviction notice from Clarke Innovations. I have until Friday to get out.

My grandfather's company is kicking me out of the building he owns.

Like Rupert did with Connor's scrawl at the hospital, I wad up the love note and throw it across the room. I'll just call my lawyer, explain what's going on, and everything will be fine again. This is simply more of Rupert's posturing. He's trying to force my hand, but I'm not going to stand for it. My grandfather would *never* do this to me—he would never uproot me from this loft. He knows how much I love living downtown.

I *could* always have Olivia book us a charter and head to Denmark, out of Rupert's reach. Grandfather loves it there.

Loved it there. *Past tense, Lara.*

Archie would never do this ... kick me out onto the street, or worse, into some low-rent apartment building with shared laundry and noisy neighbors. Hell, I'll bet Clarke Manor probably even belongs to me. I'm the only living Clarke heir! Rupert is probably squatting there, preparing to sell it so he can take all that money and disappear to the Caymans.

I need to call my attorney, and then Olivia. She can set us up with a room downtown. Better yet, she can meet me at the Arbutus Club and I'll treat her to a massage as an apology for all the angry calls and texts. We'll get blowouts and order bottomless crantinis, despite my ban on martinis. I think those are her favorite ...

Another long drink, and I pull myself up. I will shower, change, check my bank balance, and then go buy a new phone so I can get my lawyer and assistant busy on righting our listing ship.

No one is going to steal Lara Josephine Clarke's future away from her, not even vindictive, hateful Number Two who is only part of this family because he doesn't have one of his own.

Apparently the building superintendent already let the gas company turn off my service. Which means my shower was cold enough to restore the Greenland ice shelf. At least I still have electricity. Except my heat is gas, too, so it's colder than a witch's tit in here, and I am huddled in an igloo made of my wardrobe so I don't freeze to death.

Maybe that would be better, actually. Rupert will come on Friday to make sure I'm out of the apartment and they will find my stiff, blue body under the pile of designer clothing, and Rupert and Heather Smithe and Arthur Leyton and that girl who serves the tea will all feel instantly terrible and they'll shake their heads and whisper, *"Such a shame, we should've been nicer to poor Lara,"* and then Rupert will have a massive headache brought on by the guilt and stress of being generally horrible and some vessel in his brain will pop like a grape and that will be the end of it and they won't even bury him in a mushroom suit but will let his body decompose the slow, painful way, full of worms and weevils.

If I had a penny to throw into a fountain, that's what I'd wish for.

I manage to find a pay-as-you-go phone at the 7-Eleven down the block and immediately put in a call to my lawyer, yet another of my grandfather's cronies. But it's after hours, so his answering service said he'll have to call me back tomorrow. Calling Olivia again is equally useless—straight to voicemail, which is making me rethink the offer of massages and crantinis. She knows better than to ignore me for so long.

I use the Wi-Fi at Starbucks to check my bank balance, which is still *thankfully* intact—money from my usual monthly allowance hasn't been scraped out yet, so I'll go first thing in the morning and with-draw every last cent and take it to a bank Number Two doesn't know about, just in case he conjures any more insane ways to prove his cruelty.

The amount's not going to be enough to refurnish this whole apartment *and* pay next month's rent *and* give the attorney his usual retainer *and* pay whatever legal fees and fines and damages once my little criminal matter is settled. So, I'm going to have to just live like this until I can get the attorney moving on unlocking the money that is owed to me as Archibald Clarke's sole living heir.

I ignore the growling in my gut—I can't even order dinner because my credit cards have all been removed from my wallet—likely Rupert's doing while I was unconscious at the hospital. Classy, Rupert. What am I supposed to *eat*, you heartless bully?

I'll go to the Arbutus. Or even the Vancouver Club. Grandfather is a member in good standing everywhere in this city—they won't turn me away.

My phone rings. "Hello?"

"Hey, Lara—"

"Olivia, *finally*. Where have you been? Thank you for calling me back. I didn't know if you'd recognize the new number. So, there's this situation, and I need to get out of the city. If you could get us a charter to Copenhagen, we could hang out until I get all of this resolved with Rupert. Honestly, he's being so—"

"Lara." Olivia cuts me off. She never cuts me off. "I can't help you right now."

"Why? It's a weekday. I do pay you to be available on weekdays, do I not?"

She sighs through the line. "I don't work for you anymore. Mr. Bishop phoned and said I would no longer be needed."

My fingernails dig into my palms.

"Are you still there?" she asks. "Hey, can I get a reference? I'm thinking I'll go back to Toronto ..."

"Thank you for your call, Olivia. Take care." I hang up, the chilled shakes of anger—and what might be fear—renewing themselves.

Rupert fired my assistant? And he didn't bother to *tell* me?

I text Connor next, but he isn't responding, which is kind of a dick move since he's basically the only person I have left, now that Number Two has turned traitor. Maybe Rupert fired him too.

But I really need Connor, even if he's only going to talk about his stupid auditions and perfect hair. Maybe he could move his stuff into my apartment—we could finally live together, just like he's been asking—and then he could help with paying part of the rent. Isn't that what people my age do in this city? Get roommates?

Shudder.

Who would I even ask, if not Connor? I'm trying very hard not to think about the fact that I have no real friends.

Making genuine friends when you're in our part of society is next to impossible. Do people only like you because you can take them out for fancy dinners and shopping sprees and invite them to society events or fly them to Ibiza or so you can invest in their ridiculous business schemes? Even in high school, the girls I was friends with were so competitive, I didn't see the need to stay in touch after we walked across the graduation stage. It was all about who was going to collect the most university degrees or who was going to take over Daddy's corporation or who would land the richest, hottest husband and get pregnant first. Yawn.

I tried being friends with the scholarship kids at one of the (many) schools I attended—I guess they were middle class? But family dinners and sleepovers in their suburban homes made me feel even lonelier. With them, it wasn't about the money—it was about a mom and a dad and an annoying little brother or sister and a minivan that broke down a lot and a dog who smelled like socks and a house full of noise and love.

It was too much. All that realness was almost worse than the toxic reality of my society friends.

And my university adventure ended minus the pomp and circumstance after a few semesters of shit grades and blackout-drunk capers when my grandfather's chums in the alumni office could no longer look the other way. Not even the delectable offer of a blank check to rebuild the aging football stadium could buy my way back into a lecture hall.

So yes, I've never found my people. It's fine. When my mother would return home and tell me about all the beautiful things she'd seen in the wild world outside our borders, she never waxed poetic about friends or lovers or people who made her life complete. She talked about how the world was her oyster, and she was the pearl, and someday I would be too.

My mother didn't need anyone. I don't need anyone either.

All of this is why my doorbell ringing at 11:30 p.m. is a little disconcerting. And maybe a little hopeful that it *is* Connor, and he will come breezing in smelling like aftershave and high-end hair products and he will have takeout and maybe some tiramisu because he knows I've had a rough twenty-four hours …

I make it to the door and look through the peephole. No Connor, which means no takeout and no tiramisu.

I open the door anyway.

A banker's box sits on the doormat. The whole thing is taped shut, and my name has been written in thick black marker across the top—in Connor's handwriting. On the floor next to it is my plant.

Tears spring to my eyes. I kneel to pick up the plant and hug her to my chest. "I'm so sorry. I will never abandon you again."

I stick my head out the door and look both ways to see if Connor is still there—if anyone is there.

No one. Just me. And I can't even check the video footage since the camera that monitors who's at the door went bye-bye with the rest of my stuff today.

The air in the hall is too cold, so I scoot the box inside with my foot and lock the door once again. I set my plant on the floor and pull off the tape from the box's lid.

It's my stuff. Pajamas, sweats, one little black dress and coordinating heels, a toothbrush, my extra makeup kit—the things I keep at Connor's place. And yes, there's another note. I flip it open: "Hey, Lara … I think we need a break. XO, Connor. P.S. I booked the deodorant commercial. Keep an eye out for it!"

At least Connor is loyal to his narcissism.

I crumple up the note and drop it in the box.

"Come on. Let's get you a drink. But nothing stronger than water for you, little miss," I say, padding across the cold floor in my fluffiest socks. I set my plant on the counter, drip some water into her pot, and tell her she's beautiful. "People are the worst. I'm sorry you had a rough night." Gently, I rest her long, thin, white-and-green-banded leaves over my palm, inspecting for damage. "Andromache. That's your name. It means 'fighter of men.' Do you want to fight the man with me and get our lives back?" I pause for a beat, tucking my fingers into Andromache's soil. "I thought so. You and me against the world."

With the Boërl long gone, I pour the rest of some old scotch into a cup. Upon checking the fridge, I'm again gut-punched at the lack of fresh groceries—not even a parting meal left in the fridge by Vera, my housekeeper. It's a weekday—this kitchen should be bursting with food, either already prepared or waiting for Vera's skilled hands to whip it together. Was she in on this? Did quiet, unassuming Vera help them clean out my cupboards and pantry when the devils were throwing my whole life into cardboard boxes?

I find a forgotten box of stale vegan cereal Connor brought over on his last health-food kick and pour some into an oversized popcorn bowl. In between dry bites, Andromache and I strategize how we will defeat the evil Number Two.

When I can't take another mouthful of dodgy almond clusters, I grab my plant, set her on the windowsill in my room, and burrow into my makeshift bed, head spinning and comfortably numb. I'm still chilled from my arctic shower, and for a brief moment, I wish Connor were here to warm me up.

No. No more. Connor is yesterday's news. As is whiny Olivia and absentee Vera, who have both abandoned me in my hour of need.

Now I will sleep, and when I get to Dreamland, I will drop all these worries into someone else's life.

EIGHT

HAVE A FREE PEN

My dodgy new phone is ringing. Except I don't recognize the ringtone in time, and it goes to voicemail. I slither out from under my designer igloo and fumble blindly until my hand clamps onto the device. I wipe the sleep out of my eyes using the nearest available garment.

The screen reads "Missed call."

I dial my voicemail.

"Hello, Ms. Clarke, this is Bernard Allen from Allen, Shore, and Lewis. You phoned yesterday regarding retention of legal counsel. Certainly we can help you with whatever you might need. It sounds like you have two potential issues requiring my assistance, one civil and one criminal, so once you deposit the standard retainer of $10,000 for each case, we can get things started. Call my paralegal, Amanda, and she can arrange the transfer of funds direct from your bank into our trust account …"

I hang up before the message finishes.

Ten thousand for each case. That's twenty thousand dollars. I don't have twenty thousand dollars on hand.

Speaking of, I need to get to the bank.

I fly into the bathroom, wash my teeth and face, throw on whatever clothes are nearest and clean, pull my hair into a messy bun, and grab my wallet, keys, and ugly phone. "Andromache, hold down the fort. I shall return with the spoils of war!"

One of the things I love most about living downtown is the proximity to everything. Whole Foods, my bank, my favorite spa and salon, great eateries ... Why would anyone want to live on some desolate island when they could have paradise on every street corner?

It's Thursday—the bank isn't super busy. I smile at the security guard on my way past, determined to turn over a new leaf and not cause any more trouble for security guards with illegal Tasers or ginormous RCMP sergeants named Wes.

"Good morning, how can I help you?" The teller smiles brightly, revealing a full set of silver braces. I smile back as I enter my card and key in my PIN on the countertop reader.

"I need to make a withdrawal," I say. "Everything in my checking and savings accounts, please."

The teller taps her keys and then a few more keys, and her brow furrows. "Hmmm, I'm sorry, I'm not seeing anything in these accounts to withdraw."

Thud. Thud. Thud thud thud thudthudthudthudthud. "No, that's impossible."

She returns to the screen, scans and types, then looks at me again, face apologetic. "Again, Ms. Clarke, I'm sorry, but ..."

"Look *harder*."

She tries something else, mumbles how she's not sure what's happened, her lip sticking to the metal over her right incisor as she talks quietly to herself, fingers flying, but ultimately, she offers only a sheepish silver grin. "I'm just not seeing anything—"

"I'd like to speak to your supervisor, please."

The teller's hands still. Her eyes glisten like she's about to cry, and then she lifts a single finger in the air for a millisecond. "Certainly, Ms. Clarke. I'm sure we can figure this out."

My upper half feels like I'm standing too close to one of those outdoor patio heaters. I fan myself with the hand not clutching my convenience-store cell phone, hoping the customers on either side can't see what's going down. *This has to be a mistake. Maybe I've been robbed! Maybe Rupert is wrong and my identity was stolen!*

The teller returns with an older man, his glasses resting on the very end of his nose. He has a yellow ribbon pinned to his lapel above a name tag that says Andrew Chu. "So, Ms. Clarke, I understand you're trying to make a withdrawal?"

"Yes. I want all of my money out today, thank you."

"Hmmm ..."

"Can you please stop *hmmm*-ing me?"

Manager and teller look up, some of the friendliness melting from their faces. *You catch more flies with honey than vinegar, Lara.*

"Mr. Chu, I'm sorry. I've had a terrible twenty-four hours. I checked my accounts last night at around ten, and there was still money in them. Is there any chance I've been robbed or hacked?" I lean closer, lowering my voice. "There should be sums in my numerous accounts that require you to take me into a private office and offer me tea and a warm towelette. I get direct deposits on the first of every month and have since the day these accounts were opened over a decade ago."

The manager steps fully in front of the keyboard. "It looks like the balance of the accounts was transferred this morning at 6 a.m."

I can hardly hear him over the blood rushing in my ears. "Does ..." I clear my throat. "Does it say who emptied it, or how that occurred?"

More typing. "By the secondary account holder—" Mr. Chu pushes his glasses up his nose just before they fall off. He pauses to read something and then turns the screen so I can see it. "Your account has a secondary cosigner with direct, regular payments from Clarke Innovations, correct?"

"Yes, that's my grandfather's company. Archibald Clarke is—was—my grandfather. You've heard of him?"

The manager smiles and straightens his shoulders. *That's more like it. Now he knows who he's dealing with.*

"Of course, Ms. Clarke. I apologize for this as we are longtime friends and partners with Clarke Innovations. Your grandfather was the reason I bought a Prius."

I offer a tight smile. "He'd be thrilled to hear that."

"And we started our own compost exchange system in our neighborhood, all because of Dr. Clarke."

"Mm-hmm, great, that's great." I flatten my hands on the counter. "Today, I'd *really* like it if you could channel some of that affection for Grandfather into helping me. Perhaps in an office so we're not out here with all these … people?"

"Yes, I understand. Let's have a closer look." Mr. Chu scrunches his brow as he diverts back to the computer and tabs through different screens. "I'm so sorry, Ms. Clarke. If there is a secondary on the account, they have the same access to withdrawals and deposits as you do. As I said, it appears they accessed this account since you checked it last evening."

"But it's *my* account."

"Of course, yes, you're the primary, but there is a secondary person with authority over its contents and management." He types some more, eyes scanning small print I can't see from where I'm positioned. "It's been there since the account creation, uhhhh … twelve years ago."

Twelve years. When I turned eighteen. I never even thought to look at who was on my account. I signed a document Rupert gave me, the money appeared, I was given credit cards in my name—just as Grandfather promised.

"You don't understand—there has *obviously* been a huge mistake. That's *my money*, and I need you to perform some bank magic and have your machine spit out the cash that belongs to me."

Mr. Chu slides the keyboard aside and points to the monitor again. "I'm sorry, Ms. Clarke, but there is nothing in the account to cash out. Is it possible for you to contact the secondary and see if the money was perhaps moved in error?"

I close my eyes and open them only to stare at the slight bruises on my wrists—from the handcuffs. The handcuffs the police put on me last night. After I lost my mind and destroyed the second floor of Nordstrom.

"Fine. I will make a call. Thank you for your help."

"Would you like a complimentary pen?" the young teller asks, offering it over the counter.

"The ink is eco-friendly, and the pen shaft is compostable. Made of paper!" Mr. Chu adds, grinning like a dog waiting for a pat on the head.

The teller places the pen on my open palm, her metallic smile blinding me.

I glue on my own fake smile as I bend the pen. My cheeks heat again as the seconds tick by while I fight to break the pen shaft made of compostable paper. I bend it harder until finally it sort of tears in two ... and coats my hands in blue ink.

"Shit," I mumble, dropping the destroyed, leaking pen onto the pristine counter. "Thank you again for your help."

I can't let them see my embarrassment, so I tuck my goopy, ink-covered hands into my jacket pockets and hurry out of the bank before anyone spots the tears of humiliation streaming down my face.

I run to the end of the block and tuck into an alley, chest heaving to get a deep breath. I wipe my eyes on my sleeve and hold my hands in front of me—they're blue like the blueberry girl in the Willy Wonka movie—so I wipe what I can on my now-ruined jacket, my stomach growling in protest of this latest assault on my dignity.

I need to eat—Vera will have lunch in the fridge ...

Except I don't have a Vera anymore. Or an Olivia.

Oh my god, I have to buy my own groceries? I have to make my own food?

"What's wrong with you, princess?" I about jump out of my skin at the gravelly voice. "Your chauffeur call in sick?"

"Hi, Burt." Camped out on a bed of cardboard, an old hat in front of him for donations from passersby, Burt has one leg, one eye, and enough meanness for an entire city. I can't tell what color his trench coat is supposed to be.

"Where's your wheelchair?" I ask, straightening my shoulders.

"Someone nicked it while I was sleepin'."

"Can ... you get another one?"

He laughs once, a sharp, angry bark. His breath wafts toward me. I shiver.

"You look like you're havin' a bad day," he says. "What happened to your hands?"

"The bank ..." I throw a thumb over my shoulder.

"Did you rob it? The ink cartridge exploded on ya? Give me some of that!" He laughs again. I have to get out of this alley before his halitosis kills me.

I open my bag and dig through my wallet. "I don't have much today, Burt. Sorry." I hand him a twenty.

"Thanks, princess," he says. Our eyes meet for a moment as I give him the note. An ocean of sadness lies within his face.

"Take care." I run off before I can feel anything else.

The sobs threaten to overwhelm me again. *Get something to eat. Food will help.*

Despite my grandfather's insistence that I learn my way around a kitchen, I hate cooking. Plus I've always had a housekeeper, and they've always been excellent cooks. But given the sad state of my pantry at this moment, I need to figure out how to feed myself, at least until everything is worked out.

I can do this. I can be a grown-up.

I walk the extra blocks to my usual Whole Foods and slide a basket over my arm. Thank all the gods they have a tub of complimentary wet wipes at the front of the store. I pull and scrub and pull and scrub until I have an embarrassing pile of bluish towels from the futile attempt to erase my tantrum at the bank.

When a young kid in a dark green, store-branded apron walks by, I stop him. "Take care of these, will you?" I dump the pile of soiled wipes in his hands. He looks confused, and his lips part as if to speak. I walk away before that happens.

The blue isn't gone, and now my skin has that sticky, old-lady-perfume residue, but I can muscle through until I get home.

OK, what do I need to survive the next two days until Vera comes back?

Soup, fruit, skim milk, coffee, tampons, and scotch, which I can't buy here ...

I pause in the organic aisle, set my basket on the floor, and open my wallet. Since I don't have my cards and my bank accounts are empty, thus rendering my debit cards useless, I should probably see how much cash I have on hand.

Including the emergency hundred-dollar bill behind my driver's license ... $178.55.

My heart pounds and my sticky hands tingle.

I can live for a couple days on $178.55, right? Just until I convince Rupert to loosen his stranglehold on my inheritance?

I look in the basket at the items I've already picked up. I didn't bother to check the prices on anything.

Once I've got some food in me and I'm calmer, I will call Rupert and we'll talk this out like adults. Maybe I can even get Connor to come over and we can kiss and make up and I'll let him concoct some weird role-play scene for us if he wants and then we can talk about sharing his apartment—except he already has a roommate. All right, well, then maybe I can talk him into getting a place together, our *own* place, like he's harped about for the last year.

Hell, maybe I will surprise them *all* and get a proper job and then they'll all see just how horrible they've treated me. Rupert will see that I AM trying to be someone my grandfather could be proud of, that Archie didn't mess up or whatever Number Two was rambling on about last night ...

I'll show them.

In the pasta aisle, faced with too many choices, I realize I have no idea how to prepare a meal that doesn't come from a takeout container. I *do* know how to warm up soup and arrange a delectable charcuterie board with cheese and meats and olives and tiny tomatoes, however. See? I can do this!

Satisfied with my selections, I head to the front of the store. The self-checkouts are busy, so I pop into a lane with a real human cashier, a middle-aged woman with more gray than brown in her frizzy mop.

Someone needs to introduce her to the wonderful world of hair products.

"Find everything you need today?"

"I did. Thank you," I say.

"Oh, this soup is my favorite. Our in-store deli cooks are so good." She holds aloft my plastic tub of chicken noodle. "And these cheeses! Mmmm … You should get a loaf of French bread to go with everything. On special today," she says, pointing to a display at the end of her conveyer belt.

"Sure. Why not." Connor's not here to remind me not to eat carbs.

The cashier smiles and grabs a loaf, tucking it into the bag. *Single-use plastic bags for my groceries, Grandfather. How d'you like them apples?*

"Hey, can I ask you a question?" I adjust so I can read her name tag. "Molly?"

"Ask away." She talks and bag my groceries at the same time.

"Do you like your job?"

"Yeah, it's fun. I get to talk to nice people all day, and who doesn't love being surrounded by food?" She chuckles. She reminds me of Mrs. Claus.

"Does it pay well?"

Molly purses her lips for a beat. "This company is great. I've been here fifteen years, and I'm making just over twenty an hour now."

"Twenty dollars? An hour?"

"I know—pretty good, right?" She finishes ringing up my items. "Your total is $142.40. How are you paying today?"

That's almost everything in my wallet. "Um, cash." I dig it out and hand it over.

"Are you looking for a job?" She speaks as she sorts my money into her drawer. "I know they're hiring weekend cashiers. That's where you start, at least, and then work your way up."

I take my receipt, the lump in my throat preventing me from speaking. "Yes, maybe. Thanks, Molly."

I grab my bags and hurry out of the store. She makes $20 an hour. A forty-hour week means $800 a week; four weeks a month means $3200, before taxes.

Rupert said the lease on my loft—or rather, Clarke Innovations' loft—is $6000 a month. That doesn't include any of the utilities, and I don't even know how much those are because, yes, the company pays them. My grandfather's company pays for everything in my life.

How can I stand on my feet for forty hours a week and smile at people and ask them inane questions about their boring lives and pretend I'm not dying inside for twenty dollars an hour?

I'm ten steps outside the grocery store when the sky opens up.

I can't even run because the handles from the plastic bags are cutting into my blue-stained hands. And Molly overfilled the bags so when the bottom tears in one of them and my tub of delicious chicken noodle soup explodes on the sidewalk, I have no choice but to leave it for the seagull bathing itself on the sidewalk garbage can.

By the time I reach the front door to my building, the loaf of oven-fresh French bread is completely soaked. I shake the soggy paper wrapping until the bread blobs onto the porch and then kick it into the flower bed for the birds. "At least someone will eat well," I mumble, rain streaming down my face.

Like some sort of sad-sack Gretel, I trail water across the lobby and into the elevator, a puddle gathering around my feet. When the doors open, another resident gives me a wary glance.

"Take an umbrella," I say as I exit. I fumble with my remaining bags, trying to fish my keys from my jacket pocket, a task made more difficult by shivers of cold and humiliation. I pause to still my whole body, my head against the door, looking for my center to calm the chills vibrating my muscles, like my trainer instructs me to do when I work out too hard and feel faint.

Please, Grandfather, I get it. If you're somewhere out there watching, I'm sorry for being an ass. I will try harder. I will make you proud. I will pass out backpacks of school supplies and chocolate milk to underprivileged kids. Please, please, just let me open the door and see that this has all been a big nightmare, a test for me to see the err of my ways, like Jimmy Stewart in that sappy Christmas movie you loved so much.

I click over the dead bolt and open the door.

As expected, the apartment is still empty, still freezing, and still a reminder that I'm going to be squatting in the Arbutus Club locker room in twenty-four hours.

I drop the remaining groceries in the kitchen, pulling what's left out of the bags to dry on the counter. Considering I'm soaked to the bone, too, I strip and dump my clothes in a sopping pile in front of the stainless steel dishwasher. Whoever cleaned out the place yesterday left one of my heavy knitted couch throws, so I grab it from the floor and wrap it around me. It's itchy, but warm.

"Hey, Andromache." My plant is right where I left her in the bedroom. I plop into my pile of clothes, digging through to find a pair of heavy socks. "The bank didn't give us our money back. With your fancy Greek name, do you have any marketable skills? Anything that could get us a job paying more than twenty bucks an hour? I don't think I have it in me to make small talk over maxi pads and laundry soap, kiddo."

Andromache sits quietly, absorbing whatever light the thick, gray clouds allow through.

"You're already doing your job, I know. Photosynthesis is no joke. You're a good girl."

I curl up in my itchy blanket, pausing only for a moment to consider that maybe I could sell these designer clothes instead of using them as a mattress, but my eyelids have other ideas.

"Today has been too much already. Wake me up if you have any great ideas," I say to Andromache before nodding off.

NINE

THE FELONIOUS PHILANTHROPIST

I'm on the toilet when the doorbell rings. Again.

"Go away!" My voice echoes through my bedroom and into my mostly empty loft, answered by heavy knocking. "Go AWAY!" Knocking gives way to pounding. "Gaaaaahhhhhh, this better be important." I finish my business and wash my hands, fumbling around for my thick bathrobe while hollering at the door that I'll be right there.

I don't even bother to check the peephole. It's probably Connor crawling back on all fours because he can't stand to live without me after all. Thank the gods—I'm saved.

I yank open the door. "Ugh. What do *you* want?"

"Lara." Rupert nods once and pushes past, inviting himself in. Raindrops have coalesced on the shoulders and sleeves of his finely tailored overcoat, his ever-present cactus-leather portfolio tucked under one arm. "You haven't started packing?"

"I'm not going anywhere." I slam the door.

"You do not own this apartment, Lara. Your grandfather allowed you to live here, and now that permission has been rescinded. Did you not receive the notice from the building super-intendent? Was the disappearance of your furniture not enough of a suggestion that perhaps it's time for you to consider your options?"

"I'd offer you a chair, but you took them all."

Rupert stands on the bar side of the huge kitchen island, calm disconnection painting his narrow face.

"This is blackmail. You're blackmailing me to move to that ridiculous island and do your bidding. My grandfather would be disgusted if he saw what you're doing to me."

"But he wouldn't, Lara, because all of this was his idea."

My eyes sting as I twist at Grandfather's ring on my finger, and I'm pissed at myself for showing weakness, furious that my emotional control center chooses tears instead of strategy when I'm angry.

"Have you given a thought as to where you're going tomorrow? This unit has already been leased, and the new tenants will be taking possession this weekend."

I tighten the belt on my bathrobe and walk past Rupert into the kitchen. I need a drink.

Except the scotch and champagne bottles are empty in the sink, and I didn't have enough money in my wallet after buying groceries to stop at the liquor store. And speaking of groceries, everything has dried from the deluge, but like an idiot, I left the tipped-over gelato tub on the counter, too, and it melted into a gooey espresso-flake blob. Some has run down the front of the white cabinets and pooled on the floor. It looks like a Keebler elf took a shit in my kitchen.

I place both hands on the sink's edge and stretch forward, trying to keep myself from freaking out, to keep my angry tears safely hidden in the vault. I stand straight again, still gripping the counter, and lock eyes with Rupert.

"I have thirty dollars left to my name. You cleaned out my bank accounts. Any investments I might have had, I don't even know about, and if I did, I don't know how to access them. My credit cards magically went missing from my wallet at the hospital, and they don't work anyway. The lawyer wants twenty *grand* in retainers to help me with the criminal charges and to get things moving to sue *you* for stealing my inheritance—wait—are you *laughing*? You think this is funny?"

Rupert's smile softens. "This has nothing to do with me. I am a coexecutor of your grandfather's will, alongside that team of attorneys you insulted the other day. Nothing more, nothing less. I would be glad to show you my portion of Archibald's estate, which includes a small property in England that he bought for my mother, now mine in the wake of her death, plus some stock in Clarke Innovations collected over nearly thirty-five years of service and my yearly salary as I continue in my employ with the Clarke Foundation."

"And aren't you living in the Manor?"

"No. The Manor will eventually become a hub of learning. The board and I will be working to transition the house and grounds into an institute where scholars, politicians, and other sustainability experts can convene to continue the work Archibald left unfinished."

I shake my head. My childhood home is going to become an over-priced hostel for green nerds? Awesome.

"Why are you doing this to me?"

Rupert folds his hands atop his portfolio resting on the bar and looks left out the vast windows that, evidently, no longer belong to me.

"Fine. Why is *Grandfather* doing this to me?"

Number Two again meets my eyes. "I explained everything two nights ago. While you were handcuffed to the hospital bed. Before you were arrested." He moves into the kitchen and opens cupboards until he finds the tea tin, sniffs its contents and grimaces, and then pushes me aside to fill the electric kettle.

"Help yourself," I say.

"It's tea, Lara. Or at least something resembling tea."

The apartment is cold and silent, other than the occasional horn blare from the busy street below. When the kettle nears boiling, the water bounces inside like it's trying to escape.

"What, you're not going to offer a useful anecdote harvested from your bullied boyhood at some second-tier English prep school? No sage advice from the almighty Number Two?" I want to hurt him. I want Rupert to feel my dagger in his chest, just like the clawing, nagging ache tearing apart my insides.

"Would you like your tea bag left in?" He moves like the well-trained butler he is, dropping one bag each into two handcrafted mugs the movers didn't abscond with.

I ignore him. He still slides a mug in my direction, steam dancing skyward.

"You can finish your tea, but then you should leave. This is still my home for the next"—I pause and look at the microwave clock—"eighteen hours."

He takes a dainty sip and then resumes his position opposite me. He talks as he unzips his portfolio and extracts a MacBook. "Your grandfather never stopped looking for Cordelia."

I almost choke on the scalding mouthful of orange pekoe.

"He believed that when her plane went down, she made it out. He did everything he could to find the people who might have had anything to do with the incident—he hired people to search, even flew down to Mexico himself and scoured the towns around where she was last seen, where the plane was discovered. No one would talk to him. Everyone there is afraid of outsiders, of the cartels, of the government. Except one woman. Jacinta Ramirez."

I don't want to talk about my mother with Rupert. He didn't know her like I did. My mother was an adventurer, a world-class photographer, a traveler and pilot.

"Your mother built schools. Did you know that?"

I snap my head up. I did not know anything about any schools.

"The woman who spoke to Archibald—Jacinta—she knew your mother. Very well, apparently. Cordelia spent a lot of time in Mexico helping people in the poorer areas, places where schools and basic necessities and medical care weren't a priority. The cartels have a chokehold on many parts of that country, and government infrastructure is sporadic in remote villages, so your mother, alongside Jacinta, did what they could to help."

"What, like, help police arrest drug dealers?"

"She flew their products out of the country."

A siren screams by on the street below.

"Products—"

"Drugs. She spent some time as a drug runner. In turn, the bosses would give her huge sums of cash and she would then give it to the village councils who would build schools and bring in technology and access to clean water and medical care."

I feel like laughing, but I can't tell if this is a joke. A sick joke, but a joke, nonetheless.

"My grandfather never would have tolerated her doing that."

"Your grandfather had very little control over anything Cordelia did. Even you should know that."

"This ... this doesn't make any sense."

"Your mother was wild. She did wild things, including have you without benefit of a husband or even a steady boyfriend. But after you were born, something changed. She didn't care so much about what Archibald was doing because he had a whole team of people working to save the world. But she spent a fair amount of her misspent youth in Mexico and saw firsthand how difficult life was for a lot of people there, so she found her own cause."

"Did my grandfather fund this? She was smuggling drugs into America—how could he be OK with that?"

"Of course he didn't approve. He was furious. He offered her a different path, one where he would help her raise money legitimately, but she knew that would make her a target. If the cartels caught wind of a rich white Canadian woman down there trying to 'save' their country, they'd kidnap her, collect the ransom, and send her back to us in pieces. But if she was one of them, if she proved that her only interest was helping the Mexican people and nothing else, then they would gladly use her airplane and know-how."

I need to sit. All my chairs are gone. I abandon my tea and shuffle out of the kitchen to the lonely area rug in the center of the living room. Rupert stays by the bar but turns to continue his conversation.

"Why are you telling me this? Why now?"

"Why not?"

He then grabs his laptop and deigns to join me on the rug, folding his spidery legs in front of him. "Cordelia was a complex woman."

"Sounds like she was a criminal."

"Flying narcotics into the United States was definitely not one of her wiser choices."

"I don't understand … I thought she was just working a lot. She said she was a photographer. Her assignments took her all over the world, and that's why she was gone all the time."

"It did, at first. But she was so like Archibald—she had that stripe in her personality that made her see injustice in a different light from most. She wanted to do something to help."

"So why not do something that *didn't involve smuggling drugs?*"

Rupert shrugs and then pecks at his computer keyboard. "Have you ever seen Thalia Island?"

"Here we go again."

He turns the screen, now filled with a postcard-perfect aerial scene of a lush island. He hits the arrow button to advance to the next photo: a picturesque marina with small, bobbing boats, rocky outcroppings dotted with seabirds, serene ocean water lapping a pebbled beach scattered with seashells and baby crabs, sea otters floating together, the dorsal fins of a pod of orca, lighted, paved walkways, sprawling fields of wildflowers, acres of crops and grapevines and orchards, a quaint, small-town main street lined with shop fronts and a shiny red Canada Post box on one corner, tiny electric cars and even two golf carts parked along a bank of electric charging stations, narrow neighborhood streets featuring modest homes I recognize as structures my grandfather has championed in his green building initiatives …

"That's the island?"

"It is." Rupert turns the laptop around again and folds it closed. "No one is trying to cheat you out of your inheritance, Lara, least of all me. But Archibald spent his whole life building this empire to help humanity, and even your mother, in her own felonious way, found a way to carry the torch. You are the last Clarke. There is no one else to continue this work."

I'm clenching my teeth so hard, pain shoots in lightning bolts from my jaw to the top of my head.

"I'm not Archibald. I'm not Cordelia."

"No, but you are homeless as of noon tomorrow."

Rupert's gray-blue eyes don't leave mine, even as I glare back at him, willing my emotions to steady. He unfolds himself from the floor, tucks away his Mac, and sets his mug in the sink. "Thank you for the tea." He then slides into his overcoat, but from the inside pocket, he extracts an envelope. The little voice in my head hopes it's full of money, that maybe Number Two is relenting with this nonsensical fiscal austerity.

His oxfords are silent as he moves across to the door, exiting without a look over his shoulder.

I wait to hear the elevator ding before I get up to tear open the envelope.

Not money.

A thumb drive, and a note I accidentally tore in half that reads, "Maybe this will help you find what you're looking for. Love, Mom."

TEN

WINDFALL

I'm at the liquor store, one of the government-run outfits instead of a private shop, because I have thirty-six dollars and change left, and I need a drink. The price of booze always shocks my American friends when they visit—it's *expensive* in Canada. No Japanese whisky today—can't afford it. Even the Jack Daniels is too rich for my thin wallet, and they're out of the mickey bottles, so I'll have to settle for the sample sizes in the rack near the register. I don't make eye contact as the guy rings me up.

As soon as I'm out the front door, I open one of the samplers and pour the contents down my throat, followed quickly by a second. By the time I reach my doorstep, I'm four minis down—I'll have to ration the last three for when I stuff my remaining worldly possessions into the stack of gigantic paper lawn-waste bags someone left on my floor.

The thumb drive is still sitting on the kitchen island. I have no idea what I'm supposed to do with it, and if I'm going to plug it in, I need a dongle for my MacBook, which is somewhere amongst the Rupert-created chaos. As for the ripped note—I examined it before heading out to the liquor store and it's definitely my mother's writing. A callous move on Rupert's part to wait until now to share this with me.

What is he hoping to achieve? What, I will plug in the drive and see whatever is on it and then I will have a stirring change of heart and find it within to follow in the hallowed footsteps of the Clarkes who've come before me?

Maybe I will go back to my bank and rob it and then take the bags of money out into the streets, Joker style, and throw it all to the poor, overworked masses.

"What do you think, Andromache? Should we play Robin Hood like Cordelia did?"

I collapse onto my cold bedroom floor, fighting to open one of the ginormous lawn bags. It won't stand up or stay open on its own. Chores like this—*this* is why I have a housekeeper and an assistant.

Why you HAD a housekeeper and an assistant, Lara. Past tense.

I don't have enough suitcases for all these clothes—plus, all but one Vuitton rolling case are in the storage unit on the top floor, and I'm too tired to go get them myself—so this is going to have to do. And once the paper bags are full, I can cover them with blankets and sleep on them for my very last night in the apartment that isn't actually mine.

My throat hurts from the strain of reality. I crawl to my purse and pull out the remaining samplers. Finish them one after another. I don't want to feel any of this.

I shuffle back to my room. Once I'm situated in the pile again, I discover this garbage phone has no music app on it. And since Rupert's flunkies took my stereo system, I will have to pack accompanied by nothing but the songs playing in my head.

I can do this. Despite the alcohol sloshing in my belly, I'm remarkably settled and prepared for the task ahead. One at a time, I pull my beautiful clothes from the wrinkled igloo, shaking and folding and tucking into the awkward paper bags. On a solid shake of a pair of black Jil Sander trousers, something falls out of the pocket.

"Money!" I yell, holding up the fifty-dollar bill to Andromache. "Maybe there's more!"

And like a woman possessed, I'm unfolding everything I've already stuffed away, shaking the clothes and checking pockets. Then I move on to the pile of purses, the trench coats and sweaters and sports jackets—anything with pockets.

By the time I'm done checking every conceivable hiding place, I have a pile of cash waiting to be counted. How foolish Lara of Yesterday was to forget where she left her money—but Lara of Today is eternally grateful!

"Andromache—$1175! We have $1175!" From my seat in the middle of the calamitously messy room, I scoop the bills and coins and shower them over my head. "We're saved!" Well, at least for a few days.

One of my many little black dresses hangs askew from the long, open closet. "Connor loves that dress on me …"

A plan forms.

Between this money and Connor's affinity for my boobs, I will save myself from destitution and laugh in Rupert's face when I don't have to crawl on all fours and beg forgiveness.

Instead, maybe I'll send Number Two a wedding invitation with no RSVP card.

Connor won't know what hit him.

I'm less generous with my tip this time, partly because the driver screamed into his Bluetooth headset the whole trip into Burnaby but mostly because I have to be careful with my newfound windfall. At least until Connor and I can sit down and have a talk about our individual money situations and how soon we can afford to boot out his roommate and until I can find a job that pays more than Molly's amazing grocery-store gig.

It's just after eight, and a Thursday night, so Connor is home— some celebrity reality show he loves is on Thursday nights and he always races home after his acting class to watch it, even though he could DVR it like a normal person. He calls it his weekly "alone time" and says he needs decompression space after the grueling emotional workouts elicited during his workshops.

I packed my Vuitton suitcase and another overnight bag with everything I absolutely didn't want to leave behind—my favorite clothes and books, my few keepsakes, the sole framed photo of my mother and me together, makeup and hair products I won't be able to replace until I get a proper job, my plant daughter, and yes, the thumb drive and note. My whole life is with me in this cab—or at least the stuff I would be sad to lose. I stopped at the building superintendent's office on my way out and offered him cash if he would pack up the rest of my apartment and store everything for one week until I could get back to retrieve it. He seemed reluctant, until his seventeen-year-old kid popped in over his dad's shoulder and offered to do it—for $500! —because he's saving for a computer and could really use the money.

At least total strangers won't be going through what's left of my life come Saturday morning. Just some hormonal seventeen-year-old who will probably wear my panties on his face.

The rain has resumed, but at least I remembered an umbrella this time, so when the driver double-parks in front of Connor's apartment building—and I see the lights on in his front-facing unit—I don't get soaked. This is good, because I am dressed to impress. Silky black shift that leaves little to the imagination, my highest Valentino heels, the nylons with the seam up the back because they're Connor's favorite. I'm drenched in the perfume he bought me for Christmas last year, even though I find it slightly nauseating.

I need this to work. I need him to see that I've changed, that I'm ready to come together as a team and make this relationship go the distance.

The driver drops my suitcase on the sidewalk, accepts his fare in cash, and climbs back into his car without interrupting his Bluetooth argument. Deep breath, shoulders straight, I hurry toward the building's front door to catch it just as another resident exits. I used to think this place so shabby and pathetic—built a million years ago with that pebbled stucco and the leaky windows and the lobby and hallway carpeting soaked in the odors of every style of cooking known to man —but I could see myself here. I could see myself here with Connor, just the two of us embarking on our own journey to discover our truest selves. Farmers' markets on the weekends and brunch on the Drive in Burnaby, me hanging out at Companion Books while Connor is at auditions downtown. We could run lines at night, and I could help him dredge his path to stardom while I find my own way to prove to Rupert and my dead grandfather that I'm not a spoiled layabout.

The elevator judders as it carries me to the third of four floors. I quickly pull off my trench coat, fluff my hair in the dull, scratched reflection of the emergency phone cabinet, check my teeth for lipstick and my breath for freshness, and fluff my boobs in this push-up bra. When the car jolts to a stop and the doors screech open, I am ready for the spotlight.

Connor's apartment is left, then the second door on the right. My suitcase is made heavier by the overnight bag cradling Andromache draped over its pull handle, and the carpet in this hall bunches up under the wheels. And yet, I am undeterred. Lara is on a mission, world! Look out!

I'm shaking with nerves and excitement, the earlier buzz from my samplers long burned off.

Knock knock knock.

Someone is definitely home—I can hear the TV, followed by Connor's laugh.

I knock again, pulling my hair over my right shoulder. I want Connor's eyes to pop out of his head with desire the second he sees me.

The lock unbolts from the inside and the scratched, tarnished knob wiggles. At last, the door opens.

"Surprise!" I announce, my voice bouncing down the hall.

"Heyyyyy, Lara," Connor says. He's wearing the gaudy Versace pajama bottoms he begged for on his last birthday, his sculpted torso bare except for the $4000 gold, double-sided Celtic cross I bought him on our trip to Dublin last year, his hair perfect as usual. For as dumb as he can be, he sure is pretty to look at.

"Are you going to invite me in?" I pop out a hip, push my chest toward him.

"Ah, L, you should've called first ..." His cheeks flush and he looks past me, down the hall.

"I didn't realize I needed to call ahead to see my *boyfriend*."

"Tonight's not a good night."

I step closer, reach forward, and tuck a finger into the waistband of his pajama bottoms. "It looks like an excellent night. And you're already half-naked, so invite me in and I'll finish the job."

"Baaaabe, didn't you get my note? With the box and stuff?"

The elevator screeches and offers its dull *ding* behind me just as I reach on tiptoes to meet Connor's lips. He pulls back before we connect, his face paling as his eyes dart down the hall. I follow what he's looking at.

I know the woman walking toward us. And she's dressed not unlike I am—high heels, tight dress, only hers is red—she's adorned for business of the carnal variety, and she's moving toward us with her fit body, pixie-cut brown hair, huge brown eyes, and pouty red lips.

"Hey, Suze," I say so I'm not rude, then turn back to Connor. "Are you guys rehearsing or going out or something—"

His former pallor is overwhelmed by the flushing of someone who's just been caught with his hand in the cookie jar.

"Hey, Lara," Suze says, insinuating herself between me and Connor and brushing her hand against his bare chest as she walks into the apartment.

"Um, Connor?" I ask.

"Con, dinner should be here in about twenty. I ordered from the car," Suze says, then disappears into the depths of the crappy apartment. Connor steps out into the hall and closes the door behind him.

"Suze. From *Super George*? From acting class?" I say, words laced with dangerous anger. "The body's not even cold, Connor. How long have you been screwing her behind my back?"

"Lara, please ..." Connor reaches for my wrist, but I yank it away. "Come on. Don't yell. I have neighbors with kids. Don't cause another scene."

"Another scene? Really?"

Connor swallows hard. "Lara, we haven't been good for a long time. It's best if we take a break."

"Oh, you mean, now that I'm no longer soaked in money to keep you in acting workshops and fancy clothes and champagne-fueled weekends in Tofino."

He doesn't deny it. "But, like, what are you going to do now? You don't even have a job." He looks down at my suitcase and bag sitting next to me.

"I guess I'm not staying with you to talk about our options, am I? Seems you have one vagina too many to deal with." I disentangle my trench coat from the handle of my suitcase—careful not to disturb Andromache's pot from her tenuous spot in my open bag—and stuff myself into the sleeves, feeling at once stupid and enraged. *This* is why it's a good thing concealed weapons are illegal in this country.

"When you figure things out, Lar, give me a call. Maybe we can get a coffee or something."

I reach up and snatch the cross from his neck, breaking its gold chain. "Fuck you, Connor. I hope she gives you herpes."

ELEVEN

SSSSHHHH ... CHARDONNAY

When the Lyft driver pulls up, I'm in the rain with just my suitcase and bag, hair dripping down my back, my mangled umbrella tossed post-tantrum into the unkempt flower bed along the front of Connor's shitty building. I can't believe I ever thought I'd be able to live in this dump.

Since the evening did not turn out as expected, I instruct the driver to drop me at the Fairmont. Maybe Benny the Cannabis Cowboy will be bar-side and generous with his stories and cocktails.

Traffic is light for a rainy Thursday night, and the driver is a young guy who doesn't ask intrusive questions or offer knowing glances in the rearview mirror. At a stoplight, he quietly reaches over the front seats to hand me a box of tissue.

"Thank you." I dab at the mascara scoring my cheeks and use a wad of sheets to soak up the dripping ends of my hair. I can't go into the Lobby Lounge looking like a drowned rat.

He pulls into the front turnaround, I pay cash for the ride, and the driver is quick to unload my case from the trunk. He opens my door for me, offering a pleasant smile as he reaches into his jacket and pulls out a brochure. "I'm looking for venture capital for my start-up, so if your grandfather's company is looking for sound investments ..." He pushes a brochure into my hand.

"What are the odds that YOU would be my driver, out of all the fares in the city?"

"I know! It's fate! I can't believe it either! But when I saw it was you getting into my car—"

I flatten his brochure against his chest. "I'm penniless. You're barking up the wrong tree. Good luck." I grab the handle of my Vuitton and shiver as the warmth of the lobby wraps around me. The lounge is hopping, but all I require is one little seat at the bar and a willing mixologist to put this evening behind me. Maybe I'll spend one last hurrah in a waterfront room before I have to move into some shanty bachelor basement suite out in the suburbs surrounded by minivans and moms in Disney-inspired clothing and dads in Kirkland-brand sneakers and screaming children named after the cities where they were conceived.

Like I even have the funds for that.

I slide into the lounge just as a swanky older gentleman helps a buxom blond young enough to be his granddaughter off her white bar stool. "I'll take that, thank you very much," I say, hopping onto the chair in my very tight dress and still-wet shoes. The girl harrumphs as I knock my elbow into her and Andromache's long leaves brush her shoulder, but Fairmont Barbie needs to move faster. I've got some drinking and forgetting to do.

Andromache again rests on the bar beside me. "I'll bet you didn't mind getting wet, hey?" I ask her as I unzip my purse, pull out the Purell, and clean my hands. The bartender—it's the woman from the other day who wasn't as friendly as Benny—raises an eyebrow. "She's old enough to be in here, I swear," I say, wrapping a protective arm around my plant's pot.

The bartender smiles. "What can I get you two?"

"She'll have water, no ice. And me? Something tasty but budget conscious. Also, can you wash this?" I point to the polished bar top before me.

"Girl, you know nothing here is budget conscious," the bartender says, obliging my request with her bleach towel. "I can do a Mission Hill chardonnay or Cabernet Sauvignon for fifteen a glass."

"Ugh. Wine."

"The hard stuff is expensive. Why don't you just go to the liquor store and grab something there?"

Because I have nowhere to drink it and I don't want to get arrested again by consuming outside. I can't show my face at any of Grandfather's clubs. I can't even call Vuitton or Hermes and arrange a private try-on session during which they'll ply me with champagne because they're closed and Olivia isn't here to cajole managers into opening for me.

Plus I'm essentially homeless, and my boyfriend is humping his costar.

"I'll do the chardonnay. But if you *tell* anyone ..."

She mimes zipping her lips.

"Where's Benny tonight?"

"He's having a baby!" The bartender pours and slides the glass in front of me.

"He didn't look pregnant the last time I was here." I sip. It's not terrible. It'll do the job just fine.

"He and his girlfriend. Her water broke around lunchtime, so he called me to cover for him—they're at BC Women's right now."

"Wow ... he didn't mention it the other day."

"Bartenders gotta keep a few secrets. Besides, we're in the business of listening to *your* secrets." She smiles, wipes more of the counter, and moves on to help someone down the way.

The lounge is near capacity. Among the reasons I like this place—despite their drink prices that I've never before questioned but now see are ridiculous—even when filled with local young professionals and the occasional celebrity or hockey player or traveling businessman looking for a booty call, the atmosphere is controlled, not raucous. I can disappear in here without someone asking about my grandfather or Connor Mayson or if I can get them an autograph from either or if I want to invest in their start-up.

Tonight's Lyft driver the exception, obviously.

Plus, when I drink too much, I can pop upstairs and sleep it off and then hit the spa the next morning where they work their magic, and no one is the wiser. It's actually perfect. I'd live here full time if it were an option.

Only now I'm down to around six hundred bucks, after deducting the money for the superintendent's kid to pack my apartment and after paying for the cab to Connor's and the Lyft here. And the wine is going down smooth and quick. Four glasses should do it—sixty dollars, plus tip? I can probably afford a fifth glass. I just won't eat anything. I can always pop into the Arbutus after hours—or I could head out to Vancouver International Airport, buy the cheapest ticket, and eat my fill in one of the first-class lounges.

Except ...

Where am I going to sleep?

I check my phone. Nine p.m. The bar closes at midnight. I have three hours to figure out where I'll rest my head, now that it's not going to be on Connor's lumpy futon.

"Another one, please?" I point to my now-empty glass.

And so it goes for another hour, and then another. The TV over the bar has sports on, the talk nothing but Stanley Cup Playoff action (the Canucks are still in) interspersed with the same five commercials. A few randoms take seats next to me and try to strike up conversation, but I am in no mood to play. "I'm mourning the death of a family member so if you could leave me alone, that would be great." Or "My boyfriend is screwing his coworker, so right now, I hate all men. Save your breath."

I do let one guy buy me a drink, but only because I'm at my limit, and this bartender isn't as pliable as Benny was. But even he gets tired of my non-response to his lengthy sob story about his wife who won't give him blow jobs anymore, so he swallows the rest of his Gold Label and excuses himself.

I don't even realize my head is resting on my wrists until the bartender taps a long fingernail on the bar next to my ear. "Hey, sweetie ... Can I call you a cab?"

"What?" I wipe the back of my hand across my mouth. My lips are numb. "What time is it?"

"Eleven thirty. We're wrapping up for tonight."

The bar is practically empty. A glass of ice water sits on the counter in front of me alongside two Advil. The bartender smiles. "Figured this would help get a jump on that chardonnay hangover."

"What's your name?"

"Eugenia."

"That's a great name." I smile and the room spins. "My name is Lara. Lara Josephine Clarke."

She smiles again, smaller.

"You know who I am."

"Your family is kind of Vancouver royalty."

"*Was* Vancouver royalty. They're pretty much all dead now. Just me now, Eugenia. The only Clarke left. That's what Number Two said."

"That sounds very lonely, Lara." Eugenia doesn't move from her spot, doesn't look like she's trying to hustle away to clean glasses or wipe down tables.

"Benny's lucky. He's got a real family."

Eugenia pulls her phone from her apron and taps the screen open. She turns it to me. It's a picture of a red, squish-faced newborn, mouth open in a howl. It's the most beautiful thing I've ever seen.

"A girl! Benny's a dad!" she announces. A few staff cleaning the tables behind us hoot and clap.

And then I'm crying, and Eugenia's smile melts and she reaches for a stack of cocktail napkins. "Oh, sweetie, it's OK. Everything's going to be OK."

"But it's not, Eugenia," I say through a sob. "My grandfather died. And my boyfriend—you know, that crappy actor I was here with the other day? He's totally sleeping with that Suze girl, his costar on *Super George* and I went to his apartment tonight to make up after our little fight we had the other night when I sort of smacked him in the nose at Nordstrom but that wasn't my fault—it was Betty Boop's fault because she wouldn't put my stuff into the bags because my credit cards were broken and anyway, I went to Connor's and *Suze* showed up and she was, like, beautiful and tiny and perfect and she was like *I ordered dinner, CON,* and she touched him right in front of me and yes, now I know he's a cheating dirtbag, but he's all I had and now he's dumped me because I've been cut out of my grandfather's will unless I take some dumb job on some weird island full of hippies and I'm homeless as of noon tomorrow because Number Two took away my bank accounts and my amazing apartment, and I spilled my chicken noodle soup all over the sidewalk so I didn't have any dinner, and this suitcase and Andromache here are all I have left in the whole world—"

Eugenia's face pales a bit.

"Oh, no, don't worry, I'll pay for my drinks." I reach for my purse —it takes a few attempts because there are two of everything—and finally extract my wallet. "Here. Figure out what I owe you. Take a big tip because you are my only friend in the entire world, Eugenia. I'm not even kidding."

I watch as she counts out the money for my tab. She only gives herself a 10 percent tip. "More than that, Eugenia. You're super good at your job."

"No," she says, zipping my wallet closed and placing it under my hand. "You need this money right now, more than I do."

"Where am I gonna go tonight?"

The bartender's huge brown eyes look at me, and all I see is pity. For once, I'm going to take it. All of it. I'm going to let it soak into my skin because I deserve to have someone feel sorry for me for once.

"What's the job your grandfather wants you to take?"

"I don't even know. Something to do with an island." The word *administrator* comes out right on my third try.

"Will there be a place to live on the island?"

"Yes …"

"And food? And a salary?"

I shrug. "Probably."

"Doesn't sound too bad."

"Uggghhhhh." I drop my roaring head onto the counter again. The music stops, replaced by the clinking of glasses and flatware and the hum of vacuums as the hotel staff preps the dining areas for tomorrow.

"Ten minutes," a gruff voice says from the lounge entrance.

"Lara," Eugenia says. I look up at her. "Let me call someone for you."

"I told you—there's no one to call."

"Who is this Number Two you mentioned?"

"Oh, god, *Rupert*. He's my grandfather's valet or butler or servant or whatever you want to call him. He's so bossy and English."

Eugenia chuckles. "Lara, look at me. Eyes on my face."

I do. She's older than I am, her dark hair in tiny braids with a rainbow of beads, all pulled into a thick pony at the back of her head, and the smoothest skin I've ever seen. "You're beautiful, Eugenia. What moisturizer do you use?"

She smiles again. "Listen to what I'm going to say, OK? Can you focus on my voice?"

I nod—and regret it. The room tilts.

"I know who you are. I've seen you come in here a hundred times before. And I saw the video on Twitter of what happened the other night at Nordstrom."

"Oh noooooo …"

"You're a good person, Lara. Underneath all that trouble is someone who needs and deserves love. I don't know what happens in your world behind closed doors—I only know what the tabloids and gossips show the rest of us. But I've worked in this hotel for a long time, and I know how toxic and awful rich people can be to each other. Even you have been known to ruffle some feathers around here." She leans on the counter. "But I believe every single person deserves a second chance. Or a third. Or a hundredth—a chance to prove their mettle, to prove who they really are inside." She jabs at her own heart with her long, rose-pink fingernails. "You gotta know when opportunity's knocking. And it sounds like it's knocking now, Lara."

"Is it, though?"

She nods vigorously. "Go to this island. Go do whatever it is your grandfather has asked of you. Find some peace. Get away from this shitty, fake, elitist scene down here. Get away from Connor Mayson—who can't act, by the way, just between you and me—"

I laugh through tears I didn't mean to let loose.

"Go find Lara. Because sitting at my bar every night, drinking your-self silly—throwing temper tantrums in department stores and yelling at our spa staff and punching boyfriends in the nose—I don't think that's what your grandfather would have wanted for you."

I nod and nod and nod. "He would be so disappointed in me right now."

"Yes, he probably would be."

"But ... what if the job is too hard? What if I don't know how to do it? What if I fail?"

Eugenia hands me more cocktail napkins for my nose and then shrugs with great exaggeration.

"Then you fail. Who cares? At least you tried. At least you *did something.*"

"But I will be alone there. I don't have any family left."

"You'll be alone here too. And family is what you make of it. Benny and I are clearly not related"—her laugh echoes off the ceiling as she pulls her braided, beaded hair over her shoulder—"but he's my little brother. I'd do anything for that guy. And now I'm an auntie!"

She raises a hand for a high five; it only takes me two swings to meet it.

Eugenia leans against the bar again and lifts a couple of my plant's long, healthy leaves under her fingers. "This plant is your family now. Looks like you're taking good care of her, yeah?"

I bob my head again.

"What did you say her name was?"

"Andromache." I sniff.

"Like, Andromache of Scythia? From the comic book?"

I shake my head. I don't know anything about comic books. "Just Andromache."

Eugenia stands straight again. "What's the name of your island again?"

"Thalia. Thalia Island."

"Then this here little sweetie is Andromache of Thalia Island."

In the short time I've known this bartending philosopher, I've learned one thing: when Eugenia smiles, you can't help but smile too.

"I like that. That's a good name," I whisper, brushing a light finger under Andromache's leaves.

"So, let me ask you again—is there someone I can call for you?"

I meet Eugenia's eyes and know that the battle is over. I dig through my purse once again and find my crappy phone and hand it to her. "Number Two. He's in there. Maybe he will come get me."

Eugenia opens Contacts. Shouldn't take her long to find Rupert's number because I have no one else's saved.

"Is he the one listed as Posh Nosferatu?"

I pull the trigger on my finger gun. "Bingo."

TWELVE

KEYS TO MY FUTURE

T his has been the longest, hardest, most uncomfortable week of my life.

Number Two has forbidden me from consuming a single drop of alcohol, not even a sip of bubbly for my thirty-first birthday, which passed without fanfare despite my prior plans for an obscene party filled with friends, food, and fabulous French wine. Instead, I marked the occasion by coughing so hard, I blew a blood vessel in my left eye, thanks to the virus I picked up sitting at the Fairmont in wet clothes with wet hair and my now-ruined Valentinos. He disallowed NyQuil but permitted Tylenol, and even then only every eight hours. I don't know what they taught him in his bargain-basement boarding school in bloody old England, but it feels like maybe he graduated from a military academy full of jerkfaces.

Although ... he did tend to me while I stewed in my fevered juices for four days, kindly offering the spare room in the airy, spacious Kitsilano townhouse I didn't even know he owned. He delivered fresh-squeezed juice, a daily pile of vitamins from his personal physician, and meals I could swallow without aggravating my inflamed tonsils. The morning of May 2, he slid onto the nightstand a single chocolate cupcake with buttercream frosting alongside the acetaminophen and whispered *"joyeux anniversaire"* just before I fell back asleep. Andromache was given a spot near the window, and the new growth in the middle of her pot suggests that Rupert lavished her with attention too. I managed to squeak out a thank-you, and in return, he offered a small smile I haven't seen since I was a kid.

On day five, when the viral assault had waned and the coughing didn't make me gag and my body was finished shaking from probable alcohol withdrawal, Rupert threw open the drapes in my room, patted a pile of clothes on hangers draped over the end of my bed, and pointed at the en suite bathroom. "You have one hour before we leave." And then he exited, his steps quiet thanks to plush rugs underfoot.

When I emerged feeling almost normal, that almost-normal feeling went away when I realized we were leaving for Thalia Island *right then.* Rupert had his Tesla packed with my suitcases, and Humboldt the bullmastiff was already slobbering all over the back seat.

"Look lively. We're meeting the lawyers on board the ferry in ninety minutes."

"I was hoping to get my hair done before we go. I cannot show up looking like—"

Rupert stopped moving, turned slowly, and gave me The Look.

"Fiiiiine." So I climbed into his car and didn't ask questions as he yammered on about everything and nothing, only half listening since I still wasn't feeling great, and his lecture sounded kind of terrifying and overwhelming anyway.

And I must've dozed off during the ride from his place to the Horseshoe Bay marina because now Rupert is nudging my arm. "Lara, almost time to board." The tiny flicker of hope that he would surprise me with a belated birthday visit to the salon extinguishes. I'm sure the hippies living on the island won't notice I haven't had a proper blowout and straighten. Will they?

"This is a super big boat."

Rupert smiles. "Lara, meet *Lara II.* Our dedicated ferry. All electric."

"He named a boat after me?"

"A *ferry*. Not just any boat."

As we pull closer, I see my name painted in huge letters across the rear. It disappears as the car ramp moves into place.

My grandfather was a huge watercraft nerd in general, especially when it came to vessels that don't use fossil fuels, which is why I only took the seaplanes to Vancouver Island for long, romantic weekends when Archibald wouldn't find out and nag about my familial obligation to save the world. Clarke Innovations has a lot of money invested in watercraft projects that use alternative energies, so I shouldn't be surprised about the ferry. I *am* surprised, however, that he named such a beast after me. Am I supposed to feel honored?

I can hear the jokes already: *Did you get a ride on* Lara? *I had the longest ride ever on* Lara. *She's smooth and generous, that* Lara. Lara's *ride is electric, I'm telling ya*. It will be like senior year all over again.

Rupert explains that Thalia Island has a dedicated marina large enough to accommodate one of the smaller interisland vessels in the BC Ferries network, but Thalia has her own ferry system. Twice-weekly crossings can accommodate up to four hundred people, thirty cars, as well as regular shipments of food and supplies. "Those items we can't yet make or grow ourselves," he adds.

"How am I supposed to get things I order online?"

Rupert lifts an eyebrow and launches into a sermon about carbon emissions and setting an example of ethical shopping habits. He also reminds me I no longer have any credit cards, so shopping won't trouble me for now. "Take Humboldt to that patch of grass, would you?" As he says it, the bullmastiff shoves his head between the front seats and wipes his frothy jowls along my formerly clean and slime-free AllSaints black leather biker jacket.

It's going to be a long year.

As we move to the narrow foyer that encloses the stairs connecting the car deck to the first floor, we're greeted by our gray-haired captain named Cathy who chats with Rupert for a moment and then promises fifty minutes from boarding to docking. Close enough to be convenient, but far enough that we won't have squatters finding us in their dinghies. "Quietest ferry in operation, I promise!" she says, waving to return upstairs.

The space she vacates, however, is immediately occupied by three other humans in fine suits who've climbed out of the only other cars on the ferry. Number Two greets them and reintroduces me—as if these lawyers need a reminder of who I am—the estate attorneys from last week, plus the guy I called about my criminal charges. Three attorneys, one Rupert, and me.

Pretty sure they call this an ambush.

What was I saying about Rupert the jerkface?

And it's all been perfectly orchestrated. I am now trapped on a ferry that is zooming into open water and thus I cannot storm out unless I'm willing to swim for it. I hazard a quick glance out the wide windows, realizing that even if I *were* to jump into that very cold water, I have nowhere to go should I make it ashore.

"Go find Lara." Eugenia's words from the hotel bar last week float through my head. Seems I have retained whispers of her sage wisdom, in spite of that dastardly chardonnay haze.

There is no time to enjoy the beautiful scenery—Rupert has me on an invisible leash, leading our entourage to the conference room located on the passenger deck. The lawyers are close behind, as if they're all afraid I *will* fling myself into the Salish Sea.

A steward opens the conference room door and shows us inside, offering beverages and coffee as we take our seats at the ovoid table. A bank of windows stretches along both sides—we must be right under the captain's bridge—and for a second, I luxuriate in the beauty of the British Columbia coastline, the cloudless blue skies, the pristine Strait of Georgia stretching ahead and behind. Even in my most cynical moments, this really is a gorgeous part of the world.

But then a cup of steaming black tea is slid in front of me alongside two weighted pens and another blank legal pad, and any hint of gratitude disappears like mist.

The lawyers and Rupert waste no time, probably because we don't have much to waste before arriving at the island. Rupert explains quickly and succinctly as Bernard Allen from Allen, Shore, and Lewis places a stack of documents before me, detailing that they've managed to get the criminal charges dismissed, as long as I promise to pay damages and not shop at any Nordstrom location for a period of one year. Apparently there was also some back-and-forth with the judge about an anger-management program, but Rupert opted to pay the extra fine and promised both the judge and Mr. Allen that I would be too busy over the course of the coming year to have time for any long-term commitment here in the Lower Mainland.

With Mr. Allen's portion of today's matters settled, he takes his coffee to the window, sighing contentedly, clearing the stage for Heather Smithe and Arthur Leyton to plop down the next pile of papers. On top is an actual employment agreement—the first I've ever seen with my name on it—detailing the responsibilities of the "Thalia Island Project Administrator," my official title, apparently. The salary is still in the five-figure range, but at least it's better than the $30,000 stipend I was otherwise going to receive. Included, too, is housing, food, a cell phone plan, dental, vision, and medical care not covered by provincial health services, and use of an electric vehicle, already imported to the island.

I open my mouth to protest the paltry sum, given my clothing expenditures alone will eat this so-called annual salary in a single season. But Rupert lowers the blinds and dims the lights so he can cast another of his ridiculous slideshows of Thalia Island—including photos of all the hard work still left to be done—onto the screen that lowers from the ceiling.

I swallow my protest and twist Grandfather's ring around my finger to remind myself to stay silent. By the looks of things, fashion is going to be the least of my concerns, unless that fashion embraces denim and flannel and steel-toed boots and ball caps made of bamboo fiber emblazoned with the Thalia Island logo.

"Excuse me, Number Two, but will we have at least one aesthetician and/or manicurist living on the island? A stylist at the very least?" I lift a few strands of my sad hair.

The chuckles that follow are just quiet enough to qualify as polite.

So I shove my pride into my back pocket and sign their noisome employment agreement, paving the way for Heather Smithe and Arthur Leyton to hash out additional details with Rupert about how the next year will go down. It's like they're trying to cram a lifetime of information into my head before we drop anchor.

And in a way, I suppose they are. It's not like I've been tuned in to what dear Archibald has been getting up to all these years, and especially not as it relates to Thalia Island.

My new position as project administrator is going to be exhausting. I haven't even spent a single night on the island, and I'm already pining for a massage on a faraway, white-sand beach kissed by the aquamarine sea. Apparently in addition to the endless physical tasks I must undertake and oversee, I have to manage *people*—people who have been living on the island for the last year building, planting, cleaning, preparing … It's not that I'm not *good* at telling people what to do, it's that I'd rather they just know what they *need* to do and leave me alone.

What was Grandfather thinking? Why didn't he hire someone with an actual background in project management or human resources? It's like they all want me to fail—the lawyers, Rupert, maybe even my grandfather—and the terms of my employment arrangement are very specific about milestones I must meet by the end of this first year, a.k.a. Schedule A, or else I'm discharged from my duties, booted off the island, and we revert back to the $30,000 annual stipend.

The stakes here are real. There's *no way* I can live on thirty thousand *Canadian* dollars a year. It's like they didn't even consider the exchange rates in this laughable sum!

"Lara." Rupert's voice pulls my attention back to his face, and he points at the pad and pens before me. "This is information you might need." He closes the slideshow and raises the blinds, again flooding the conference room with light.

"Can't you just email everything to me? I'm tired."

"You can nap later. Your new position starts imminently." He then opens his briefcase on the table, pulls out a brand-new iPhone still in its box and a huge set of keys, and slides both items across the table.

"Great. I'll look like a janitor. Happy now?" I jangle the heavy key chain in the air, raising Humboldt's attention from where he's stretched on the floor. He farts thoroughly and then drops his head again, returning to whatever dream he just left behind, which probably involves a place filled with worm-infested dirt, terrifically ugly work boots, and smelly people who desperately need showers, all of whom are waiting for me to figure out which of these million keys opens the island's only indoor-plumbed bathroom.

THIRTEEN

BOUNCING BABY BULLMASTIFF

I make sure to wipe the awe off my face before Rupert sees it as the ferry eases into her spot. Sand-and-rock beaches cuffed by lush forest stretch in either direction of the new, state-of-the-art marina, the northern shore arching around and out of sight as it morphs into a high-walled, rocky outcropping topped by more woods. These beaches would be amazing for bonfires—like English Bay, only wider, and no people. I'm not even sure if we're allowed bonfires here ... probably too much smoke or happiness for the ozone layer.

Our gathering returns to the vehicle deck, but the lawyers aren't disembarking—they took this midday meeting as a courtesy after the earlier meeting was postponed by my head cold. I'd thank them for their accommodation, but their billable hours are all the thanks they need.

I cajole Humboldt back into the Tesla and climb in myself, settling Andromache on the floor near my feet so Humboldt won't eat or slobber on her as we wait for Number Two to stop jawing with the sharks. I settle into my seat and open my new iPhone. When Rupert delivered my last phone upgrade, I gave him hell about how environmentally destructive these little devices are—a quick Google search, ironically on your phone, reveals that smartphones are loaded with mercury, chlorine, lead, arsenic, cadmium, and on and on. He told me my grandfather recognizes that phones are a "necessary evil" until such time we can develop more sustainable technologies not reliant upon cheap labor and dangerous chemicals to manufacture. "Let's focus on the demon in front of us, shall we, Lara?" Rupert said. I didn't actually care. I just like watching him get flustered.

This phone is the latest model. I dig into my wallet and pull out the folded napkin with the number scratched on it. Upon texting this number with my 7-Eleven phone last week, I was relieved to learn it was indeed Eugenia the bartender's number, and not that weird dude who kept going on about how fellatio makes a man perform better in the boardroom.

The thank-you text I tentatively sent was, in fact, received by Eugenia, and now, amazingly, I seem to have made a friend. *Send pics of the new place. I'm so happy for you! And stay away from the chardonnay.*

Not a problem.

It's not just Eugenia who I've added to Contacts. She looped Benny the Cannabis Cowboy into our quick conversation so now he's on Team Lara, too, although mostly he's just spamming us with photos of his new baby girl who they named—seriously—Sativa. That kid won't have any issues at *all*.

Though I don't like kids, this is way better than the dick pics that usually populate my DMs. Gross. And I'm not going to lie—it *has* been weird to not have my phone blow up with Connor's smutty texts and gym selfies or his whiny pleas for funding for some acting class with a has-been coach here from LA trawling for "the next big thing" or him shit-talking some other actor who booked a job he says he *totally* should've gotten ("I mean, have you even *seen* his hair?").

What's even weirder is that I miss him, and my heart does hurt that he's already moved on, that he was clearly only with me because of my family's status.

What does that say about me that I miss someone who treated me like a human ATM?

Nothing good.

Is that why my mother never stayed in one place for too long, before she could get close to any one human in particular? Is that why she chose the life she did, so that people would write her off and leave her to do whatever she needed to feel whole?

Then again, how many lives did she ruin by helping the drug lords funnel that poison into the US and likely Canada? Did she feel it was justified when she built a school or medical clinic or whatever she was doing down there? Did Cordelia have some sort of warped scorecard to rationalize whatever pain her actions caused?

And who was Jacinta Ramirez? Was she just some woman in Mexico who cared about her people and saw an opportunity in my mother, or was she more than that to Cordelia?

My head aches with so much thinking. I'm not used to it. Usually I do everything I can to *avoid* thinking about heavy topics. And I am in no way ready to look at whatever is on that mystery thumb drive. Someday. When I'm more evolved. For now, it's fine where it is, to be forgotten in the inside pocket of my L'Inconnu bag alongside emergency tampons and my favorite discontinued lip color.

Finally, Rupert stops talking, shakes hands, and slides in behind the wheel. I'm trying to look indifferent and maybe even bothered, but a small flame of excitement burns in my stomach—the good kind of flame, like that feeling you get when that A-list hottie you've had your assistant low-key stalking drops a quick hello in your DMs and asks to meet at the top of the Eiffel Tower on the summer solstice so you do and he's just as gorgeous and muscled in real life as he is on the movie screen but then he turns out to be super needy and actually kind of icky so you decide to bid him *adieu* but not until one last delicious, hard-body, ab-filled naked selfie before shooing him out of your suite at Hôtel de Crillon …

What were we talking about again?

Rupert pauses and thanks Captain Cathy. Window up, we roll off the boat, leaving the lawyers behind, nothing but my new, A-list-hottie-deficient life ahead.

"From our private marina, the drive to downtown is only ten minutes. Note that nearly all the main roads on the island are made from PlasticRoad, versus standard asphalt, made exclusively from recycled drink containers. We sourced it from a Dutch company with a one-hundred-year guarantee—we're one of their pilot locales to test the PlasticRoad under the drenching BC fall and winter seasons."

"Cool." It actually *is* cool, but again, less is more. I don't want Rupert to think I'm enjoying this.

We pass a Watch for Deer sign as Rupert explains the sustainable farming and irrigation practices underway that will eventually allow the island to be a hundred percent self-reliant for pretty much everything that can be grown or raised for food. What can't be grown in fields will be nurtured in four, four-story vertical farms mid island that have been integrated into the surrounding environment for minimum footprint and maximum protection from weather-related exposure. Within one of the vertical farm buildings is a lab where the first British Columbian "clean meats"—beef, poultry, and pork—are being grown as a hopeful alternative to traditional meat sources.

"Is all that part of my job too?" The warm, fuzzy excitement is shoved aside as panic rushes forward. I don't know *anything* about food sourcing or vertical farming or lab-grown cheeseburgers. Food comes from Vera or Olivia or the grocery delivery service. Meat comes from the city's finest butchers. Meals come from the housekeeper, chef, or caterer.

"As detailed in the employment agreement you signed"—Rupert purses his lips—"your primary responsibilities will be in municipal management. I already have a team in place to handle the external affairs, which include farming and roads and the underbelly of the island's day-to-day resources, such as plumbing, wastewater management, zero-waste mandates, that sort of thing. Consider yourself the first mayor of Thalia Island."

"So, paperwork—no dirt?"

Rupert chuckles. "Mostly human resources. You're good at bossing people around. You should fit right in."

He slows as we approach a junction. It leads into the downtown core I recognize from the photos he displayed at my loft last week. So perfect and clean, it's almost eerie. "Did you hire the Hallmark set designers?" Even the planter boxes along the sidewalks and storefronts are packed with spring flowers.

"This, of course, is the hub of Thalia. Most of these spaces will eventually be occupied by shops and service providers for the residents. Since the focus of our mission statement trends away from a heavily consumeristic lifestyle, shops and business owners will serve the specific needs of the islanders—food, clothing, farming supplies, hardware, and of course, technology. We won't have any regular commuters living on the island for the first few years. If you live here, you have to be able to work here too. A number of residents will be telecommuting from their companies on the mainland."

Rupert pulls alongside the curb and points to a log cabin-ish structure. "Made of wood logged from the island. That is the town hall."

"I figured that. By the sign along the front that reads *Town Hall*."

He ignores me. "This is where you will be spending the majority of your time." He pulls back onto the street and loops a block over to the first completed neighborhood. It's not unlike a typical suburban subdivision—finished sidewalks and a road wide enough for two cars—but instead of unnaturally green, hypermanicured lawns, the yards are planted with either wildflowers or rows of young crops. "We are very bee friendly here," Rupert says, nodding. "The North American preoccupation with the perfect lawn is bizarre."

The houses themselves range in size from tiny homes to bigger structures capable of comfortably housing a family of five, but nothing the size of the McMansions so popular in the greater Vancouver area. "Every house has a Tesla solar roof wherein the individual residents can monitor their energy intake and output via an app on their phones. As of last month, the entire island is grid-free," he explains.

"Grid-free?"

"We are independent of the BC Hydro power grid. Thalia Island harnesses wind, water, and solar to power the entire island. What we don't use, we will eventually sell back to the Hydro corporation. Nothing here is wasted, Lara. Make that your mantra."

Damn. Grandfather *has* been busy.

At the end of this long lane flanked on both sides by houses sits a schoolhouse-slash-community centre that matches town hall—graced by a doe with twin fawns chewing on the tall grasses.

"You brought the deer in to impress me, right? Picture-perfect scene and all that?"

"The BC islands have abundant black-tailed deer populations. They're not as helpful as you'd think, and unless a cougar shows up, there are few predators. Voracious appetites, those buggers. And the non-native European fallow deer are even worse. Definitely something you will deal with during your tenure."

The next lane over is more houses, though not all are finished. Number Two again unhinges his jaw into explanation mode about how the first seventy-five "settlers" will be arriving in two weeks with a second wave next month and subsequent residents trickling in as their homes are finished.

Settlers to Thalia Island were chosen from a huge pool of applicants, people with the right credentials to serve a purpose on the island who are also willing to commit to a slower-paced, small-town lifestyle that requires communal cooperation, i.e., you have to put in a certain number of hours toward the island's upkeep in exchange for stabilized rent and/or mortgage rates, free electricity and heat, and a universal basic income to spend at local merchants.

Among the residents already here, beyond the crew of agriculture techs ("agritechs") and laborers, are the four members of the town council—two men and two women, who I will meet shortly—as well as a certified nurse practitioner, four firefighters, and the island's lead engineer who is in charge of overseeing all the crews. The crews apparently don't live here full time and are not, in fact, settled residents but rather professionals who've spent their careers learning, developing, and employing sustainable construction and farming practices. Those who wish to live on the island after their contracts are fulfilled have first dibs on homes as they come available.

"Number Two, my brain is already full. Can you just show me where I'm going to be sleeping so I know you're not pulling a fast one?" I roll down the window, fanning my hand in front of me. "Also, I think your dog needs to poop."

He smiles. "I'll show you to your new home, but we're not done for the day. You still have to meet your team."

"There'd better be food involved."

"Only if you're on your best behavior." He turns the car around in a cul-de-sac and exits the small neighborhood. "Lara, I'm not sure if you read the fine print on the will documents, but Humboldt belonged to your grandfather. Which means he now belongs to you."

I whip my head in Rupert's direction.

"Congratulations. It's a boy!"

FOURTEEN

GET UP, LARA JO!

Two miles south of the quaint residential area, on the east side of the main two-lane road, lies an expanse of land with three dwellings spaced about a half acre apart. They've been built in the same log-cabin style with solar roofs and long gravel driveways, the surrounding natural landscape left in place, other than the fields in front that have been marked off and tilled, "ready for you to plant your own functional gardens." I laugh behind my hand. Mm-hmm, *that's* not going to happen.

The house in the middle, at the top of a small rise, its driveway flanked by black ash saplings, is apparently mine. A line of trees visible along the rear of the property are, according to my tour guide, young Port Orford cedars and dawn redwoods, "which will eventually grow into a terrific windbreak to protect the house and the farmland in front of it from the winds that frequent Thalia Island."

The house itself ... yes, fine, it's *super* cute.

Rupert parks and unfolds himself from the driver's seat to set Humboldt free to do his business before we die of asphyxiation. I tuck Andromache under my left arm and watch Rupert retrieve my bags from the trunk, still playing the bored socialite so he doesn't ever get the chance to say, "I told you so."

But it would be totally justified if he said that at this moment. I sneak a few photos of the house to send to Eugenia later ... she's not going to *believe* this.

"Would you like to go in?" Rupert's face shines with what might be pride, maybe a little excitement of his own. "That one over there is where I will stay when I'm here—I still have duties in Vancouver to manage—and that one over there belongs to the lead engineer. You'll meet him"—Rupert regards his Apple Watch—"oh dear, soon. We're running late. Let's get you settled."

From the outside, the house looks bigger than a woodsy cabin or ski chalet, but only just, with a peaked roof on what looks like a second story. Three steps lead to a covered porch that extends across the entire front of the house, and twin Japanese maples decorate the front flower beds on each side of said steps. A reddish Adirondack chair sits along the left front windows.

"All of these porch lights are solar powered. They'll come on when the sun goes down. You have them along the drive, too, so you can always find your way home." He pauses at the front door. "Keys?"

I dig into my purse for the huge key chain bestowed upon me during our ferry meeting. "This would only be better if you gave me one of those leather-studded chains so it could hang off my belt. Complete the look."

"Snob," he says, taking the keys and looking for the one that apparently fits my front door.

"Do we even need keys here?"

"Once you're moved in, you can decide that for yourself," Rupert says, "but you are correct. We don't have a crime issue presently. It'll take some getting used to, all this peace and quiet." He pushes open the door, and my breath catches.

My furniture, my rugs and paintings and mirrors and knickknacks and books—my whole apartment has been moved into this house. "But ..."

"It was a gamble. I'm glad you were able to see reason." Rupert's outstretched arm invites me in.

The living area with a huge stone hearth welcomes us. Inside is cozy, already warm, and the smell of new wood from the exposed but sealed log walls perfumes the air. The living room blends into a dining area, my dining table just barely fitting in the allotted space. The spacious, bright kitchen is a mix of polished concrete, wood reclaimed from old boats, and more recycled plastics made into cupboard fronts. "The old is made new again," Rupert says.

Like a kid in a candy store, I leave him behind to check his phone and throw myself through the rest of the cabin. Two bedrooms on the main floor and an office upstairs (the big window in the peaked roof overlooks my front yard), a big bathroom with a clawfoot tub, a corner glassed-in shower with wall-mounted waterfall faucet head and low-flow toilet. The bigger of the two bedrooms has a decent walk-in closet—it's not the closet I had at the loft, but it's workable.

Brown paper lawn-refuse bags stuffed to bursting cover the hardwood floor. I tear into one, and sure enough, it's my clothing from the loft. "Sneaky bastard," I say under my breath. I'll eventually thank Rupert for rescuing my collection from the landfill or charity shop, for moving all my stuff over here from Vancouver without me knowing it, for believing I would do what he sees as the right thing.

I'm still not convinced this is the best option for me—or for Thalia Island—but given the choice between homelessness and this place? I guess I should google *project administrator* and figure out how to not screw this up.

But first, I flop backward onto my bed, taking the first deep breath in what seems like an eternity. I close my eyes for a minute, and I swear I see my grandfather leaning against one of the massive trees outside Clarke Manor, giggling behind his hand, like he used to do when I was learning some new skill, whether it was riding my bike without training wheels or skateboarding or archery or tennis, or the time I got stuck in my new treehouse and he made me figure out how to get down on my own. I went through a phase where I would purposely try to injure myself, just so I could get his attention. It worked on the first broken wrist, but not again after that.

Instead, he would yell, "Get up! So what if you fell! Get up, Lara Jo! Get up a thousand times!" He believed in me, even if I was a giant pain in his ass.

I twist his ring, safe on my middle finger. "I see you, Grandpa ... I'll try not to burn your island to the ground."

FIFTEEN

HIKING BOOTS ARE FOR HIPPIES

On the short drive back into town, Number Two makes me download Lutris, the app that everyone on the payroll uses to stay in contact. It's not fully functional yet, which is why contacting the IT company is among the many tasks on my to-do list once I'm officially on the job.

As we cruise along what qualifies as downtown, I notice that several businesses are already open—a grocery and general supply, a pub called the Wandering Salamander, and a '50s-style diner plainly named Tommy's. "Who is working in these places?"

"Our first settlers. They've been here about eight months."

"This feels a lot like make-believe," I say, my mouth watering at the idea of a grilled cheese on homemade bread, fries, and a cold beer as advertised on the sandwich board outside the diner.

"It's not far off. Thalia Island is a grand experiment, like a giant dollhouse. But if we make it work, we can be a model of environmental sustainability and neighborly cooperation for the rest of the world."

Rupert pulls into a spot in front of town hall and turns off the car. "You ready?"

I'm surprised that my usual stoicism has been replaced by a sheen of cold sweat; even a kaleidoscope of butterflies fans their anxious wings in my chest. I can't remember the last time I felt nervous about anything important.

Number Two moves to get out of the car, but I grab his arm. "Wait."

He turns to me, and our eyes meet. "You'll be fine. Just don't stick your foot in your mouth, don't throw any furniture, and don't call anyone the F-word."

"Great pep talk."

I climb out and open the rear door for Humboldt. "Doesn't he need to eat or something soon?"

"Later. I have dog food in my office."

I follow Rupert to the double glass-and-wood front doors, another streak of panic whooshing through me, a reminder that once again, I am in way over my head. But he holds open the entrance, and I know there's no way out.

An airy lobby to the left hosts a bank of mailboxes, wide windows, and two blank walls in need of decoration; a reception area sits to the right, but no one occupies the chair behind the tall, wood-topped counter. I pause at the hand sanitizer dispenser and squirt goo into my palm. "Mmm, orange."

"We make it here."

"You *do?*"

Rupert snickers.

Voices and laughing filter from down the wide hardwood hall straight ahead, so I pull back my shoulders and prepare my best society smile. Offices with glass walls line the hall on both sides, and Humboldt runs ahead, like he knows where he's going. It's probably the smell of food that pulls him forward—it's doing the same to my growling stomach.

"To the right here is council chambers and our interim courtroom," Rupert says, pointing. "After introductions, I'll show you to your new office." He points over his shoulder toward the doors we've just passed. *I have my own office.* Gulp.

He then pivots left and enters a conference room that is more windows than walls, the thick glass framed by long sheers and drapes pulled far aside to let in maximum light. The theme of Thalia Island seems to be honey-colored wood—it's everywhere, from walls to exposed beams to flooring.

At the center of the room sits a huge, live-edge conference table—I can't even imagine a tree big enough to make something this size—and around it are five new faces in the midst of a cheerful meal and conversation, all of whom pause to offer warm welcomes to Humboldt and Rupert, and yes, even me.

A middle-aged blond woman wearing more flannel than should be allowed on such a petite body hops out of her chair, hands pressed together in front of her. "My beautiful English prince has returned, and he's come bearing gifts!" She hugs Rupert and kisses him once on each cheek—which is odd because Rupert is, like, super weird about people touching him.

She then turns her attention to me. "Oh, I have not seen you since you were nothing but skinned knees and wild braids." The woman adopts a solemn frown as she touches my arm. "Lara, I am so sorry for the loss of your beloved grandfather." She then wraps herself around me in a hug, but I'm frozen. I don't know this woman, and it's uncomfortable that she seems to know too much about me.

Then again, everyone knows too much about me. Hazard of being a Clarke.

She steps back, but her incense-like fragrance lingers. "I'm Kelly Lockhart, one of the town councillors for Thalia Island. Welcome home, Lara!" Kelly Lockhart claps, and the others join her, though less enthusiastically. She then turns on her hiking-booted heel, her hand clasped around my upper arm, and introduces the other humans in the room.

"This is Stanley—he runs the Tipping Point, our grocery and general store, and is the island's shepherd—goats mostly right now because they make the best milk. This is Thomas—but everyone calls him Tommy—he's our poultryman with the most delicious roasters and the *most* gorgeous brood of laying hens you've ever seen. He also runs the diner. His wife Catrina is our nurse practitioner—you'll meet her later at dinner—she'll be working with our doctor once he arrives.

"And this beautiful creature is Ainsley—she's here for a year on loan from Edinburgh to finish her dissertation on organic farming practices, and she grows the most incredible carrots in all of Canada!" The room chuckles, and Ainsley blushes a fierce red that matches her hair. "We'll all be working closely with you and Rupert to get Thalia Island running at top speed," Kelly says.

She finally releases my arm and moves to the other side of the table, positioning herself behind the final person I've yet to meet. She drops her hands on his shoulders, and I swear he stiffens under her touch. "And of course, I cannot forget this diamond in the rough, Finan Rowleigh, our lead engineer and Thalia Island's most eligible bachelor." Kelly says his name and title slowly, almost seductively, as she rubs his shoulders. It's pretty clear Kelly Lockhart would very much like to show young Finan Rowleigh more than just some blue-prints for the best place to grow eggplant.

Certainly enough, her left ring finger is devoid of precious embell-ishment.

Finan pushes his chair just enough to get her to let go of him, and then stands—shit, he's as tall as Rupert but twice his bulk. He reaches across the table to shake my hand. He's the only one who does, his redwood-brown eyes crinkling with a quick smile. When our hands meet, I'm not surprised that his grip is strong, his palm rough with calluses. He is, after all, the lead engineer—whatever that means. He, too, is outfitted in flannel and denim, a tawny Carhartt work coat hanging off his chair. His dark brown hair is thick on top but closely shaved along the sides; the facial hair is a little more than I usually like, but it's well-manicured. Not quite hipster, not quite mountain man.

I wipe my hand off on my pant leg; he notices and lifts a brow, the polite smile melting. What? I don't have to explain to him that I'm not into germs from strangers, especially strangers who have dirt on their clothes and who might be romantically linked to Kelly of the Flannel.

"Nice to meet you," he says and sits again to finish the slice of pizza resting on his plate.

"Are you hungry? Have a slice—this is gluten- and dairy-free. Even finicky Finan likes it." Kelly moves alongside the table and giggles. "And over here we have different kinds of salads—kale, quinoa, even a vegan macaroni. We're helping Tommy with the new menu. Of course, we eat meat here, so you don't have to be a vegan, but we want to make all our new residents feel at home with their dietary needs. Oh, you don't have a peanut allergy, do you?" Kelly asks, lacing her fingers together in front of her face.

"No. No allergies," I say.

"Oh, that's just excellent. Although soon we will have the cutest doctor you've ever seen—single, I might add." She wiggles her eyebrows. "And he will have EpiPens!" She giggles at herself again. "So—Lara—did Rupert show you your new place?" Kelly launches into twenty questions, and I'm careful with answers because I'm not sure how much she knows about the circumstances around my appointment to Thalia Island's town council. Is everyone in the room aware that Rupert and the lawyers basically resorted to blackmail to get me here?

I'll need to talk to Number Two about this—the last thing I want is to give Kelly and her crew ammunition for later.

Yes, I have trust issues.

Thankfully, the lunch meeting wraps, and Stanley and Kelly tidy the mess and then disappear down the main hall, heads bowed as they discuss timelines and schedules and details I am completely clueless about. Rupert has been pacing a circle in the corner, talking on his phone during most of my interrogation, but finally he hangs up and raps his knuckles twice on the conference table.

"I'll show Lara her new office, but then, Finan, can I leave it to you to give our new project administrator the grand tour of her domain?"

Finan, mid drink from a reusable water bottle, offers a thumbs-up.

"Lara, this way," Rupert says, moving toward the doorway. Humboldt's nails make more noise on the hardwood than the butler's soft-soled shoes. Guessing Rupert doesn't get muddy often while he's here, which makes the box with the clunky, lace-up hiking boots sitting on my new desk all the more annoying.

"You don't expect me to wear these," I say, holding one boot by the loop at the ankle.

"You can wear whatever you want, as long as you get the work done." Number Two nods at my feet, currently in a pair of brown Chloé Goldee goatskin ankle boots. "*Those* won't last one day in the field."

"I don't plan on *being* in any field."

Rupert invites me to sit in my chair—a Steelcase Gesture made specifically for Clarke Innovations, complete with bamboo seat fabric and recycled plastic parts. A cozy bamboo-fiber blanket embroidered with the Thalia Island logo is draped over the back of a gray canvas-and-pine couch along the wall. My new desk (all reclaimed wood) has a brand-new Mac, as well as a landline and all post-consumer recycled paper products. Behind me is a wide, double-paned, Argon-filled window treated with solar-cell tint that looks out onto what will eventually become a huge community garden but right now is a muddy patch filled with stacks of railroad ties and stakes and twine marking out plots.

"This"—Rupert pulls the lid off a banker's box—"is filled with everything you will need to acquaint yourself with your new position." I stand and look inside, and my stomach clenches.

"How will I ever read all this?" Binders, spiral-bound manuals, file folders stuffed with papers ... "Please tell me there's a flask hiding in here somewhere."

Number Two slides the lid back on. "Speaking of, it would be best for you—for everyone—if you abstained from intoxication during your time here."

I shake my head. "This is a job, Rupert, not rehab."

"Perhaps, but can we agree that drunk Lara is not always conducive to a peaceful and productive environment?"

"I am not spending this entire year sober. That was not part of the deal."

"Always so dramatic." His phone buzzes in his pocket again.

"Dinner will be at Tommy's Diner at 8:00 p.m. I'll text you a reminder." He answers the phone but then tells the caller to wait half a second. "Also, I'll have someone drop Humboldt's food on your porch. There's a backup bag in my office closet for this afternoon. If you don't feed him, he will eat whatever he can find, including furniture. And couches give him the runs."

Then Rupert is off, and I realize he did not, in fact, show me to the car I was promised. "How am I supposed to get home?" I call after him, but he's long gone. Humboldt whines once from the floor beside my desk, his puppy-dog eyes watching the open door and then looking up at me. "He's crazy if he thinks I'm going to be sober during this whole twisted experiment." Humboldt snorts, as if he's exasperated with me, too, and flops his head onto his giant paws, a line of slobber oozing over his fur and onto the rug.

"We're really going to have to do something about your saliva issues if we're to spend time together."

I recline on the couch and yank the Thalia Island blanket over my shoulders and chest. I am so effing tired.

My lids close for a second, but my next inhale is replete with the charming aroma of dog breath. I peel one eye open. "What ..." Humboldt has rested his head on the couch next to my face. "You are super gross, do you know that?" He snorts and licks my forehead just as the lead engineer stops at my doorway.

"You ready to get to work?"

"Do I have a choice?" I throw off the blanket and lunge for the tissues on my desk hutch. "Humboldt, never lick my face again." Another line of spit drains onto the area rug. I shiver.

Finan smiles, wide and white, and kneels next to Humboldt, who immediately whines with glee. "You're a good boy, aren't ya," he says, scrubbing Humboldt's head and scruff.

"Oh my god, stop petting him. You're making him drool more."

"Little dog slobber never killed anyone."

"I'll likely be the first," I say, dabbing at my forehead with the powder compact pulled from my bag.

Finan stands and points at the hiking boots still sitting in the box. "Might want to put those on."

Without taking my eyes off him, I lean forward and with the side of my left forearm, I slide the box into the wicker trash can next to my desk.

Finan laughs and shakes his head. "Suit yourself." He then plods down the hall and whistles once, pulling Humboldt to his feet and out the door.

"Traitor," I mumble after the dog, throwing my biker jacket back on and stomping out like a tantrumming five-year-old.

SIXTEEN

MT. MAGNUS

I follow Finan out of town hall and down the block, past unoccupied storefronts, noting that the sidewalk under my feet is not like any sidewalk I've seen before. "Is this—are these solar panels underfoot?"

"Yup. Dutch innovation. Solar roads, too, here in town. Every ounce of sun power keeps us warm and bright." Finan offers that tight smile again, and my hackles rise. I'm guessing he's not excited about babysitting me today. But I'm also guessing I'm ranked higher on the food chain, so he'd better smarten up.

He finally slows and moves toward the driver's side of the weirdest-looking truck, a huge silver toolbox stretched across its utility bed.

"Let me guess: electric."

"Atlis XT. Fully electric. A prototype from a small company in Arizona that will eventually give Elon's Cybertruck a run, if they can get the funding together," Finan says, unlocking my side with a stab of his key fob. He opens the dual-cab rear door and pats the seat; Humboldt lumbers in, though not without Finan's help. "Your grandfather couldn't have loved Chihuahuas?"

Comedy. So Finan the glorified handyman is funny.

I start to climb in, but note that my seat—the entire inside of the truck—is dirty, and some sort of cutting device sits on the floor behind the driver's seat. Fine sawdust has settled everywhere.

"Is there a problem?" Finan asks.

"Do you have, like, one of those little vacuums? Maybe a cloth or something?"

Finan pushes in front of me and wipes off the passenger seat with the sleeve of his jacket. "Clean enough for you?"

Uh, no.

I hop in and buckle up just as Humboldt inserts himself between me and Finan, his paws already coated with whatever is on the floor in the back. "Humboldt, sit." I snap my fingers and point; the dog yawns at me but obliges, thankfully. There's no way I can tolerate riding the twisty island roads with dog breath in my face.

"Did you bring anything to write on?"

"I have my phone," I say. I then open the Notes app and press the little mic icon to dictate a note. "First item on my to-do list: Buy small vacuum for handyman's truck."

Finan laughs under his breath. "Whatever you say, boss." He starts the engine and backs out.

"I *am* the new boss, aren't I. I guess that means I can make up whatever rules I want for this place."

"We are still governed by the laws of British Columbia." Finan gestures to the dash control center. "Help yourself if you're warm or cold." The main street area is short; within a minute, we're on the road leading out of downtown. Finan, like Rupert did earlier, switches to tour-guide mode.

We head back out to the marina, now quiet of boat traffic. He explains the moorage rules here, how vessels must belong to registered residents and day passes to Thalia Island are not issued for private citizens. "It's not Salt Spring or Vancouver Island. Thalia is privately owned—we're not a tourist stop."

"Will we have security to deal with curious civilians?"

"Eventually. We'll have a private security officer—Derek Irving— he's late moving to the island. Something to do with family in Abbotsford. Sister getting married or something?"

"Bummer for her."

Finan chuckles. "Boats not registered with town hall we report to Derek and the town council, and if we need to get Fisheries or the closest RCMP detachment involved, we will. The wildlife on and around Thalia is federally protected, everything from sea otters to transient orca to seabirds who nest on the western side. We don't have any bear on the island, but we do have a ton of deer—and the occasional cougar, since they swim between islands in search of food. Your grandfather worked with the federal government to make sure everything that lives here would remain undisturbed by our presence."

An unexpected twinge bites at my throat. Grief is the shadiest thing. Pops up at random, inconvenient times and takes away your ability to speak or even breathe for a minute.

"Onward, yes?"

I nod, clutch at Grandfather's ring, and scold my emotions.

Finan then routes us around the western side of the island, and it's much wilder than the downtown and residential areas. He explains again how habitat preservation is key, but of course, in the real world, not all these concessions would be possible simply due to urban sprawl. "Still, the hope is that we can take lessons learned here and apply them in urban development settings." The winds are quite strong along the perimeter road, spinning the thingies on the lamp-posts that Finan explains are vertical axis turbines. "They were intended for highways and freeways, to harness the energy of passing cars, but these are part of a pilot project to see if they're more efficient than the big-blade wind turbines we already have. The small ones are a hell of a lot cheaper and much easier to service."

The view of the sea and Vancouver Island beyond takes my breath away. For a few minutes, I forget that I'm breathing recirculated bull-mastiff air and that I'm in a job I am totally unqualified for and that my grandfather is gone and I'm alone in the world.

"When you get a chance, we'll come over to this side in a boat. The birds here are amazing. Cormorants, loons, grebes, auklets, bald eagles, osprey—if you're a birder, this area is a gold mine."

"I'm *definitely* not a birder," I say, laughing at how ridiculous that sounds. Me and a pair of dorky binoculars and a guidebook for nerds? Can you imagine?

"Thalia Island is about a fifth the size of Vancouver Island, around fifty miles from tip to tip and fifteen miles across at its widest." According to Finan, my grandfather bought the whole island sixty years ago in a unique agreement with the provincial and federal government in the hope that once the technology was available, he'd be able to do what we're doing right now. "It's large enough to house farms for food, wind, and solar, and small enough that we can limit the population to maintain the control group necessary to complete the mission."

"The mission? That's what you guys call this?"

Finan smiles. "Archibald was a visionary, as you know. I cannot imagine what the government folks thought when he bought the island all those years ago. Probably thought he was out of his mind."

"Sometimes I wondered that too," I say.

"Visionaries usually are a little nuts, but look at all this. Pretty incredible."

A warm memory surfaces of my grandfather hunched over his desk late at night, brow furrowed as he worked on one of his crazy plans, sipping steaming chamomile, laughing when he discovered I was hiding from the nanny in the empty liquor cabinet—again.

"Archibald was very clear about the parameters set forth for Thalia, the objectives we are to meet, the reports and results that other countries will study in the decades to come. Rupert gave you plenty of reading material to catch up on, yes?"

I clear my head of nostalgia. Now is not the time to reminisce. This is my new reality. "And not a drop of whisky to be had," I say under my breath.

Finan snorts. "That's what the Salamander is for."

I bite my tongue before the snark escapes. I don't know how much Finan Rowleigh knows about me and my boozy shenanigans. Probably best not to open the door to gossip.

He slows the truck and then stops—there's no one on the road behind us to block, but it's still weird.

"Everything OK?"

"Want to see something cool? I think we have time."

"Sure?"

He smiles and then makes a U-turn, surprising given the narrow road and the big truck. A few minutes back in the direction we just came, he flips a right onto a gravel road that has been sliced through the thick trees, and we're climbing, my ears plugging slightly with the uptick in elevation.

After about ten bumpy minutes on this twisty road, the trees thin and we're on a flat, wide-open stone ridge. Ahead is ... hard to describe. Finan looks over at me, all smiles. "Come on." He hops out and releases Humboldt from the back seat. The dog bites at the wind that hits me hard in the face as soon as my door opens, bringing tears to my eyes that might not only be from the cold.

Finan moves closer to the ridge edge, pointing out everything my eyes cannot believe. "That's Vancouver Island over there. All this water is the Strait of Georgia, which you know, and south of here, it eventually dumps into the Pacific Ocean, which you also know since you're from BC. Down there"—he leans and points at a sandy stretch with lapping waves way below—"is Cordelia Beach. That's where the best birdwatching is."

I swipe at a tear escaped from the corner of my eye. "Windy up here," I say, covering the reason for my unexpected emotion. *Cordelia Beach.* Rupert never mentioned that my grandfather named part of his island after my mother. I get an electric ferry—she gets a beach. *Archibald, you sentimental nutter.*

"It's not always so windy." Finan zips his jacket and sighs, a happy sound. "This is my favorite place on all of Thalia."

"I can see why." The sun breaks through the clouds over the water; seabirds catch an updraft, wings wide as they hover. Now we only need a breaching whale or Poseidon himself to wave from the current between here and the next island.

Finan turns and points toward what remains of a tree, a big stump about three feet high and two feet across. I walk over to it. Embedded in the surface is a bronze plaque. "'Mount Magnus, 420 metres above sea level, named in honour of Archibald Magnus Clarke I and his unyielding pursuit of a better life for all creatures of Earth.'" Just below this, in smaller raised block script, is half of Archibald's favorite Carl Sagan quote: "'Survival is the exception.'"

I pull off Grandfather's ring and look inside the band. The engraving is worn but still present: "Extinction is the rule."

"Huh," I say, running a hand over the bronze. Half the quote is on the plaque, the other half on the ring. Together, it reads, "Extinction is the rule. Survival is the exception."

He's left a piece of himself everywhere.

Finan gives me a second, pouring some water from his reusable water bottle into his hands for Humboldt. When I've finally composed myself, I rejoin them on the summit lip. Finan has a pair of binoculars pushed against his eyes. When he drops them, his brow furrows.

"Something wrong?"

"I don't know." He hands me the binocs. "Look down at the beach —do you see that big pile of driftwood?"

I find the pile. "Is it not supposed to be there?"

"Driftwood doesn't wash ashore in neat piles."

I return the binoculars. "Maybe the maintenance crew was cleaning up the beach?"

Finan shakes his head. "There's no direct access to Cordelia Beach by road. They'd have to come by boat. And they'd have to be off-islanders."

"Do people do that? Squat on our beaches?"

"They're not supposed to"—he looks again—"but someone has. Looks like a firepit has been dug too."

"Does the island have any sort of surveillance system? Cameras or drones or anything?"

Finan lowers the binoculars. "No. That's part of the appeal of being here. We're not living under constant watch like you are in the city."

"Yes, except here, we can't monitor what people are up to if we don't have cameras. Not everyone will have good intentions."

Finan replaces the caps on his binocular lenses. "Ah, the city girl is a cynic." He snaps his fingers and Humboldt lumbers to his feet.

"The city girl is a realist. And if you had surveillance of some variety, you'd know who's been building driftwood forts and roasting s'mores on Cordelia Beach."

"Fair enough," Finan concedes as he helps the dog back into his spot behind us. I'm glad to be in the truck again. Mt. Magnus is wonderful, and I will figure out how to get here on my own, but maybe with a heavier coat.

"Thank you. For showing me this," I say. "I appreciate that you understand ... about me missing my grandfather." I can't say anymore. My voice won't cooperate.

"He was my friend," Finan says. "Welcome to Thalia Island, Lara."

SEVENTEEN

PRINCESS LARA OF THALIA ISLAND

Once off Mt. Magnus, we resume our prior course and wrap around the southern end of the island just as a passing spring shower darkens the sky overhead. Finan follows the road that cuts through the heart of Thalia, flanked by farmland on either side. "This is where the magic happens," Finan says, slowing to pull right onto a gravel and dirt road before stopping the truck. "Everything you're used to finding in the produce department, we can pretty much grow here."

"Even bananas?"

He leans over the steering wheel and points south across the field. "Those structures—the vertical farms. You can get your bananas from there." He smiles again.

"I wouldn't have noticed them if you hadn't pointed them out." The four structures match the surrounding environment.

Finan turns off the truck just as a few raindrops hit the windshield. So much for this morning's clear skies. "Come on. I'll give you a tour."

"No, that's fine. I can see it from here."

"Nonsense. It's a short walk."

Ugh. "Do you at least have an umbrella?"

"Come on. You won't melt."

How do you know?

Humboldt is more than happy to gallop along the muddied path abutting the fields, bright green with early growth. "Corn here. Over there, Ainsley has more traditional garden fare, stuff we can pick and eat on the spot. The next fields up are grain crops, which can be milled here for flour or sold as an export, depending on yield, and then closer to town are orchards—pears, quinces, and a dozen varieties of apples. Cherries and nectarines in the summer. Wild blackberry and raspberry grow everywhere, *and* we don't have to compete with the bears for the fruit." Finan continues talking about stuff that goes right over my head, but I'm hardly listening—my attention is focused on the rain soaking my leather biker jacket.

By the time we reach the covered porch attached to the second vertical farm, marked with a bright green *B*, my Chloé boots have transformed into mud socks hiding my feet in their sloppy, freezing-cold depths.

Finan looks down, a smirk tugging at his lips.

"Not a word, sir."

"Wouldn't dream of it," he says. "Humboldt, stay." The slobbery mutt shakes, sharing a spray of water and dirt with us, and then plops down on a floor mat on the covered concrete slab. He rests his head on his legs and sighs.

Finan holds open the front door. "Except—" He stops me right inside the building. "You can't walk through here with those on your feet."

"Am I supposed to go barefoot?"

He reaches into a cupboard and pulls out paper surgical booties, slipping a pair over the soles of his Timberlands. "That's a lot of mud. Maybe just wear these and we'll sort out how to get you back to the truck when the tour is over."

"Lovely." I free my icy feet with a sucking slurp and slip on the paper booties.

The tour includes Finan explaining more about the tech behind the vertical farms, followed by introductions of more people who work and live on the island—mostly graduate students, it seems—even a few stops for taste tests of strawberries, oranges, and yes, a banana, all delicious.

"I cannot believe we can grow all this in these buildings. How do the roots go deep enough on the fruit trees?" I cradle a lemon still attached to its branch. "This is incredible, Finan."

His smile is full of pride as he caresses the leaf of a nearby orange tree. "Science is kind of awesome, Lara."

I don't want to admit it, but Thalia might yet work her way into my cells. Here I feel a new clarity—there are bigger things going on in the world than who I'm sleeping with and where I'm going to get my next drink, if the paparazzi is going to pick up the story of Connor banging his costar or try to snap pictures of me being helped out of some swanky bar, again, by the bouncers.

"Lara?" Finan has walked ahead.

I gently release the fragrant lemon and shake out my damp ponytail, trying not to notice the confident swagger in Finan's step as he leads me to the stairwell.

We say goodbye to the new faces I've met and once again, at the front door, I am reminded that I have no shoes. My ankle boots are unrecognizable under the build-up of half-dried mud and gunk. It will take an industrial power washer to make those wearable again.

"Ummm ... is there any way you can bring the truck over closer?" I ask. Finan's face splits into a grin as he pulls off his paper booties.

"No need. How much do you weigh?" And before I can answer, Finan has me over his shoulder, my butt in the air as he exits the building.

"Put me down! Oh my god, what are you doing?"

"Come, Humboldt!" The giant pooch pulls himself up, stretching briefly before plodding along behind Finan. He even hops once toward my flailing hands, and I swear, the dog is *laughing* at me.

"Finan, this isn't funny."

"I'm offering you transport to the truck so your feet don't get dirty —or dirtier. You can thank me later."

"I am perfectly capable of walking to the truck myself." My voice shakes with every step, his shoulder jammed into my gut.

"Lara, I know enough about you to be aware that your life has mostly involved expensive high heels and glittering evening gowns. I'm going to guess that walking on gravel isn't something these sweet society feet are used to."

I raise my arm to smack him, realizing that the only real place I can reach is his butt, and even for me, that seems a little forward. "Have you ever spent hours in a pair of four-inch Louboutins sucking up to wealthy nerds?"

He chuckles.

"My feet are probably a lot tougher than you think."

He then grabs one of my ankles, manhandling my lower leg to get a look at my wet, dirty foot. "You have big feet."

Now I do punch him in the ass.

"Violence in the workplace will not be tolerated. I may have to report that." I hear the smile in his voice just as we reach the truck. He digs into his pocket for his keys, opens the rear cab door for Humboldt and then my door, dropping me onto the seat.

"As the new head of Thalia Island, my first official decree will make it punishable by death for anyone to look at my feet."

He looks down at them again; I hurry to hide them from view. "And pink toenails." He bows deeply. "Strike the killing blow, Princess Lara. I am ready."

I flip him the bird as he rises and shuts my door and moves around the front. When he climbs into his side and turns on the engine, heat full blast, I've already got my phone out, thumbs flying.

"How long is the ride back to town?"

"Fifteen minutes."

"Good. That will give me plenty of time to brainstorm the list of punishments I will employ when my subjects misbehave."

Finan's laugh is loud enough to startle Humboldt, who woofs loudly in my left ear. "Starting with making this bullmastiff into sausage."

EIGHTEEN

MAYBE WE NEED A MOAT TOO?

After our arrival back at town hall, Finan grins but remains quiet as I pull the hiking boots out of the trash basket and slide my bare feet into them. He offers a pair of socks from his stash in his office, but no, eww, and I remind him to prepare for his imminent death under the sheen of my sword.

Kelly doesn't take long to insert herself into our otherwise pleasant afternoon. "You're back! How did our newcomer enjoy her tour?" Her voice … maybe as my first official act, I should instead pass a law about decibel limits while indoors.

"Hey, Kelly. It was beautiful."

"I took Lara up to the lookout, and I noticed some changes down on Cordelia Beach. Looks like driftwood stacked and a firepit. Has there been mention of any unusual activity over there?"

"No, no, no one has said a thing." Her smile is cheesy. "But remember, we talked about doing some beach tidy over there, maybe to put in a covered picnic spot for island residents to use during boat outings?"

"Did we?"

"Yeppers. Don't worry about it. Your list is long enough. I'll check in with the maintenance crew."

Finan nods, but the line scored between his eyebrows as he walks away suggests this conversation isn't over. He seems to be in charge of all the crews, so wouldn't he *know* if there was some sort of cleanup or repurposing happening on the island?

Kelly waits until he disappears into his office before flapping a hand at me. "That Finan sure is a scrumptious bite of pastry, isn't he?"

I'm not going to tell her how said pastry picked me up and carried me across the muddied field or how my pants are still damp from the surprise rain, despite the heated seats in his truck.

I look over my shoulder at Rupert's banker's box. "I should probably get some reading done."

"Always plenty of that around here," she says. "Though it's probably not as interesting as your usual fare."

Which is ...? "Hey, do we have someone here to make coffee? Is there staff for that sort ..."

Kelly is giggling before I've finished my sentence.

"Sweetie, I know your life in Vancouver was much tended to, but around here, we serve ourselves. No housekeepers here to plump your pillows or assistants to froth your milk." In the span of two sentences, Kelly Lockhart reveals exactly what I need to know about her. She's one of those fake-ass women who will take great joy in watching me, the spoiled heiress, fall flat on my face. I can almost visualize her dancing on the ferry dock as I leave in defeat 364 days from now.

"Not a problem. I'm sure I can figure it out. Do we have a coffee machine? Or you probably prefer Folger's Crystals."

Her smug smile melts a little, and then she points behind her. "Kitchen's on the left. We have an espresso machine."

"How cosmopolitan." I give her a snotty smile of my own and move past.

"One more thing, Lara."

I turn around but keep moving to let her know she's not important enough for me to stop. "You might want to grab a shower and change your clothes before dinner. First big get-together here for you—probably want to freshen up. Maybe something other than ... that." She drags her eyes up my body, from the new boots on my feet all the way to the top of my still-damp ponytail.

These pants cost more than your monthly salary, you clearance-rack serf.

"Looking forward to it, Kelly!" I announce over my shoulder as I slide into the kitchen.

And the "espresso machine" she mentioned? Hardly qualifies. Doesn't look like the steam wand has even been used. Whatever. I've spent enough time at coffeehouses to know how to load and pull my own espresso, even with this third-tier knockoff. Caffeine is caffeine.

"Want to make two while you're at it?" Finan's voice behind me makes me jump. He opens the fridge and leans in to grab a glass bottle of milk.

"I'll be lucky if I can get this machine to make *one*," I say, pounding the ground coffee into the porta-filter.

"Sorry, no Starbucks here, Princess Lara, but this thing does the trick, believe it or not."

I whip around, wielding the coffee tamper like a weapon. "OK, you need to stop calling me that." I lower my voice. "Especially around Kelly Lockhart."

"Trouble in paradise already? That's a new record." He feigns looking at his watch and slides the glass bottle onto the counter beside me. He then opens one of the overhead cupboards and from it pulls a stainless steel pitcher. "You like goat milk? It hides the taste of the espresso a little, but we don't have cow milk or nut beverages at the moment."

"Is it nonfat?" I slide the porta-filter into the machine as Finan chuckles at me. Again. "Just espresso for me, thanks."

Finan turns so he's leaning against the counter, the silver pitcher cupped in one giant hand. "Kelly is an acquired taste."

"Sort of like rubbing alcohol."

His eyes widen. "You don't drink that, do you?"

"Har har."

"She'll probably give you crap for a while. Do what you can to not antagonize her."

I face Finan as my espresso dribbles into the shot glasses. "Ahem. Lest I remind her—and you—that this is *my* island."

"Technically, it's not."

"*Technically*, it is. My last name is Clarke. No one else's here is. I'm basically the mayor."

Finan's laugh is louder this time. "So, I should call you Madam Mayor instead of Princess Lara?"

I open cupboards until I find a demitasse to hold my newly poured, crema-rich shot.

"I'm teasing, Lara." Finan wipes down the steam wand and prepares to heat his milk. "You're new. We've been here better part of a year. Kelly is territorial and maybe a little possessive—she's been the big momma bear on Thalia since the first foundations were poured, so forgive her if she's a little smarmy."

"Finan, I can respect that. But what she thinks she knows about me, she's learned from the internet or the tabloids. And I can feel it when people are looking sideways at me—I've been in the spotlight my whole life. I am well acquainted with what it feels like to be judged before someone even knows you."

Conversation quiets while the steam wand works its magic on his goat milk. He then turns it off, sets the pitcher aside, and wipes down the wand. "OK, so, let's you and I agree right now that we know nothing about each other, and I will drop any preconceived notions I might have gleaned from Kelly's gossip—"

"See? Oh my god, she's already gossiping about me?"

"—and *you* will let me get to know the real Lara Clarke. There's a reason you're here. Archibald was a very smart man. He would never leave anything to chance."

The battle flame in my chest dims a little. Maybe that could work. If Finan is willing to get to know me outside all the bullshit he *thinks* he knows about me, I might be able to figure myself out alongside him.

"Fine." I empty the porta-filter and pull another shot for his drink. "But if Kelly Lockhart thinks she can go around the island making things difficult for me just because of the family I was born into, she's in for a rude awakening."

"I don't doubt it," he says, smiling as we watch the espresso pour into the shot glasses. He offers a hand in front of him. "Shake on it?"

"Oh, a secret pact? Already? Absolutely." I clasp his hand, trying to ignore the stutter in my pulse as our eyes meet. "Just don't forget who's princess around here."

"I can't wait to get started building the dungeon, my lady."

"As long as it has a dragon that eats middle-aged busybodies who smell like dollar-store incense."

"Your every wish is my command."

I throw back my espresso in a long swallow, trying to hide my smile behind my tiny white cup.

NINETEEN

IT MEANS "GREEN" IN LATIN

The subsequent two weeks fly by in a blur of binders, paperwork, meetings over long lunches and even longer dinners—and no alcohol in sight, contrary to Finan's tease about the pub. But everything's been surprisingly … good. Might even be the first time I've felt like a real grown-up, though when my brain threatens to overflow from too many things I absolutely must know, Finan or Kelly and the council throw something else at me. Though I've long since drained my collection of hidden flasks transported with my belongings, I'm so tired at the end of every day, I fall asleep without need for the lulling warmth of Suntory or Black Label.

And Rupert has been gone dealing with Foundation business in Vancouver—I'm sort of disappointed he's not here witnessing my newfound maturity—so whenever I nod off during an interminable report on early crop-yield predictions or issues with the solar array on the western side, Finan has been kind enough to nudge my chair with his boot and wake me before anyone notices.

Dare I say I might have made a new friend?

I'm in the parking lot attached to the marina with said new friend, and Humboldt and the rest of town council, as we await our first big batch of "settlers." My big-girl job still stresses me out, but I'm slightly more confident I'll be able to handle whatever new challenges are walking off the ferry right now, given that Finan answers my questions without snide undertones or subtext like *some* people.

Suffice it to say, Kelly and I are keeping each other at arm's length. Per my earlier inkling that we definitely need surveillance on this island, I have half a mind to order and install security cameras within town hall so I can prove to Rupert that she really *is* an obnoxious cow when everyone else is out of the room. He says it's in my head, that Kelly is a hundred percent on board with the mission; I counter that while her dedication might be legit, her attitude sucks. If I were truly the mayor, I'd move her to wastewater treatment *posthaste*.

But as Rupert sharply reminded me, I have a mandate, a list of goals known as Schedule A, and unlike the solar power that keeps our lights on, time is a nonrenewable resource. "Focus on the task at hand. You're better than to engage in playground politics."

But ... am I, really?

Because it's clear that playground politics are very much underway here. Already people are taking sides, especially since I, in my first big, official project—finalizing the plans for the settlers' welcome-home party—overrode the council's earlier plans and called in a favor from the owner of my favorite Vancouver restaurant, Viridis, who will be catering tonight's big street party. We're not using Tommy's menu of diner food; I insisted we needed something fancier, given the huge milestone this evening represents.

The debate was heated, but in the end, I pulled my Clarke card. "It's my grandfather's island. I'm the project administrator. This is what we're doing." In hindsight, I don't know if it was the right thing to do, and sure, Tommy's is great for daily fare—burgers, sandwiches, the best egg-white omelet I've ever had—but tonight ... tonight is special.

Thalia Island becomes a real home tonight. The settlers are an integral part of my grandfather's vision. So even if Tommy and Kelly are pissed because they don't get to make kebabs and cheeseburgers on the giant new barbecues they bought, tough. We can do that for the next batch of residents due to arrive next month.

Tonight, we will eat like the royalty we are.

The seventy-five new residents—singles, couples, and a few families, all vetted and chosen based on specific skill sets, income and education levels, as well as their commitment to community cooperation and the environmental movement—are actively disembarking, luggage pulled behind them, waving with their free hands to our welcoming committee. We have two party bus–size electric coaches to transport everyone downtown, plus Finan's and another two electric trucks with big beds for overflow luggage.

Once everyone is checked in, they will be escorted to their new homes by the council members and island crews. Furniture is part of their housing deal, but anything too big to carry that they wanted to bring from the mainland will follow in a container delivered via ferry next week.

My job right now is to hurry back to town hall in the ultra-compact Toyota EV Rupert imported from Japan and then assigned to me—he said I had to earn anything bigger—to greet the new settlers in person and hand out welcome packets. Though I have refused to succumb to the unofficial island uniform of flannel and hiking boots, I am enjoying the less formal daywear of skinny slacks and cute tops with matching jackets, coordinated with whatever designer heel feels right for the day. Just because everyone else here dresses like every day is casual Friday doesn't mean *I* have to.

"Humboldt, get *in*," I say, trying to pick him up around his midsection. Finan laughs as he passes behind me. "It's not funny. He's the same size as the car!" I release the groaning, overstuffed creature and wipe my hands on my black pants now covered in dog hair.

"He can ride with me." Finan snaps his fingers and Humboldt gives me a quick, apologetic look before trotting over to Finan.

"Archibald should've left you the dog."

Finan hoists Humboldt's back half into the truck like he's a piñata and not a 110-pound bullmastiff. "Race you back?"

"Ha." I climb into my Hot Wheels. On the Humboldt-free passenger seat sits a long line of fresh drool. I yank a moist towelette from the tub stuffed behind me and wipe it down as Finan grins, honks once, and pulls out of the lot toward town.

I'm starting to think of that smile before I fall asleep.

With everyone checked in and other island staff showing the settlers to their new domiciles, I hustle back to the marina to meet the Viridis team so I can escort them into downtown. Émile shuffles off the deck, black scruff and white sunglasses, thick black hair standing in stylish, smooth waves, his usual perfection from head to toe in a black Yohji Yamamoto distressed sweater and draped Buddha pants. He's successful enough now that he fully embraces the role of chef and restauranteur, allowing his team of underlings to do all the dirty bits while he bosses them around and sips from whatever top-shelf beverage happens to be nearest.

I'm so excited to see him, I can hardly stand it—even if I *did* have to break about a dozen rules to get his two gas-powered catering trucks on to Thalia Island. His staff who don't fit in the truck will be in the electric coach that I've only had one driving lesson in, so … fingers crossed.

Émile offers condolences about my grandfather, followed by condolences about the state of my hair, and then proceeds to fill me in on gossip I've missed in our shared social circles over the last couple weeks. "Vancouver is so boring without you," he says. *Without my temper tantrums giving everyone something to laugh about, you mean.*

The ride is too brief, but he does manage to squeak in that Connor and Suze have gone Instagram official. I already knew—I'm not above stalking my exes on social media—but I act like it doesn't matter. Because honestly, it doesn't. They're perfect for each other.

Our convoy of three pulls along Main Street, and I show them to Tommy's where they will be taking over his kitchen for the rest of the day. Tommy, surprisingly, is polite and glad to meet my friend and his team. He even offers to help wherever he can and mentions he's "excited" and "would be a blazing idiot to turn down the opportunity to learn from such an experienced chef." I thank him with hands clasped, prayer-like, against my chest.

Kelly was not so polite when I introduced her to Émile and his staff, and once she left, I apologized until Émile placed a shushing finger against my lips. "Not everyone is happy," he said, followed by a wink and a kiss to both cheeks to get me out of "his kitchen." Now I just cross my fingers that the Viridis people don't go back to Vancouver and whisper that my new life isn't as great as my own Instagram feed suggests.

I'm no more than two steps beyond the wide gas stove when Émile launches into the pointing and yelling and organizing in the way only he can. It's why he's so good at what he does—a demanding leader with a good heart and an unparalleled instinct for what makes food great. That raw talent is what earned him his first Michelin Star before he turned thirty.

Finan, exiting town hall, waves as I approach from Tommy's. "Everyone settled?" he asks.

"Yes. Just wait. Best food you've ever had."

"Looking forward to it."

"Now if we can get through tonight with everyone fed and happy, and without Kelly making a big deal about not serving Tommy's menu or the fact that their catering trucks run on gas."

"Maybe she'll fall in love with the food and forget about that other stuff."

"A girl can hope."

"Plus, your chef friend—he's male?"

"Pansexual. French. And handsome too."

"That's all Kelly needs, then."

"It's still harassment, you know—her constant handsy crap. If a dude did that, he'd be run off the island."

"Probably."

"I'll warn Émile," I say.

Finan's phone buzzes in his pocket. "Duty calls. Oh, and Humboldt is napping in your office. Gave him fresh water."

"Thanks for bringing him back. The ride there was ... slobbery. Rupert gave me that clown car on purpose."

"It fits your personality."

"What, tiny but potent, or—"

"The clown part."

"Just wait until Humboldt is in your truck and he shakes his head and those goopy, gross strings go all over *your* face and head."

"Don't slobber-shame the dog." Finan smirks as he responds to a text and then walks backward away from me. "Save me a seat?"

"Are you going to annoy me through the entire five-star meal?"

He mimes that he's shaking a Magic Eight-Ball and then pauses to read it. "Signs point to yes." He smiles again and turns, and I unabashedly watch until he hops into his truck, smiling myself until I hear my voice called on a shrill breeze otherwise known as Kelly Lockhart.

"These tables aren't going to set themselves up, Lara. We could use your help!"

Ugh. Only eight hours until bed.

TWENTY

WHO ORDERED THE OYSTERS?

É mile and his white-and-green-clad crew are just as efficient as I knew they would be—and by the looks on our new residents' faces as they bite into their meals, worth every penny, even if Kelly almost blew an aneurysm when she saw the budget for tonight. The weather has cooperated brilliantly—as if the mental memo I sent the weather gods was received and approved. It's a bit chilly, as per usual for a mid-May evening in British Columbia, but the blue sky stretches endlessly, floating into a purplish-blue, the first stars flickering as the sun exits stage west.

The insanely fresh air carries a mix of aromas from the culinary masterpieces before us and the woodsy scent from the newly built picnic tables (wood sourced from Thalia Island herself!), covered in red-and-white-checkered tablecloths. They're in rows, in a half circle in front of town hall, facing a small stage situated in the middle of the street, its edges lined with potted plants bright in their colorful spring outfits. Grapevines nestled in half barrels full of enriched soil have been woven up and over a temporary trellis along the stage's sides and back. A narrow podium with a skinny mic awaits its first victim, which, per the schedule distributed to the council members, will be

Rupert, returned from Vancouver just in time to serve as master of ceremonies.

Above the dull roar of the excited new neighbors getting to know one another, the folksy-rock band, Marmoset Hats, ferried over from the mainland, sets up on the second stage farther down the block. The maintenance crews even stretched solar-powered light strings in diagonals across the two-lane street, and benches have been placed along the curb edges for dancers to rest between twirls. It actually does look like a Hallmark movie set.

As Rupert takes the stage to commence the post-dinner welcome speeches, a line of Thalia Island's under-eighteens bounce on tiptoes for their turn at the sundae bar manned by Tommy and his wife Catrina who seems to be as comfortable with a canister of whipped cream as she is with a stethoscope.

Everything looks perfect—just as I knew it would. And people thought all those years as a pampered princess wouldn't come in handy. Look at this place! I'd polish my nails on my shirt if my manicure wasn't such a disaster. I might be getting the hang of bossing people around. As if there were ever any question.

At my table near the stage, I adjust so no one can see me loosen my belt—I ate as much as my stomach would hold, but now I'm regretting it. Plus it's almost my turn at the podium, and my gut is crampy and unsettled with nerves. I should've waited to eat.

And while I saved Finan a seat, he didn't make it to dinner as promised. I texted, and his response was a quick "Save me a plate," followed by a photo of what appears to be a broken irrigation pipe and a partially flooded field outside one of the vertical farms. Not great. Add that to tomorrow's to-do list.

The order of tonight's speeches was hotly debated among several key members of the council (ahem, *Kelly*). She demanded she be allowed to go right after Rupert, since she's been here the longest; I said it should be me as I'm the only surviving member of the Clarke family and my grandfather would've wanted it that way.

Kelly put it to a vote—naturally—and I wasn't surprised when Stanley and Ainsley raised their hands for her to go before me. Rupert refused to vote in what he mumbled was "egocentric nonsense." Finan and Catrina weren't present, so it was just me and Tommy left. We were overruled.

As such, Rupert is up there now welcoming everyone and reiterating my grandfather's mission statement. He *finally* finishes talking after having to pause twice to take a drink of his water bottle. He looks a little off tonight—I'm guessing he, too, overindulged, probably as pleased as I was to have *actual* culinary couture.

When Kelly takes the stage, it's to hoots and hollers from more than half the crowd, which is odd because everyone just arrived, so how do they already know her well enough to react so warmly? Maybe she's been in touch with them during the selection process? I really should talk to Rupert more about how the settlers were chosen, who was in charge of interviews and vetting, get a more thorough rundown of promises made to new residents and by whom. Last thing I need is an insurrection of Lockhart Loyalists taking over the joint.

Because I'm not afraid to remind them who owns this island.

Kelly's speech goes on too long, my stomach knotted nervously as I wait for her to finish with her store-bought platitudes about community, friendship, personal spirituality, and the bond between "the brothers and sisters of Thalia Island." I turn away so no one sees me sprain my eyeballs.

If she ever stops talking, I will basically repeat what Number Two said and thank everyone for being here and *if you have any questions or concerns, don't hesitate to ask* when I really just hope everyone figures out their lives and leaves me alone because—let's be honest—unless it's a party that needs organizing, I can pretty much guarantee I won't know the answer to their questions or concerns. I still have too many of Rupert's encyclopedic binders to get through.

Finally, after Kelly takes a selfie with the cheering crowd behind her, she gestures to where I stand at the bottom of the three short steps on the stage's right side. "Now, if you please, help me welcome Thalia Island's First Granddaughter, Miss Lara Clarke!"

The crowd puts out a lot of sound for not many bodies—not as much as when Kelly bounded up here, but a shiver of pride buzzes under my skin. It's fleeting, however, lasting just long enough for me to take my spot behind the podium and see all the expectant, smiling faces, as if they're waiting for me to reassure them that I know what I'm doing. These people uprooted their entire lives for the Thalia Island mission—and somehow, I'm supposed to lead them to environmental victory?

I offer a pleasant wave as nausea judders through my midsection, weakening my knees. The applause quiets, the only sound an errant strum of a guitar from the band behind us. It makes everyone jump. "I think that's the song they wrote for me. I told them to keep it short," I tease. The audience laughs politely. "OK, well, you are here. Welcome!" More applause, followed by the speech Rupert wrote, words I probably wouldn't have said on my own given that the last time I was invited to give a speech, it was at a lunchtime fundraiser for the Clarke Foundation and I was three double martinis down by the time they handed me the mic.

I find myself pausing to drink from my very own Thalia Island water bottle, wishing it were a martini instead. The nerves in my stomach just won't settle, even though it's clear no one here is laughing or holding their phones to record me screwing up, not like they do back in the city when I'm on a bender—or tearing apart a Nordstrom.

Except Kelly. She has her phone aloft. Of course she does.

A sheen of sweat coats my upper lip. "Please know, you are most welcome here. My grandfather would have given anything to see this day … but since he can't, I am the witness in his stead, and I look so forward to the days, weeks, and months ahead wherein I can get to know every one of you."

The back of my throat feels tight.

I blot at my upper lip with the back of my long sleeve, smiling as I grip the slender podium with one hand and fan myself with the other. My lower gut gurgles dangerously. "Is it just me or is anyone else feeling a little warm with all these good vibes?" It's then I see Finan standing at the back of the still-seated crowd. His arms are crossed over his chest, his brow furrowed.

And I've lost my place in my speech because I am feeling *very* not right.

"Please, grown-ups, when the kids are done, help yourselves to the dessert bar, and then get ready to dance the night away with our first real-live concert on Thalia Island, brought to you by Marmoset Hats! Thank you!"

A pleasant applause rolls through the crowd as they turn back to their tables, though a family of four in the front row looks about as green as I feel, and then their daughter—maybe ten?—drops the ice cream cone in her hand, doubles over from her spot on the bench, and vomits. Everywhere.

That's all it takes.

I stumble away from the podium, barely managing the steps before I've got my head in one of the azalea bushes, reintroducing my own meal to the flower bed.

And then more, and more, and more people behind me are throwing up.

An arm around my middle keeps me balanced just as I'm about to fall over from absolute weakness, my entire body overcome with shivers and those horrific cold sweats. "Let me help you," Finan says, leading me away from the crowd. But I pause and turn back to look at the seating area, and certainly enough, it's a sea of vomit. All over the tables, on the ground. Those who aren't actively puking are holding the hair for those who are. Some people are running away, terror in their eyes, while the little girl who vomited earlier screams as a brown stream runs out of her shorts and down her legs.

"Finan …"

"Come on."

I pause so I can puke again. "I … I need a washroom. Right *now*." Finan has a strong arm wrapped around my midsection as we skip-hop toward town hall. He helps me through the front door, basically dragging me at this point because I'm barely able to stand.

He slams open the door to the single-stall restroom and helps me inside. "Do you need …"

"Oh my god, go. Get out before it's too late."

He doesn't linger. I lunge at the heavy wooden door to lock it and manage to get my pants down and my butt on the commode in the nick of time.

"Whatever deity is listening, please let me die ..."

 ∽

Untold hours later, I wake to a slight knock on the door. I'm curled on the washroom floor, in town hall, under one of the Thalia Island fleece blankets. No idea how that came to be.

"Lara? Can I come in?"

I try to lift my head. The smell in here ... "Oh my god, please stay out. I've destroyed this bathroom. We're going to have to burn the whole place down."

When the door opens, it's Catrina, Tommy's wife, wearing a surgical mask over her face. We're friendly enough, given we're on council together and have shared meals and after-meeting chats, but not so familiar that I'm not mortified for her to see me like this. Regardless, she looks like a backlit angel descending from on high. "You OK in here?"

"I think I'm dying."

She kneels next to me, her cool fingers against my blazing forehead. "Here. Can you manage a sip of water?"

I shake my head no. Nothing else is going in until I'm sure everything is done coming out.

"Finan has offered to drive you home. You might be more comfortable in your own washroom."

I can't even keep my eyes open. I am *so weak*. "The settlers ... who else is sick ..."

Catrina stands and moistens a stack of paper towels that she then wipes over my forehead, cheeks, and lips. I mumble a thank-you. "Unfortunately, it seems that a fair number of residents have been afflicted, and as the night goes on, my phone keeps buzzing."

I finally do manage to open my lids. "Was it the food? Did we eat something bad?"

"That's the only thing I can think of. To have so many people get sick with these symptoms so quickly. And then some folks are just fine, which is helpful as I only have two hands. Even Tommy is at our place hugging the porcelain."

"Oh god ... poor you. I'm so sorry."

"It's not your fault, Lara."

But it is. If only I'd just shut up about having the food catered. If we'd just eaten Tommy's hamburgers and french fries, no one would be puking out their spleens.

"Who *isn't* sick?" I ask, hoping it's more than Finan who can lend a hand.

"Hmm, let's see—Stanley and Kelly seem to be OK, and about thirty of the new residents are fine. Those who are able have been helping me at the clinic to hand out Gravol and bottles of electrolyte solution. We're definitely going to need more of that within the next twenty-four hours. I'm making a list for Ainsley to go across to Vancouver with two of the maintenance team."

Of *course* Kelly didn't get it.

"Rupert?"

Catrina purses her lips and shakes her head.

"Damn it." I try to push onto my elbow, but I'm very shaky. "Did Émile and his staff leave?"

"Ohhh yes, they hightailed it to the ferry as soon as they saw what was happening. He couldn't stop apologizing—he was crying, Lara."

I lie back on the hardwood floor and rest my forearm over my eyes. Even the scant light from the hallway is too much. This is like being hungover without the fun that comes before. "Yes, well, Émile is an incredible chef. This sort of thing could destroy his reputation if it got out."

"I don't think anyone on Thalia is that sort. No gossips here to worry about. Besides, we have no proof that it was the food from Viridis. Could've been something picked up in our kitchen, or maybe the oysters were, you know ..."

Our eyes meet. There's no way it came from Tommy's kitchen.

And not everyone ate the oysters. It had to be something else. We both know that without saying it.

"Let's see if we can get you sitting up without too much trouble, and then Finan can help you home, shall we?"

Gratefully, I take Catrina's offered hand and move into an upright position. Big mistake. "Nope. I'm staying here for the night." I let go and lie back down, the nausea resurfacing. "I think I need a minute …"

Catrina nods and exits quickly, just as more of my insides make it to the outside.

No gossips here to worry about, Catrina said. Sure. We'll see about that.

TWENTY-ONE

A SNITCH IN THE MIDST

I shuffle weakly out to Finan's truck under the early morning sun. A couple of maintenance guys outfitted in full Tyvek suits with mops and buckets and bottles of bleach in hand pass us on our way out of town hall. I keep trying to apologize to anyone who will listen, but instead, I am hoisted into the vehicle, a care package of ginger ale and various over-the-counter medicines at my feet, the outside of the paper bag marked "Feel better soon! Catrina [smiley face]."

Finan doesn't talk during the drive to my cabin, which I'm so glad for. I don't have the energy for anything more than breathing. He helps me into the house, into the bathroom, and quickly grabs fresh towels from the hall cupboard, as well as the plush bathrobe from the end of my bed.

"I'm going to wait until you've showered to make sure you don't faint," he says. His face is flushed, he won't meet my eyes, and he sounds a little flustered.

"Are *you* OK?" I ask.

"What? Yeah. Yes. It was a long night, that's all," he says. "And, uh, your shirt ..."

I look down. Somehow I must've unbuttoned my top when I was trying to pull it off mid-barf. My left bra-covered boob is saying hello

145

to the whole world. I pull my shirt closed. "You've seen one of those before, haven't you?"

Finan lifts a brow. "I'll wait until you're clean."

"Thank you, Mr. Rowleigh. You may go. I won't faint."

He flicks his fingers toward the bathroom door and sits on the couch, lifting one boot-clad foot onto my coffee table. I don't have the reserves to scold him.

The shower is long and hot, and while I did feel a bit woozy toward the end given there is nothing but blood left in my skin bag, I manage to wash all the detritus from my body before drying off and wrapping in my robe. I brush my teeth for approximately ten minutes to erase the taste of the last fifteen hours. I haven't had food poisoning like this since a trip to Beijing when I was eleven. It's somehow less disgusting when you're a kid.

I open the bathroom door and let the steam billow out behind me, not even ashamed that I probably drained the island's reservoir. The care package from Catrina is on the counter, so I open it and pull out a can of ginger ale. I pop the top and realize I am one bullmastiff short. He is always interested in the opening of food, even carbonated beverages.

"Where's my dog?"

"Oh, so, now he's your dog."

"Are you offering to adopt him?"

Finan smiles. "The shower help?"

"Immensely." I sink into my matching overstuffed chair across from the sofa, my eyes fixed on Finan's boot until he gets the message and lowers his foot to the floor. "Catrina said a ton of people got sick."

His head bobs once. "Like I said, it was a long night."

"But not Kelly."

"Nope. Not Kelly, not Stanley or Ainsley, not me—but that's because I missed dinner dealing with that pipe."

"What happened out there?"

Finan runs a hand through his hair that looks like it also could use some shower time. "It's weird. Like someone took a shovel or ax to it.

Split it right in half where it comes out of the giant rain barrel and stretches to the watering lines."

"Seriously?"

"Could've been an accident, but we haven't had any heavy machinery in that field in a few months. And we lost a ton of water. I'm worried about what got washed away. That whole area will have to be replanted once it dries out."

"I'm telling you ... we need cameras here."

Finan chuckles. "A real police state, hey?"

"Not police. But people can't be trusted. If that pipe was severed on purpose, then someone here is not on mission."

"Try not to be too suspicious, Lara. I'm sure there's a logical explanation."

That, on top of the food poisoning last night? Sort of hard not to be suspicious.

"Anyway, I'm not sure what the final count was as far as sick residents, but everyone will be fine. Catrina was on the phone all night with the doc who's going to be arriving in a few weeks. They managed between the two of 'em."

"Bet he's glad he wasn't in the first batch of settlers."

"Shit happens."

"Literally."

Finan snorts.

"I'd offer to make you breakfast, but food is the last thing I want to think about right now," I say.

"Aaaand I'm going to guess you wouldn't know how to cook breakfast, even if you wanted to."

"Wow. Is that what you think of me? Just some helpless socialite who can't scramble an egg?"

"Well ... can you?"

"Yes. I can. I wake up, saunter into the kitchen, and tell Vera the housekeeper I'd like a scrambled egg. Voilà! Perfect eggs every time."

Finan laughs out loud. He then stands and walks into my kitchen to the window above the sink. "Speaking of flooded crops, you're overwatering this plant," he says.

147

"Hmmm?" My eyes are heavy again. I need sleep.

"Your spider plant—"

"Andromache."

"You named your spider plant Andromache?"

"She's a warrior. I saved her from terrible barbarians."

"Hello, Andromache. Tell your mother she is overwatering you and that's why you have leaf burn."

I hear him in the kitchen, but I have no idea what he's doing. "Please, no food. I cannot."

"Broth only. You need to rehydrate. That's the biggest concern with food poisoning."

"Hmmm …" I again close my eyes, serenaded by the sound of him making himself at home among the dishes and pans. If he wants to make me soup so I don't die, I guess that's OK. "Connor never made me soup."

"Are we talking about exes now?" The burner on the stovetop *click click clicks* alight.

"No. Just a thought that made its way out of my mouth." I'm so tired, I don't know how I will ever move again.

About ten minutes later, Finan appears before me carrying a breakfast tray with a bowl of steaming broth and a napkin with four saltine crackers. Our eyes meet—his remind me of the bark of a redwood tree when the sun hits it just right. "I didn't even know I had food in the cupboards."

"Sit up, Madam Mayor. You need electrolytes."

"I don't want electrolytes. Can't I just go to bed?"

He sets the tray on the coffee table. "You need to find some strength somewhere," he says, pulling his phone from the pocket of his discarded jacket. He scrolls for a second and then hands it over.

My stomach clenches anew. "Oh, you've got to be kidding me."

TWENTY-TWO

THE GLACIER CLEAVES

Already the major local news sites have picked up the story of a
mass food-poisoning event on the "super-exclusive Thalia
Island, built as a living experiment in search of a more sustainable way
of life."

And the comments on the online articles ... I know better than to
read the comments. Ever.

"We need to call the PR people handling this."

"You *are* the PR people handling this."

"No! Clarke Innovations has—where is Rupert?" I return Finan's
phone and stand in search of my own, though I'm still wobbly. Finan
leaps to his feet, as if he's going to catch me if I swoon. "I'm fine. I
don't need help." It comes out nastier than I mean it to. "Sorry."

He signals his surrender and sits again. I find my bag and dig
through until I find my phone, dead, of course, so I plug it in and wait
until enough juice flows into the battery for the screen to wake up.

And boy, does it ever.

Google alerts, text messages, twenty missed calls, mostly from
Canadian news outlets. "I can't bring myself to look at all this. Please
don't tell me we're trending ..."

"Only for about two hours."

"Awesome. This is fantastic." I scroll, light-headed and nauseated again. "Who leaked it? Oh my god—Émile—he's probably devastated." More scrolling. "Oh god, this is so bad. I have to call Rupert—he has to get CI's PR people on this. This is way out of my league—"

"Come on, Lara. Sit. You're practically see-through. At least drink something. It's that, or I'll take you to Catrina for an IV."

I leave my phone to charge and collapse into my armchair, feeling like a scooped-out avocado. I sip the broth and eat one cracker, my forehead resting against a shaky hand. "What could it have been? Like, did we all eat the same thing and that's what caused it? This is a nightmare."

"It'll be fine. We'll go into town, meet with the council, check on the settlers to make sure everyone's OK—because they are our first priority, not some internet gossips."

"I know that, Finan." I drop the spoon on the tray. Seems I don't have enough energy to slurp soup and be polite to this person who is trying to help.

"Once we know everyone is on the mend, we'll have an emergency town meeting." Finan leans forward and scrolls through his texts. "Rupert said health inspectors from the BC Centre for Disease Control will be coming over later today. They'll investigate the whole situation —who ate what, if there was something in the kitchen, if it was bad seafood ..."

"That can't be good—they can't shut us down the first week of people actually living here!"

"No one is coming to shut us down. We just have to make sure this doesn't happen again."

I close my eyes and count my heartbeat pounding against the inside of my skull. "I will never live this down. Kelly will never let me forget this. If I'd just let Tommy feed everyone instead of insisting on Viridis coming over—she's going to use this against me forever, you know."

Finan exhales and sets his phone on the coffee table. "Lara, I don't mean to sound like a dick, but we need to put your ego aside for a second and make sure our residents are all right."

I lift my head long enough to glare at him. Like I need to be scolded right now. I'm a victim too! "I'll get dressed," I say coldly.

"I'll wait for you in the truck." Finan stands, and it's the first time I notice how dark the circles are under his eyes. He grabs his coat and exits quietly.

I really need to learn how to not be an ass, and hopefully in the next twenty minutes before I'm faced with a town of angry, dehydrated hippies.

Nary a word passes between Finan and me on our short jaunt to town hall.

"Whatever the maintenance crew is making, double it," I say as we walk past the washroom, now scrubbed sparkling clean, no lingering evidence of the malfeasance I cast upon that poor toilet last night. I stop in my office to grab a pad to write on and am greeted by Humboldt whining and jumping to greet me. "Hey, buddy … sorry I abandoned you last night."

Catrina's head pops through my office doorway. "He spent the night with Auntie Cat, didn't you?" He wags his tail.

"Thank you. I don't even know where to begin—"

"Don't exert yourself. You still look like hell. Well, except for the shoes." She smiles softly.

I twist my leg and present the gorgeous YSL Blade slingback pumps in patent leather. I may look like a walking corpse, but my shoe game is strong.

"You ready for this?" she asks.

"Are they all waiting for me?"

Catrina nods and steps into the room. "Stand firm. This wasn't your fault, so don't let anyone make you feel like it was," she says, voice lowered.

"If I'd just let Tommy grill up plant burgers and free-range chicken, no one would've gotten sick."

"Maybe, but who knows?" Catrina rests a hand on my arm. "Think of this as your first opportunity to prove to the residents and council that you have the mettle to withstand the storms as they come at you."

I bob my head, fear biting at me. "Hey, have you checked on Rupert?"

"He's here. Green around the gills, but that stiff upper lip firmly in place."

Naturally. Rupert's been around my entire life, and I don't remember him *ever* taking a day off due to illness or vacation or anything, frankly. "Thank you. For your help last night, and the care package. I'm so embarrassed about—"

"Honey, I've seen it all. A little vomit, *et cetera*, doesn't scare me." Catrina winks and then turns to leave. With a pat against her leg, Humboldt moves in beside her and trots down the hall.

"I have the mettle to withstand the storms," I whisper to myself as I approach the conference room's open door.

What I don't expect is the Kelly-shaped storm walking in a tight circle at the head of the table, her face red like an overripe tomato, phone pressed against her ear as she yells at someone on the other end. Rupert pulls out the chair beside him.

"How are you feeling this morning?" he asks as I sit.

"Been better. You?"

"As long as we don't talk about food, I shall recover in due course."

In looking at him, dressed as usual in a finely tailored suit, he definitely does have that greenish tinge Catrina mentioned. He pulls peppermints from his inside pocket, pops one in his mouth, and offers me the packet. "It helps with the nausea."

"Thanks." I take it gratefully and lean closer, angling my body so Stanley, Tommy, and Finan across the way can't see my lips moving. "What happened? Have you been able to get ahold of Émile?"

"Frankly, I have no idea at this point. And calls are going to his voicemail."

"What about the PR people downtown? Can they help us manage this?" Kelly's shrill voice interrupts me as it bounces off the arched ceiling. "Who is she screaming at?"

"Who hasn't she been screaming at this morning?"

"She's not even sick. That's honestly not fair," I say.

He smirks. "Be nice."

I flick my fingers at him like I'm shooing away a bug.

Catrina sets cups of steaming tea in front of us. I thank her again for her help and concern and then turn back to Number Two. "Did Finan tell you about the ruptured pipe near the vertical farms?"

He nods.

"Rupert, we need surveillance. Cameras, drones, whatever—we can't be everywhere at once, and something like that could devastate crops as we head into summer."

"One burst pipe does not mean we have saboteurs on the island, Lara."

"I'm just saying—"

Our dialogue cuts off as Kelly finishes her call and claps her hands to get our attention. I feel like I'm in Mrs. Ripper's first grade class again. I wonder if Kelly will put my name on the dry-erase board followed by a series of check marks (one check mark equals five minutes off lunch recess) because I won't stop chatting with my neighbor.

"I don't need to tell you what a major calamity we have on our hands today," she says, leaning on bony knuckles against the tabletop. She's worked herself into a sweat and peels off her bamboo fleece Thalia Island jacket. The short sleeves of the white shirt underneath reveal the bottom half of a tattoo on her right upper arm—I never would've pegged Kelly as the type. I can't make out what it is—a black, blue, and red blob of what might be the lower half of a mermaid with black wave squiggles?

No idea.

Kelly takes a deep breath and then launches into how all the news channels are carrying the story. She lists the social media accounts we've been trending on sporadically overnight, how we're being skewered on Twitter (*everyone gets skewered on Twitter, Kelly*), and how there are renewed calls from housing advocates and social justice warrior groups to shut us down.

"The war cry has started again about our so-called exclusionary process for settler selection, how we only let the super-rich live here, how we're taking advantage of loopholes in the law to avoid taxation ..."

I lean over to Rupert. "Is any of that true? We really have people who hate this place?" I whisper. He purses his lips and lifts an eyebrow before returning his attention to Kelly's ongoing rant. She covers more problematic ground for another few minutes before turning her attention to last evening's debacle.

"The suspected food poisoning could have been avoided altogether if we had relied upon the resources we have here on Thalia Island, as Archibald intended for us to do. If Tommy had provided the menu last night"—she pauses long enough to migrate her angry eyes in my direction—"we wouldn't be in this mess this morning. After we're done here, I have to go deal with the musicians from Marmoset Hats who are still on the island, half of whom are still sick this morning. The money we lost last night, between the overpriced catering and the fees for the band that we *didn't even get to listen to*, plus the fees to Dr. Stillson for his time spent on the phone all night helping Catrina—he's not even due to move over here until late June, but I think we need to offer him a bonus to come sooner. And that, too, will take a big bite out of our quarterly operating budget."

Kelly finally pauses to inhale before she passes out. As she guzzles from her reusable water bottle, no one says a word, and no one will make eye contact with me.

She refreshes her bright pink gloss plucked from her pocket and smacks her lips before resuming. "I will thus be adding an item to the agenda for our first town hall meeting, to be held once everyone is able to leave their bathrooms, about banning outside caterers from future island-wide events. If we want to eat it or serve it, the food either has to come from here or as part of our regular grocery shipments. Period. No more outsiders. I mean, how do we know that this wasn't intentional? That someone on the outside who has a grudge against our mission purposely poisoned our food? What if it was someone from Lara's friend's restaurant, a jealous sous chef or catering assistant or something?"

"Oh, come on," I mumble.

"What? You've not been here long enough to understand fully the vitriol directed at our mission, Lara," Kelly says. My face catches fire as Stanley and Ainsley bob their heads in agreement. Tommy sips at the tea Catrina placed before him as well, but again, he won't look at me. Finan is bent over his phone, thumbs flying.

"Does she want me to apologize or something? Émile would never intentionally do this!" I whisper to Rupert.

"Save your breath, for now," he murmurs in return.

"Do you have something helpful to offer?" Kelly asks, her voice begging for a fight.

I sit up straighter, willing myself to look braver than I feel. "We'll need a list of everyone who is sick. We'll need a statement to send to the press—"

"For what? To give them more fodder?" Kelly snorts.

"I've drafted something already," Rupert says, opening his cactus-leather portfolio and extracting his MacBook. "I will handle all press calls as well as the statement for our official social media channels. Further, I will facilitate the representatives from the BC CDC upon their arrival this afternoon."

Kelly clasps her hands behind her back. Part of me wants to see her challenge Rupert. She might be blustery and loud like a *T. rex* but Rupert, even under the weather, is like a vampire—sleek, quiet, stealthy. He'll bite her with his politely venomous, needle-sharp fangs before she sees him coming, like some long-lost British Cullen.

"And I'll talk to Émile, as soon as he'll answer his phone. I'm sure he's torn up," I interject. Kelly makes that annoying nasal sound again. Maybe she was a sow in her last life?

"Like I care what happens to your cook," she says.

"He's a Michelin Star *chef*, and this could destroy his business. Do you not care about that?"

Kelly's smug face answers for her. I stand—I must show her I'm not going to back down from her bullying, even if I really want to hop on the next ferry to Vancouver and move to that damp suburban basement suite and get a tacky mermaid tattoo of my own and forget Thalia Island ever existed.

"If Rupert is handling the media statement and the CDC investigators, I will work with Catrina to make sure the residents have what they need. That way I can offer a personal apology to every afflicted household." I look down at Rupert, and I *think* his mouth tugs into a partial smile. "No one has died. This is just a hiccup. We can overcome this, and quickly, so we can move on to bigger matters."

Finan, finally finished with whatever was occupying his attention, slides his phone on to the table. "Lara's right. Let's manage this and move on. If I may, I'd like to discuss the urgent issue regarding the severed irrigation pipe leading from the rain reservoirs near vertical farm B. Yes?" The buzz of agreement floats around the room from everyone except Kelly. Rupert excuses himself to tackle his to-do list, Kelly hot on his heels, her face flushed anew.

Finan stands and gives me a quick wink as he assumes Kelly's former spot at the table head and clicks on the huge monitor to cast photos of the damaged piping from his phone.

And with that single gesture, a Finan-size piece shears from my frozen heart and melts at my feet.

TWENTY-THREE

BRAVE NEW FRIEND

Catrina and I spend the entire afternoon going door to door, making sure everyone who fell ill is recovering, stopping every half hour so I can sit in her car and sip ginger ale and nibble Digestive cookies for quick sugar. During these breaks, I field emails from Rupert, mostly cc's for the statements and press release he's sent out, as well as a few texts from Finan checking on me and sending a video of Humboldt gleefully frolicking in the sloppy mud pile in front of vertical farm B.

"I think that's the first real smile I've seen from you," Catrina says, sipping from her insulated coffee mug. I hold up the phone to show her what my inherited canine child is doing. "Your cabin has a bathtub?"

"Ugh." This muddy mutt in my pristine bathroom? I don't think so. I text Finan: **Please tell me you are hosing him down before dropping him off.**

The bubbles dance for the count of five before his response: *Maybe …*

Another real smile, followed by a deep inhale of the clean, fresh air. Mist hugs the tops of the forest behind this strip of homes, and even this late in the afternoon, the dampness pervades, another reminder we're near the water's edge. I can only imagine what this is doing to my hair—we *have* to get a stylist over here—but I don't bother looking at my reflection in the visor mirror. Who's here to see me anyway?

It dawns on me that this is the first time since I learned about such creatures as paparazzi that I haven't checked for their presence hiding behind a tree or in a parked car. Certainly we have fewer opportunist photographers in Vancouver than, say, LA or NYC, but my grandfather attracted a strange lot. His brand of environmental clamor was viewed through different lenses, depending on the agenda of the person looking. Typically, people who follow science have always been staunch supporters of his efforts to mitigate the effects of climate change, whereas those who refute the evidence are more interested in squawking about his excessive wealth, picking apart every single thing he did—every flight he took, every fundraiser he held, every political candidate he supported that they didn't like. "You can't make them all happy, Lara Jo. That's just a fact."

But after my mother disappeared under mysterious circumstances, and I became the lonely orphan living in Clarke Manor with the gregarious but mildly eccentric grandfather and the quiet, imposing valet, the public interest transformed—less chatter about what brand of electric car Archibald Clarke was driving and more gossip about what mischief I was making or what celebrity I was hobnobbing with, evolving viciously into exposés on how much greenhouse gas was emitted during the manufacture of the evening gown I wore to the latest society event or how many overseas trips I took during a given year, thereby undermining my grandfather's efforts to save the planet.

The whispers got louder, and the photographers got cleverer—and crueler.

"If your shoulders creep any higher, your head will disappear," Catrina says.

"Sorry ... it's just so quiet here. I can hear myself think."

"Not a bad thing, I hope? To hear yourself think?"

I chuckle and tuck my phone away and follow Catrina to the next house, asking myself her question over and over again.

Of the people who got sick, only five or so were really angry, and even they calmed down once we explained how the situation is being managed and thoroughly investigated by the proper authorities. However, there were a *lot* of questions about the safety of the food supply on the island, when the full complement of medical professionals will arrive, and when Lutris, our on-island digital communication units (like Alexa, but for our private network) installed in each residence, will be fully functional.

By 7:00 p.m., every resident has been attended to. We stop at town hall to collect Humboldt just as the sky finally decides what it wants to do with the heavy gray clouds it's been packing around all day. The wipers of Catrina's electric Toyota can hardly keep up as she navigates the road out to my cabin. When CBC News reports the story of the fancy island with a recent suspected salmonella outbreak sickening its brand-new residents, Catrina clicks off the radio and offers a friendly smile.

"Don't let it get to you. There will be bumps in the road. It's like *Brave New World* here, minus the mind-control drugs and mass orgies."

I look at her, not sure if I'm supposed to laugh—but hearing kind, motherly Catrina talk about mass orgies is sort of hilarious.

"What? You've never read that book?"

"Uh, *no*."

"Oh, you should. It's terrific. Aldous Huxley. Published in 1932. We read it in university—changed my world view."

"Wow." I don't tell her I didn't bother to finish university because Advanced Mixology and How to Attract Hot but Dumb Guys 101 weren't offered as credit courses toward graduation.

"I can loan you my copy if you want. Might be an interesting read for you, considering we're creating our own utopia here. Maybe it'll give you some perspective on what could go wrong, beyond food poisoning and broken irrigation pipes."

"I'll take whatever help I can get at this point."

Catrina slows and turns into the long gravel drive that leads toward my cabin. She finally stops in front of the knee-high, rough-hewn lumber fence that surrounds my front flower bed, the electric car's engine completely silent, the only noise the rain battering the car's sunroof. She turns in her seat and examines my face.

"Did Archibald ever tell you that I knew your mother?"

My heart skips a beat. "No. We never talked about Thalia or who would be living here, so …"

Catrina looks forward again, a warm smile crawling across her face. "I met Cordi at UBC. I was head down in the books—the nursing program is competitive—and your mom, she was the wild child, never without a camera, always looking for causes to join but only the ones that involved marches and banners and bullhorns. The ones that would make your granddad pinch the bridge of his nose."

My own smile emerges, imagining my mother in her usual army-green cargo pants and long-sleeved white shirt, standing atop a cafeteria table waving some protest sign.

"We were unlikely friends. She was brilliant. Never took notes during classes and still managed to get the best grades. A real knack for math—did you know that?"

My eyes sting and a tentative laugh stumbles from me as I try to hide my emotion. "She did not pass on that trait."

"I was failing calculus, and she helped me squeak through so I could move forward in the program. But then she vanished third year —didn't even clean out her on-campus residence. We all thought something terrible had happened. And then a letter arrived with a picture of her in a cockpit. She dropped out of university to go to flight school! We kept in touch off and on … I met Tommy and then graduated and went to work at a Vancouver hospital, and your mom was flying around the world, earning her stripes as a photographer. Had a real talent for it."

I lean my head back, watching raindrops race each other down the windshield.

"I invited her to our wedding, but she sent her regrets—turns out she was having a baby girl around that time." She chuckles. "We tried to keep in touch after that, but you know how life gets. Plus she was always off on some adventure."

"That she was …"

Catrina's smile slowly fades. "It must've been hard for you, not having her around all the time."

"That's what nannies are for." My voice sounds hard in my ears.

"She loved you. And your grandfather, well, he just adored you. Your mom was a bit feral. Nothing could contain her," Catrina says. I can't meet her eyes. She may have known my family longer than I have, but that doesn't mean I trust her with the sadness bubbling under the surface.

"Thank you for all the help, and for the ride home." I unbuckle my belt and reach for the door handle, but Catrina's hand on my arm stops me.

"I just want you to know that I'm here for you. Me *and* Tommy."

I nod quickly, flash a practiced smile, and free myself from the car before things get any mushier. I'm not used to talking about my feelings with people I'm not paying $350 a session.

Once inside, I shed my raincoat and peep through the front curtain to make sure Catrina's car is bouncing down the driveway and that she's not going to knock on the door to tell me more sad tales from the past that happened before I was a sparkle in my mother's wanderlust-infused eye.

I melt into the couch, almost too tired to see why my phone is buzzing—again—afraid to see who's harassing me now. I'm very happy to find it's not harassment but my new friend Eugenia, checking in with a photo of her holding Benny the Cannabis Cowboy's daughter, Sativa.

Thought you could use a smile. Hang in there.

Eugenia looks every bit the auntie with that tiny, shriveled bundle smooshed against her smiling cheek. Honestly, I do not understand why people think babies are so cute. Sativa looks like a sunburned old man.

So adorable! Hope everyone is doing well over there. I miss the big city!

It's definitely quieter without you, but it looks like trouble took the ferry to visit.

It did. So gross. I don't know if I will ever eat again.

Fresh ginger, either as tea or with white rice. And NO BOOZE. You'll be right as rain in no time.

Just the thought of a drink makes the room tilt. Chalk one up for salmonella! **Thanks, Eugenia. Hello to Benny and family from me.**

She responds with a smooching emoji just as my stomach growls. "No way. I'm not feeding you yet," I say, rising from the couch to grab the last ginger ale from the fridge. I treat myself to another hot shower to chase away the chill and lingering malaise, and just before clicking off my bedside lamp, I shoot a quick text to Finan: **Pretty please with sugar on top, will you babysit the beast until tomorrow? I need sleep.**

I'm out before his reply comes in.

TWENTY-FOUR

THE LIST

My front door whooshes open. "Good morning, sunshine."

I'm hunched over a cup of black coffee at the kitchen counter, still in my robe and stocking feet, tired eyes heavy, stomach less achy but still grumbling at me. "Why are you here …"

Rupert holds aloft a stainless steel travel mug. "I've brewed you some tea from fresh ginger. Why are you not ready? It's after nine. You are already late for work."

I groan. "I need a sick day."

"Then you should have negotiated one in your contract," Rupert chides. "Quick, quick, there is fire afoot."

The nervous jitters enliven in my chest. "Wait—what fire?"

"As they say in your beloved Netflix dramas, I'll tell you on the way."

Tell me, he does. I have no idea where my car is—I think I left it downtown?—so I ride in with Rupert, who is looking far less Kermit green than he did yesterday. Thankfully, we both are. And my

163

seat belt is hardly on when he reaches into his ever-present portfolio and hands over a page black with ink, today's date in bold at the top.

"Why are you giving me a numbered list of problems?"

"Because our current problem list requires numbers, and likely more than are on this page."

I scan—certainly enough, we are still managing fallout from the suspected salmonella incident. According to the list, Rupert has to finish up with the two BC CDC investigators today. In addition to the broken irrigation pipe out at vertical farm B, which I was formerly assured was no big deal but actually *is* kind of a big deal, the list also includes problems with the electric grain harvester, a rockfall on the west island road, malfunction signals going off in the unfinished solar array field, and on and on. The fifteenth item on the list reads "Malfunctioning HVAC system, VFs C and D."

"This all looks like stuff for Finan and his crew."

"The mechanical issues, yes, but when he's overwhelmed like this, you need to pick up the slack and delegate."

"Why can't you do that?"

"Refer to problem number one." Right. The CDC people.

"Fine, but what about Kelly? Isn't she the queen of delegating?"

"Kelly has her own list overseeing the completion of the last set of residences before group two arrives. Ainsley is out helping with the issues at the vertical farms, doing what they can to prevent irreversible damage to the young plants in the affected buildings. Tommy has to run the diner, and Stanley is at the general store, now that we have residents on the island. Catrina is again following up with anyone still feeling unwell, plus she has to prepare the clinic for Dr. Stillson's imminent arrival."

"He's coming over early?"

"First week of June now. We need him. And until the food-poisoning investigation concludes, I'm tied up." He reaches into his inside pocket and hands me his pen. "Add to the list: call Jeremiah."

"Who is Jeremiah?"

"The technician who handles our IT matters—internet connectivity, Lutris, our island-wide Wi-Fi—we need to schedule a Zoom call to talk about when Lutris will be fully operational. It should've been up and running already. Plus the Wi-Fi is spotty now that we have more humans connecting to the network. This won't stand, not for what we've paid him."

"Is there a file on this somewhere so I know what I'm talking about before I call him?"

"In the binders."

Of course.

Rupert pulls into a diagonal spot in front of town hall and glides out of his seat, pausing long enough to plug his car into the curbside charger. I rush to catch up to his long stride, surprised that my stomach growls with the smell of freshly baked bread wafting by. "Rupert, wait." He stops.

"I know I'm new and clueless about pretty much everything, but this list"—I hold it in front of me—"is this *normal*? Like, this is a ton of stuff going wrong all at once. Is that expected? Because if it is, I think we might need more help running this place. And I seriously want to talk about installing security and surveillance. We'd be naive not to do so."

"This week has presented unforeseen challenges, for sure. And I understand the logic behind wanting to surveil and protect our precious resources. But we have promised our residents a more peaceful, para-urban life, and if we start installing cameras and piloting drones, how is that any different from what they left behind?"

I again scan the page in my hand. Maybe he's right. The people living on Thalia are striving for a new ideal, one that doesn't involve constant governmental interference and monitoring or the constant eyes-on found in a more metropolitan environment. "Who leaked the photos of people puking? Have you seen them? And what people are saying on social media, about how the settlers were picked ... is it true? Did we only pick the best of the best, the people who could afford it?"

Rupert regards his Apple Watch and resumes walking. "No idea who leaked. And you are more than welcome to peruse the settler files. They're in the cabinets in Kelly's office—tell her I've asked you to review them, to get to know the new people living here."

"Ha. She's not going to let me into her office."

"So wait until she's gone. That giant key chain of yours is the gateway to everything. And"—Rupert holds open the front door and waves me through—"no surveillance cameras for her to see you in there." He winks, but before I can ask another question, he's shaking hands with the man and woman in off-the-rack suits, their BC CDC ID badges clamped to breast pockets, his business face firmly affixed.

I should affix mine as well, but not without caffeine.

A quick stop in my office to stash my bag and shed my coat and then to the kitchen. It seems I'm the only one here at the moment—everyone else must be out handling the maelstrom. I stop in front of Kelly's darkened office and jiggle the handle on the closed glass-and-wood door. Locked. A quick scan of the hall reveals that hers is the only door that is shut. Rupert's is open; Finan's too, his lights off because he's out saving bean sprouts. Tommy, Catrina, and Stanley share a space, since they are only here during council business, also open.

I suppose I could go into Kelly's office and have a look at the settler files. I should probably get to know who is living on my island —because *someone* among them leaked the food-poisoning story and photos. I should start looking for who would do such a thing, right? Especially since I've yet to meet Deputy Derek, so we have no official "police" presence on Thalia yet ...

I slide Rupert's numbered to-do list onto the round wooden break-room table to review while I caffeinate. As I wait for the kettle to boil, I scan the faces in my head from the other night, the few I can remember. It's mostly a haze—between my nerves about giving a speech and my tempestuous stomach, the only person who stands out is that little blond girl in the front row who ralphed up her dinner and set everyone else's gag reflexes in motion.

I swallow hard and open the cupboards, looking for anything inoffensive to nibble on.

No way would anyone on Émile's team leak info—he'd have their heads. And they all signed NDAs before they were allowed to step foot on our ferry.

Woof!

"Jesus!" I startle hard enough to drop the open foil bag of roasted coffee beans, which Humboldt immediately saunters toward.

"Not Jesus. Only me," Finan says, hooking a hand around Humboldt's collar before he ingests the beans and then poops everywhere. "You look about a thousand percent better today."

I grab the broom. "Thank you?" I pour the half-full dustpan into the green waste. I'm too lazy to wash these beans, and eww, they've been on the *floor*. "Coffee?"

"Is there enough for two?"

I shake the bag to answer. He nods. Finan, dressed in Levi's that fit *very* nicely, pulls off his Carhartt jacket. A black, three-button Henley hugs his shape, the sleeves pushed up to his elbows. He drapes his coat, pulls out the chair, and sits. His entrance into the space introduces new smells that override the coffee beans in the grinder—soil, water, fresh air, a natural cologne comprised of sweat and leather and maybe aftershave? It's nice. Connor only ever smelled like the cologne counter at Holt Renfrew, and only because he doused himself in Tom Ford's "Noir De Noir" to mask the smoke emanating from my credit cards.

"Quite a show out there today," I say, focused on not spilling the hot water as I pour it into the French press. The espresso machine sucks. I stir the grounds to sit for a minute and lean against the counter.

"Yeah ... Rupert briefed you?"

"We need more help around here."

"You sound like Kelly."

"Oh god, please never say that again."

He smiles, and I try very hard not to notice the fine layer of dark hair on Finan's strong forearms or how it stops just above his hands. Connor waxes everything. He spends more time manicuring his personal gardens than I do. He would never allow scruff on his face, not even a five o'clock shadow, unless it was for an audition or a role, and his weekly standing appointment with his hairstylist could feed a family of four for a year.

In looking at Finan—thick, dark, messy-tapered hair begging for my fingers' attention, a well-manicured but lush beard, a faint scar I've just now noticed running through the fade on the left side of his head near the temple—that flip low in my belly suggests I might actually like a manly man.

I turn away to press the coffee and pour before Finan spies the warmth that undoubtedly is coloring my complexion. "Cream or sugar?" My voice sounds too high. Did he see me gawking?

He pulls out some coconut-based creamer and then sits again. "This stuff's pretty good." I slide a filled mug in front of him and he lightens his coffee, offering me the creamer. Our eyes lock and I forget how to breathe.

"Just sugar for me." My chair scrapes against the wood floor as I slide into it. "Thanks for taking Humboldt home with you. Again. I passed out as soon as Catrina and I finished our rounds yesterday."

"I'm glad you're feeling better." Finan grabs and unzips a sizable bag of dog treats stashed in the lower cupboard and offers Humboldt a green, bone-shaped cookie the size of my foot. "Try to give him one of these every few days. They keep his breath from fouling up the place." He resumes his seat and scrubs a hand down his face, dropping his head back for a second. "I don't know what the hell is happening out at the vertical farms. They've been running perfectly for months, and now it's like everything is falling apart."

He sips his coffee, and I notice how tired he looks.

"Are *you* getting any sleep?"

"Sleep is overrated."

I stir another spoonful of sugar into my cup—this dark roast tastes burnt. "So, why do I sound like Kelly?" I wrinkle my face.

"About more help. One of the new residents is like her golden boy who allegedly has experience in a hundred different specialties, and she keeps pushing him toward Rupert, saying we need to split my job in half."

"Would that be a bad thing?"

"Wait until you meet this guy."

"Are you afraid you'll be squeezed out? Because I *can* remind dear Kelly that I am the actual boss around here, and if anyone does any squeezing, it'll be me." I lift my coffee mug, as if in salute. Finan chuckles.

"It's not about ego or even job security. I've been here the longest —Archibald recruited me for this place."

"Damn. I did not know that."

"I just don't like it when someone fresh out of technical college tries to tell me how to do things I've been managing for months."

"Is that what's happening?"

"Have you seen the *Shrek* movies?"

"I'm sorry?"

"The movies about the ogre and the donkey and—"

"Yes, I've seen *Shrek*."

"This new guy is like a nerdy Prince Charming. Comes in waving his hair and his diplomas around, talking over everyone else, not listening to much of anything."

"You've learned this much about him in, what, a few days?"

"Nah, he's been here off and on for a few months—he did his practicum here, working on the vertical farms' ventilation and lighting systems. He's just finally moved over permanently, now that's he's graduated."

"He's young, then?"

"Midtwenties? But he and Kelly"—Finan holds a hand up, his fingers crossed—"tight. The sun shines out of his ass, as far as she's concerned."

"She's old enough to be his mother."

"Pretty sure she doesn't see it that way."

"What's this guy's name? And why haven't I met him yet?"

"He arrived with the settler group. And *you've* been a little preoccupied with your friend salmonella."

I swallow a sip to soothe my touchy throat.

"His name's Hunter."

"Solid frat-boy-douche name."

Finan smiles and nods. "I'm all for working together but don't come in and start telling me how the sausage is made, you know?" His phone buzzes against the table. He looks at the screen and holds it up for me to see. I cover my mouth to muffle my laugh—Prince Charming's face smiles cartoonishly back at me, overlaid with the caller's name: HUNTER.

"Finan here ..."

A loud, excitable male voice pours from the phone. Finan doesn't even have to put it on speaker for me to hear the conversation. When he tries to respond, Hunter rolls right over him like a wave, allowing a few *mm-hmms* to squeeze through. Finan, meanwhile, makes faces as Hunter talks, giving me a thumbs-up, raising his brows in mock surprise, pursing his lips like he's kissing someone's butt.

"I'll be there in a few." He ends the call before Hunter stops talking.

"That went well."

He raises his arms to his sides, as if showcasing my prize. "Welcome to nirvana." Humboldt takes that as his cue to hoist his front half onto Finan's thighs. "Ohhhh, come on, man, you are not a lap dog."

Finan scrubs Humboldt's forehead and muscly sides, the soft whine and long slobber strings dangling from his jowls indicative of canine bliss. I can't help it—I stand and grab paper napkins.

"So gross," I say, trying not to let the drool touch me. Finan chuckles as I wipe Humboldt's face. "Get down, you lump." I push him to the floor, and not without effort.

Finan drains his coffee, stretches again, and pushes out his chair. "Thank you for the conversation. Glad to see you're on the mend."

"Yes. No problem." My cheeks flame again, and my tongue feels thick in my mouth. "Let me know if you need me. If you need help. If you have more for my to-do list or whatever. I'm supposed to be delegating ..."

Finan spins Rupert's list on the tabletop and whistles. "Looks like you have plenty to handle today." He winks, grabs his coat off the back of his chair, and heads toward the door. "You care if he hangs out with me?"

"Please. Take him and his farts out of doors."

"Come on, Humboldt." Finan waves as my derpy dog follows him out of the small kitchen. My coffee cup cradled in my hand, I smile when an image of Finan without all those manly work clothes floats through my brain.

Until my own buzzing phone throws me back onto planet Earth with a heaving thud. "Yuck."

I clear my throat and answer. "Hey, Kelly ..."

TWENTY-FIVE

THALIA ISLAND, MELTING POT

I cherry-pick through Rupert's list for stuff I know I can manage, making calls and moving maintenance crews around where they're needed per Finan's and Kelly's urgent texts and calls. I spend two hours on the phone with Jeremiah about Lutris and the Wi-Fi, and he's actually super nice. I'm relieved he isn't a jerk, considering I know very little about networks or IP addresses or servers or Wi-Fi towers or a bunch of other terms and checks he tries to walk me through.

When we're off the phone, I quietly download a countdown app for my office Mac and sync it to today's date—and the date I will be finished with Thalia Island. Assuming I will be leaving by noon on my last day here, the clock sits at 349 days. There's an option for hours, minutes, and seconds, but I'll switch to that when I'm feeling petty and desperate. So, like, in an hour.

I pause to unload the Canada Post bag shuttled to town hall by one of the maintenance crew who met the mail boat at the marina. As I slide letters into the lockboxes in the front lobby, it appears I'm now the postmaster too? Unloading other people's mail reminds me to reclaim my credit cards from Number Two. If the town council won't approve a drone, I'll buy my own.

Also, Kelly Lockhart has a ton of mail. Like, most of the mail in this bag is for her. One letter has been covered in stickers of sparkling gemstones and beaches and waves and sunshines, as if someone depleted their sticker collection just to send a letter to Kelly. Who in the world could like her that much to go to such effort?

I can't even get her lockbox closed. Whatever. They can hire a postal worker if they want perfection.

Lunch—chicken salad on a fresh-baked croissant with Thalia Island-grown lettuce, delivered to my desk from Tommy's—is consumed while I prioritize emails. Catrina doesn't stay to chat, other than to ask obligatory medical questions about my stomach, fluid intake, and bowel movements—and to drop off a well-loved and annotated copy of *Brave New World*.

"We can be Thalia Island's first book club," she says as she waves goodbye.

It's almost like having a real mom around.

Also, this sandwich is the best thing I've ever eaten in my thirty-one years of consuming food. My appetite! It hath returned!

By three in the afternoon, my fuzzy eyeballs are skipping over words on the screen. I'm still alone in the office, other than a few residents stopping by now and again to collect their mail keys, ask about ferry schedules and when the containers of household furnishings will arrive, collect the seed kits for their front and backyard garden plots. It's been quiet and blissfully fart-free since Finan and Humboldt shoved off to deal with the vertical farms.

I log into Lutris to check functionality after my long call this morning. One of the neat tricks Jeremiah walked me through is the ability to track where Thalia employees and council members are on the island, if they have their Thalia-issued phones with them.

Sure enough, my ID tag (a cute little orca icon, thanks to Jeremiah's help) shows me at town hall. Rupert's, a fir tree, has him at Tommy's, still with the BC CDC folks, I presume; Finan's—a beaver, no joke—is at the vertical farms' field; Ainsley's orange carrot is smack-dab in the middle of the farmlands; and Kelly's mermaid is moving—she seems to be driving, along the island's west side. Probably out dealing with the rockfall? I will need to get the software onto Hunter's phone too. I very much like the idea of keeping an eye on people. And if they won't let me have cameras …

Given that Kelly is at least a twenty-minute drive from where I am, there's no time like the present to let myself into her office for a look at those settler files. I need to know who's here, and I need to be able to answer honestly when people accuse Thalia Island of only catering to the wealthy.

I grab my huge key chain out of my drawer. I flip through, looking for any marker that indicates which key belongs to which office. "Seriously, Rupert?" I find the one that opens my door, note the others identical to it, and then try each in the lock to Kelly's.

After the tenth attempt, the door clicks open and I am immediately awash in that cheap, perfumey incense Kelly likes so much. We're going to need an air purifier if she doesn't tone it down—this *mauvaise odeur* does *not* seem very eco-friendly.

Light clicked on, I check my Lutris app again to see where her flashing mermaid is—still out on the west side.

Why am I so nervous? Rupert said I should do this. I'm not breaking any rules. "It's *your* island, Lara," I mutter.

Kelly has four filing cabinets—one tall, four-drawer, beige metal cabinet, and three longer, two-drawer wood cabinets—all covered with mermaid collectibles, some artful but mostly cheesy with sparkling fish tails and huge boobs, the nipples covered by tiny clamshells. Even her chair has a mermaid-graphic T-shirt stretched over its back.

I start with the tall cabinet, careful not to disturb her toys. The top two drawers hold the same collection of binders still sitting in messy stacks on my desk and floor. The third drawer is filled with rolled, rubber-banded sheets and cardboard mailing tubes of engineering plans and blueprints. The fourth is extra office supplies, an old pair of running shoes, and more of that god-awful incense. I pick up one of the packages—sure enough, it has a Dollarama sticker on its front. "Why am I not surprised …"

I move on to the first of the wooden cabinets, pulling the top drawer's handle only to find it locked. Again with the key chain from hell, I flip through until I find a tiny key to fit the tiny lock. Finally, the drawer releases with a quiet sigh. The files within are organized alphabetically by last name; all of these are marked with red stickers along the folder edges. Scanning the tabs, I don't recognize any of these folks. Probably a safe assumption that a red sticker means these applicants weren't accepted as residents.

The second drawer of the first cabinet also contains folders demarcated with red stickers, so I move on to the next cabinet, repeating the key hunt until I find a winner. Bingo—these folders have green and blue stickers on their folder edges, and flipping through, the recognition is immediate for nearly all the surnames.

Upon checking both drawers of the second and third cabinets, I find them full to the brim with files, so I have my work cut out for me.

I grab a sizable stack of folders and tuck them against my chest while closing the drawer with my hip. I leave the office door open—since I'm the only one here—and retreat to my desk.

I flop open the first file, this one with a blue sticker on the name tab. G. Abbells: single male, age thirty-two, no kids, works on the maintenance crew, degree in livestock and ranch management, specializing in animal husbandry, on Thalia Island under a temporary one-year permit. Flipping up the page on the left-hand side of the folder held by a horizontal pronged fastener, I recall that I've seen the face smiling back at me.

So the blue stickers must be the people working on Thalia, and the green stickers must be residents. Good to know.

I therefore separate them into two piles and return the blue-stickered folders to Kelly's cabinet in exchange for just green-stickered files. She'll probably get pissed I've messed up her filing system, but it makes more sense to have employees separate from residents.

The first green folder I open is the Allen family of four. Dad is a life insurance broker, Mom is an analyst for a solar energy company, and obviously both careers allow them to work from home or else they wouldn't be here. Two kids, a boy and a girl, ages eight and ten. Cumulative gross household income: $225,000.

So, middle class, right? I don't even know what the middle class is in this country. I've never paid attention to such things because I've always known where I—or rather, my grandfather—sit on the financial food chain.

I google it. The upper-class range in Canada starts at $236,000. The Allens are just under this.

The folder also contains pages and pages of handwritten answers to questions someone—or some committee—deemed worthy of asking, including the personal mission statement for each of the persons applying to live here. In addition, there are questions pertaining to mental and physical health, commitment to environmental causes, a credit report, even an RCMP criminal background check.

So, in essence, we *did* pick the cream of the crop. Not necessarily the richest but definitely the most wholesome, which I suppose isn't terrible—it's not like my grandfather would've gone to all this expense and decades of planning and effort just to let some hoodlums come tear apart his island.

Next folder: Lucy-Frank Makamoose, single female, no children, age thirty-eight, First Nations visual artist, gross household income $68,000. And beautiful.

On and on through the stacks, I scan and make my own notes—data only with no names attached to preserve privacy—and then return and replace with the next batch. Of the eventual one hundred and fifty permanent settlers we will have on the island during my year here, it looks as though we will have a wide cross-section of Canadians represented, including many ethnicities. I'm also glad to find they didn't exclude people who've had a serious past medical history (other than those needing ongoing care in the Lower Mainland), a history of mental health issues, or physical challenges. The entire island was designed with accessibility in mind, something Rupert pointed out the first day I was here. I didn't really think about the people who might need curb cuts or widened hallways or grab bars in public bathrooms ...

Then again, there are a lot of things I haven't thought about in the last fifteen years, mostly because I've been too busy thinking about myself.

With regard to income and the assertion that we only let the super-rich live on Thalia, it's not completely true. The few residents who *do* make over a million a year (and one woman who makes significantly more than that) skew the all-island average into the lower-upper class range, but most everyone else would be considered comfortable middle class or even against the upper echelons of the lower-class figures—which also explains why Thalia Island has instituted a universal basic income for all residents who qualify, subsidized by the Clarke Foundation and the voluntary taxation paid by the island's multimillionaires.

Some random pile of ooze on Twitter called Thalia Island "a living, breathing progressive liberal circle jerk."

Lovely. Crawl back under your bridge, troll.

What IS good is that we have a huge variety of skills, careers, and talents among us—painters and potters and sculptors, the livestock guy, a well-known Canadian author and her professor husband on sabbatical for a year from Simon Fraser University, a small crew of scientists working on biomedical and bioagricultural research (including the team growing cultured meat), four teachers for the school that will run kindergarten through grade 12, financial professionals, a dietitian, a contractor who runs his company remotely with his wife here and adult son across the strait in Squamish, two plumbers, actual farmers, and a swath of renewable energy professionals whose jobs enable them to work from home and whose skills will help keep the island functional.

It's quite fascinating how many really smart people are—

"ExCUSE me, what the *hell* are you doing?"

TWENTY-SIX

LUNCH DATE

"Hey, Kelly," I say. My cheeks burn, even though they have no reason to. I'm not guilty of anything.

"*What* are you *doing*?" Kelly Lockhart charges my desk, fumbling with her bulky, oversized pleather purse on one shoulder, her phone in the left hand, and her own massive key ring in the right.

I swallow and remember that she is not the boss of me. "Rupert thought it would be good if I reviewed the settler files, to get to know who lives here and understand how they were chosen."

Kelly stops short of grabbing the folders spread across my desk. She squishes her thin lips together and tucks one side of her messy bob behind her ear. "Rupert told you to do this?"

"Yes."

"How did you get into my office? These files are confidential, Lara —did you break in to get them?"

I hoist my own key chain and jiggle it loudly.

She drops her phone into her purse and leans on stubby, dirtied fingers on the edge of my desk, rage purpling her sun-mottled complexion. "I did not give you permission to go into my office."

"I needed the files. You weren't here." I stand, as tall and straight

178

as I can, not at all timid about reminding her I'm easily six inches taller than she is. Maybe eight with these power heels. She has to look up to meet my eyes.

"You are to stay *out* of my personal space, do you understand? If you need a file from in there, you will *ask* me before entering."

"*Actually*, Kelly, I'm going to have those settler files moved into my office," I say, surprising myself. I hadn't even considered such a thing until just this second. "You're always out dealing with the hands-on stuff, and I'm now the contact person at town hall, you know, the real face behind Thalia Island. That is why Archibald chose me for this role, don't you think? My innate ability to connect with people given my background?"

Kelly smirks and shakes her head. I swear I can hear her hiss behind her teeth. "Those files are fine where they are. And just because you're some rich old man's orphaned problem doesn't mean you're going to be mine."

My heart hammers against my sternum. "What did you just say?"

"You heard me." Kelly lowers her voice and leans in. "We all know why you're here. Grandpa Archie couldn't bail you out fast enough, could he? And after he dropped dead, now you have Rupert shushing all your legal troubles. I've seen that video, your little tantrum at Nordy's—we've *all* seen it, Lara. You're not special. You're only here because your grandfather's personal servant was told to keep you out of prison."

My eyes burn with my anger, but I'm shaking so hard, I'm not sure if I can speak without revealing that she's gotten to me. So I don't.

"Mm-hmm. That's what I thought," Kelly says, her grin wide and malevolent. "Keep your mollycoddled ass out of my office, or I will find a way to make you disappear."

A laugh jumps out of my mouth. "Disappear? Oh, wait—I know my line—I'm supposed to ask you, *Is that a threat*, and you'll growl back, *It's a promise*, trying to keep your forked tongue behind your yellowing teeth and then I will run around scared of big, bad Kelly? Yes, sorry, Kells, high school was about forty years ago for you, wasn't it? And if you recall, it's MY last name on the deed to this place, *not* yours."

Kelly slowly tucks her keys into her sweatshirt pocket and sets her huge, ugly bag on the floor. I'm watching her, if she's about to throw a punch, but instead she keeps her eyes on mine, folds closed the file on my desk, and neatly stacks the others in a pile. "I won't warn you again."

A large human steps into my doorway, moving aside long enough to let Humboldt pass and trot over to lick my hand, now trembling where it hangs at my side. "Am I interrupting?" Finan asks.

"No, not at all, Fin," Kelly sings, her demeanor changing from viper to vixen in record time. "Lara and I were just talking about the filing system." She glares at me once more before turning and walking out, her ass swaying like a pendulum as she slides past Finan, making sure she leans into him more than necessary as her body squeezes through the open door.

His eyes are on me but mine are on where Kelly was just standing, wishing I'd stabbed her in the temple with the bamboo-handled letter opener or stapled her wrinkly lips together so she'd shut up forever. Instead, I grab the Handi Wipes from my desk drawer and wash where her filthy fingers touched.

Finan waits for me to finish and then clears his throat. I look up; his face is concerned. "You look murderous. What did I miss?"

"She needs to *go*." I slide into my chair, still unsteady from the confrontation. Humboldt whimpers and drops his giant head in my lap, slobber strings dampening my pant leg. My hand hits my mouse, waking my computer. Lutris is still active on the screen, showing Finan's icon here at town hall.

But Kelly's indicates that she's on the west side of the island, which makes no sense because I know for a fact she's eight feet down the hall. I squint at the open app.

"Something wrong?"

I look up at Finan. "Remember when you mentioned the area on the west side, just below Mt. Magnus, that has good birdwatching?"

His face softens and he nods. "I'll grab sandwiches from Tommy's. You OK with beer?"

"We'll meet you at your truck in twenty," I say, rubbing Humboldt's soft ears as Finan and his perfect ass waltz out of my office.

TWENTY-SEVEN

OSSEOUS DISCOVERY

Finan meets me at his truck, holding the handle on a sizable wicker basket full of food. Four sweating beer bottles peek from the open top. My mouth waters—I haven't had a beer in a million years. Honestly, I've had hardly *any* alcohol since I've been here, which may not be a big deal for most people, but come *on* …

I'm not going to be swoony and dramatic about it, but Thalia Island is asking new things of me, showing me that maybe I'm not a total spoiled screw-up like everyone thinks. And for the first time, maybe ever, I don't want to let Rupert down. It's a weird feeling. I'll be sure not to tell him.

Although he may be let down when he learns I've already put my feelers out among my Vancouver stylist friends about anyone interested in setting up shop over here—or at least someone willing to visit once a week to fix this neglected nightmare sprouting from my scalp. Certainly I can renegotiate my contract to include a health-and-wellness allowance. It's the humane thing to do, given that I'm trapped with all these moon-bathing alfalfa sprouts.

I fed Humboldt the last of the kibble from the spare bag at town hall, enough to hold him over until later tonight. The two giant dog cookies in the basket will help—Tommy bakes them specifically for this squishy loaf of fur and slobber. And chances are good he'll finish whatever food Finan and I don't. Talk about spoiled.

I had just enough time to splash my face with cold water to calm the angry red from my run-in with Kelly, reapply some light makeup, finger-brush my teeth, and run a comb through my hair before pulling it into a loose bun. It would've been nice to change into something less yawn-worthy, but I remind myself it's just Finan and we work together and we're only going on a boat ride to find out why the hell Lutris says Kelly's over *there* and not over here and also it's still spring so wearing anything that doesn't involve multiple layers, on a boat, in British Columbia, would be stupid.

Finan unlocks the truck and gets the passenger door for me. I open my mouth to tease him about how Connor never opened anything but my wallet but then remember I don't want to talk about Connor, not now or ever, with Finan. Not unless he wants to talk about exes. Because we're friends, *new* friends, and I don't want to blow it by being weird.

I mean, do friends talk about stuff like former flames? The friends I've had over the years only ever talked about their vacations and new cars and their plastic surgeons and who's cheating on whom. I wouldn't talk about Connor, or whoever I was sleeping with, because it would end up in the gossip sphere almost before I'd finished saying it. I've never talked about relationships or my family or my innermost feelings with anyone outside my therapist's office, and sometimes not even then. Trust is hard to come by when everyone wants something from you.

As Finan drives toward the marina, I am again taken aback at how beautiful this place is. I've lived on the West Coast my entire life, with countless stays in other big cities around the globe, but I feel most at home near water, trees, and fresh air. Sure, Paris and London and Tokyo are dazzling and exciting and alive with humanity, but have you seen Vancouver during cherry blossom season or skied Whistler on New Year's Day?

I lower my window, not just because Humboldt reeks like wet dog and kibble but because I love the way the air smells. Another thing not to admit to Rupert: I do *not* miss having to keep my apartment windows closed because of the car exhaust and obnoxious downtown clubbers. Here, I throw open my cabin's windows whenever I can, especially when it's raining. The fresh air helps me forget that I'm living on a rock burst from the ocean with a hundred other people instead of in a bustling metropolis filled with my favorite shops and access to the airport on a whim.

Only 349 days to go.

I lean my head against the door frame, eyes closed, and let the cool air stream over my face, trying to relax the Kelly-caused tension in my cheeks and jaw.

"You want to tell me what was going on when I walked in?"

Aaaand the tension returns.

"Kelly is an ass."

Finan bobs his head once. "And?"

"Number Two told me to go over the settlers' files so I can better respond to questions and criticisms about how the island's residents are chosen."

"Number Two?"

"Oh. Rupert. Have you not heard me call him that before?"

Finan chuckles.

"From *Austin Powers*. I started calling him that when I was a kid because it pissed him off."

He shakes his head, grinning.

"Anyway, Rupert said I should go through the files, so after my brain started to ache from all the real work I did today, I decided to spend the remaining afternoon reading up on the residents. The files are in Kelly's office, which is always locked—and that is super weird, Finan. No one else locks their office. So I let myself in. She was *not* impressed."

"And that's when I showed up."

"If you hadn't, I might have been forced to unleash the MMA moves my trainer taught me." I land a soft blow to Finan's arm not holding the steering wheel. Humboldt watches, and when Finan fake yelps, the dog chirps at me.

I rub Humboldt's head. "Don't worry, Big Dog. I won't hurt your buddy."

Finan steals a look before slowing and pulling into the marina parking lot. He finds a spot near the docks where the smaller water-craft are moored. "I brought an extra coat for you—wasn't sure if you'd have one at the office."

"I did not. Soooo, thank you." I hop out and help Humboldt onto the ground just as Finan rounds the bed end of the truck and hands me the coat. It's his size, so even though I'm tall, I swim in it. When he turns away to reach for the picnic basket, I steal a sniff of the fabric. Mmmmm.

"This way, Madam Mayor," he says, locking the vehicle. Humboldt trots ahead, between Finan and me, down the docks.

"I take it he's has been on the boat before?"

"A few times." Finan and the dog stop in front of a decent-size cruiser complete with swivel fishing seats at the rear, a canopied cock-pit, and a small, enclosed cabin up front. It's not a yacht, but it's not a dinghy either. "This is us."

I pause when I see the boat's rear end. *The Lady C.* It's named after my mother? "Gentlemen first," I say, my heart squeezing at seeing my grandfather's nickname for Cordelia painted in elegant script on the fiberglass. I board once the boys have, after a quick but subtle calming breath.

"Fridge is in there—can you stash the sandwiches and beer?"

I do as asked, pleased to see the front cabin is bigger than it looks from the dock. Two cozy couches, stacked with nautical-themed pillows, arch together and join at the bow. Underfoot is scratchy waterproof carpet in a soft blue. A tiny bathroom I can't quite stand up straight in holds a narrow toilet and sink, but not much else. At least if a girl has to go potty out on the ocean, she doesn't have to hang her fanny over the side of the boat.

With the food put away, I feel the motor's soft rumble under my feet.

Back out at the wheel, Finan reviews a laminated checklist before untying the final rope that will release us from the dock. He then pulls out life jackets, tosses one to me, and wrestles Humboldt into his very own.

"I cannot believe you have a life jacket for the *dog*."

"Just wait until we get to the beach. He *loves* the water."

"It's freezing! He can't swim in this!"

"Try telling him that." Finan points to the jacket he tossed at me. "Life jacket, please."

"Seriously?"

"I don't know what kind of swimmer you are."

"I completed Red Cross lifeguard training in the tenth grade. Does that count?"

"OK, but once we're in open ocean, just humor me and put on a jacket under your coat. This water is cold, and you can't swim if you're hypothermic."

I ignore him. "This boat is electric?"

"It's hybrid. One of the earlier models your grandfather brought over, but she's trusty."

"Of course she is," I say to myself, settling into the copilot's seat. Humboldt moves awkwardly down the few steps, sniffs about near the couches and fridge, and then turns around to position himself on the floor at the mouth of the cabin.

"I usually bring him a dog bed," Finan says. "Sorry, bud."

Humboldt lowers his head onto his paws, sighs, and his eyes grow heavy.

"He doesn't get seasick?"

"Nah. The biggest problem is keeping him in the boat once I slow down."

"He's over a hundred pounds. How does he not sink like a stone?"

"That's why he wears a life jacket." Finan navigates expertly around the other sleeping boats and toward the open water, careful to mind the no-wake signs. Once we're clear of the launch area, he throttles up, tipping the boat's nose ever so slightly. Even from under the canopy, the wind plays with the hairs that have gone rogue from my bun, tickling my cheeks and eyelids. Again with the fresh air ... I will never get tired of this.

We're heading around the northern end of the island, surprisingly rocky and steep, resilient trees growing from the cracks in the rock face and hugging the edge above. This area has been left untouched, other than the fog beacons to warn oncoming craft that there is, in fact, an island here. It's too steep and rocky to build or plant anything on, plus it's home to a colony of seabirds who enjoy relative safety, other than threats from the eagles, hawks, and osprey who patrol the Strait of Georgia island chain.

Thalia Island is considerably narrower at this northern tip than she is across her midsection, so it only takes a few minutes to round the bend and point south as we move along the western side. We're far enough out in the strait to see Mt. Magnus in its entirety—from here, it barely looks like a mountain at all. The first half of this west side, however, is much like the northern tip—great for rock climbers or novice rappelling, but maybe not picnicking.

And then the island smooths out about halfway down, the iceberg of rock ramping at a soft angle, giving way to a pebble-and-sand beach, plenty wide for anyone adventuring this way for a relaxing afternoon. With the boat slowed to a crawl, Finan continues to point out landmarks and areas of proposed development, mostly relating to solar and wind projects rather than residential structures. In alignment with my grandfather's mission, Thalia will never be widely clear-cut or logged for profit or human habitation. The only trees to be felled (outside of those in the established neighborhoods and farm fields) are to make space for renewable energy apparatus or in the event of tree disease or death.

"We're keeping it as pristine as he wanted," Finan says. I smile, grateful that he understands and believes in Archibald's vision. "You hungry?"

"I could eat."

He slows down and steers so we're now perpendicular to the wide beach, crawling toward shore until the depth finder indicates we're close enough in to be able to get out. "Again with the heels. Did you not learn your lesson last time?"

"I didn't know I'd be getting wet today!"

"It's shallow enough up there for you to take the ladder off the bow."

"Into the water? These are Jimmy *Choos*. I am NOT getting them wet."

"Would you like me to carry you?" he asks as he pulls on a pair of chest waders that fit like ugly green overalls.

"You're going to have to figure out something because you'll have to kill me before I'll wear a pair of those."

He snaps the second buckle over his left shoulder and adjusts the waders so they don't bunch around his groin. "Lara, I will have you know, these are the height of fashion."

"Maybe among hillbillies."

"Says the girl who's about to jump into 15°C water in nothing more than skinny jeans and suede heels." Finan's smile is so full of mischief, sometimes I feel like I'm talking to a ten-year-old. "Here—" He lifts one of the side-seat benches and hands me a thick blanket. "For the beach. Those pebbles can be rough on a princess's underside."

Splash!

"Humboldt!" I yell. "Oh my god, how did he—"

"Told you."

My giant mutt is in the water, his girth buoyant because of the life jacket, but it shallows quickly. He's already trotting out of the soft waves lapping the shoreline, shaking the sea free from head to tail, though futilely since the life jacket fits like a glove.

"Is there anything that can hurt him?" I ask, surprised by my sudden concern for my walking saliva factory.

"We don't have any big predators here. Plus he's a bullmastiff. Even if a cougar had made its way over to Thalia, it'd be a hell of a fight."

"That's terrible!" I run to the front of the boat. "Humboldt! Come back here, now!" Of course, he ignores me. Finan chuckles from where he's kneeled, refilling the picnic basket with our chilled meal. He stands, closes the small refrigerator with his booted foot, and sets the basket on the bow before lowering himself into the water.

"Come on, princess. Let's get you ashore."

"If you tell anyone about this ..."

"Aren't you the one who wanted security cameras?"

With the blanket clutched tightly under my left arm, I carefully lean forward and drape myself over Finan's shoulder, my ass once again skyward as he packs me through the water like a sack of flour, depositing me on the dry beach. He then shuffles back to the boat to grab our food just in time for Humboldt to return with a long, thick hunk of driftwood clamped in his jaw.

"Humboldt, come." Finan hands me the basket and then grabs the driftwood from my dog's mouth.

"Something wrong?"

"It's been burned," he says, showing me the wood's charred end. "We have a burn ban anywhere outside of designated firepits." He again takes the picnic basket, although the look on his face has morphed from playful to worried.

"Is this bad?"

"I don't know." We walk farther up the beach, finding the neat stacks of driftwood we spied from the top of Mt. Magnus during my introductory tour. Sure enough, there's a huge firepit in the sand, complete with a stone perimeter, that someone has haphazardly buried.

"Maybe just some people out on the water who stopped for a break?"

Finan slowly spins in a circle, looking around the beach, kicking his boot at the firepit. "Maybe ..."

My stomach growls loudly enough to be heard over the quiet waves. Finan snaps back to the present. "Someone's hungry." His face again softens as he takes one side of the blanket and helps me spread it. He slides out of his waders to sit as I unload the basket, offer Humboldt a dog cookie so he doesn't steal our sandwiches, and pop the caps off two beers.

Finan takes his and offers it in a toast. "To Princess Lara of Thalia Island. Long may she reign."

"And to the court jester, who would be wise to remember his promise to build the princess a dungeon."

Our bottle necks *tink*, and Finan bows his head before taking his first sip. "At your service, my lady."

We tear into Tommy's delicious sandwiches, and I am again grateful for the return of my strong stomach, even if I'm still carrying a little of the nervous tension from the situation with Kelly. I don't want this to become a thing where I'm afraid to run into her in real life. It's an *island*. Not like I have a lot of places to go to avoid her, and it's not like I can leave anytime soon.

The partially cloudy sky looks like she's going to behave and hold on to her moisture. While the wind is stronger on this side of Thalia, the strait is free of whitecaps, just the soft murmur of waves brushing against the long, pebbled shore.

"Finish telling me what happened with Kelly," Finan says, popping a red seedless grape into his mouth.

"Not much else to tell, other than she didn't want me in her files." I swig my beer, pausing to savor it. I love a quality microbrew. "Oh! Wait! Yes! OK, so, Lutris—you know what it is?"

He nods.

"I talked to Jeremiah, the IT guy, for, like, two hours today, and he's crazy nice. Very helpful. Didn't even get frustrated when I didn't know what he was talking about because, duh, like I've ever had to deal with anything IT related."

"You've had people for that?"

"Naturally."

Finan smirks as he cracks open a glass Snapwear of homemade brownies and helps himself.

"Anyway, don't interrupt. The Lutris system is installed on all the island-issued phones—did you know that? We can tell where people are based on the built-in GPS tracker in Lutris."

He nods again. "We all have it."

"Yes, but it wasn't working properly until today, until Jeremiah and I fixed it."

"That's good. It'll help me keep an eye on the crews."

"Exactly. But—and this is the weird part—" I dig through the basket, hoping Tommy packed some wet wipes or at least a cloth towel for my sticky fingers. It's very distracting. "I know Kelly has a Thalia-issued phone, so before I decided to go into her office, I checked the system to see where she was, and her little mermaid icon showed her *here*."

"She was dealing with the rockfall this afternoon."

"*Allegedly.*"

Finan smiles. "Why *allegedly?*"

"Because after she went all Wicked Witch on me, when she walked away, I checked Lutris and it didn't show her at town hall. It showed her out here, on the island's west side."

Finan finishes his brownie and wipes the chocolate off his fingers. I can't stop thinking about how we need wet wipes.

"I'm not sure I understand ..."

"I don't either. Why would her Lutris tracker show that she's on the west side of the island when, in fact, she was just down the hall in her office?"

His brow furrows. I can't take it anymore. I grab a cloth napkin from the basket, run to the water's edge, and get it wet. I then hurry back and offer the dampened napkin to Finan. "For your fingers."

"You have a ... thing ... about dirt, don't you."

"Shut up." I wipe my own hands as best I can, but they still don't feel clean.

"You *do* know that's a mix of salt and fresh water, right?"

I'm not going to admit that I didn't even think about that. I crumple the cloth and throw it back into the basket. "I think Kelly's up to something."

"Because her Lutris tracker isn't working? That system hasn't been working for months."

"Maybe, but it's working *now*. Jeremiah assured me it was, plus I saw you when you came in. I saw where Ainsley and Rupert and everyone else were. The only person not where their tracker said they should be was Kelly."

Finan leans back on one hand and takes a long pull from his beer. "Maybe she disabled it. Removed it somehow."

"Can you do that?"

"I don't know," he says.

"Maybe she ditched that phone somewhere and she has her *own* phone that we can't track or monitor. You can forward calls from one number to another, right?"

"OK, it's a little weird."

I smile with satisfaction, happy that he agrees with my Sherlock Holmesian assessment. "Plus, have you ever noticed how much mail she gets? Why is Kelly Lockhart—who has a degree in, what, city planning?—why is she getting SO much mail here? Finan, it was over half the Canada Post bag, all for her."

"I've never handled the mail."

"Does she have a fan club of some sort? What did she do in her life before Thalia? And where are the personnel files for the council members?"

"They should be in her office too. Have you talked to Rupert about any of this yet?"

I shake my head no and scoop up a brownie with a napkin so my fingers don't get even stickier. "This whole thing just feels off. And the shit she said to me today ..."

Finan sits forward to put his empty beer bottle back in the basket. "What did she say?"

I don't want to repeat it. I don't want Finan's pity, and I don't want to explain my prior legal woes, in case Finan doesn't know anything about them. Although that's wishful thinking. Of course he knows. *Everyone* knows. The worst part? Kelly's not entirely wrong. I'm here on Thalia Island because I'm an orphaned troublemaker.

"Hey, your face just got really dark. Did I say something ..."

I force a fake smile and bite into my brownie. "I really should've let Tommy cater the welcome-home party. These brownies are incredible."

Before Finan can respond, Humboldt trots toward us, again carrying something branch-like in his mouth. He flops down next to the blanket, his prize gripped in his jaw.

Except this time, it's not a piece of burned driftwood.

It's a bone.

TWENTY-EIGHT

CAVE ART

"What the hell …"

Finan moves to take the bone—actually, *bones*—from the dog. "Wait! Don't touch it!" I yell, my voice bouncing off the massive rock wall that serves as the backdrop for this lovely beach. He pulls his hand away. "Do you have any gloves on board?"

"It's probably just from a dead animal."

"Exactly! Gross!" I rummage through the basket for the napkins, even the used ones, and wrap it around the end of the bones firmly clamped in Humboldt's *very* strong jaw. "Humboldt, release."

He doesn't release.

Over my shoulder, Finan dangles the last of Humboldt's dog cookies. It works. The bullmastiff abandons his bony bounty and throws himself toward the treat. I, too, let go, and the bones drop onto the pebbled sand. "I've not spent a lot of time outdoors or near dead things, but do animals have long, skinny bones like this? Maybe a deer?"

Finan scoots closer and pokes at them with a twig Humboldt chewed off a bigger branch earlier. He's then careful to pick up the bones with the soiled napkins.

"Oh, so now you don't want dirty fingers?"

"This doesn't look like an animal ... and if it isn't, I don't want to tamper with evidence."

My skin goes cold. "Evidence? Of what?"

"This is an ulna, and this is a radius, and the only reason why they're still together without the rest of the bones or the meaty stuff is because of this." He points to a metal plate fastened with tiny screws.

"How do you know that?"

"In my youth, I was a daredevil with a knack for gruesome skateboard injuries. These are arm bones."

"Wait ... Finan, these are *human*?"

He's already at the picnic basket, removing the cloth Tommy lined it with. He quickly shuffles back over and wraps up the bones. He then pulls his waders back on since without them, he has no boots. "Did you see what direction Humboldt came from?"

"No, but this beach isn't huge. We could look ..." We tuck the macabre treasure into the basket and then fold in half our heavy picnic blanket to wrap around the whole thing so Humboldt can't get to it. "Maybe this is one of those cases we hear about on the news, about bones washing up in shoes along the shores of Vancouver Island?"

Finan fastens the second shoulder clasp on his waders. "Maybe. But those are usually detached feet. And these bones look too fresh to have been in the water for long. Still a little meat on them." I shudder. *Meat. As in human meat.* "Humboldt, come on." Finan pats his leg. The dog snorts and reluctantly stands again, the unfinished half of his cookie hanging from his foamy mouth. "You have your phone? We might need the flashlight."

I pull it from the upper left breast pocket of my borrowed down coat. "Battery's at 40 percent. And—look at that—zero bars of service. I hope no serial killers are hiding here."

Finan's smirk isn't as light as I was hoping for, sending my mind spinning like a malfunctioning turntable about how in the hell *fresh human bones* are on my grandfather's beloved island.

We walk up the beach, past the stacked driftwood and buried firepit, about midway between the shoreline and the rock wall. A copse of trees reaches in a northerly direction, growing from a ledge just above the beach. We continue on until we can't go any farther without climbing, our sole accompaniment the soft *shushing* of the waves and the back-and-forth of seagulls catching drafts over the open water.

"No way he climbed that—Humboldt's not that nimble," Finan says. So we turn and head in the direction we came, moving beyond our picnic spot and boat bobbing offshore, southerly around another organized stack of driftwood we hadn't yet discovered. Someone has also dug four holes in the sand, thick chunks of driftwood planted upright to create a square. The driftwood pieces, at their tops, have lengths of sisal rope tied through drilled holes about the size of an egg, carabiners on their ends, as if used to fasten some sort of material to provide shelter.

"Someone's definitely been here," I say. Finan nods.

Just as we're rounding a bend on the beach, under a canopy of some sort of leafy tree whose new growth is still coming in, an upstart stream etches its own path in the heavy sand, trickling ambitiously toward the strait. Humboldt takes off at a gallop along the slip of water, toward wherever it might originate. "Big Dog!" I yell, and we run after him, though we don't get far before discovering the source of his curiosity: a cave.

"This isn't weird at all," I say, moving closer to Finan. Yes, I am a city girl, and no, I am not adventurous and brave like Cordelia was. The most adventurous I've ever been—other than parasailing drunk with a couple of hockey wives I befriended in the Maldives—was at this ridiculous summer camp Rupert convinced my grandfather I would love and, in fact, I did *not* love and when I broke out with a full-body rash, likely due to the foliage and clumps of dirt hidden in my sleeping bag by my charming cabin mates, I demanded the head counselor call my grandfather to have me picked up immediately or else I would go online and tell everyone in the world she was drinking gin behind the girls' bathrooms while we were at archery. Even if it wasn't true.

I know. I was a spirited eleven-year-old. Hey, cut the orphan some slack. Not all of us can be Bruce Wayne.

"Humboldt, sit!" Finan hollers, so loud it bounces off the rocky cave opening just ahead and echoes back at us. The dog ceases his frenzied digging and plants his wide butt in the sand, tail wagging sheepishly as he looks up at Finan. "Good boy," he says, crouching next to Humboldt's freshly excavated hole.

Finan moves his hands through the sand. "Nothing here. Or maybe this is where the bones were?"

"Without the rest of the skeleton?"

Finan stands, and I'm like a wimpy girl from a Jason Vorhees movie, sliding in behind him, my fingers clamped on the back pocket of his waders as my heels sink into the cave's mushy floor. "Phone," he says over his shoulder. I open the lock screen, activate the flashlight, and hand it forward.

The cave's opening is probably ten feet across and deep enough that a group of boaters caught in a storm could shelter within. No vines or other foliage block the entrance, and a few feet inside is another firepit. Only this one hasn't been covered up, ashes and charred wood piled in its belly. The air is stuffy, as one might expect, the deeper in we walk. Finan spins the flashlight around the cave interior, throwing light against the rough rock walls, but we both inhale a startled breath when the illumination hits the southern side.

It's smoother than the rest, and not without decoration.

"Is ... is that a wave?" I step closer, but I don't dare touch. A crescent-shaped claw of black water, akin to a wave about to crash upon a beach, with sprawling black squiggles upper right and lower left—like snake tails—take up most of the wall. At the wave's center is what looks like a rectangular gemstone in a deep red. What isn't covered by the symbol is covered by red handprints, as if someone, or a lot of someones, dipped their hands in red paint—or something else—and pressed them against the cave wall.

"Finan, what in the living hell is this?"

He's shaking his head. "Can I use the camera?"

"Please."

He snaps photos for ten minutes, from every possible angle, but the sun is going down and the cave is getting too dark, even with the flash. Plus my battery is down to 21 percent and I'm assuming Finan's phone is still on the boat and this formerly pleasant beach is starting to feel *very* creepy.

"Could this be ancient? Like, First Nations or something?" I ask.

"No. No way. This land was completely surveyed and examined for artifacts and anything else that would have blocked the sale. Plus, the bones have a plate and screws in them. Definitely not ancient."

"Would Rupert know anything about this? He's been involved with Thalia since the beginning."

"Has he ever mentioned anything that would be remotely connected to what we're seeing?" Finan asks. I shake my head no. "And you trust him—you trust Rupert to tell you the truth?"

My head snaps up. "Of course. I trust Rupert with my life. He's the only family I have left."

"I'm just thinking out loud here—"

"Don't think out loud about Rupert," I say, tiptoeing out of the cave and taking a deep breath of fresh air. "In fact, Rupert is the ONLY person we should talk to about this."

Finan joins me on the beach and whistles for Humboldt, who fell asleep from the boredom of watching his humans wander in circles among the big rocks. "I agree."

"What about the bones? Don't we have to give those to the island's constable or sheriff or—"

"Derek."

"Right."

Finan shakes his head. "He was hired after me. Only met him once, months ago, so I don't know if we can trust him. Plus he keeps pushing his start date. Still dealing with some family thing, according to Kelly."

"But they're *bones*, Finan. Human bones. We can't just not tell someone." We've now reached our picnic spot. I unwrap the basket and fold the blanket over my arm. Finan's face looks like he's still thinking.

"Let me get Humboldt and the stuff on board. Then you."

I feel dumb that he has to carry me back to the boat, but it's colder now in the purpling twilight and I'm not in the mood to ride back to town soaking wet due to my pride. Plus, Jimmy Choo. I love these shoes.

Once we're loaded and the anchor is pulled, Finan follows the current and we travel around the southern end of the island, both of us watching the shore for any other evidence that non-Thalia visitors have made themselves comfortable.

Nothing else obvious.

Finan speeds us along the southeastern flank, slowing as we approach the no-wake zone. The marina is lit like Christmas, walkway and overhead LEDs illuminating every step to keep returning boaters from falling into the frigid water. The engine slows to a putter as we slide back into the alley and finally our moorage slip. "Keep Humboldt's life jacket on until we get to the truck. I'll take it with us to wash out whatever he's gotten into today," Finan says. His eyes are dark and worried in the weak cockpit light.

I follow his instructions about closing down the boat for the night, emptying the fridge of whatever food we didn't eat, making sure the cabin is locked, and of course, covering the basket containing human bones with the picnic blanket. Again, just in case we run into someone between here and wherever we're going next.

Which has yet to be decided.

By the time Finan is behind the wheel of his truck, my teeth are chattering, a mixture of cold and fear. He cranks the heat and pulls out his phone, scrolling as the messages that didn't come through on the west side populate his screen.

I'm afraid to check my own phone to see what new calamities have surfaced during our brief absence. But I need to talk to Rupert—in person. There's a text from Catrina, which is safe to open because she's not scary: *Humboldt's Korna order arrived. BIG box at town hall— too big to drag into your office! Spoiled doggy. :)*

"Can we stop at town hall real quick? Humboldt's order arrived." Finan *mm-hmms*, eyes and index finger still scanning his screen. "Anything that can't wait?" I ask as he exhales heavily and rubs one eyebrow with his thumb.

"Kelly's sicced her puppy on me."

"Hunter?"

He holds up his phone and scrolls with the other finger to show me the stream of messages that go on and on and on.

"I dated a guy once who used to do this to my DMs."

Finan smirks. "And?"

"I sent him the link to the bridal registry I set up in our name and asked him to fill in his parents' details so we could get our family tree started on the right foot. Oh, and I gave him choices for baby names."

Finan laughs loudly and taps his temple with the corner of his phone. "See? *That's* why they pay you the big bucks."

TWENTY-NINE

SOMETHING ROTTEN

Downtown, the zigzagging light strings brighten the street and sidewalks busy with people. A handful of new residents are having drinks at the patio tables outside the Wandering Salamander; even more are inside Tommy's Diner, which, at night, looks like something out of the 1950s with the LED neon and bright, throwback décor. The Tipping Point is still open for business, and when we park in front of town hall, I'm surprised to see the interior lights on in there as well.

"Did we miss something tonight?"

"Don't think so. It's busy," Finan says.

"That's good, right?"

"Better than having everyone at home puking their guts out and threatening to sue." Finan climbs out but tells Humboldt to stay—he smells musty from his beach adventures.

"I can probably get the Korna box in my car," I say, pointing at the tiny Toyota that's not moved out of its spot in days.

"No way. I ordered extra bags so we'd have them strategically positioned wherever he's hanging out." Finan gestures for me to follow, and I again remind my dog to sit when he tries to escape through the front seats.

Town hall's front doors are unlocked, and in the middle of the hallway, a young man with shiny hair so blond it's almost white is on his knees, a power tool in hand. "Oh, Finan, *there you are*. You are a difficult man to get ahold of. Did you get my messages? I needed to talk to you about what's going on out at farm B, but you didn't answer, even when I called, so I'm glad you're finally back from wherever you've been for the last two hours. Lutris showed you on the west side of the island, but that's weird, since I thought you were supposed to be at the farm. I mean, seriously, what if it was an emergency? Next time, if I can't find you, we could have real trouble." The kid raises and lowers his voice in accordance with the noise he's making when he pulls the trigger on the contraption in his hand.

The hair. The nonstop talking. The whiny tone.

This must be Hunter.

Finan points to the huge box with the Korna logo sitting next to the unoccupied reception counter. He's right. This will never fit in the clown car.

"Finan"—the kid stands—"oh, hi, you must be Lara. I've heard a lot about you. Nice to finally meet in person. I'm Hunter Parrish. I'm working with Finan on the HVAC and UV lighting systems for the vertical farms, though my talents are more aligned with specialized electronics for self-regulating hydroponic systems so I'm hoping I can use my expertise and knowledge to help Thalia Island meet her potential one day. Lots of work left to be done here, but this is a good start. Did you know I spent time advising your grandfather on hydroponics? It's the system of growing plants without a medium such as soil. I've instead concocted my own aqueous solution to provide the nutrients plants need to sustain life. If you would like me to explain further, I'd be happy to give you a virtual tour of the system I've designed—"

"Hi, Hunter," I interrupt, smiling tightly as I gesture at the door he's kneeled before. "What are you doing here, exactly?"

He looks down at his hand, as if he forgot he was holding a power tool. "Oh, this is a battery-operated screw gun."

"I know what a screw gun is. But what are you doing with it?"

"I'm replacing the lockset on Kelly's office door."

202

"Are you now."

"She said her key broke off in the other one."

Yeah, no, it didn't, and if it did, it was intentional.

Finan and I look up when the door to the town council chambers opens. Laughter—from multiple bodies—floats toward us. "Did we miss a meeting?" I ask Finan.

"Not that I'm aware of."

I start down the hall, Finan keeping step. "Tomorrow, I'm taking the door off her office. She's changing the lock to keep me out—which means there's something in there she doesn't want me to see."

"Or she's just being stubborn and territorial, two of her more sparkling traits."

Finan pushes open the chambers door. At least thirty people sit in the half-round gallery, Kelly holding court in front of the elevated councillor area, her short stature augmented by the help of a two-step wooden stool. Her bleached-blond, chin-length bob is messier than usual, her face red with exertion, the underarms of her tight-fitting T-shirt dark with perspiration. Her animated hands freeze and her expression ices when she sees me. The residents on the padded benches look where she's focused and sit straighter, their own faces slinking behind a layer of frost, at least until they see Finan and offer a politer countenance.

"Hello, Finan," Kelly sings. "Lara."

"Did we miss the memo about a meeting?" I ask.

Kelly laughs theatrically. "Oh no, we're just having a little get-together, talking about some of the residents' concerns ahead of our inaugural town hall tomorrow night."

"Concerns that couldn't wait until the actual meeting?" I move halfway up the aisle of pew-style gallery benches so I can better see the people in the seats and close the distance between myself and Kelly.

"Lara, I know you're new here, so you wouldn't have had the chance to get to know the residents like I have, like Rupert and the other council members have, during the lengthy selection process.

Some folks feel more comfortable expressing their thoughts in smaller groups, like this one—among friends. You understand?"

Kelly talks to me like I'm a three-year-old who's being scolded about eating Play-Doh. She then turns her caustic gaze to Finan, again softening. "Fin, did you get a chance to talk to Hunty about the problems out at farm B?"

"I'm sure it's nothing we can't handle," Finan says. "Be sure to lock up when you leave." Finan's hand squeezes my wrist lightly and then moves to my lower back as he steers me out of the chambers and back into the hall. One look up at his bristled face and even through the beard, I can see his clenched jaw.

"So, Finan, I have time right now if you want to go into the conference room and talk—"

Finan walks right past Hunter, now apparently finished with Kelly's door situation, and pulls a multitool from his back pocket. He then leans over the Korna box, unzips the seal with an extended blade, yanks out a bag of dog food, and then maneuvers the box with his feet behind the reception counter, out of the way. Hunter continues to yammer on, his phone cupped in his hand, thumb scrolling as his lips move—does he ever pause for a breath?—but Finan nods me toward the door. I'm not sure what we're doing, but it's clear we're not stopping so he can have a chat with Hunty in the conference room.

And I sure as hell don't want to go back into council chambers and be condescended to again.

I push open the front door for Finan to pass through with the huge bag of kibble over one shoulder. Hunter calls after us; we keep walking.

"Pretty sure I don't like that guy," Finan says, flopping the dog food into the truck bed.

I climb in on my side, immediately assaulted by Humboldt's sloppy tongue and excited whining. You'd think we were gone for days. Even before the driver's side door is closed, Humboldt pivots from me and assails Finan with affection.

"OK, so, 'private' town hall meetings just for Kelly and her besties?"

Finan's eyes are fixed forward; he gnaws at one side of his lip.

"And 'Fin'? As if your name is so long, she can't muster the energy to pronounce both syllables."

He still doesn't say anything, his thumb playing a beat only he can hear against the steering wheel. After an eternity, he finally looks at me. "Do you have the Lutris app on your phone?"

I pull out my device, now at 12 percent battery, swiping open the app and handing the phone over. Finan looks at it, zooms in and zooms out, moving the map of Thalia Island around under his fingertips. "It's still showing her tracker on the west side. Everyone else is in town or around here or where they should be, at their residences."

"That's not weird at all."

He hands my phone back. "Let's go talk to Rupert."

THIRTY

VIOLIN CONCERTO NO. 1 IN D MAJOR

I throw Rupert a text on our way out of downtown, but he doesn't respond. It's still early—just after eight—and I know he's usually up late working. He's prone to reminding me how lazy I am for needing eight or more hours of sleep when he is "perfectly fine" with five due to his "vigorous constitution and commitment to a personal wellness regimen consisting of regular exercise and a diet free of sugar, alcohol, and processed foods," thank you very much.

We arrive at my place, unload dog and dog food and the picnic basket carrying some poor soul's arm bones, and still no response. Number Two doesn't answer my call either, though from my porch, I can see his place across the adjoining grassy field—the interior lights are on, his Tesla is plugged in, and my Lutris app shows that at least his Thalia-issued phone is there.

"Maybe he fell asleep watching TV?"

I snort. "Rupert would never lower himself to do something as pedestrian as watch the *tele*, young Finan." My British accent isn't terrible, considering I was basically raised by a Londoner. "If you give Humboldt a bedtime snack, I'll walk over and see if he's ignoring us."

"He's a genius if he is," Finan says, opening my front door. The first week, I stopped locking it as per Rupert's comment about no crime on the island but after today? I think I'll resume with the dead bolt.

"Hey, plug my phone in for me?" I hand it off and bounce down the porch steps toward Rupert's.

With spring fully underway, our sunsets get later and later as we approach the solstice. Crickets serenade me across the field of new, stiff grass—and maybe the beginnings of wildflowers—brushing my exposed ankles. I'll have to ask Rupert if the maintenance crew handles the mowing because there's no way I'm doing it. The span of earth between my cabin and Rupert's is slightly hilly and shadowed by the trees that line the back of the property; it won't be used for gardening since we have plenty of space out front for that.

As I approach Rupert's cabin, Paganini's *Violin Concerto No. 1 in D Major* floats from an open window. I knock hard, in case he's fallen asleep—I don't want to be presumptuous and let myself in. He doesn't answer, so I knock again. Still no answer. A wiggle of the knob reveals it unlocked, so I push open the front door a couple inches.

"Number Two? You home?" I stick my head through—smoke billows out of a pot on the cooktop. I push all the way in and hop across the open-plan living room, looking for a towel or oven mitt to yank the scorched pot from the gas burner. The range hood hums above, the only reason the entire place isn't filled with smoke.

"Rupert?" I holler, moving out of the kitchen to the hallway that leads to the bedrooms and bath. I poke my head into the master bedroom—not there. Maybe he's in his home office. "Rupert?" I yell up the stairs.

Nothing.

The bathroom door is slightly ajar; I pause and knock, heart hammering in my ears. "Hey, Rupert, you in there?" Again, quiet.

My armpits are now damp with worry. I flatten a hand against the door to push it open. "Please tell me I won't be scarred for life—"

The door stops. Something is in the way. I nudge a bit harder, widening the gap so I can look into the bathroom to see what is going on.

"RUPERT!"

THIRTY-ONE

PLEASE BE OK

I shake and shake and shake him, but he won't wake up. "Rupert …
Rupert, please!" I lean close to his nose. He's still breathing. Ear
against his chest as I check his wrist for a pulse. His heart beats, but
faint and slow. His face is deathly pale, his hands cold. I again press
my head to his chest to make sure I don't need to start CPR before
screaming for help.

"Rupert, please, wake up," I say, patting his cheek. He groans but
won't open his eyes. "I'm going for help. Please, please do not die
on me!"

I run out the front and scream so hard and so loud, something gives
in my neck. "Finaaaaaaan! FINAAAAAAN! Help me!" I fumble around
my pockets for my phone but remember I gave it to Finan to plug in. I
scream again, knowing I can't run across the field and leave Rupert
alone. Just as I'm about to bolt back in and search for Rupert's phone
and check if he's still breathing, Finan appears on my front porch.

"HELP! HUUUUUUURRYYYYYY!"

He takes off at a sprint and I'm so relieved, a sob catches in my
throat. I rush back inside, searching for Rupert's phone—any phone.
The Lutris portal is propped on the counter, but I don't know if it's

even plugged in or if anyone will think to answer it, so I race back into the bathroom—maybe he had his phone on him? Maybe he was trying to call for help?

"Rupert, where's your phone? I need your phone!"

He groans again and tries to open his eyes. I rest a gentle hand on his cheek. "Heyyyy, I'm here. It's Lara. Can you look at me? Can you tell me what's happened?"

His eyes remain closed, though his cheeks regain a slight pinkish tint. A buzz vibrates against the floor under his left arm. "Your phone!" Gingerly, I lift his wrist and grab the device just as Finan's voice echoes through the cabin. "In here! Help me!"

Finan stops in the partially obstructed door, realizing we can't get it open any farther with the way Rupert's long body is sprawled. "What happened?"

"I don't know. He's barely breathing. I don't know who to call—"

But Finan's already on his own phone. "Catrina, Rupert's collapsed. We'll need an air ambulance. Yeah … yeah, OK, thank you. See you soon."

"Air ambulance?" My voice squeaks.

"Do you know CPR?"

"Ummm … yes, but it's been years—"

"I need you to go to my truck—in the toolbox in back is an AED kit in a neon-green case. You can't miss it. There are also LED flares. Bring me the AED and then wait for Catrina—she's on her way. As soon as Catrina gets here, you need to put the LED flares in the field for the helicopter to land."

"I—I don't know how—"

"Catrina does. Just get the defibrillator and the flares. I know CPR so I'll stay with Rupert." Finan reaches down and lifts me under my elbow, but my legs feel so weak all of a sudden.

I lean over Rupert, again cupping his cheek and whispering in his opposite ear. "I will be *right back*. Don't you dare die."

Finan helps me stand and then takes my place, pressing his hand against Rupert's cheeks and forehead. He takes Number Two's pulse at his wrist, watching the second hand on his Apple Watch to calculate the beats. "Go, Lara."

I'm stunned frozen as I look down at the last link to my disintegrated family, lying on his back, his white button-down shirt soaked with perspiration and stained with drops of what might be blood. I look at his aquiline nose and certainly, there is dried and fresh blood around his nostrils—

"I don't know what I will do ..."

Finan shakes his head before I can finish the sentence. "He's going to be all right. Just please, go get the kit and wait for Catrina. And if you're going with him in the ambulance, gather whatever you need." Finan reaches with the hand not holding Rupert's wrist and wraps it around my closed fist, giving me a reassuring squeeze. "We'll make sure he's OK, Lara. I promise."

I break my stare at Rupert's wan face and look directly into Finan's redwood-brown eyes. "Promise?"

He nods.

And I run out the door.

The air ambulance takes a hundred years to arrive, but when it finally does, it settles in the middle of the flare-demarcated field, just as Catrina said it would. The EMTs on board are quick to pile into Rupert's cabin and shoo us out. Catrina offers her help, including what she knows about his recent and past medical history. Rupert's pulse is very slow, his temperature is high, and the rest is all Greek to me so I make myself useful by finding his wallet with his medical services card and ID and both of his phones plus chargers.

While they attach Number Two to EKG wires and an IV and slide an oxygen mask over his pallid face, Finan helps me pack a bag with clean clothes, a challenging task given that Rupert only ever wears suits. He has nothing casual in his closet. In the event of a prolonged inpatient stay, I'll send someone out to shop for him while I'm waiting at the hospital.

Because there's no bloody way he's going to Vancouver without me.

We reenter the living room just as the EMTs are maneuvering Rupert's lanky, blanket-wrapped form out of the bathroom, down the hall, and through the cabin. "Finan, please keep Humboldt? And can you water Andromache?"

"I'll take care of them." He cups my face in his hands, forcing me to hold still and look at him. "Call me later after you find out what's going on?"

I nod, hot tears racing down my cheeks. Finan opens his huge arms and pulls me tight to him. I'm surprised but so grateful, I can't hold on hard enough. "Everything will be all right, Lara," he says next to my ear.

I nod against his chest, squeeze him back, and then run out the door and across the field to catch up with Catrina and the EMTs loading my surrogate father into a giant dragonfly.

THIRTY-TWO

STORMY SKIES

The air ambulance only had room for me, so Catrina and Tommy said they'd come over later in their personal boat. Until their arrival, I'm in a private family-care room outside the ICU, pacing until someone comes to explain why Rupert is so sick.

Upon our arrival, he was ushered into the ER while I perched on my seat's edge in the waiting area, fidgeting with the surgical mask they insisted I wear, in case we brought something contagious with us. It didn't take long for the supervising physician to emerge and inform me they were moving Rupert upstairs and they would give me more news as soon as they had it.

"Are you next of kin?" the doctor asked.

"Rupert is my family."

He flipped through the chart, as if looking for someone other than me he could talk to.

"We are the only family we have left, especially since my grandfather's recent death, and sizable legacy contribution to the Vancouver General Hospital Foundation," I said, reminding the doctor it wouldn't be in his best interest to question my legal right to see Number Two.

It worked. He closed the chart and nodded.

"I'll bring an update as soon as I can." He turned to leave, but I grabbed his arm.

"Please, I honestly don't understand what's going on. He was fine this morning. There was a recent bout of food poisoning—could it be related to that? Is it his heart? Did he have a heart attack? He's in such good shape, I can't imagine—"

"Again, we're still running tests, Ms. Clarke. Try not to worry." He patted my hand, offered a gentle smile, and quietly shuffled out of the waiting room past other people watching to see if it was their turn for bad news.

~

"Lara ..." A voice from afar. My eyelids are weighted down with dumbbells. "Lara, I brought coffee." The aroma of freshly brewed beans wafts under my nose.

"Hi, guys," I say, sitting up in the uncomfortable vinyl chair, grateful to see Catrina and Tommy smiling down at me. My neck has a kink in it, and the band from my displaced surgical mask is tangled in the baby hairs on my neck. I yank it off. "What time is it?" I ask as I accept the white-and-green takeout cup from Catrina.

Tommy looks at his phone and sits. "About three thirty."

I glance out the nearby window—still dark. Three thirty in the morning. "You didn't need to come over so late. You could've waited until the doctors updated me."

Catrina looks at Tommy and then back to me. She sets her cup down on the faux-wood coffee table and slides into the chair next to mine. "I spoke to the oncologist on call when we got here."

"No one has come to talk to me since the ER doc—wait ... oncologist?"

Catrina nods.

"Is Rupert OK?" I push Finan's borrowed coat off my lap and move to stand. "Is he dead? Did they not come in because they were waiting for you—"

"No, no, no, he's not dead. He's in ICU for now. They're waiting on blood work and in the morning, they'll do a bone marrow aspiration and biopsy as well as some scans."

"For *cancer*?" I couldn't even stand if I wanted to. The dumbbells on my eyes have transformed into a pair of elephants now resting on my shoulders. "How is this even possible?"

"They're looking at non-Hodgkin's lymphoma. Did you know he had a history of cancer?"

"What? No. Oh my god, no. This is *Rupert* we're talking about. He hasn't been sick a day in his life—I've known him since I was born."

Catrina nods. "He's very good at hiding what he doesn't want people to know."

"But lymphoma—people die from that. How would I not KNOW if he's had this before?"

"I don't know, Lara. Apparently he had leukemia as a child. He beat it and was healthy for years. I only have what little information I've been able to chisel out of him—you know how private he is."

My eyes fix on a thrift-store painting on the wall across the room, the abstract image replaced with the scroll of my memories as they pertain to Rupert, when he might have been sick and hiding it, when he might have been on vacation but actually receiving medical treatment, when I was away at one of a handful of failed boarding school experiments or on a vacation where he wasn't involved, when I might have missed that he was ill and Grandfather covered for him …

As if conjured from thin air, a doctor appears, introduces himself to Catrina and Tommy, and asks if he can sit. I try to listen to the words coming out of his mouth, but everything suddenly feels very surreal, almost numb, as if I'm watching this unfold behind a Plexiglass wall. I should've paid closer attention in science classes instead of flirting with hot boys. The doctor's words are flying right over my head.

I force myself to focus on the doctor's lips as he speaks, twisting my grandfather's ring to keep me grounded in the moment. He's talking about tests they want to do, how Rupert is dehydrated and underweight, how he's going to be in the ICU for at least another few days until he's stabilized and they have time to devise the appropriate course of treatment if it is indeed lymphoma, and that the swollen nodes and enlarged spleen are significant signs that he has some unto-ward pathology going on …

"But when can he come home? Can you just give him chemo or something? I can take care of him—I can hire the best care."

The doctor folds his hands reverently, like doctors are wont to do when they're about to tell you something shitty. "Ms. Clarke, I know this is impossible, but try not to worry. We will have our top people working on Mr. Bishop's care, I promise you." Catrina drapes a comforting arm over my shoulders.

I lock eyes with the doctor and notice that his wire-framed glasses need cleaning. "Is he going to die?"

The doctor's soft smile seems genuine, but maybe that's just something they teach in medical school so people like me don't freak out. "Mr. Bishop is stable now. He's not in any pain and he's resting comfortably. We are monitoring everything, and in the morning, once we have records from his private physicians, the oncology team will begin their thorough review of his case. I *promise* we will do everything we can to help him regain his health."

"But if it's cancer—you think it's cancer, right?"

"Let's not talk in hypotheticals until we have more data, OK?"

"When can I see him?"

"It's best to let him rest for tonight. Do you have somewhere you can stay?"

I nod, wiping the tear off my chin before it lands on my dirty pant leg. I've only just realized I failed to pack clean clothes for myself, and I've been wearing these for almost twenty-four hours. Twenty-four *very weird hours* that I need to talk to Rupert about.

And now …

"We can stay at Rupert's. He has a place in Kitsilano," I manage, barely above a whisper.

"Perfect. Just make sure we have all your phone numbers so we can get in touch." The doctor then stands and shakes our hands before sliding out of the small waiting room, clicking the door closed behind him.

The three of us sit quietly for a few minutes and when I finally look up at Catrina, her warm blue eyes are filled with tears. Without another word, she closes the distance between us and wraps me in a hug. I hang on because I am afraid if I let go, I will float away and be lost forever.

THIRTY-THREE

THE PATIENT PATIENT

I listen to make sure no one else is showering and head into the bathroom. Upon checking my phone, I'm relieved there are no missed calls from the hospital—only missed texts from Finan checking in to see how Rupert is. I shoot a quick reply that I don't have much info yet, but he's in ICU and I promise to call as soon as I know more.

After bathing, wrapped in one of Rupert's very soft bamboo towels, I find my clean, folded clothes from yesterday on the bench at the bed's end. I smile and hug my shirt to my face. "Catrina ..." She must've stayed up after I crashed and washed them. The little harpy who lives in my head questions why this virtual stranger would do something so nice for me—maybe she wants something.

"Shut up," I whisper. I don't have time for my insecurity monsters today.

I follow the aroma of fresh-cooked delights downstairs and find Catrina and Tommy at the marble kitchen bar cradling coffee cups and talking in low tones. Plates with evidence of a finished breakfast are pushed aside. "Morning," I say, pouring myself a cup from the French press. "Any news?"

"Rupert called," Catrina says. "He's mad at us for making a fuss."

I set my cup on the counter so hard, hot coffee splashes onto my hand. "Damn it ..." I quickly wipe it and the counter off. "And? What did he say?"

"He said he'll explain what he can when we get there."

"But he sounded good?"

"He sounds tired and a bit weak, but he's lucid."

"OK, good. This is good. We should go." I pour the untouched coffee down the drain.

"Lara—eat first. There's a plate in the oven."

"Honestly, I'd rather just go."

Thankfully, Catrina and Tommy have a car here on the mainland because I again remember I don't have any credit cards so I can't order a cab or a Lyft. Gonna have to talk to Rupert about that— once I'm sure he's not dying on me. Jerk.

From his apartment to Vancouver General is only about fifteen minutes, but my nerves stretch the journey into an infinity. Every red light makes me want to punch something, ratcheted up by endless winding through the parking garage as we look for a spot. I miss the days of Town Cars and stoic drivers wearing smart black suits.

Catrina can't park fast enough. When she does finally find an empty electric-only slip, I'm out before she's pulled the E brake. I'm at the elevators jamming the button with my sleeve-covered thumb when they walk up behind me. The traffic and blaring horns and hollers from passersby on the street below are jarring—it's overwhelming being back in Vancouver, even after such a short time on Thalia. The edginess and anxiety slither under my skin like an unwelcome invader. It makes me want a drink.

This is probably not the best coping mechanism. Also a bit unnerving that I so easily slip back into old temptations.

Inside the hospital, we check to make sure Rupert is still in ICU. We can't all go in to see him at once. Catrina and Tommy agree to wait in the little room from last night while I visit first. Then we'll trade so

Catrina can talk about medical stuff with the doctors and explain it to me like I'm five.

The ICU nurses are very kind, helping me into a paper gown and mask and shoe booties, showing me to a sink to wash and use hand sanitizer. Given the virus problems we've had in the last few years, there is no shortage of precautions. I'm just so glad they're actually letting me see him in person rather than via a grainy, unreliable messaging app.

The nurse slides open the glass door and I step in behind her. As soon as I see Rupert, my breath freezes. He looks about a hundred years old, attached to wires and tubes, two blankets covering his long body. His hair is in need of combing—a fact that would horrify him if he saw his reflection—and his color is worrisome. A tray of untouched food sits on a wheeled table on the opposite side of the bed. One look at the offered menu and I know I will be ordering his meals in for however long he's here. No way he's going to get strong on this dreck.

"Mr. Bishop, you have a visitor," the nurse says, gently touching his wrist. His eyes open, but they look so, so tired.

"Lara," he says, his smile not without effort, his eyes heavy. "Welcome to my lair."

The nurse does her checks, taps notes into a tablet near the bed, and then leaves.

"How are you feeling?" I ask.

"Probably will delay my plans to climb Everest for another week or so," he says. I chuckle and take his dry hand, so relieved that he has enough energy for his stupid jokes.

"Why didn't you tell me you weren't feeling well? I found you in your bathroom, and I thought you were …"

"*Hmmm.* Not yet. Still have work to do."

I squeeze his hand. "How long …"

"I suspected a few months ago. I've been seeing my own doctor and we've been watching things, and then Archibald passed, and I got sidetracked."

"Sidetracked? Seriously, Rupert?"

He points to the box of tissue on the nightstand. "Save your tears for the rainforest, Lara."

"Don't make fun," I say, snorting into a wad of Kleenex. "Is it cancer? They're talking about lymphoma or something."

"Seems not even I am invincible."

I lower my head against his wrist so he doesn't see me cry, but it doesn't matter because my tears land on his skin.

"Honestly, Lara, I have the best kind of beastie. Very treatable. I'm only in here because I let things go and missed a few appointments and then the salmonella poisoning threw me for an inconvenient loop."

I lift my head. "Why didn't you *tell* me?"

"You've had your own issues to grapple with as of late."

I'm immediately ashamed, my face on fire as I think about what a spoiled ass I've been in the last few months. Honestly …

"Now, now. Let's focus on the present tense, shall we?" He manages to pat the blanket. "Can you ask the nurse for some apple juice? They're very stingy with the refreshments here."

"I can't believe no one's offered you a mimosa," I say, blowing my nose before replacing my surgical mask and going in search of a nurse.

"Nothing a tersely worded letter won't remedy."

In a jiffy, I return with the apple juice, only to find Rupert with his phone in the oximeter-free hand. He gratefully accepts the juice, sipping it like an old lady, but once finished with the small carton, he seems more awake. "Update me on what I've missed."

"You've only been gone overnight."

"Yes, but with you around, there is never a dull moment."

Seeing that he's not on the brink of death, everything comes pouring out of me: what happened yesterday with Kelly and the settler files, with the weird Lutris tracker showing her elsewhere, the evidence of people hanging out on the western beach and the insane cave art, Hunter and the new lockset and the secret council meeting—AND HUMBOLDT FINDING HUMAN BONES. I talk so fast, he makes me stop and repeat myself a couple times, but most especially about the bones.

"Every detail, Lara. Slow down. Give me *every detail.*"

I feel shitty dumping all this on him right now, but I explain that Finan and I agreed: no one else can be trusted. *No one.*

He nods, his eyes distant for a moment—I hope he's thinking deeply and not in pain.

"We need to call the RCMP, don't we? And where is that Derek guy? Aren't we supposed to have our own cop on the island?"

Rupert picks up his phone and scrolls clumsily with one long thumb. "I want you to call Wes Singh." He hands over his phone, the screen open on Wes's info.

"Wait—no. The sergeant from that night at Nordstrom? Oh my god, Rupert, seriously, no."

"Wes is a dear friend. Explain everything you've just told me—but in person, here in the city. Do not talk to him over the phone, do you understand?"

Unease prickles my skin. "Are you being paranoid or is it the medication they're giving you?"

"The man who is supposed to be providing security services on Thalia Island is young and inexperienced, a recommendation from Kelly Lockhart and Stanley Johnson. And he was supposed to have reported for work weeks ago."

"Did he get a different job and just not tell us?"

"I have no idea. He allegedly had some sort of family issue in the Fraser Valley, but my calls and emails have gone unanswered. I certainly am not going to hand this over to someone I don't trust, someone who hasn't even shown up for his first day of work."

I nod. Rupert's right. Ugh, I cannot believe I have to call the cop who saw me at my absolute worst. I copy Wes Singh's information into my phone.

He tries to sit up a bit straighter. "First, you will talk to Wes. He needs to come to Thalia and see the bones. Finan has them?"

"They're at my cabin."

"Wes can handle the forensics quietly—the last thing we need is a swarm of RCMP on the island, combing it for more remains. One bad PR event per month, thank you very much."

221

"Do you have *any* idea where the bones could've come from?"

"Not a single clue. Hoping they've just washed ashore from somewhere else." His face pales again. "Be a dear and grab me another pillow, would you?" I snatch a spare from the ugly vinyl chair in the corner and then help him tuck it behind his back. "Thank you. These beds are dreadful."

"You are *very* thin right now," I remind him.

"Soon I will be plump and happy and back to causing you grief," he says, pulling the coarse white blanket higher on his chest. "Until then, I need you to be a Clarke. Thalia Island needs you. It needs a strong hand protecting her interests and the interests of the Clarke Foundation until such time that I can return in full glory and continue my reign of terror."

I smile. "As if you've ever been a terror."

"My first headmaster would roll over in his grave if he heard you say that." He looks to the nightstand and then the tray table alongside the bed. "Did my wallet make it over with me?"

The bag I packed is on a bench under the window that looks out onto the city. I retrieve his pristine cactus-leather wallet and hand it over. From it he pulls two credit cards, both belonging to the Clarke Foundation. "Do not buy anything I have to explain to the accountants."

I smile. "So much for the sex swing for Kelly's office, then."

"The horror of that suggestion will haunt me forever. Thank you." He looks pale again. "Fatigue hath returned, so if you could do what you need to do without blubbering all over me, that would be ideal."

I laugh. Anyone who doesn't know Rupert might find such a comment harsh, but I'm glad for it. Any evidence that my British snob is going to be all right is most welcome.

And yet I'm suddenly nervous. I don't know how to "be a Clarke."

"Lara, please go away. I'd like to sleep."

"Right. OK. When should I come back?"

He turns his head and squints at me. "You need to see Wes and then get back to the island. Today, if possible. Tomorrow at the latest."

"Absolutely not. I'm not leaving here until I've talked to your doctors."

Rupert sighs heavily. "Lara, darling, I appreciate your fervor, but obstinance is not something I have energy for. I am not dying today, I promise. My own physician will be assuming my care, and within forty-eight hours, I will be back in my lovely townhouse awaiting whatever fresh hell is coming at me in the form of treatment."

"But—"

"At which time I will have a team of very handsome nurses looking after my every whim." His smile is broad and genuine. "I promise you I will not die without your permission." His hand lifts from the bed, and I take it.

He squeezes it. "Now get out of my room and go take care of our island."

I laugh through the fresh tears dampening my cheeks and lean over to give Rupert an awkward but heartfelt hug. "I love you, even if you're a pompous asshole."

"Takes one to know one," he says, and then closes his eyes.

THIRTY-FOUR

DEA VITAE

Phoning an RCMP sergeant who last saw me drunk, crying, and combative and asking him to meet me in a public place because we can't chat over the phone is probably the weirdest thing I will ever do. Well, except for that time I went home with that hottie from the Rivoli Bar at the Ritz London and when we got to his flat, his wife was waiting for us, dressed in leather and a ball gag. I had to pretend I had diarrhea so I could escape. *That* was definitely weirder.

But here we are, sitting in the quiet rear booth of a coffee shop in downtown Vancouver. Though Rupert wanted me to get back to the island posthaste, I had to wait for Wes to be available, which meant I had to hang out for an extra day and drive Number Two even crazier.

Wes is wearing the same black-on-black ensemble as that ill-fated night at the hospital, but his face is dressed in worry for Rupert. I tell him what I know so far from the doctors and explain who Catrina is and how she will be helping out with his care. He asks when he can visit or if he can offer his help; I advise him to text Rupert.

"Anything he needs, I'm there," Wes says, his smile tentative.

"He's lucky to have your friendship." I sip my cappuccino, delighting in the pleasure of a quality coffee I didn't have to make myself.

"You're lucky to have him as your caretaker," Wes counters, drinking from his own cup, black, no milk or sugar. "So. Your call sounded very cloak-and-dagger."

"Rupert's a bit paranoid about this, but I think maybe for good reason. You're the only person he trusts for me to tell, which is why we're here."

I relay the story of the bones my dog found, explain their condition and the metal holding them together, show him the photos to prove that they are actual human bones and not some wayward animal that starved to death on the barren west side of Thalia Island. And then I show him the photos Finan took of the cave, mostly to round out the story. I doubt that bizarro graffiti has anything to do with this, but Rupert instructed me to tell Wes *everything*.

And Wes's reaction to the cave art takes me by surprise. "Where did you say this is?"

"Along the island's west side. The terrain there isn't suitable for building, plus my grandfather wanted it left untouched. But this cave and the area around it—clearly someone has been there. And it wouldn't be First Nations or older because they would've found it during the assessment of the island years ago."

Wes stares at the photos, scrolling through, enlarging and turning his head to inspect from every angle. "Definitely not First Nations. This is the work of Dea Vitae."

"I'm sorry?"

"This wave with the snake tails. The red handprints. The ruby in the center of the wave. These are all hallmarks of Dea Vitae."

"Again, not following."

"Can you send me these photos?" He continues to scroll and examine, and I continue to be completely confused.

"Wes, I've no idea what Dea Vitae means. I can't google it because you have my phone."

"Means 'goddess of life' in Latin. And I wouldn't google anything to do with these guys. If you want to look it up, use a private web browser. You should be using one anyway." He finally clicks off the screen and returns my phone. "Dea Vitae is a cult. They worship the

Babylonian goddess Tiamat, but they follow a doomsday prophecy that will welcome Tiamat back to Earth to avenge the murder of her husband at the hands of their children. These Dea Vitae folks have taken it a step further. They actively encourage their followers to take over towns and open land, especially in coastal areas since Tiamat is considered the primordial goddess of the salt sea. That way they can be the ones who control everything when she returns to usher in the end times. By then, nonbelievers will have been eliminated."

"Uhhhh ... okaaaaay."

Wes points at my phone where it sits on the table. "Someone has been to your island, surrounded by the salt sea, and left their signature, which basically equates to an intent to occupy. If they're not there now, they're coming back. Thalia Island has been marked."

"That's ridiculous. Thalia is private property. My grandfather bought it, and the Foundation holds the deed, at least until I prove I'm worthy of it."

"Maybe. But when the world ends, there won't be such a thing as land deeds or governments to enforce them, right?"

I don't mean to laugh. "Honestly? A cult?"

"I'm just telling you what I know. We've been seeing an uptick in their Canadian activity in the last four or so years. A lot of unfarmed land out in the Fraser Valley, especially around rivers and lakes, has been taken over by Dea Vitae squatters. Tiamat's husband was Abzû, the god of fresh water. So these Dea Vitae nutjobs pool their resources, buy the land legitimately so they're not chased away, and then they build their"—he air-quotes—"'temple' and elaborate communal living structures. They start farming the land, making babies, recruiting followers, especially followers with political connections, tech and science backgrounds, or who are famous. Like that dude who ran the sex cult out of New York, the one with the girl from *Smallville*. She was recruited here, in Vancouver."

"This is too nuts to be believable."

"But then again, it's not. This is exactly how most major religions have come about. Hell, it's not so different from government parties. Ideology, recruitment of vulnerable populations, then financial control.

That's where power comes from. The biggest difference with Dea Vitae from other bona fide religions is that their leadership is modern and forward-thinking. They don't eschew technology—they *embrace* it, and they go to tech schools around the world to recruit hackers, analysts, engineers, web developers, you name it, by promising them a share of the pot once they start taking the money away from their so-called enemies—the capitalists. Which is, in itself, ironic, because then they in turn create their own capitalist-based economies while also controlling everyone who lives under their roof. It's Cult 101."

"And you think these cultists are on Thalia."

"No, I think someone has been on the island with the intent of marking the territory. I have no way of knowing if they're there now. Didn't you guys do some serious background investigations of your potential residents?"

I nod, thoughts racing as I try to remember the names and details of the settler files I was able to review before Kelly showed up and scooped them away.

"Why do you know so much about this?" I'm suddenly nervous—maybe I shouldn't have trusted this guy after all.

"I did a project on the 1993 Branch Davidian Waco siege in grad school, so I have a special interest in cults and religious movements and what makes people fall into them. Plus I have a cousin who's a Scientologist—they're basically a cult." Wes smiles.

"Don't let Tom Cruise hear you say that."

"Great actor, crackpot everywhere else." He chuckles. "Anyway, when the Dea Vitae graffiti started popping up around the city, different divisions within Vancouver PD and the RCMP noticed an increase in other incidents—hate and cybercrimes specifically, even a theft at a UBC biolab of some pathogenic samples. Nothing serious, but still not great. Dea Vitae is proud—they always take credit, like Al Qaeda or Daesh would. They want us to know it's them. They're sort of everywhere, like crazed, scary Robin Hoods, and they're growing."

"And yet we've not heard anything about them in the news."

"Which is intentional. The thing about cults—give them a spotlight, and they grow. Like fungus."

I swipe my phone open again and scroll to the hurried photos Finan and I took of the bones. "But what about this mystery arm? Could it be related to Dea Vitae?"

Wes shrugs and drinks from his heavy ceramic mug again. "Hard to say. Could be bones the tide carried from some wholly unrelated situation, a boating accident or separated remains from a tsunami or disaster on the other side of the world. Could be a body someone wanted to get rid of and they chose your island to do it, until your dog found it. Or ..."

"Or what?"

"Or it could be related. Dea Vitae is not above animal or human sacrifice. Some say they offer up people who try to defect or who squeal. People do crazy things in the thrall of religious zealotry. Babylonian gods and goddesses are no different from Christian or Hindu deities—harmless on paper. It all depends on the worshipper."

"You're kidding me. That is *insane*."

Wes shrugs again and drains his coffee cup. "But is it? Creation gods are found throughout human history. Tiamat is seen as a symbol of chaos or of primordial creation for the Babylonians. The Egyptians have a bunch of creation deities, including Amun, god of the air. The Māoris have Papatūānuku, which is the land, the Mother Earth figure who gives birth to all things. Monotheists have a singular deity— Christians have God, Muslims have Allah, Sikhs have Waheguru. Creation gods are found everywhere, in every culture."

I stare at him, wide-eyed.

He laughs under his breath. "I told you, I'm a huge nerd under all these muscles. When I find something that interests me, I learn everything I can about it—got that from my mom. Self-taught, that woman. I just happen to know a little more about Dea Vitae because of the law enforcement interest in their activities here in British Columbia."

This is *very troubling*. "OK. OK. Umm ..." I don't even know what to say. This meeting has not gone the way I'd expected and, speaking of tsunamis and other natural disasters, I have a whole new level of shitastrophe on my hands. The first person who pops into my head: Finan.

What I would give to have him here right now.

The thought sends an unexpected warmth through me.

But I must concentrate. I must be the Clarke Thalia Island needs. Rupert's orders. "Is there any way you can come to the island? To see the cave and then bring the bones back here? Rupert said you'd be able to handle the forensics quietly. The last thing we need is more media attention."

Wes smiles. He's handsomer than I'd noticed before, probably since this time he's not handcuffing me to a hospital bed.

"If Rupert is asking for help, I will do whatever I can. Is tomorrow soon enough?"

"You tell me," I say, chuckling nervously.

He flattens a hand on the table. "They're bones, Lara, not a corpse. We'll figure this out."

I nod quickly, trying to keep my anxiety behind the drapes and not flashing in my eyes. "What if Dea Vitae is actually on the island, though? How will I know?"

"You'll know when someone stages a coup."

THIRTY-FIVE

MARKED

Wes and I exchange all pertinent info, and then I advise him about transportation for tomorrow, that I will make sure our ferry is at Horseshoe Bay to deliver him to Thalia. If anyone sees us, he's a family friend invited for a day visit and tour—no other information will be offered to my fellow council members or island residents. No one will know he's an investigator, except Finan. Without Rupert, I need backup, so lucky Finan is my guy.

Now is when I start wondering if Finan is somehow involved with Dea Vitae and I'm being played.

Now is when I suspect that *everyone* is involved with Dea Vitae, and this is just a giant Hitchcockian joke on dumb, spoiled, bratty Lara.

But before I can start side-eyeing anyone and everyone, I have to get back to the island, even though every part of me wants to stay in Vancouver with Number Two.

I return to the hospital and talk at length with Catrina and our illustrious patient about his prognosis and what the doctors said in my absence. The plan hasn't changed. Once his blood work stabilizes, the diagnostic scans and bone marrow biopsy are done, and his kidney function returns to normal—lo and behold, the salmonella likely is responsible for his current kidney dysfunction too—he'll be moved out of ICU to a regular ward and then discharged home, under Catrina's watchful eye until a home health nurse can be hired. Rupert will commence treatment protocol per the BC Cancer Centre in conjunction with his own private physicians within the next week, care that may include immunotherapies and clinical trial regimens, none of which I understand. Even in a country with socialized medicine, money still buys the best, promptest, most innovative care.

Catrina excuses herself to the washroom, and while she's out, I quietly tell Rupert about my meeting with Wes. "Have you ever heard of Dea Vitae?"

"No. Should I have?"

"Wes says it's a cult, that the water-and-snake graffiti in the cave is like their brand or whatever. They've *marked* our island, like, they want to take over and kick us off."

Rupert's face blanches and he closes his eyes for a long blink. "Your grandfather's brand of extremism, however well intended, has always collected the oddest assortment of humans."

"How do we know if any of them are living among us? What if someone is there right now, setting the stage for their takeover? I have NO idea how to fix this!"

Number Two is too tired for my questions. I need to unburden him so he can focus on getting well. "Wes is coming over. Tomorrow. We'll handle this, Rupert, I promise. I'll figure it out." I squeeze his hand and offer my bravest smile just as Catrina reenters the room, draped in a fresh yellow protective gown.

"Tommy's ready to go whenever you are, Lara," she says. The surgical mask hides her smile, but the crinkled corners of her kind eyes reassure me I'm leaving Rupert in good hands.

"Thank you. Thank you for staying with him," I say, offering a hug. All this physical contact lately has been very weird ... but also not terrible.

By six o'clock, Tommy and I are on their boat, heading back to the island. I'm beyond exhausted, and while I am torn about leaving Rupert behind in Vancouver, I know Thalia needs me.

Especially right now.

I text Finan and let him know we're coming home; he replies with a picture of Humboldt asleep on his couch. **Big Dog is so bad**, I reply.

Do you need a ride from the marina?

Tommy said he'd drop me off downtown to grab the clown car.

Dinner?

Starving. Been a long day. So tired.

I'll feed you. BBQ OK?

BBQ perfect. Mouth already watering.

See? Your dog child does take after you. ;) See you soon.

I look out the side window of the enclosed cockpit, sharing my smile with the passing landscape, happy to know that someone other than a houseplant and orphaned dog is waiting for me to come home.

THIRTY-SIX

INCENDIARY

The bags under Tommy's eyes as he drops me downtown tell me his bed beckons. He promises to call if he hears from Catrina; I reciprocate.

Upon letting myself into my cabin, I almost fall onto my face with relief and exhaustion. Finan's text of ten minutes ago advised me to hop across to his place where food awaits, but I want to freshen up and change into different clothes that don't smell like hand sanitizer and sadness.

The Lutris portal on my counter pulses green around her edges—this is new. I tap the dark screen and am happily surprised to see it come to life, welcoming me with our custom vector logo of a sea otter. A little red bubble indicates that I have messages. "It works!" I say to the quiet.

I tap the bubble and scroll through the received messages, the first from Jeremiah offering me a virtual high five that we got Lutris up and running and also that he heard about Rupert and to let him know if I need anything. Nice.

Two more messages follow—one from Kelly and the council to all residents updating them about why there was an air ambulance on the island. A generic statement, signed by Catrina, reports that Rupert was suffering ill effects from the food poisoning and needed urgent treatment in Vancouver. Good. The fewer people who know about the cancer, the better.

The subsequent message details that the first town hall meeting, originally scheduled for last night, was postponed, pending new information about Rupert's intended return. I consider replying to all that we should wait a couple weeks at least, but I don't want the residents to start asking questions about where Rupert is—plus, Kelly and her band of BFFs in the council chambers the other day would probably pitch a fit if I delayed too long.

Whatever. I can't think about this right now.

I change clothes, brush teeth, slather on fresh deodorant and a spritz of Chanel No. 5, and release my hair from what's becoming a chronic bun, rubbing my sore scalp. A few twists with the curling iron and some fresh lipstick, and I almost look ready for prime time.

As soon as I step outside, the smell of barbecue wafts my way. Sure enough, Finan is on his front patio, an apron around his tall frame. From a distance, he waves, metal spatula aloft. Humboldt sees me, woofs once, and lumbers in my direction, probably saving whatever energy he has for yummy morsels Finan might "accidentally" drop from the grill.

We meet halfway, and he licks my hand like it's a Popsicle. So gross. I need to refresh the Handi Wipes supply in my purse. "Hi, Big Dog. Did you miss me?" He whines as I scrub his head. From the grayish-white clouds, a light mist falls, basically undoing the effort I expended with the curling iron, but I cannot summon the will to care, especially when Finan's smile practically breaks his handsome face in half.

"Welcome back, Madam Mayor," he says, offering a half-assed bow. I bump him as I walk past to flop in one of the Adirondack chairs on his covered porch. "I've got chicken and beef here. And beer in the fridge."

I wave a hand at him. No beer. Too tired.

It's in that moment that I realize the razor-like buzz of anxiety that crawled under my skin back in the city has disappeared. Out here, sound is nothing more than a calming hum, the whooshing of trees in the wavering wind, the chitchat of birds, an owl warning the other creatures that he's awake and open for business.

"Heyyyyy," Finan says. He kneels in front of me, the plate of barbecued food in one hand, his other on my knee. "You OK?"

My face is wet. I didn't even feel the tears fall.

He takes my hand and helps me up. I follow him into the house, our fingers still locked as he sets the platter of cooked meat on the reclaimed-wood island. When he pulls me against him, I melt.

We stand in his kitchen, his arms wrapped so tightly around me, I feel like nothing could ever touch me again. I will be safe as long as I stay here, just like this, forever. He whispers that everything will be all right as he strokes my hair, his lips pressed against the top of my head, his left hand rubbing softly up and down my back.

Finally I have to let go for a napkin because my nose is running and this stupid drug store–brand mascara burns my eyes. Finan takes the opportunity to cover our dinner and slide it into the oven set to low. "Come sit. Tell me what's going on."

He again entangles his fingers with mine, and I stare down where our hands are connected. "I don't want to talk anymore."

"That's fine. Do you want to eat? We can watch Netflix or order a movie—"

I don't let him finish his sentence but instead grab the front of his shirt, yet another off-white Henley that hugs all the right places, and pull him down to me. Our lips connect, softly at first, and then with a hunger I haven't felt maybe ever. Connor never kissed me like this. I've never wanted to kiss *anyone* like this.

Finan's hand is in my hair, his other at my hip, squeezing me as I position myself as close to him as I can get, my arms around his waist, fingers digging hungrily into his muscled back. His hand moves from my hip and he cradles my face, pulling his lips from mine, both of us breathless. He looks down at me, his eyes ablaze with desire but also tentative.

"Lara … you're in pain right now. I don't want you to think I'm taking advantage of that."

"Maybe I am. Maybe this—maybe you are the only thing that will make me stop thinking about everything else." About Dea Vitae, about Rupert, about my grandfather, about how alone I feel in the world ... except when I'm with Finan.

His smile is new to me, not polite or one he'd offer to someone walking by at work. This smile is playful and teasing, but also sensuous and warm, like he's looking at me for the first time. We stand like that, leaning against the kitchen counter, our bodies touching, our eyes exploring each other's faces. I trace a fingertip down the scar along his left temple; he follows my collarbone with his thumb, smiling when I shiver under his touch.

He pulls my loose-necked cotton shirt aside and kisses the flame his thumb started, and my entire body breaks out in goose bumps. I move my hands to undo the top two buttons of his shirt, hoping that will be enough to get it over his head because I'm *very* interested in what's underneath—

WOOF!

We both startle, pulled from our intoxication long enough to chuckle and note that the dumb dog is still out on the porch, yet another huge chunk of wood in his jaw. Finan kisses my forehead and releases me; I'm instantly colder as he walks across the living room and opens the screen door to let Humboldt in and wrestle free the branch so it doesn't end up splintered all over the floor. Big Dog saunters past into the kitchen, more interested in the deliciousness fresh off the barbecue than the fact that he just interrupted the hottest moment of my life.

"Humboldt, man, we gotta talk. You can't do this to a guy. Can't you see I have a beautiful woman here and she was unbuttoning my shirt? Do you not understand what that means?"

The dog yawns and flops in front of the oven. "Pathetic," I tease. "Honestly, I should've stuck with plants. Andromache would never be so rude."

"I'll feed him," Finan says, picking up a huge ceramic bowl standing in as Humboldt's dinner dish.

With the moment cooled, we decide instead to feed ourselves too.

236

We share a beer and stuff our faces with Finan's scrumptious cooking, laughing about everything and nothing, the conversation steering away from more pressing topics. I know I should tell him what's going on with Rupert and Dea Vitae and Wes's arrival tomorrow, but I don't want to.

Not yet.

I just want a few minutes to pretend that this perfect bliss is exactly that—perfect—before I have to back up the beeping dump truck of calamity and ruin what is quickly sliding into the number one spot on my top-ten-best-nights-ever list.

With our plates emptied and bellies full, Finan surprises me with a pan of double-chocolate brownies. He makes quite a show of scooping homemade vanilla ice cream on each chocolaty square and then shaves fresh vanilla bean on top.

"Honestly. I cannot believe this. You made ice cream?"

"I am a man of many talents, Lara Clarke."

When he slowly licks the spoon clean before setting it into the sink, I almost combust.

He slides my dessert in front of me, but then pauses to stab a tiny pink candle into the ice cream and light it.

I give him a curious look. "You do know it's not my birthday."

"Actually, I have no idea when your birthday is."

"May second."

"Ah—I just missed it!"

"You did. Why all this now?" I gesture at the tiny dancing flame.

He sits and scoots his chair closer to mine, leaning in on one elbow. "Because it's almost your three-week anniversary here, and given the trauma of the last few days, I figured you could use some brownies." Again with that smile that warms me like a campfire.

"Three weeks. It feels like three years." I think of the countdown clock ticking away on my office computer.

"It hasn't been all bad, has it?"

I lean closer. "Not *all* bad."

He kisses the tip of my nose. "Blow out your candle, Princess Lara."

"Shall I make a wish first?"

"I didn't go to all this trouble to miss out on a wish."

I close my eyes and let the smile crawl across my face before theatrically blowing out the single candle. "You want to know what I wished for?"

He shakes his head. "Then it won't come true."

"Yeaaaaah, I'm pretty sure this wish will come true." I pick up his spoon and scoop ice cream and brownie together, feeding it to him, our eyes never leaving one another. I then feed myself a bite of his brownie, moaning when the flavors explode on my tongue. "Oh my god, this is the best thing I've ever tasted. You should be making these for the diner."

He smirks. "I only make these for special people. Secret family recipe."

"That right?"

"Mm-hmm."

I feed him another bite, followed by one for me. "I don't know anything about your family," I say. "I don't know anything about your life before you came to Thalia Island."

"What do you want to know?"

"Hmmm ... maybe where you learned to cook like this."

He smiles and leans back in his chair, arms crossed over his chest. The buttons on his Henley remained unfastened, and for a moment, I consider straddling him and picking up where Humboldt so rudely interrupted.

"My mom and grandmother. Both excellent cooks. They started teaching me when I was a kid. Me and my sister. Food is a big deal in our house," he says. "What else do you want to know?"

"Where did you grow up?"

"North Vancouver."

"School?"

"UBC for my bachelor's and SFU for my master's."

All at once, I feel really dumb. I hope he doesn't ask me about university. He has a master's degree, and I couldn't even be bothered to sober up long enough to go to class.

"What do your parents do?" I ask, hoping to deflect.

Finan smirks again, but instead of answering, he stands and disappears down the hall. I quickly scoop another bite of dessert into my face because it's too damn good to waste. He returns, a picture frame in hand, and sets it on the table.

It's a family—a husband, wife, and two kids hovering on the brink of adolescence, all dressed to the nines. I pick up the frame and look closer. *I know these people …*

"Is … is this you? Your family?"

Finan nods, his lips pulling playfully to one side.

"Your dad—he looks familiar."

"He worked for Clarke Innovations. You might have seen him a time or two. This was at one of the company Christmas events."

I stare at the boy in the photo, my finger running over the glass. "This is you … I know you." And it all rushes back: my mother's memorial, the plate of pickles on the buffet table even though she hated pickles more than anything in the world, the expensive crystal pickle plate …

I set the photo frame down and hop the short distance between our chairs to plant myself in his lap. My hand on his bearded chin, I turn his head to the right. "The scar on your head … you're the pickle-plate kid."

Finan turns back so our faces are inches apart. "Could that be considered our first date?"

I clasp my hands on his cheeks and adjust his head again so I can press my lips against his scar. The scar I gave him when I launched the crystal plate, intending to revel in its destruction against the wall of my grandfather's grand dining room.

"Finan, I am so, so sorry."

He wraps his arms around me again and eases his head back so our noses touch. "I know you, Lara Clarke. I've known your family my whole life. Every time I looked in the mirror after and saw this scar, I was reminded of that beautiful girl who was in so much pain. You were surrounded by wealth and privilege and everything you could've ever wanted, but even then, I knew—what you *needed* couldn't be bought. I've never seen a person look as sad as you did that day when my parents pulled me out of your grandfather's house with a cloth napkin pressed against my bleeding head. The look on your face as you sat on the stairs while Rupert scolded you … I remember it like it was yesterday."

"Why … why didn't you tell me this before?"

"It didn't come up."

I lean back. "You're not some weird stalker dude, are you?"

"If you're asking if I've snuck into your cabin to steal hair from your brush, the answer is—not yet."

I punch him lightly, and he laughs once, startling Humboldt who has now moved in front of the fireless hearth. "Your grandfather took care of my family when my dad got sick. Even though Dad couldn't work, Archibald kept him on the payroll so he wouldn't lose his secondary health insurance or his pension and so my mom could stay home with me and my sister. That's when I knew that I'd eventually work for Clarke Innovations. You come from good people."

I look away, afraid he will see right through me. *My grandfather was good people. And my mother was a drug runner. I have neither glory nor notoriety to lean on.*

"When I was in first-year university, your grandfather invited me to intern at CI so I could decide what to major in. I found a good balance between structural and environmental engineering, so that's what I did. And Archibald hired me the day I graduated."

"How did I not *know* this?"

His smile changes—it almost looks like pity. "We weren't exactly running in the same social circles."

My cheeks warm. I will never stop being embarrassed about the last decade.

Finan adjusts his hands so his fingers are laced together at my hip, holding me to him. "When Thalia Island was offered to me, there was no way I could say no."

"You've done an incredible thing here," I say. "Grandfather would be in awe."

Finan smiles and bobs his head. "I hope so. He was a decent, kind, hardworking man. And he loved you a lot. He'd mention you whenever he could. 'You remember that time Lara Jo hit you in the head with that pickle plate? She's a feisty one.'"

I chuckle, eyes stinging again, and lean my head against Finan's.

"I was engaged … briefly. To a woman I'd dated in high school and then off and on during university. At our engagement party, Archie pulled me aside and told me she wasn't the right one for me."

I pull back. "Oh my god, he did not."

"He did. And he was right. She was actually sleeping with my roommate. They're married now. Two kids. So cliché." He smirks again. "Like I said, your grandfather was a very wise man."

"I can't believe he said that at your engagement party."

"You know Archibald better than anyone. He was never one to hold back."

Finan's right. It was both endearing and infuriating how Archibald Clarke saw things no one else could.

"I took this job because I believe in the Thalia Island mission. I wanted to do my part to make sure Archibald's vision was cared for. I don't have to tell you that not everyone has the mission at heart. Money does weird things to people."

"Welcome to the story of my life," I say.

"I'd always hoped our paths would cross, eventually, here or somewhere else," Finan says, running a finger down my cheek. The longing in his eyes at this moment, the way his tongue quickly wets his lips … "I want you to know, Lara—I've always got your back. As your colleague, as your friend, as anything else that might develop, or not— I will always have your back. This place, this miraculous dream, it's a team effort." He moves his hands along the sides of my face so I have no option but to look at him. "If *you* fail, *we* fail too. I will *never* abandon Thalia Island, or you. Do you understand that?"

I nod, new tears streaming down my face. My entire life, I've been surrounded by rich people, famous people, people who wanted to get near me to serve their own ends.

"No one has ever said that to me before."

He pulls me closer, my forehead resting against his.

"I will say it every day if you want me to."

I laugh and nod my assent. "I could get used to hearing that. It would be nice to not feel so fucking alone all the time."

Finan pushes his lips against mine again, our kiss salty from my tears, sweet from the lingering taste of vanilla and chocolate. He releases long enough for me to move my leg so I'm straddling him on the kitchen chair, and finally, *finally*, I get that last button undone so I can pull his shirt over his head.

His chest is just as delectable as I'd envisioned. Muscular, his brown chest hair in light, whorled patches over each pec and running down his abs, thinning to a fine line that disappears into his jeans. His shoulders and arms and back are sculpted from the hard work that has gone into building our new home. And god, he smells so good, so, so, so good.

His lips move to my neck, the scruff of his beard against my skin sending hot spikes straight through me as he reaches the hem of my shirt and pulls it up and over, dropping it to the floor. Finan stops for a moment, leaning back slightly, searching my face, my neck, my breasts in the lace bra that does not disappoint. "I have never seen anything so beautiful."

My brain spits out a snarky comeback—*I'll bet you say that to all the girls*—but my mouth knows better and keeps it tucked inside. If he wants to paint me with compliments, I am an eager and willing canvas.

I cup my hands behind Finan's neck and push my chest forward, my breath halted as I wait for the first touch of his lips against my sternum, down to the space between. His redwood eyes look like they're lit from within as he pulls me closer and plants that first kiss, followed by a second, and a third ...

The alarm reverberating behind us at first doesn't register as anything other than a phone gone rogue, but it's persistent enough to stop our building frenzy.

Finan's head whips toward the sound coming from the long side table under his front windows where his Lutris tablet sits. Instead of the green pulsating glow I saw on mine earlier, the module pulsates red at a more urgent pace.

"Did we set off Lutris with all that heat?" I tease, but before I can answer, our phones vibrate and sing on the counter.

Rupert!

I disengage and run to my phone just as Finan, shirtless and hot as hell, crosses the living room in a few long strides. He taps Lutris, and it lights up with a huge block of warning text across the screen, "FIRE AT FARM B!" replaced by a giant dancing phone icon. Finan taps the Answer button and Ainsley's face fills the screen.

"Finan! FIRE! All hands on deck! Farm B! Hurry!" She then holds up her camera so we can see the formerly pristine vertical farm B being devoured by voracious orange flames reaching toward the stars.

THIRTY-SEVEN

VERTICAL FARM B

Finan offers me a pair of heavy canvas chest waders and a flannel shirt to go over my clothes that are *definitely* not appropriate for fire abatement. "We're going to get very wet, and no one other than our firefighters has proper gear. These will at least keep you from getting chilled."

Reluctantly I slide them on, grateful they're not so huge I can't move or even sit properly in his truck. He races across via our conjoined driveway to my cabin so I can replace my impractical but gorgeous McQueen sandals with those godforsaken hiking boots so I don't end up injured and useless. When I climb back into the truck, he's on speaker with Ainsley.

"But is anyone still inside the building?"

It's hard to hear her over the yells of people in the background, but she says everyone is accounted for. The fire suppression systems kicked on, but the fire has reached the roof, so the structural sprinklers are useless.

"I hafta go. Hurry, Finan!" Ainsley's phone cuts off.

"Vertical farm B—is that the one with all the fruit trees?"

Finan nods, his brow creased with concern as he pushes the truck faster down the narrow road. If it weren't for the solar-powered lane lines lighting our way, we could be driving off a cliff, it's so dark. "I just don't get it. These buildings have been specially designed to avoid situations like this. The latest in anti-fire tech, sprinklers, foam—you name it, we installed it."

From the look on his face, it's obvious this is more than just a fire to Finan—it's personal.

We're at the vertical farm property in record time, but as he turns the truck down the bumpy, graveled access road, our collective inhales register the shock of what's ahead. Huge fire hoses have been connected to the outside hydrants, but the flames dancing from the top of farm B look like they're enjoying themselves far too much and will not be bothered by a little water.

"What do I do, Finan?"

He slams the truck into park. "Whatever you're told. Come on."

We run across to join the fray—it feels like the entire Thalia population is here holding on to hoses, pulling gear and chickens and ducks out of a nearby wooden, barn-size shed, doing whatever the fire crew hollers at them. Kelly and Hunter are here, too, but rather than holding hoses, they're holding their phones, both standing along the edge of one of the cultivated fields.

I storm over, arms raised in question. "What are you *doing*? Why aren't you helping?"

"We ARE helping! We're documenting the fire for the insurance company!" Kelly shrieks through her nasty look. "Go do something useful, Lara, or else you're going to have another PR nightmare on your hands."

I don't know what to say or do because this is the first time I've ever seen a building burn in real life and been expected to *do* something about it other than call 911. I jog back toward the group and join where I can, grabbing tools and equipment rather than bitey, scratchy, dirty creatures, my ears alert for someone to bark instructions at me to do otherwise.

It doesn't take long. I soon learn just how strong our four firefighters are.

Over the next hours, our efforts to save farm B turn to soaking vertical farms A and C so they don't catch fire. We take turns on the hoses, which is absolutely grueling—they are heavy and powerful, and it's like holding the tail of a choleric rattlesnake forced to do our bidding against its venomous will.

Agritechs bravely go into the adjoining vertical farm buildings to pull out computers, files, and heavy metal suitcases. During a brief break wherein a settler takes my spot on hose duty, one of the crew tells me they're rescuing our seed stores, agri-bio samples and experiments, young grafts, things that will allow us to restart our crops should we somehow lose more buildings tonight.

Another thing to add to the to-do list: We need a fireproof, impenetrable vault for these precious agricultural assets. We need to look at what's been done around the world to safeguard our seeds and crop starters.

By the time the sun teases that she's waking up, every human out here is beyond exhausted. A few residents raced back into town with Stanley to clean the general store shelves of ready-made snacks—granola bars, bottled juices, jugs of fresh water, and superabsorbent cloth towels to clean ash and sweat from dirtied faces. They even brought back carafes of coffee and two huge first-aid kits to treat the minor hose burns, cuts, and scrapes we're all collecting.

But as the sky lightens, it's clear that vertical farm B's structure is a total loss.

Finan and his crew, along with our four firefighters, release everyone except a core group to go home while the rest of us stay behind until full daylight to make absolutely sure the fire is out and farms A and C are safe. I've plopped down on the only dry patch of dirt I can find, sipping some nasty health-freak juice concoction, my heart heavy as I watch the smoldering remains of one of my grandfather's dreams. Ainsley grabs a bottle from the food pile and eases herself next to me.

"I don't know if I've ever been this tired in my entire life," she says.

"Seriously."

We drink in silence, watching our fellow residents move around us, some throwing shovelfuls of dirt onto smoldering wood, others moving equipment and disgruntled birds back into the sheds now that the inferno is doused.

"What the hell happened ..."

Ainsley shakes her head. "I dunnae. I was watching random TV when the agritech lead called me. Said they were closing up for tonight and smelled something off. They opened the room that controls the electronics and were overcome by smoke."

"I don't understand. We have *so* many systems in place to avoid this. The building is completely melted."

She nods. When I look over at her, her round blue-green eyes are filled with tears. "This place was full of baby plants. My heart ..." She flattens a soot-dirtied hand against her chest. "I've spent months nurturing these tiny seeds, and now ... now they're just gone. First the chopped irrigation lines, and now this."

Though I don't know Ainsley very well, she seems very young at that moment, despite her advanced degrees and brain full of brilliant ideas. I pat her shoulder and reassure her that we will rebuild very quickly. "I'll have a fire inspector here before dinner. We'll figure it out. And then we'll get a new structure built so you can keep going with your important work."

She nods once, takes another drink from her juice, and then stands. Her flannel shirt and jeans are soaked and muddied. "Thank you for coming out to help us, Lara. I know this isn't something you're probably used to doing."

"Firefighting? No, can't say I've done much before tonight." I chuckle.

"I mean, this kind of hard work. You look really tired. So, thanks." She then walks away, finishing the juice and then sliding the empty glass bottle into a hemp bag for washing and reuse later.

This kind of hard work ... Wow. So that's what these people really think of me? That I really *am* a pampered princess?

Lovely.

"Lara," Finan calls and waves me over to where he's standing with Kelly, Hunter, Stanley, and Tommy. I pull my sore ass from the ground and jog, so tired my eyes struggle to focus. Ainsley and two of the four firefighters join the circle just as I do. A conversation ensues about getting a fire inspector to come to the island today as well as delegation of who will stay here until inspections can be done on vertical farms A and C to check for structural damage from their proximity to the intense heat.

A few theories about what happened are bandied about, but Finan is quick to shut down speculation, especially from Hunter who just doesn't know when to stop talking and seems to take every opportunity to criticize the work done by the people who've come before him.

Everyone looks dead on their feet, but there's still work to be done. Finan will remain on-site with the agritechs, maintenance crew, and firefighters; Kelly and Hunter will go open town hall. I'll take Finan's truck back to our cabins to let Humboldt out and feed him, and then I'll join the remaining council members downtown so I can get on the phone with Vancouver FD and see about an inspector coming over.

Finan hands me his keys and offers a brief smile, but any hint of what transpired—or *almost* transpired—between us last night before all this is hidden away. Probably for the best. Last thing we need is tongues wagging.

I nearly miss our shared driveway upon my return home, but when I open Finan's front door, Humboldt dashes past to the yard and relieves himself for probably ten minutes. I'm filthy, so I ease my aching body into a porch chair and check my phone.

"Shit."

Wes Singh has texted about the ferry. I completely forgot. I dial his number.

"Hey, Wes, Lara Clarke."

"Hi, Lara. Just following up on our meeting plans."

"I am so sorry—one of our vertical farms burned down overnight, so I'm just getting in from that. Is there *any* way I can persuade you to come over later today or even tomorrow while I deal with this new disaster?"

"Wow. Anyone hurt?"

"Everyone got out safe. But all the residents had to help—we only have four firefighters on the island at this point."

"Any idea what caused it?"

"None. But it's shocking given the technology that went in to building those structures. I gotta get an inspector here now, somehow."

Wes *hmmms* on his end. "How about I plan on coming over tomorrow morning?"

I exhale my grateful relief. "That would be amazing. Thank you so much for understanding, Wes."

"Lara, one more thing—what we talked about yesterday … make sure you keep that information in the front of your head when you start digging through the ashes."

My thoughts speed again as I consider what he's implying. "Do you think …"

"Talk tomorrow. Good luck today." He hangs up.

No way. Could the fire be related to Dea Vitae?

Nooooo … absolutely not. A proper inspector will find a faulty wire or electrical short or something tragic but logical.

Humboldt is now sitting in front of me on the porch, his tail sweeping back and forth, his droopy eyes pleading that he is starving and will die if I don't feed him within the next twelve seconds. Instead of feeding him here, I close up Finan's cabin and slog toward my own where I dump too much kibble in a bowl and take a water-heater-draining shower to wash the smell of fire from my whole person.

As I'm drying and running leave-in conditioner through my hair, my reflection reminds me that I'm in desperate need of salon help—I'm trying to avoid the reality that some of those hair follicles have engaged in a direct revolt, now sprouting gray instead of dark blond. Very rude indeed.

I shuffle into my room and select clean clothes—gray straight pants with a red cashmere sweater—easing my screaming muscles onto the edge of my very comfy bed to pull on warm, clean, dry socks. My pillow whispers to me: *Lara, I'm so soft and fluffy. Stop moving for a second and let me take care of you.*

"OK, pillow. Good idea. Maybe just for a second." I let the pillow wrap her feathery self around my aching head, the last image passing behind my eyelids the orange and red, Medusa-like appendages bringing about the terrible demise of vertical farm B.

THIRTY-EIGHT

WAKEY, WAKEY

Something wet and sort of rough rubs against my face. I brush it away. It nudges me again, soaking my cheek. "Stop it." Again. This time it manages to coat my lips.

I shove it and squint to see what's assaulting me. "Oh god, gross, Humboldt! Get down!" He doesn't, and in fact, he flops over and shows me his belly, his giant, slobbery head soiling the fresh pillow on the formerly unoccupied side of my bed. "I'm going to have to burn these sheets."

I push myself into a sitting position, disoriented for a moment. The sun is still up. Where am I? Where is my phone? What day is it?

And then like a reality tidal wave, it all rushes back, my stomach clenching in instant anxiety-rich nausea. Rupert! The farm fire! Finan!

I clamber off the bed and run into the living room, trying to remember where I put my bag that will, I hope, have my phone within. I dig and dump the bag onto the couch. No phone. What was I wearing? Those god-awful canvas overall things. Run into the bathroom. Check those. No luck. Did I drive myself home? Yes. In Finan's truck.

But I talked to Wes on the phone after I got here, so it has to be around somewhere.

Back in the house. I check the bathroom again—somehow my phone ended up in the tall wicker laundry basket with my dirty clothes. I tap the screen to wake it up, but it's sleeping harder than I was five minutes ago. The dead battery icon flashes at me.

"Perfect."

I plug it in, but it's super dead and will need at least a few minutes. Across the room, Lutris pulsates a subtle green. One swipe along the screen brings her to life. It's past three in the afternoon. I am awash in guilt as I see the messages back and forth from everyone during the time I was sleeping, all of them dealing with the fallout from the fire while I did my own bit of slobbering on my pillow.

My face heats up as I read through one particular message string among Finan, Hunter, Kelly, Ainsley, and Stanley, a conversation that clearly shows few are on Team Lara because "no one knows where she is" and "Never mind, I will call VFD and the insurer myself and inquire about an inspector" (both from Kelly). Finan counters with a quick "She's been up for nearly two days helping with Rupert's care"—thank you, Finan, for defending me—followed by less compassionate responses about how I'm not doing my job. Again.

I can feel my heartbeat in my face. *Why can it not be Kelly with terrible cancer instead of Rupert?*

"That's not very nice, Lara," I say to myself as I scroll through the Lutris contact list. I find Finan's name and press the Call button.

"Hey," he answers.

"Oh my god, I am so sorry. I came home to feed Humboldt and then I showered and changed to head downtown, and—"

"Slow down. Everything's under control."

"Ha. I just saw the message string in Lutris."

"One sec," Finan says. He's quiet for a count of five and then the background noise of wherever he is changes. "Sorry. Needed to excuse myself."

"You at town hall?"

"Yeah. Finished up out there and came in to grab something to eat."

"Have you had a break at all yet?" I ask, guilt shrinking my voice.

"A minute here and there. I could really use clean clothes."

I look down at my own fresh ensemble. "Finan, I feel so bad."

"Don't. You've had a rough couple days. Any news from Rupert or Catrina?"

"I don't know. My phone died—charging it now. But there aren't any emails here from Catrina, so that's good, right?"

"Definitely." His beard bristles against the phone mic.

"You want me to bring you a change of clothes?" Nervousness flutters in my belly at the idea of going through Finan's things, touching his clothing.

"That would be amazing."

"Or I can just bring your truck in and you can come home and clean up ..."

"Nah, bring your car. I can catch a ride home with you. Plus, I need to be here, even if I smell like an ashtray." He pauses. "You should probably get down here too."

"Why does your voice sound kinda scary all of a sudden?"

"Because if you don't come into town, you'll miss the emergency town hall Kelly has called for, oh, ninety minutes from now."

The one thing no one tells you when you are suddenly handed an electric car after years of being driven around in gas-powered or hybrid vehicles is that said electric car must be plugged into its little charging station every once in a while. Like a phone. And I forgot this. So my ultra-compact Toyota EV, so new and cutting edge it's only been introduced to the Japanese market, is out of juice right there in my driveway, parked inches from her charging station.

Saving the planet is great and all, but it is a LOT of work to remember all this stuff.

I now have two choices: Finan's ginormous truck, or Rupert's sleek, elegant Tesla.

Like it's even a contest.

I give Humboldt dinner early, lock up, and jog to Rupert's, letting myself into his cabin long enough to grab his keys and then check that all of his windows and doors are locked. Things are getting too weird around here. Better safe than sorry.

A quick stop at Finan's to grab clean clothes, glad no one can see when I press one of his shirts against my face and inhale. Even under the laundry detergent, his scent lingers, and my body responds. What would've happened last night had the farm not caught fire? Would I have woken this morning in Finan's bed, stiff and sore from wrestling a wholly different kind of fire hose, legs entwined with his, my head resting on his bewitching chest?

I groan and zip closed the stuffed backpack.

I head into town, trying to anticipate what's coming at me in tonight's un-postponed emergency meeting. Based on the chilly string of messages in Lutris, I'm not hopeful this event will be free of sparks.

Plenty of parking out front of town hall—maybe it's no big deal after all and it's just my neuroses getting the better of me, all this worry.

That feeling evaporates as soon as I approach the front doors.

The lobby is packed—an hour before the meeting's scheduled start.

I paste on my society smile and offer friendly hellos, but not a lot of folks reciprocate, adding to the tension racing along my nerve highways.

I bypass my office, mostly because it's the first one down the hall and I don't want to make eye contact with the frosty residents who're waiting for the council chambers to open. Finan is in his office, seated in his chair, his back to the closed door, phone against his ear. I knock and he spins around. His face lights up.

My real smile replaces the fakery everyone else gets, and my heart actually flutters. Being around Finan feels like my first crush a lifetime ago, that first beautiful boy I fell in love with when I was fourteen who, naturally, broke my heart into a million pieces. But still … fluttering and giddiness is why humans haven't gone extinct.

I hold the backpack aloft and then set it against the wall. He mouths *thank you* and continues his conversation as I settle into one of the two guest chairs before his desk. They're talking about the fire. He picks up a pen and jots on a Post-it Note: VFD. Ah. Good. I'm glad *someone* is doing the job I seem incapable of.

I clasp my hands in front of me and bow my head once in gratitude. He winks back.

The noise of people in the hall is muffled by the glass wall and closed door, but a sharp peal of laughter and a spike in the chatter and movement tells me Kelly is on the premises. Sure enough, she squeezes through the throng, pausing long enough to look at me through the glass. She's all spiffy for her big town hall debut, even wearing high-heeled sandals that reveal toenails painted magenta.

But it's the smirk on her face, the Grinch smile that pulls her lips taut, that sends a chill through me.

I turn away. Finally, Finan hangs up.

"Thank you so much for the clothes. Now if only you had a magical shower pod in your designer bag, life would be almost perfect."

I smile. "Will Vancouver Fire send someone over?"

"No, they don't handle anything not municipal, so the chief recommended a private fire and arson investigator."

"Arson?" I ask, dumbfounded. Finan nods solemnly.

"He's coming tomorrow."

So is Wes Singh. I really need to tell Finan all this.

"After the meeting, I gotta go out to the building remains and cover everything with tarps. Weather report calls for rain, and the inspector wants us to protect the integrity of the site."

I nod. "I can help."

He snorts. "Dressed like that?"

"What?"

"Nothing … I like it. You look …"

"Yes, I know, like a princess."

"Not what I was going to say," he says, leaning forward on his arms. Our eyes lock for a beat, his face softening as his gaze lingers on my lips.

Someone scraping against the glass wall breaks the moment.

"Um, so, any idea why Kelly urgently rescheduled tonight?" I adjust in my seat to cool off the fire simmering within.

255

"I think people need reassurance. It's been a stressful week," he says.

Like you have to tell me that.

"Any news about Rupert?"

"A voicemail from Catrina. He's staying another night in ICU and then tomorrow he's moving to a regular ward. They're waiting on PET scan results."

Finan stretches his arm, his huge hand flattened on his desk as if he's reaching for me. "He'll get the best care. He'll pull through this, Lara."

I nod, my throat tight. I clear it before the emotion chokes me. "So, maybe you should get changed? Looks like the chambers are open. Maybe we should …"

He nods and pulls the backpack onto his lap, unzipping and inspecting the contents. "Thanks. This is great."

"I put your deodorant in the bottom, just in case."

He smiles. "I was wondering if maybe, after the meeting, you'd like to get dessert. I hear you're a fan of homemade double-chocolate brownies and vanilla ice cream."

I grin so hard, my cheeks ache as I look down at my hands in my lap. "I could be persuaded to eat homemade double-chocolate brownies and vanilla ice cream with you."

"Excellent."

My grin is probably going to be permanent whenever I'm around him, and right now, I need to focus and get ready to answer the tough questions. I stand and pull my bag over my shoulder. "Mr. Rowleigh, I will see you in there."

"See you in there, Madam Mayor."

THIRTY-NINE

TOWN HALL MEETING

The council chambers are packed. By the looks of it, every person who calls Thalia Island home, either as a settler or crew member, is present. Of course, the two faces I wish I did see sitting alongside me up here in the council seats are still in Vancouver.

After a brief check-in with Tommy, who has the same up-to-date information I have from Catrina, I ease my sore body into my cushioned, high-backed chair and keep my fidgeting hands in my lap. The council members sit on an elevated platform behind a half-round continuous desk, skinny microphones extending from the far edge, one for each speaker. A legal pad and pen await important scribbles at each position, as does a clean glass, waiting to be filled with water from the chilled, sweating pitchers placed between every second seat.

Kelly has unsurprisingly staked her claim on the middle chair, despite the fact that it probably should be mine, given my role and relationship to Thalia Island. I'm certainly not going to say anything; if she wants all eyes on her, I'm fine with that. Her laptop is open on the desk at her spot, though her body is working the room like a politician.

The last time I stood before these people, with a mic in front of me, I followed my speech with spirited vomiting in the azaleas.

Hoping for a better outcome this time. Also, may I again state for the record that sobriety is overrated.

The other council members take their seats. Tommy drums his fingers on the desktop as if already bored. Stanley and Ainsley are huddled in conversation. Finan taps my chair as he sits in the open spot to my right. I stretch a hand toward him when he sits, confident no one out front can see, grateful when he gives it a quick squeeze.

When it's obvious not another soul will fit in the chambers—we're standing-room only, which implies we might need to look at having these meetings elsewhere—Kelly sashays through the crowd and finally climbs the dais to take her seat center stage. I don't notice the gavel until she raps it three times on its matching pedestal.

I flick a raised brow at Finan. He smiles behind his hand.

The crowd quiets.

"Welcome, one and all, to our first official town hall meeting of Thalia Island!" The crowd applauds. Kelly hardly waits for it to die down before launching into her prepared speech, again about promotion of community values, personal spirituality and responsibility, and a reminder of Archibald Clarke's mission statement, "to usher in a new age of environmental enlightenment for humans of Earth."

Another smattering of applause, a "Hear! Hear!" from the back.

"Down to business. First, thank you to everyone who came out last night to help with the fire at vertical farm B. I am sad to report that the building is a total loss, though our quick efforts saved farms A and C. Finan, our lead engineer, has arranged for a fire inspector to come over from the Lower Mainland to get to the root cause of the blaze and to make sure it doesn't happen again. As soon as we have definitive answers, and the insurance pays out"—a few people chuckle—"construction to replace the farm will happen immediately.

"Next up, again, council wishes to express its deepest apologies to those who suffered from the suspected salmonella poisoning from the catered meal served at our welcome-night fête. Council has met and agreed that all future events will be catered on-island, which means no food-service providers will be brought in from Vancouver or anywhere else, for that matter." Kelly finishes her sentence with her glare on me.

I fold my hands on the desk and sit taller. *Do not look weak here, Lara. Don't let her see you sweat.*

Kelly then launches into the agenda, though I seem to be the only one in the room without a paper copy of it. Sure enough, looking out at the gallery, it seems the residents all have a sky-blue page in front of them. I glance at Finan—he doesn't have one—but everyone else up here does.

"Excuse me, Kelly," I interrupt. "Finan and I don't seem to have copies of your agenda."

"Oh. Is that so?" She shuffles the stack of papers in front of her. "Sorry about that. I must've run out of copies. I emailed it to you, so you can just check your phone to follow along, yes?"

She doesn't let me respond before resuming. A quick look over at Finan—he shrugs but then opens his iPad portfolio. A few swipes later, he has the agenda pulled up. He slides the screen so it's halfway between us.

"Thank you," I mouth.

The first few lines of the agenda list notes about the farm B fire, an update from the BC CDC on the food-poisoning incident, followed by the long list of issues we're still handling—the rockfall on the west side, the severed irrigation line, how to check and monitor the battery banks on each dwelling, tips for our zero-waste initiatives at home, the assignment of community-based tasks and chores that will be solidified after the second wave of settlers arrives.

There's a line item about Lutris, which Kelly hands off to me to update. It only takes a few moments to slow my racing heart and remember the quick start-up tips Jeremiah shared during our lengthy call. "Lutris should be fully operational now. You can access the community calendar, request or change task assignments, send notes to council and/or to your fellow settlers. The message boards are open and functional. It also serves as the intraisland phone center, so for those of you who don't want to use your cell phones to call your neighbors, the Lutris portal doubles as a landline. You can phone, text, or email all from the same interface."

I explain how the emergency services here works differently from what happens on the mainland. We don't dial 911, but rather an on-island emergency number—*-H-E-L-P—that is monitored twenty-four hours a day. We are connected to emergency services in Vancouver, as was demonstrated with Rupert this week, just not through traditional channels.

"Will we all be given access to an air ambulance if we need it?" a resident asks from the gallery. I don't quite catch who spoke.

"Of course. Every resident of Thalia Island is equal and will be given whatever level of care is required." I swear Kelly snickers down the way from me, but I don't look her way, trying very hard to keep my stoic, strong Clarke face intact. "If an emergency dictates use of an air ambulance, one will absolutely be summoned."

"Where is Rupert? Is he coming back?" Another resident asks, a woman this time.

I clear my throat. "Rupert is undergoing treatment in Vancouver and will rejoin us very soon."

"Is this from the salmonella? Should we be worried about the safety of the food supply?" a lanky man standing in the back row asks.

"There's no reason to worry about our food supply," Tommy interjects. "Rupert will have the full report from the BC CDC upon his return, and we will immediately make that information available to you. It was just a case of bad luck." Tommy manages a quick look in my direction; I offer a grateful smile. "Rest assured that while the CDC investigators were here, they undertook a comprehensive inspection of not only my kitchen but the refrigerators at the Tipping Point as well as the kitchen and fridges at the Salamander and anywhere else on the island that pertains to food care, handling, and safety. We passed with flying colors, as we have on every other inspection over the last six months."

"So this was something the fancy caterer brought in?" asks the woman from a minute ago. I recognize her from Kelly's informal town meeting last week.

"Again, we will disseminate the CDC's conclusions when they become available," Tommy says, effectively shutting her down. By her lemon-pinched lips, she doesn't look satisfied with his answer.

For the next thirty minutes, random questions are fielded from the gallery pertaining to when the school will open, when the new doctor will arrive, when residents can start making medical appointments via Lutris, questions about shipments of ordered goods from the Lower Mainland and abroad, about planting the seed kits in private gardens …

Midway through Ainsley's detailed explanation about the maintenance of individual garden plots, the main chamber doors open, and a burst of cortisol splatters the inside of my chest like a paintball capsule.

Connor Mayson is here. With Suze whatever her name is.

"What the …"

While Ainsley rambles on about root vegetables and soil quality, my hands shake so hard on my lap, I can hardly type out the text to Finan. **My ex just walked in. WTF is Connor doing here?**

That's him?

YES. FINAN, what is going on?

"Thank you, Ainsley, for that comprehensive tutorial. Folks, you know where to go now if you have questions about nurturing your homegrown crops. No one beats our Ainsley when it comes to carrots!" A titter moves through the room as Ainsley waves once, her face again the color of those beets she loves so much.

"Now, the final item on tonight's agenda, noted at the very bottom, pertains to our current leadership structure."

I lean closer to Finan's iPad, my fingers so clammy from being clamped tight in my lap that I can't get the screen to enlarge. When it finally cooperates, the last line on the agenda reads: "Discussion of modification to current leadership structure."

A quick look at Finan—the shake of his head is subtle, but his furrowed brow suggests that Claudius is about to drip the poison into King Hamlet's ear.

"As you know, Archibald Clarke's dream of a flourishing, vibrant community of environmental crusaders is just one part of our overarching mission," Kelly says. "We want to show the outside world that not only can we overcome our socioeconomic and cultural differences but we can thrive within them to build a robust society where no one is left behind."

As she speaks, Connor moves from the seat he's just taken next to Suze—a seat a settler gave up for them—and he moves to the guest podium at the center of the gallery. "I was chosen for this role on Thalia Island by Archibald himself, as were the rest of us here on your town council. Every single settler in this room was *chosen* for their specific abilities and talents, their special gifts, the little something that makes every one of us unique among our fellow earthlings."

Kelly flicks a hand toward the side where Hunter stands next to the light panel; the chambers dim. A screen behind us whirrs quietly as it lowers. "However, not everyone on Thalia Island is here because they *earned* it. And I, for one, as a contributing member of this new society—contributing with not only my blood, sweat, and tears, but my financial investment—believe that we need to have a say in who sits on council, who is given a leadership role within the Thalia Island hierarchy."

As the last word rolls off her lips, a photo of me—screaming at the camera, mascara-streaked cheeks, being led out of Nordstrom, dress ripped, bare feet dirty, hands cuffed—fills the screen behind the council chairs. Kelly then gestures toward Connor, waiting quietly at the podium.

He clears his throat and leans too close to the slim mic, sending a wave of feedback through the space. "Sorry ... hello to all of you. My name is Connor Mayson. You may know me from television and film, but I was also Lara Clarke's boyfriend for the last two years. I think it's important that you be aware of who is running your new home, which is why I agreed to come over to Thalia Island with my fiancée, Suze, and give you some hard truths."

Fiancée? Hard truths?

"Connor, what the hell is this—"

"Lara, you do not have the floor," Kelly bites through her mic. "Wait your turn."

Connor nods and again speaks, revealing private details of our time together, how I hated charity work, how I refused to tip the waitstaff when we went out to eat, how I never left gifts for the housekeepers during the holidays, how I even demanded that my housekeeper Vera skip her son's wedding so she'd be there to coordinate the catering and decorations for my birthday soirée.

Everything he's saying is completely out of context.

Everything.

But he keeps talking, and as he does, the wave of hate and disgust rolling toward me from the gallery lassoes my lungs. The screen behind us flashes a new photo with every sensational morsel that tumbles from his lips. One unflattering photo after another, me drunk out of my mind, me hanging off some random guy, and another, and another, photos he clearly has been stockpiling, just for this very moment.

"Thank you for allowing me to have a moment to address you. Kelly and I felt it was important for the new residents of the island to know who they're putting their trust in. Also be sure to tune in Thursdays on CTV for my show, *Super George*."

Connor steps away and resumes his seat next to Suze; she kisses his cheek and rubs his arm, as if what he just did to obliterate my character was somehow taxing for him.

"Thank you for taking time out of your shooting schedule to come to Thalia Island, and for your brave candor, Mr. Mayson."

"Kelly, I think we've heard enough," Finan says, folding his iPad closed.

"Finan, you are here because you were chosen. You have dual master's degrees in structural and environmental engineering. The councilwoman sitting next to you barely finished high school, and she has been installed in the literal driver's seat, without any of us having a *say* in the matter. *Our* futures are in *her* incompetent hands."

"Kelly—" Finan growls.

"The people have a right to know, Finan." She turns away before his name is even fully out of her mouth. "Since Lara Clarke has been on the island, we have had nothing but a string of disasters—the severed irrigation pipes, food poisoning, Rupert being rushed out by air ambulance, and now the fire at farm B. Don't tell me this is coincidence, Finan. It's *incompetence*."

"Knock it off. Lara didn't have anything to do with the pipes or the fire."

"But the food poisoning that hospitalized Rupert—the man who basically *raised* her—isn't that enough? It's her fault that happened, Finan. *She* brought the caterers to the island. *She* bypassed council's wishes, and spent a small fortune doing it, resulting in a terrible illness. No one can look at the facts and deny it."

Finan's jaw clenches so hard, I can hear his teeth grind. His fist is balled atop the desk, as if looking for something to strike.

Kelly turns her chair so she's facing her beloved audience once again. "And beyond the revelations presented by Mr. Mayson, startling new information has come to light, information about a chapter far darker than an alcoholic heiress being handed the keys to our kingdom."

Another picture fills the screen—my mother in sunglasses, a tank top, and cargo pants, beaming and sun-kissed, her legs dangling from the open side door of her Cessna in the middle of a jungle, her arm draped around the shoulders of a beautiful, dark-haired woman, their heads pressed together, the sun creating a lens flare that overexposes the upper right third of the photo.

"This is Cordelia Clarke, Lara's mother. While the Clarke Foundation would like us all to believe Cordelia was the adventuring daughter of our patriarch, the award-winning photographer and eco-activist responsible for saving swaths of South American rainforest, she was, in reality, a drug runner for the cartel out of Sinaloa, Mexico."

The gallery comes alive with noise, but it does nothing to rival the roaring in my ears.

I'm going to fucking kill someone.

FORTY

JAPANESE WHISKY

For the first time since I've been here, I'm grateful for this ridiculous gorilla-size key chain.

Because it opens all the doors on Main Street.

Including the Tipping Point, our general store.

And since Stanley is still ensconced in the hatefest back at town hall, I will just help myself to whatever is in here because I am *done* playing nice.

Tonight, what I need includes this cloth tote and this cloth tote and these four bottles of wine and that bottle of gin and that two-liter jug of mixer and that bottle of Japanese whisky he said he didn't carry but clearly he was lying so fuck that guy, I'm taking the whisky.

I close the door behind me, but just barely. What do I care if the settlers pillage his store? They certainly don't seem to have a problem pillaging my life. Have at it, kids. Fill your pockets with organic granola bars wrapped in repurposed banana leaves and shitty two-ply 90 percent postconsumer recycled toilet paper. YES, pun intended.

Few have exited town hall, and those who are outside give me a wide berth as I noisily clink to Rupert's Tesla. Once behind the wheel, I tear off the sticky fabric seal on the Suntory Toki and take a long, healthy swig, my cells coming alive with the infusion of their favorite substance. I exhale as the subtle whisky burn coats my insides—Japanese whisky should be savored, but needs must. Wiping my mouth on the back of my sleeve, I screech out of my spot.

Speed limits are for chumps, and who cares—it's not like we have any cops on the island. Derek Irving is still a no-show, so no DUIs here, baby! Plus if Elon Musk didn't want me to drive like a bat out of hell, he wouldn't have created Ludicrous mode. Zero to sixty in three seconds? Yes, please.

I fly toward my cabin, sad when I reach it in record time. I still have a half bottle of whisky left—I'm out of practice—so I slide sideways into my driveway, grab my loot, and stomp into the house. Humboldt barks once and saunters toward me, abandoning his warm spot over the heat vent.

"Guess what, Big Dog? We're moving! We're going back to Vancouver! Are you excited?" He has no idea what I'm talking about, but he still wags his tail and wiggles like I've just promised him a trip to the dog park. "First, let's get some ice, shall we?"

In the kitchen, I grab the box of organic dog biscuits from the counter and dump them upside down all over the floor. "It's a party, Humboldt!" Tall glass out of the cupboard, fresh ice—*tink, tink*—just two cubes, thank you. I pour the whisky to the rim, laughing at myself when I dribble some down my front. "It ain't a party until Lara spills the Suntory!"

I throw back the glass until there's room for more. I haven't had really any booze in nearly a month, so my tolerance isn't what it used to be. *No worries*, the little devil perched on my shoulder says. *We'll get you back in shape in no time.*

Closets thrown open, I pull out my suitcases. Should probably just take the basics for now—once Rupert is better, I'll convince him to hire someone to pack and ship the rest of my stuff. He did it before without me knowing; he will certainly be able to do it again, especially once he learns what the hell is going on over here.

I sway slightly, finding my balance with one hand against the antique armoire in my bedroom, the other hand holding tight to the cool, half-empty glass. I squeeze my eyes closed against the pain of seeing my mother's memory dirtied by that flannel whore, splashing Cordelia's face over the screen like she wasn't a human, like she wasn't worthy of respect or love.

Like she wasn't my *mother*.

This is Cordelia Clarke … While the Clarke Foundation would like us all to believe Cordelia was the adventuring daughter of our patriarch, the award-winning photographer and eco-activist responsible for saving swaths of South American rainforest, she was, in reality, a drug runner for the cartel out of Sinaloa, Mexico.

"My mother wasn't a bad person," I say to no one. Humboldt comes in and looks up at me, head tilted, his droopy eyes laced with concern, if dogs are able to lace their eyes with concern. Maybe he just needs to poop again. "They didn't know her, Humboldt. They didn't know my mother. Why do they think they can say such terrible things about her?"

He waddles over and rubs up against my leg. I sink to the floor, spilling a bit of my drink—can't have that, so I finish it in one long pour. Humboldt whimpers and then bathes my cheek with his icky tongue. I scrub the back of his neck and then he flops onto me, flattening my legs with his weight, spreading himself out so I can scratch his belly.

"I don't know why Kelly did that … I am *trying* so hard to be a good person, Big Dog. What the hell is *wrong* with that woman? Why is she out to destroy me like this?"

"Because she's jealous."

I flinch at the intrusive voice, and Humboldt woofs. My hand against his ribs soothes him and he drops his slobbery head onto my leg again. "It's OK. It's just Finan. Finan who sat there and let Kelly Lockhart decimate what's left of my character."

Finan moves across the room, around the bed, and kneels next to us faster than I can lift my right hand to shoo him away. "Kelly Lockhart is a bully. She always has been, and she always will be. And you didn't stay for the rest of the meeting, so you don't know that I didn't just 'sit there.'"

"Oh, yeah? Did you yell at her about defaming me? Defaming my mother's memory? Sullying her name? Did you vote to kick her off council? Is she at her house right now—a house my *grandfather* built—packing her bags so she can run away, tail tucked in disgrace?"

Finan brushes a hand down his face and sighs.

"You smell like a liquor cabinet."

I pick up my glass and dump it upside down, a line of leftover liquid drizzling into my area rug. "An *empty* liquor cabinet, maybe."

"This is what you do to cope?"

"Oh, please. Save us all the speech."

Finan stands but perches on the side of my bed, pushing my open suitcases out of his way. "You're leaving? And going where?"

"Not really your concern anymore, Mr. Rowleigh. After all, you have lots of university degrees and I have none. You have big important jobs to do here on the island, and all I'm good for is a wild, boozy night on the town to give the people someone to point and laugh at."

I push Humboldt off my legs. My glass needs refilling.

It takes a second, but I manage to get back on two feet, a miracle considering I've had almost an entire bottle of whisky in the last hour. Maybe I'm not as out of practice as I feared.

In the kitchen, I don't bother with ice or the glass. There's only about a shot or two left in the bottle anyway, so down the hatch! Finan walks in behind me and unloads the stolen wine from the cloth tote bags printed with The Tipping Point and the inverted iceberg logo. I watch as he slides the gin and the two-liter bottle of mixer into the barren fridge, followed by the two bottles of white. I may have accidentally grabbed chardonnay, after I promised Eugenia I'd never drink it again.

Eugenia … oh man, I should call her. She's so nice to me.

Finan pauses to examine a bottle of red cradled in his hand. He puts it, and its merlot companion, in the countertop wine rack that has otherwise been bereft of occupants since my arrival on Thalia Island.

"You gonna drink all this tonight?"

"Maybe."

"Has Humboldt had actual dinner?" Finan picks up the emptied box of dog biscuits from the floor and slides it into the recycle bin.

"Hmmm …" I can't remember if I fed him. Other than the cookies. "Come on! We're having a party!" I shuffle over to the counter where Andromache sits. "I'm sorry, Andy! I forgot to give you a sip because I already drank it all!" I kiss her long, healthy leaves and tell her she's so beautiful and that of course I won't leave her when we go back to Vancouver.

"I'm going home," Finan says. "Call me when you sober up."

"What … you don't want to talk to me like this? Didn't you see the slideshow, Finan Rowleigh? I am WAY more fun when I'm shit-faced. Just ask Connor! Ask Connor and ask Kelly and ask the paparazzi who took that photo and all the other photos! All the photos they've been taking my entire life, waiting for me to get old enough so I could start screwing up like a proper useless rich girl—"

"You sound really sad right now, so I'll go." Finan turns on his booted heel and does exactly what he says he's going to do: he leaves.

Just like everyone else.

FORTY-ONE

MAGIC WALLET

It's still dark. Disorienting to fall asleep when it's dark and to wake up with it still dark.

I actually don't even know where I am.

"Humboldt …" I lift my pounding head toward the sound of his breathing.

Except it's not Humboldt's breathing—it's Finan's.

I'm on my couch, warm under one of my Merino wool knitted blankets. Finan's asleep in the overstuffed leather armchair across from me, his boots off, his sock-covered feet propped on my coffee table, a plaid wool blanket draping his torso. His head is turned to the right, and the light from the side-table lamp outlines the scar I gave him so many years ago.

I sit up and squint at the throbbing-green Lutris tablet, trying to see the digital clock tucked into the upper right corner: 3:13 a.m.

I need my phone. Gotta check for messages—what if Rupert called? Or Catrina? Did they hear about what happened at the meeting? Is Rupert going to fire Kelly? I need to call the lawyers. No one has the right to do what she did. She's not a Clarke—she can't just call for my removal. Plus it's pretty goddamn sneaky that she did all this while Rupert is off the island. How *convenient*.

And how in the world did she connect with Connor? How did she get him over here without me knowing about it?

I need water—a lot of water—and Advil. Rising from the couch as quietly as I can, I shuffle into the bathroom, drink directly from the tap, and swallow the maximum-allowed dosage of ibuprofen. I brush the whisky fuzz from my teeth and gargle with enough mouthwash to burn off what remains of my taste buds. Still maybe a little drunk, though I'm impressed with my body's impressive metabolic dispensation of so much Suntory in such a short time. Clothes off, I step into the shower and let the hot water work its magic on my aching skull.

But as the water pummels my skin, I realize it's not only my head that hurts. I've been on Thalia Island for just shy of a month and look how easily I slipped back into old habits. As soon as something got hard and mean and scary, instead of fighting, I ran. I ran and then I numbed myself because Rupert wasn't here to take the bullets for me.

What am I going to do if the cancer takes him? What can I do to save him when I'm not even capable of saving myself?

How will I ever prove to him that I'm not what Kelly Lockhart says I am? How will I ever prove that I am more than just Lara the party girl, Lara the bitch who doesn't tip her waitress, Lara the broken heiress who stomps her foot and swims in Toki Highballs when the going gets tough?

I slide to the bottom of the shower, crying so hard, I can't catch my breath. This isn't fair. I thought I'd already hit rock bottom. How many rock bottoms are there before things get better?

I cry until my ribs ache, until my stomach feels like I've gone nine rounds with a prizefighter, until my skin is coated in goose bumps because the hot water has run out. As soon as the tap turns off, I hear footsteps outside the bathroom door. I wipe the moisture from the glass enclosure, spying the shadow of two feet on the hall side, but then they disappear, moving away until the front door opens and closes.

Quickly, I grab a towel and dry off, throwing on clean panties and my plush robe, yanking open the bathroom door and hustling to the living room. The chair where Finan was asleep is now vacated. I wrap my bath towel around my head, slide into my UGGs slippers, and run onto my front porch. Finan is walking toward his cabin.

Without calling after him, I bound down the porch stairs. Whatever slice of moon watches over us is hidden by a dense cloud layer; the only light to guide my way is the dwindling glow from the solar-powered yard sconces spaced along the gravel path between our cabins. My slippers are loose on my feet without socks, so my heels scuff in my haste to catch up.

Ahead of me, Finan stops, but he doesn't turn around.

I should be worried about him seeing me like this—towel-wrapped, wet hair, face blotchy and puffy from crying, heart broken—but I'm not.

I step in front of him, pulling my robe tight against the chill. "You came back."

"You drank a lot of whisky."

I nod. "It was a rough night."

His head bobs once and he looks down at his untied boots.

"Finan ... I'm broken. I *feel* broken."

His eyes meet mine, and they're bright with emotion. "But you're not. You're scared."

A flame of indignation lights in my chest but before I can parry, he continues. "What Kelly did tonight was unforgivable. And it won't go unanswered." He reaches for my hands, encasing them in his much-warmer grip. "But when things get hard, you cannot just run away. You can't go pack your shit and drink yourself into oblivion and take off, Lara." He steps closer, moving one hand to cup my cheek. "This has been a really, really fucked-up year for you so far. I *know* that. And I know how worried you are about Rupert—when my dad got sick, the only reason he lived as long as he did was because of your grandfather and Rupert. And when my dad died, your grandfather and Rupert made sure everything was OK in our household. They *cared* about what happened to me and my mom and my sister.

"You may not have seen me facing off with Kelly tonight at that meeting, but that doesn't mean I'm not on your side. I've already told you—I will *always* have your back. You just have to believe that you're worthy of that kind of loyalty."

Finan's fingertips trace my jawline before he again envelops my hands with his.

"You can finish packing, and I will drive you to the ferry myself if going back to Vancouver is what you want or need right now. Humboldt can stay with me. I know your old life is in the city—Rupert is in the city, and I know he's very sick. But if you leave, there is no Clarke on Thalia Island. There is *no one here* from your family to protect her."

I pull my hands free and tuck them into my robe. "I can't do this, Finan. This job is bigger than I am. I didn't earn my spot—like Kelly said—and I'm not like you, or anyone else here who worked for years to *earn* their place. It was given to me to keep me out of jail."

"That's ridiculous. Your grandfather willed it to you, which means he saw something in you, something you can't even see for yourself."

"But you *heard* Kelly—you saw what she did. What do you think will happen once the media gets hold of the truth about my mother? What do you think is going to happen to this island, to Clarke Innovations, if the myth around Cordelia Clarke is true?"

"That's for the lawyers to worry about. YOU weren't running drugs or doing whatever Kelly says your mom did—you were just a kid! A kid whose mother was flying all over the world and leaving her in the care of nannies and valets and an aging grandfather. I don't want to talk shit about Cordelia, especially since I met *you* at her memorial service, but you, Lara, you are *blameless* in this. You were a *child*."

My eyes burn and my throat aches as new tears threaten. "And what about since then? I'm not a child now, and I haven't been for a long time. And Connor had no problem telling everyone how thoroughly terrible I am."

"Is what he said true?"

"About what?"

"The housekeepers, all that."

I shake my head and sniff, wishing I had some tissue in my

pocket. "No. Well, mostly not true. I did get a little insane with my housekeeper about my twenty-fifth birthday party, but what Connor didn't mention is that I gave her $15,000 for her son and his partner to go to the Bahamas for their honeymoon in exchange for her help."

"Connor only shared the salacious bits, the parts that make him look like the long-suffering boyfriend and you the spoiled heiress."

"He's very good at that," I say, teeth chattering. "Always the victim."

"But what about you? Is that a role you're willing to continue to play?"

I can't look at him. I wipe my eyes with my sleeve.

"Come on. You shouldn't be out here with wet hair." Finan takes my hand and we walk back toward my cabin. "You are not broken, Lara. You're just a bit lost. You have no idea who you are because you've never had to *be* anyone other than Archibald's granddaughter or the drunk airhead splashed on vicious tabloid sites." He opens the front door to my cabin, and I quiver as the warmth wraps around me. I let go of his hand so I can grab a wad of tissues.

My throat aches worse against the strain of emotion. "I don't know what to do, Finan. I don't know how to be anyone other than Archie's granddaughter or Cordelia's kid or Rupert's troublemaker. Or the drunk airhead." I pause and look up at him. "Do you think that's what I am?"

Finan closes the distance between us and pulls the towel off my head. He finger-combs my wet hair as tears slide down my cheeks; he arranges the untangled strands over my shoulders and down my back. Whenever his fingertips brush my neck, I shiver all the way to my feet. He steps behind me, gathers my hair, and braids it, gently, without pulling the baby hairs at the nape like my nanny used to.

"You are Lara Clarke. You're funny, creative, clever, hardworking, kind, and wicked with a spreadsheet. You are learning to be a good dog mom, though you still have some work to do when it comes to plants."

I laugh under my breath as he nears the end of the braid. "But I tell

Andromache every day how beautiful she is. Not just when I'm drunk."

"And she hears you. Plants listen. It's science."

Finan releases my hair and moves in front of me again.

"You have a good heart under all your designer labels. I see it in the way you worry about Rupert, how you've done whatever has been asked of you here on the island, how you've risen to the challenge, even when you didn't think you were capable of it." He takes one of my hands again. "I know because I saw how much it hurt you tonight for those people to say such terrible things."

"Even if some of it was true."

"Maybe ... but you try to make the world believe this is granite in here"—he taps my chest with a gentle fingertip—"and it's not. It's soft and squishy like the rest of us. Maybe a little bruised, a few scars here and there ..."

"Just a few."

Finan smiles, the smile he reserves for me when no one else is around, and it feels like the sun on my face. I reach up on tiptoes and push my lips against his, tentatively, hoping I'm not making a fool of myself. Again.

But he kisses me in return, and then his hand cradles my head and his other hand drops to my lower back to close the gap between us. The kiss deepens as our breaths accelerate, and I break only long enough to push him against my couch. He sits but doesn't let go. Straddled across his lap, I'm only wearing a robe and panties, and the fire in Finan's eyes says this is exactly how he wants me.

He kisses me thoroughly, biting at my lip, our tongues exploring one another's mouths before his lips migrate down my jawline, to my neck. I giggle and break out in gooseflesh when he bites my ear. He eases me back gently, unties my robe, and lowers the plush cloth off my shoulders, exposing my chest to him as the robe drapes behind me. His breath stutters—if I didn't know better, I'd think the mighty Finan Rowleigh might be nervous.

I take his right hand and flatten it over my heart. "I want you, Finan. I want all of you."

That's all it takes.

Both hands are on my breasts, his mouth taking turns on each one, the scruff of his beard a new pleasure. He buries his face against my sternum, taking a deep breath, inhaling me, before kissing across my collarbone, across my left shoulder, and then back up and over to the other side. By the time he reaches my neck again, I'm dizzy with need.

I clamp both hands on his face and kiss him harder, releasing him only to shed my robe fully.

"Are you sure—"

My lips stop his question; he smiles against my mouth. "You have too many clothes on," I whisper and lean back, pulling off his shirt. I take a moment to run my fingers over his muscled pecs, the carved collarbone, where the muscle at the shoulder meets his biceps. He shivers when my fingertip flicks at his nipple. "Finally. I have wanted to touch this chest since the moment I saw you."

"You have not."

"Oh, but I have, Mr. Rowleigh. You see"—I unbuckle the black leather belt at his waist—"I have a thing for engineers, especially engineers with not one but *two* master's degrees who look like you do in a Henley and Levi's." I pull at the button fly of his jeans. "Few specimens have an ass like yours."

"I feel so objectified."

"You should," I say, pulling at the second button.

"You only like me for my fancy clothes, then." His breath hitches as I tug at his pants.

"I'd like it better if your fancy clothes were *off* your objectified body."

He grins and maneuvers clumsily to remove his jeans, hanging on to me with the other arm, as if he's afraid to let go. When his pants are crumpled on the floor, and we're both sitting in nothing but thin layers of silk and cotton, his desire is obvious.

"Calvin Klein. I should've guessed."

"Costco had a sale," he teases, pushing his bearded face against my sternum again, nipping at my breasts as he flips me onto my back. "I

276

should be a proper gentleman and ask if you'd prefer to retire to the bedchamber, but I think it's overrun with *les valises*."

I pull him fully onto me, a shock wave of searing need coursing through my body, my legs wrapped around his waist, hips teasing against him. "A proper gentleman gives a lady what she wants without making her wait for nonsense like moving suitcases," I say, shrieking when he sinks his teeth into my neck.

He kisses me then, less voracious than a minute ago, slowing to feather his lips along the periphery of my mouth, along my jaw, his thumbs caressing my cheekbones. My hands can't get enough of his muscled back, his shoulders, the biceps that flex with every touch against my body.

I've never felt anything like this with any other man. Incendiary, like walking into an open flame, but safe and lighter, like the battle armor and chain mail have been peeled away and I'm nothing but flesh, waiting to be consumed.

I slide my hand between us to touch him; Finan's low growl suggests he's as ready as I am. Thumbs in the waistband of his Calvins, I slide them down. He helps kick them free, groaning against my mouth as my hand finds its mark.

He pulls his lips from mine, our foreheads pressed together, each of us inhaling the other's breath, the sweet-and-spicy aroma of our bodies finding their groove. "Lara …"

I *hmmmm* against his lips. "We're supposed to have that talk before we get naked."

He smiles, his cheeks flushing. He leans on one arm and reaches for his jeans with the other, digging for his wallet.

"Eww, tell me that hasn't been in there since high school," I tease as he extracts a foil packet.

"Only since prom." He waggles his eyebrows. I take and tear it open, sliding the condom over him as he again reacts to my touch. Our lips reconnect, but he breaks to lean back and free me of the last piece of cloth in our way.

"I want you," I say again. Finan lowers himself over me, his redwood eyes sparking with need. I wrap my left leg around his waist, opening myself to him. When he settles between my thighs, neither of us breathes as he eases into me.

Finan is generous, taking his time, making sure I find the release my body craves, kissing me through the shuddering waves, pulling me closer to him, beautiful words no one has ever said floating into my ear, whispered reminders that he is safe, and together we are whole and there is nothing he wouldn't do to keep me near him.

At last we reach the final peak together, panting through the exhilaration, kissing like we will die if parted. Finan's weight on me, I want to keep forever. I don't want to move. I want to feel his arms holding me against him, around my back, behind my head, his hand against my face, his form united with mine.

He kisses the tear from the corner of my eye.

"It's a happy tear," I whisper.

"Naturally."

I reach around and pinch his bare ass. He strokes the hair off my forehead, his finger tracing my eyebrows, the silhouette of my nose and lips, in figure eights around my eyes. When the sweat on our skin cools, he gently slides free of me, and I'm already longing for him again. Unabashedly, I ogle his beautiful body as he stands and moves to the bathroom, returning after a moment to pull a blanket from the back of the couch and slide in next to me, covering us both with the soft wool as I nuzzle against his broad chest, inhaling his essence.

"Good thing you have such a big couch," he says.

"One more word about the suitcases on the bed and I'll pack you in one of them," I tease. He kisses the top of my head.

"Forgive me, my lady. Humblest apologies, my lady."

I can hear his smile in his words. I twist his nipple, making him jump and grab my hand. He turns onto his side so we're facing one another and pulls the blanket up so my shoulders aren't exposed. Now that we're not moving, the room's chill lurks, looking for uncovered skin.

Finan again maps my face with his index finger. I study the lines of his perfect lips, his jaw, his nose, run the back of my fingers against his beard.

"You're my first, you know," I say.

He hikes a doubting eyebrow.

"My first engineer. My first with a beard."

His deep laugh warms my chest. "You've never been with a guy with a beard?"

"No. Contrary to popular belief, I'm actually pretty choosy about who gets to see my panties."

He laughs again and kisses my forehead. "We don't have to do that —talk about past conquests."

"You've seen the type of men I attract."

"Hey, now. You attracted me …"

"Present company excluded."

Finan brushes his lips across my knuckles. "Connor Mayson is a weasel. And he can't act for shit." He then wraps his arms tighter around me. "I don't want to talk about him. If we're going to talk about anything, it should be how I'll get through my days without thinking about the way your body fits around mine."

"If you keep talking like that, you'd better have another foil wrapper in your magic wallet."

Finan drops a hand under my leg, pulling it over his hip, renewed hunger in his kiss. "As a matter of fact …"

Suffice it to say, the magic wallet delivers.

FORTY-TWO

UTMOST DISCRETION

A kiss against the nape of my neck. Big hands on my bare shoulders, sending chills down my arms and across my chest covered only by a silk camisole, under my matching silk panties, down my freshly shaved legs still waiting for me to decide on today's outfit.

"God, you smell good," Finan murmurs against my ear.

"If you keep doing that …"

"What? This?" He nibbles my skin.

I brace myself on the open armoire door. "I need to get dressed."

"Clothes are overrated."

I lean into him—ironically already clothed for the day—before turning in his arms for a proper kiss. When his fingers brush under the silk, my hand on his chest pushes him back. "Don't start something you can't finish."

"I wouldn't think of it, my lady." He kisses me again, his fingers roving under my camisole, across my belly button, moving upward—

"We have to meet Wes at nine," I say, removing myself from his grasp for real this time.

"Just be glad it's me kissing you and not this bullmastiff who has decided digging in our unplanted fields is his new favorite thing."

Finan leans to the side, and just behind him sits a grinning,

WELCOME TO PLANET LARA

growling Humboldt, tail wagging, saliva-soaked, multicolored rope toy clamped in his jaw—and his front legs filthy to his elbows.

"Ewwww! Oh my god, get him out of here! Did he track dirt through the whole cabin?"

Finan laughs. "I'll clean it up. Come on, Humboldt. Time for breakfast. Let your mom get ready in peace." Big Dog growls playfully as Finan tugs on his toy and then follows his best buddy into the kitchen.

We'll be out in the boat with Wes this morning, so a black silk button-up blouse and off-white cashmere pullover should be warm enough; the layers will allow me to lighten up if the sun makes an appearance. As I step into my dark gray skinny pants, the delicious soreness of specific body parts reminds me that we didn't get much shut-eye. And I'd be quite contented to go for long, sleepless periods if it meant we could stay in this cabin and revisit the activities of a few hours past.

I hear the kibble pour into Humboldt's metal dog bowl just as Lutris rings. "I'll get it," Finan says.

Clasping my earrings, I move into the hallway so I can hear who's on the line.

"Rupert!" I yell, shuffling into the living room, grateful Finan tidied the mess we made overnight. I'm sure there will be questions about why our lead engineer is answering my Lutris this early in the morning, but bigger matters are on the immediate agenda.

I'm so relieved to see Rupert's face filling my Lutris screen. "Oh my god, you look so much better," I say. "How are you? What's happening?"

"Did you misplace your phone?"

"Um, sort of. It's here somewhere." I look behind me, not actually sure where I left it. "Last night was … eventful."

"I've heard. Tommy filled me in when he phoned Catrina."

"Tell me what's going on with you—"

"Yes, it's B-cell non-Hodgkin's, slow growing and very treatable. Yes, I'm still in hospital but not in ICU. Kidneys are fine. Home today, and my first monoclonal antibody immunotherapy treatment is in three days. It's managed."

"Rupert …"

"No, no time for blubbering. We need to deal with what happened over there."

Finan rests a hand on my lower back. "She's a psycho, Rupert. Connor was here and he said a bunch of super-mean stuff about me. And Kelly outed my mom—told everyone about the cartel. How can I face her without tearing out her screeching throat?"

Number Two's face looks too pale through the screen. I don't know if it's the cancer or Kelly Lockhart's bullshit. Probably both.

"Finan, farm B—you have an inspector coming over?"

"Yes. I've hired a private firm. He'll be here this afternoon. I covered the site with tarps last night, after leaving Kelly's little performance."

Rupert nods. "And Wes?"

"We're picking him up from the 9 a.m. ferry," I say.

"I'll have him to the house the minute he's done with you."

"Rupert—"

"I will send Catrina back to Thalia with a more secure mode of communication. Until then, nothing on Lutris, nothing on your phones. Do you both understand?"

Finan nods beside me.

"But why is Catrina coming back so soon? Don't you need her?"

Rupert's smile suggests he's got a canary tucked in his cheek. "I have a private nurse starting this afternoon."

"I'll bet you do," I tease. "Update me every hour."

Rupert flops a hand at the screen.

"Fine. Every day, then."

"After Catrina arrives tonight, retrieve the care package I'm sending with her. You can phone me then."

"But … what am I going to do about Mom? How am I going to handle this?"

Number Two leans back against the pillows of his hospital bed. "You're not. Not a word. You don't owe anyone anything. Your mother's life was hers, not yours." Finan squeezes my shoulder and then rubs my back. "I'll get the CI PR department, and the lawyers, on standby. And it looks like you have a trustworthy ally over there, so the two of you ... be careful."

A glance at Finan shows a mild blush coloring his face. It's cute. "We'll talk tonight. And take care of yourself," Finan says.

"Take care of our girls, young Finan. I'm relying on you."

"Yes, sir."

Rupert ends the call.

Our girls ... Thalia Island ... and me.

An unfamiliar warmth wraps around the aforementioned chunk of granite in my chest.

"Last night—I didn't tell you what Wes told me about the cave paintings. He thinks we have a *cult* on the island, Finan."

He utters a sound that is not quite a laugh and very much incredulous. "A *cult*?"

"I meant to tell you everything after I got back, but the vertical farm fire and then Kelly's big show last night—"

"Can you give me bullet points on the drive to the ferry?" Finan asks, looking at his watch. I nod. "Finish getting ready. I'll make you a smoothie to go. And grab a coat. We'll take Wes right to the beach—I don't want him in town if we can help it."

"He would certainly attract attention—a handsome, very muscled Indian man with a beard even more impressive than yours. Pretty hard to miss." I slide into the bathroom to deal with hair and makeup while Finan opens my fridge in search of smoothie ingredients.

"You have nothing to eat, unless you want a wine smoothie."

"Grapes are fruit. Breakfast of champions," I say. I hear the fridge close.

Finan appears at the open bathroom door. "Where's the picnic basket?"

The picnic basket with the bones Humboldt exhumed. The actual reason for Wes Singh's urgent visit today.

"In the closet in my room. I didn't want Big Dog to get into it."

Finan nods and moves into my room, retrieving the basket. On his way past the bathroom, he stops and leans in for a kiss, his lips soft against mine, his free hand against my cheek like he's cradling a Fabergé egg. "I'll take Humboldt and go across to my place where there is actual food. Meet you outside in twenty."

I kiss him back and then swat his ass before he escapes. "You forgot to bow before making your departure."

He turns and bows deeply, his hand flat against his heart. "Forgive me."

"I'll punish you later."

"I look forward to it, my lady."

FORTY-THREE

THREE-HOUR TOUR

Sergeant Wes Singh is a formidable man, even when he's not overseeing your arrest for public intoxication and a rather spirited bout of chardonnay-fueled vandalism.

He strides off the ferry walkway and into the grassy greeting area of the parking lot where we're waiting, offering his hand as I introduce him to Finan. He then turns to me. "Update on Rupert?"

"I spoke to him this morning. It's non-Hodgkin's lymphoma"—I swallow my sadness because now is the time for business—"but you know Rupert. He said he wants to see you as soon as we're done. They're discharging him today."

"That's good news, yes? Being discharged already?" Wes kneels to give Humboldt his undivided attention or else risk losing the skin on his hand from sandpapery bullmastiff tongue. "Whatever Rupert needs."

Finan gestures toward the marina. "Shall we? We're trying to keep a low profile today."

"Seems you folks already have your fair share of drama." He nods at the blanket-wrapped picnic basket in my left hand.

"You have no idea," I say, falling in line behind Finan and Wes. Humboldt is all too happy to be bouncing toward the boat again. I'm glad to let the men handle the launch of our vessel while I wrangle the dumb dog into his life jacket. Wes explains he spent childhood summers on Vancouver Island with his cousins, so boating is in his blood. Small talk fills the time until we're clear of the marina, out of the no-wake zone.

Then Wes switches gears. "Show me what you found."

I move into the cabin, gesturing for him to follow and sit. It's remarkable how much smaller the below-deck space is with Wes Singh hunched inside. I pull the picnic basket out and uncover it, revealing the bones. Wes extracts purple nitrile gloves from his jacket pocket and slides them on before gently removing our ghoulish find.

"Definitely human," he says. "I think we're going to need a forensic anthropologist on this."

"Not a pathologist?"

"Not yet. There's no body and not much in terms of remaining tissue. An anthropologist would be the best place to start. We work with a few up at UBC. They specialize in postmortem osseous examination and could quickly tell us if these are from a male or female." He flips and examines the opposite side of the bones. "They're pretty fresh. Doesn't look like they've been in the water, and they're not sun-bleached. Should still have viable DNA. Plus the hardware here"—he points at the metal holding the bones together—"it should have a serial number or at least a company name and date of manufacture on it. And if the person these bones belong to is in the system, we should have a pretty quick ID."

"And if not?"

"Then we start looking at missing persons' and accident reports, a more comprehensive DNA profile search outside Canada—believe it or not, if the decedent ever used one of those ancestry DNA analysis companies, forensics can search those too. If this person has been reported missing by family or friends, we can ask for DNA samples from personal effects and then make the comparison."

Wes returns the bones to the basket and recovers them. "You have anything more inconspicuous than a picnic basket wrapped in a blanket?"

"I think we have compostable garbage bags on board—"

"Are they paper?"

"Of course. Welcome to Thalia Island, sir."

As Finan pulls up to the island's west side, it's clear someone has been here since our visit last week.

"Any surveillance at all on this side of the island?" Wes asks, leaning against one of the fishing seats as Finan drops the anchor. I turn and lift an eyebrow at Wes's question; Finan smirks.

"No surveillance. At least not yet," I say, pivoting back to Wes. "I've been overruled. Something about how the new residents don't want to live in a police state."

"Sure they don't. Until they're in a state when they need the police." Wes takes the waders Finan offers and steps into them. They won't fit over his chest or shoulders, but he's quick to improvise with the belt from his black cargo pants. He catches me smiling. "I'm used to it. I was basically born with a full beard."

"Your poor mom."

"From your lips to her ears." He grins.

Humboldt again launches himself into the water and trots up onto the pebbled sand. As Finan drops into the strait and reaches for me, I point a finger at Wes. "If you ever tell anyone I'm being carried ..."

Wes feigns zipping his lips and laughs as I lean over Finan's shoulder. "At least she's wearing boots today," Finan teases.

"These are Bottega Veneta. They cannot get wet, Mr. Rowleigh."

Wes snorts and follows us out of the boat and up the beach.

The firepit is where we left it, though blackened evidence of a fresh fire sits at its center, the perimeter rocks unburied. I point in the direction Humboldt came from after he found the bones; Finan and I tag-team recounting the details from our prior visit. Wes is careful to walk along the harder sand at the waterline, his phone out for photos. The four upright driftwood posts are still in place, except from one hangs a wilted canvas.

"That's new," I say.

Wes stops and pulls more nitrile gloves from his pocket for Finan and me. Gloves on, he carefully tugs on the canvas and looks at the other three posts. "Maybe someone's using it as a picnic area?"

"Maybe."

"Do you guys do that? Have people over here for picnicking and campfires?"

Finan shakes his head. "There's no access to this side of the island other than by boat. And only a few residents have their own water-craft." He steps back and cranes his neck at the rock face. "Unless someone rappelled down the side from the forest above. But even that would take a huge effort since there's no access road through the wooded area. This swath of the island is untouched, other than a few clear-cut spots for the wind turbines."

Wes nods and takes a handful of photos of the unremarkable canvas.

"You said there's a cave?"

"Over here." I lead the way.

Finan calls Humboldt and makes him sit so as not to disrupt anything inside the rocky armpit. Good thing too—this firepit has also been recently used. Wes pulls a narrow but powerful flashlight from his cargo-pants pocket and illuminates the wall. He exhales slowly, scrubbing a hand down his face and beard.

"Holy shit," he mutters.

"Do you think this is Dea Vitae?"

"Definitely." Wes takes dozens of photos, asking me to hold our flashlights so he can get every detail. "I don't think I can keep this to myself. Vancouver PD will want to see this too." He pockets his phone and tiptoes around the cave, looking for anything else that might be of use. My heart thuds; my feet feel too heavy.

"Can we see about the bones first and then tackle the markings? I'm afraid if your guys swarm the island, whoever this is will get spooked," I say.

Wes rejoins us at the cave's mouth, one hand on his hip. "Yeah. I'll get my forensics contact going first. Any way you can get me a list of your residents?"

I look at Finan. I don't know if that's even legal.

"I'll talk to Rupert," I offer. "He'll know what we're allowed to do. I'm not sure what kind of confidentiality agreements we have in place."

"Given what's happening in here, subpoenas and warrants will likely follow. Just so you're aware."

I nod.

"The staff sergeant heading the Dea Vitae task force is a good friend. I'll show him what I've got from today. As long as you don't feel like anyone is in danger on the island, we can do this nice and slow. Need to establish chain of custody so we don't screw up any potential future prosecution. And the best way to track cults is quietly, under their skin when they're not looking. We'll need more before we can get warrants, and I don't want to make a big show of coming to the island with a van full of constables unless we absolutely have to."

"Oh my god ..." I press a hand to my forehead against the flood of panic. "Honestly, Wes, we cannot handle another PR problem. We had the food-poisoning situation, and then the vertical farm burned down the other night."

"I think all this is connected somehow."

"You do?" Finan asks, releasing Humboldt's collar so he can run. Though I raced through the Dea Vitae highlights for Finan during our short drive to the ferry, there's still much to add for the full picture.

"As I told Lara, Dea Vitae is like an infection. Once they target where they want to be, they actively move in, doing whatever is necessary to scare off anyone who's already there. Out in the Fraser Valley and beyond, if there's land they want, they cause all kinds of problems for the people who already own it. Poisoned cattle, ruined crops, torched barns—these are not nice folks."

"And Rupert pooh-poohed me when I said we might have saboteurs on the island," I say.

"In this day and age, never say never. Especially with the run of bad luck you've had."

"Do you think the vertical farm fire—or the salmonella—could those things have been done *intentionally?*" Finan asks.

Wes shrugs. "There was a situation in Oregon back in the '80s where a religious group poisoned the salad bars at a bunch of restaurants in a small town. Over seven hundred people got sick," he says.

My stomach clenches anew with the reminder of my own bout with the suspect food, the devastated reputation my friend Émile is still dealing with—and the idea that someone could have done this on purpose.

"What Lara and Rupert and I are concerned about *right now* is what all this means to Thalia Island, if our residents are in danger, and who those bones belong to."

Wes bobs his head once and scratches his bristled chin. "I can't tell you that no one here is in danger. You don't have a police presence on the island, and no surveillance to speak of. If it were me, I would definitely keep one eye looking over my shoulder until we get some answers."

"I can't believe this. Do you think it's one of our residents?" Kelly's face flashes in my head—of course it does, after what she did last night. But I'm afraid to mention the town hall fiasco to Wes. Last thing I need is him sniffing around my mother's past missteps.

"Hard to say," he says.

"I really need to get my hands on those files in Kelly's office," I say to Finan.

"Let's do this one step at a time," Wes says. "You get me whatever you can about the people living here. I'll do some digging about anything weird happening on the other Southern Gulf Islands, see if there have been any reports that could be related to Dea Vitae but haven't yet been connected."

He turns again and surveys the cave, mumbling to himself about the size of the mural. "Finan, any chance you can get me back to Horseshoe Bay in your rig instead of via the ferry?"

FORTY-FOUR

A VERY GOOD BOY

Finan navigates up to the outermost dock to drop off Humboldt and me so he can taxi Wes back to the mainland. I'll take his truck into town—as much as I don't want to face anyone after what happened last night, or gods forbid, run into Connor if he's still here, I can't be a coward today. I have to take care of Thalia Island.

As I pull up to town hall, my stomach falls into my feet. Sure enough, Connor and Suze are still here, chatting and smiling with Kelly and Hunter in the round, blossom-filled courtyard to the right of the town hall entrance. Kelly's flirty smile dissolves when she realizes it's not Finan behind the wheel of his truck.

I know how to handle this. I've grinned through tempests before.

Humboldt hops free from the back seat but sticks close to my side instead of running to greet the new faces. Even my dog is a good judge of character.

I look at the time on my phone. "Last I recalled, it's a workday, Kelly, Hunter, not a vacation day. Paychecks here are *earned*," I say, walking past without a second glance at Connor or his fresh-faced fiancée.

"Lara, wait," Connor calls behind me. I don't stop moving, instead pulling open the front door to town hall, stepping aside for Big Dog to enter ahead of me. "Lara, please."

Connor has the nerve to grip my upper arm. I glare down at it. "Remove your hand."

He does. "Can we talk for a second?"

I continue my path into the building, not bothering to acknowledge any of the residents inside collecting mail or standing about chatting. After last night, I don't owe these people a thing, and in fact, if I have it my way, our residents' list will undergo a significant shift before the next full moon.

I drop my keys and bag onto my desk and poke my mouse to rouse my Mac. The countdown clock on the screen adjusts itself: 344 days to go.

"Lara, please, can you just stop moving for one minute?"

Fingers poised on my desk's edge, I deign a glance at Connor. He looks skinny and short, and his fake tan has left a stain on the collar of his wrinkled button-down. "I think you said everything you needed to last night, Mr. Mayson. Get out of my office. And get off my island."

Connor instead slides into the room, but then Humboldt is on his feet, hackles raised. A low warning rumbles from his throat. Connor flinches and subtracts his presence by two steps. "Is that dog going to bite me?"

"It *is* past his lunchtime. Anything's possible, I suppose."

Connor freezes in the doorway, his eyes on Humboldt but his words directed at me. "Lara, please, I'm sorry for how everything went down at that meeting. When Kelly Lockhart contacted me, she said it was because she was worried about—"

Humboldt graduates from the growl to a snarl, intimidating canines exposed, followed by a menacing single bark.

"I'd leave if I were you." I sit in my chair and move the keyboard in front of me, clicking my Lutris app open to start my day, offering no outward clue that I am up to my ears in a shit tsunami.

Connor exhales his defeat. "I didn't know that stuff about your mom. I didn't know Kelly was going to say all that." He offers his palms in front of his legs. "Good doggy. You're a good doggy."

Humboldt's ensuing chain of warning barks echoes off my office walls—extra cookies for the dog who says all the things screaming inside my head.

"If you want to talk—"

"I don't."

Humboldt charges, sending Connor skittering out and down the hall. Big Dog only chases a few steps outside my door before returning and squeezing in behind my desk to lay his giant sloppy muzzle in my lap. I scrub his cheeks and neck with my shaking hands and smooch the top of his head, smoothing my lipstick from his fur. "Thank you, Humboldt. You're such a good boy."

I rise and dig through the delivered pet-store box. "What did Uncle Finan order for you, hmmm?" There's a huge bag of Greenies, his favorite snack, so I give him one. Plus a red chewie thing filled with very stinky chunks of meaty treats. I swear my four-legged bodyguard smiles at me when he flops onto the area rug.

I lean against my desk to calm my racing heart.

Because the day's not over.

Courage, Lara Jo, my grandfather says in my head.

A quick glance out my door reveals a quieter lobby. Maybe Humboldt scared everyone else away too. I look in the opposite direction to find Kelly's office dark; her new Hunter-installed lockset shines under the overhead LED lights.

The kitchen has lots of drawers and cupboards. Surely one holds a toolbox?

After a thorough inspection, I do indeed find a small collection of maintenance implements in the small pantry closet—along with some organic red licorice I would be happy to ingest. Hammer and flathead screwdriver in hand, I tuck the licorice packet into my back pocket and return to the hallway.

Hunter is a terrible handyman. With the flathead jammed against the keyhole, it only takes one solid punch with the hammer on the screwdriver's wooden handle to pop the whole lockset clean off. I extract my massive key chain and open all the filing cabinets, helping myself to the settler files in heaping armfuls, scooped and deposited on my desk.

I've got the last load in my arms when I hear the clicking of cheap heels on the hardwood floor. Kelly's shrill voice rings in my left ear as I push her out of the way with the weight of folders in my arms. "What are you doing? You have no right to those!" Her shrieks follow me down the hall. I turn left into my office, dropping the last load onto my desk, eyeing where the hammer and screwdriver are, you know, just in case this gets weird.

Kelly storms in behind me. "You shouldn't even be here—everything I said last night at that meeting is true. No one wants you on the island. We took a vote after you left. The majority of the settlers want you to leave."

"Do they." I sit on the edge of my desk, in front of the mountain of files, and pull a single rope of licorice from the paper package. I take an aggressive bite but don't offer Kelly any. Petty, but I'm fine with petty.

Kelly crosses her arms and stands defiantly in my doorway where Connor was a few minutes ago. "You are nothing but the bastard daughter of the worst kind of human. You're just like your mother," she says with a nasty snicker. "I knew her. Oh, indeedy-do, I knew her years ago. Always a sneaky piece of work, trying to get away with everything, breaking your grandfather's heart, spending his money like he owned the World Bank. How many lives do you think she ruined flying drugs all over the place? How could your grandfather even *look* at you without wanting to drown you?"

"Are you done here, Kelly? I have a lot of work to do," I say, gesturing to the files behind me. I keep tearing bites from the licorice; I don't dare wipe at the nervous sweat gathering on my upper lip.

"Those files aren't meant for your eyes."

"I am the project administrator of Thalia Island. Rupert Bishop, the actual person in charge of *all* of this"—I circle a hand in front of me —"my immediate superior, and yours as well, has asked me to review settler files to better field questions from the media about the composition of our population. And since you refuse to give me the password to the database where all of this is compiled, I have to create my own."

"Rupert may have all sorts of things to say about this, but Rupert's not here. And that makes me second in command."

I tilt my head. "Not quite sure where you got that organizational chart, but my last name is Clarke. My actual name is on the deed, the official documents filed with the province of British Columbia and with the federal government of this great big, beautiful country, regarding physical ownership of Thalia Island." I drop the last chunk of candy on my desk and stand, stretching to full height, grateful for the three-inch heels on these boots, my hands clasped behind my back, mostly so I don't accidentally punch her stupid face. "So, if you would please get your polyester-blend flannel out of *my office*, I have much to do."

Kelly's haphazardly lined lips tug into a sinister grin. "All the money in the world can't buy you out of what's coming next."

"Like I haven't heard that before," I say, stepping closer until Kelly shuffles backward. As soon as her ugly, magenta-painted toenails cross the threshold of my office, I quietly click my door closed in her face and retreat to my chair, careful to keep composed until she stomps off, her eyes burning a hole through my office's glass wall.

I spin in my chair so no one in the hall can see me, just in time for the first furious tear to race down my cheek. I fumble for my phone to check for messages, hiccuping with relief to see a note from Finan, and attached to it, a photo: a pod of orca that followed them across the strait.

I laugh through the fury and tap out my own text: **No fair that you get orcas. I've had a weasel and a shark in the last hour.**

Just throw a pickle plate at them. Works every time.

And me, fresh out of pickle plates.

Happens to the best of us.

How far away are you?

I'm going to wait for Catrina. Plus the boat needs a charge.

You guys need a ride from the dock?

Tommy will grab us. Stand guard against weasels and sharks. I'll see you tonight. Maybe for dinner?

As long as there's dessert too.

Count on it.

The brief text exchange calms my quivering hands and thundering pulse. I pluck a tissue from the nearby box to dab at my eyes and nose, followed by a quick dig through my bag for a pressed-powder compact. Upon unzipping the interior side pocket, my hand freezes.

The thumb drive from my mother. I'd forgotten all about it.

How can I look at it now? What if there's information on it that proves everything Kelly said last night? Where did she even hear about my mother's exploits?

God, I would give anything for Rupert to be here. And I know how selfish that sounds—he's engaged in an actual life-or-death battle, whereas I'm just feeling sorry for myself because a bully said some mean stuff about my dead mother.

Still …

As soon as Catrina arrives tonight with whatever "care package" Rupert has put together, calling him is the very first thing I will do. He'll know how to fix this.

I tuck the torn envelope back inside the pocket, pull out my compact and smooth my foundation, and spin my chair so it is again facing this bushel of paper. I give my grandfather's ring a twist on my middle finger so the gemstone shines up at me—and kiss it.

"For luck," I say to Humboldt, watching me from his spot next to the couch. "It's going to be a long day, partner."

Big Dog responds by rolling onto his side, stretching his back leg, and farting.

FORTY-FIVE

TIAMAT MEA FORTITUDINEM

When Finan said I am wicked with spreadsheets, he wasn't wrong. With breaks only long enough for Humboldt and me to manage our bladders and grumbling bellies, I'm three-quarters through the settler files when my phone buzzes against my desktop at 5:02 p.m.

We're leaving Horseshoe Bay. See you in 60 or so.

Motor safely. Bring me an orca—I need a hug.

An orca would love to hug you … with its teeth.

They don't hunt humans.

No, but they'd make an exception. You are very tasty.

Perv.

Not a perv. Truth teller.

The spreadsheet open on my huge screen contains baseline identifying information for nearly all the settlers, but upon scanning through it, my eyes cross. Nothing in these files indicates that anyone on the island is involved in anything untoward, and certainly not a dangerous cult like Dea Vitae.

Banking data, listed so qualifying island residents can receive their monthly stipend, doesn't show anyone doing business with any offshore or unknown financial institutions—only familiar Canadian banks and credit unions. The island's wealthiest residents, the Corwins, list two American banks, but she's a well-known author and her husband is a respected, tenured professor at a major local university. Certainly if they had ties to an insidious cult, people would've figured that out ages ago.

The one thing I don't have in the spreadsheet are photographs. Maybe cult members have some unique physical identifier—a tattoo? A specific haircut? An unusual piercing? A branding like that icky sex-cult guy out of New York? Though I haven't spent a lot of time hanging around the new residents, I've not noticed anything I would consider unusual. Kelly has a tattoo, but I'm almost positive it's something related to Disneyesque mermaids.

Based on what Wes told me—Dea Vitae targets smart people with tech and science backgrounds—I scroll through my columns to find residents with occupations that might align. A whisper in the back of my head remembers that among the list of recruitable occupations, Wes mentioned engineers.

Finan is an engineer. Times two.

No way. Finan isn't insane.

I hate that I have to suspect everyone, especially someone I let into my body last night.

I'm glad no one's here to see my sly smile.

I pull from the stacks the folders of residents with big brains. Everyone had to submit photos with their applications, so there are at least a few in each physical file. Even going on social media and looking at who has accounts and what photos they've posted—nothing stands out. These people look so normal, it borders on boring. Other than some questionable hairstyle choices, they all look healthy and well-adjusted and accomplished, and no one seems creepy or like they belong to a cult that would sacrifice a human to appease some ancient avenging goddess.

Eventually, that gritty, gnawing ache settles in behind my eyeballs from too long staring at the screen. I need a break. And maybe some eye drops.

"I don't think there's anything here, Humboldt." I close the folder in front of me and sink back into my chair. Big Dog lifts his head long enough to look up at me, thump his tail against the floor twice, and fall back asleep on a sigh.

Clicky heels in the hallway pull my attention to my glass wall. Kelly hurries past, her huge, tacky purse over one shoulder and Hunter in tow, an iPad settled against his arm, the opposite hand typing away as Kelly utters something I can't hear over her shoes. Neither of them looks at me when they pass.

Good.

I cross my arms on my desk to rest my head for a minute. Upon reopening my eyes, I see my purse sitting on the floor near my feet. The purse that holds the thumb drive from my mother.

I really need to see what's on it. I need to be able to defend myself when the next wave of attacks comes, since it inevitably will as long as Kelly and I are still both on Thalia Island. And it's only a matter of time before the press gets wind of yet another Clarke family scandal and starts digging up the past. Maybe they already have. I'm surprised Wes Singh's friends haven't come knocking on my forehead in the wake of Kelly's sell-out show.

But like Rupert said, I need to worry about the island right now.

Before I lose my nerve, I grab my bag and pull the torn envelope from the inside pocket. The thumb drive fits into the USB port on the back of my computer. Once it registers on the desktop, I double-click to open.

Five labeled folders appear, just waiting for me to release the ghosts living within: *Lara, Photos, School Info, Financials,* and *JR.*

My pulse plays a beat in my ears, and my face burns.

Do I really want to do this?

I need you to be a Clarke.

"Here goes nothing," I mutter, clicking the folder with my name on it, my hands clammy on the mouse.

Inside are photos of me—photo after photo after photo of my infancy and childhood, my skinned knees and messy uniforms and ripped pants and tangled braids and toothless grins and even me sleeping ... so many photos of me sleeping. The photos are named and organized by date, which makes it very easy to see the pattern of when Cordelia was around, and the long spans when she'd disappear. There are no photos during those blackouts of motherhood, at least not in here, but if there had been, the emotions expressed would've been the opposite of the smiling Lara in the other shots.

Farther down the dated list are more pictures of me but she didn't take these—they're from other sources. School photos, photos my grandfather or Rupert took at special events, the day I got my braces on, and off, my short-lived horse phase until I learned how incredibly boring dressage was and how much it hurts to get bucked off a stubborn Westphalian, a photo from the prom I almost shut down when a prank involving silly string, lab mice, and vodka went sideways, as well as shots taken from my own social media accounts and even more recent photos from the tabloids.

But that makes *zero* sense. Cordelia has been gone since I was ten. Who would've compiled this database of my life after her death? It has to be Rupert—my grandfather was useless with computers—plus, who else would take the time? And why did he give me the thumb drive *now*?

Another subfolder pops up in the Lara main folder. I open it—not photos, but letters. Some handwritten—journal entries and notes written on stationery from hotels in distant lands, scanned or photographed—others typed up, as if Cordelia paused her adventures long enough to borrow a typewriter or open a laptop and bang out a few lines for the kid she left behind.

Hello, my baby Lara Jo, I met a tarantula today named Spike. A Goliath bird-eating spider. SO big! I didn't even scream ... he was actually very sweet.

I click open the next file:

Hey, hey, Lara J, it's your mom. Just landed in northern Bolivia. We'll be here for a few days to hike into the jungle before we head down to La Paz to help our South American sisters continue their fight toward passing Law 071, the Law of the Rights of Mother Earth. I'll be taking my camera into the jungle to document native endangered species—just wait until you see the giant otters, Lara! They make our BC sea otters look like house cats!

And the next:

Hello again from high above the clouds, my Lara … Rupert says you got into a fight at school again. I'm glad you're standing up for yourself, but come on, kid —I told you that punches are for after the bell rings …

Letter after letter, note after note—why the hell have I never seen these?

I don't know if I should be angry or sobbing—or both—and I've only opened three of probably a hundred or more pieces of correspondence in this subfolder. Why did they keep these from me when they *knew* how much I missed her? My fists clench so hard, my unmanicured nails dig into my palms.

I click back to the thumb drive's main directory. The *Photos* file is full of exactly what it says, except they're my mother's photographs from around the globe. Stunning images fill my screen, everything from the endangered giant otters she mentioned in the letter to aerial expanses of Amazon rainforest, farmed steps carved into verdant hillsides, snaking brown rivers flanked by green shores, smiling citizens in colorful ceremonial clothing. She's photographed so many jungle scenes, I have no idea what countries these were taken in. When the landscapes change in tone and texture, the flora and fauna change with it—instead of bird-eating spiders and saucer-size insects, they're lions and elephants and cheetah and giraffes and the fearsome open jaws of lunging hippos. I knew she spent time in Africa from the massive, framed elephant photos in Grandfather's house, but this folder contains a treasure trove of world-class photography.

One name near the top of the alphabetically organized list catches my eye: "Cordi and Jacinta, Mexico." I click on it; it's the photo from the town hall meeting the other night, the one with my mom sitting in the open side of her plane with her arm draped over the shoulders of another woman, both of them young and healthy and gorgeous, as if neither had a care in the world.

I AirDrop it to my phone. I want to have this photo with me all the time, even if Kelly Lockhart tried to make it part of her slanderous puppet show.

I could spend hours scrolling, and eventually, I will. I'm also going to see about prints—even if some people accuse my mother of terrible deeds, her art deserves to be displayed.

The *School Info* folder isn't about me at all (a relief to not revisit the disappointing grades and frustrated notes from teachers throughout my academic "career") but is instead filled with documents mostly written in Spanish—these must pertain to the schools she had a hand in opening down in Mexico. The *Financials* folder contains dense spreadsheets detailing business expenses for what looks like two different planes as well as the money spent to open and maintain the aforementioned schools and maybe a medical clinic?

I don't know what I'm looking at, and I'm guessing income and outflow of dirty money isn't something one lists in Excel. If I was hoping to find evidence in this folder to indict or exonerate Cordelia Clarke, I'll need to consult a forensic accountant who knows far more about money laundering than I do.

The final folder, *JR*, is password protected.

"Seriously?" I say to the quiet.

I try my name. I try my mother's name. And Grandfather's. And Rupert's. All our middle names. Our names backwards. Our names with our birthdates. The names of my mom's beloved menagerie of childhood pets she told me stories about when she was around. Even the name of her friend from the photo—Jacinta Ramirez, in case that's who the *JR* represents.

Nothing.

My buzzing phone scares a squeak from me.

Just docked. Tommy's here to drive us out. Catrina has a package from Rupert.

I'm still at town hall. I'll lock up and meet you at home.

I eject the USB drive and slide it back into my purse, realizing that time got away from me and I didn't drag Kelly's filing cabinets into my office. I do, however, have a small coat closet that locks.

Humboldt watches curiously as I toss aside the two trench coats hanging within so I can organize the residents' folders in tall stacks inside the closet. "That'll work for tonight, hey, Big Dog?" He tilts his head at me. I lock the knob from the inside and give it a test pull once closed to make sure it's secure. Unless someone reenacts my earlier malfeasance and knocks the doorknob out with a hammer, we're probably good until morning.

With my things gathered and Humboldt stretched and ready to move, I lock my office after us and then take a quick stroll to see if I'm the only person left in the building. Seems that's a yes. I've not seen Ainsley or Stanley at all today, nor did I think to check their Lutris avatars; I know Tommy was busy at the diner before picking up his wife and Finan. I check over my shoulder again and walk into council chambers, my heart thudding as last night's ambush replays in my head.

The room has been tidied, though the recycle bin near the door is full of folded and crumpled meeting agendas. I pull out one of the sky-blue photocopied pages and stuff it into my bag. Humboldt moves through the aisles of the empty, half-round gallery seating, his snorting nose pressed to the merlot carpet. This is the only room in town hall with synthetic floor covering—I'm guessing it's intended to dampen the noise of bodies walking and maneuvering about the padded benches.

I walk along the top of the room, stopping in the middle, just behind the back row, and take a slow 360° view to see from where the slideshow was projected, where the light controls are, how I managed to miss that Kelly was up to no good.

This row had the best seats in the house to watch the drunken meltdowns of the misdirected, motherless heiress cast upon that screen.

Guess I should be grateful Finan didn't have his camera phone out when he found me in my bedroom last night, half a bottle of Suntory Toki galloping through my bloodstream. Wouldn't want that image to feature in the next presentation.

Humboldt ambles down to the podium, sniffing with more vigor, which suggests he needs to pee. "Come on, Big Dog. Let's go home." He lifts his head and moves toward the wide carpeted steps. He's three stairs away from meeting me at the door when something two rows down catches my eye. A dark red strip of fabric, wedged into the seat crease of one of the padded benches.

I shimmy between the rows and pull it free. It's a woven bracelet, sort of like the embroidery-thread friendship bracelets we made in middle school arts & crafts. Instead of braided strings to tie it to a wrist, silver clasps have been clamped to the half-inch-wide ends, though one is missing, which probably explains why it's here and not on the person who owns it.

But it's the black metal charm stitched in place at the bracelet's center that catches my attention.

It's a wave. And not just any wave—the wave from the cave on Cordelia Beach: a claw of imminently crashing water with snake-like projections and a red gem in the middle. Words have been etched along the circle's outer edge: *Tiamat Mea Fortitudinem.*

I'm shaking again, and I suddenly feel like I'm being watched.

My first instinct is to google this phrase—it is Latin?—but then I remember what Rupert warned: *"Nothing on Lutris, nothing on your phones."* I'll have to wait until I get back to the cabin to see whatever secure device he's sent over with Catrina.

"Humboldt, come. Time for dinner."

As I lock up town hall, I remind myself to take normal steps and regular breaths, to pull out of the parking space and drive down Main Street at a reasonable speed, just in case someone *is* watching.

Once the truck's front tires hit the town limits, I floor it.

FORTY-SIX

SPECIAL DELIVERY

I park Finan's truck in front of his cabin and then jog with Humboldt over to my place so I can feed him and maybe pour myself a glass of wine to calm the head-to-toe jitters.

I'm just pulling the cork when there's a knock, met by a single bark as the door opens and Catrina's face pops through. "Oh, tell me you have a glass of that to spare," she says.

"Of course! Come in!" I hurry over to relieve her of the familiar cactus-leather satchel. Definitely from Rupert. And when I take it from her hand, she almost wilts against me. "Hey, you OK?"

She wraps her arms around me in a tight hug. I hear her sniff against my shoulder. Then she pushes away. "I'm exhausted."

"Is Rupert …"

"He's a fighter, Lara. And he's feeling better already, or so he said when he shooed me out of his townhouse this afternoon."

"He said he had a nurse starting today?"

"I helped arrange a revolving schedule of care with home health. He has his underlings at Clarke Innovations, plus our Rupert has a *lot* of friends."

"He does?" How did I not know this?

"He knew you'd fret, so call him after I leave. He can fill you in."

I loop Catrina's arm through mine and pull her to the breakfast bar, practically lifting her onto one of the high stools. "BC Pinot OK?"

"You would be my very favorite person on the planet," she says, clasping her hands before her. "Finan is cleaning up and then he'll be over. He bought some live crab from a guy at Horseshoe Bay. I hope you're hungry."

"You staying for dinner?" I slide a freshly poured glass in front of her. As much as I love Catrina's company, I really need to talk to Finan, and I *really* need to see what's in Rupert's bag of tricks.

"No, no, just a quick glass with you. Tommy's popped into Rupert's cabin, checking the Powerwall and watering his succulents. He'll be over in a sec. He's gotta get back to the diner, and I have to follow up with the growing list of settlers wanting to make get-to-know-you appointments."

"When's the doc arriving?"

"Dr. Liam Stillson. Week from Thursday. Thank heavens."

I lean against the counter and clamp my hands around Catrina's. "Thank you. For everything."

"Not another word." She lifts her wineglass. "To Rupert's restored health, and to Lara, fighting like hell." Our glasses *tink* and we sip. "Kelly Lockhart is a menace," Catrina adds, taking another healthy swallow. When she sets her glass down again, her face is filled with storm clouds. "What she did at the meeting ... if Rupert has anything to do with it, she's not long for Thalia Island."

I'm so relieved to hear Catrina say that, but it needs to come from the horse's mouth for me to believe we can actually boot Kelly off, hopefully right into the hands of Clarke Innovations' high-powered legal team.

"She told everyone ... about my mother," I say. "I don't know how much of it is true. But you can't just go around saying terrible things about people, not like that. Cordelia is still my mom."

"Whatever she got herself involved with was her business. The Cordelia I knew was a good woman with a huge heart who loved fearlessly and often. I see that in you," she says, tapping the back of my hand with her finger. "And for Kelly to drag your ex-boyfriend into the fray—"

"I'm sure he enjoyed every minute of making me look pathetic."

"You're not pathetic. And it says far more about that young man's character that he was willing to participate in such a charade—"

"Knock, knock." The front door opens behind us. It's Tommy. I signal for him to come in as Catrina impressively downs what's left in her glass.

"Thank you for this. I needed it." She stands and meets me halfway, again granting a tight hug. "Call me later. And as soon as I hear from Rupert's oncologists, I'll give you a buzz to translate." She squeezes my upper arms and looks me square in the face. "You are not alone here, Lara. Thalia Island is your home. We will stand by you."

I nod, unable to speak.

"Let us know if you need anything," Tommy says, wrapping his arm around his wife's tired shoulders when she meets him at the door. "And enjoy those crabs. Finan shared, so I know what's on the menu tonight!"

I follow the couple out onto the porch. As they're climbing into their car, Finan, en route to my place with full hands, hollers a thanks and lifts the arm holding a huge pot. Humboldt nearly knocks me over to get past and down the stairs. He whimpers and wiggles his wide butt at Finan, his tail like a whip against his favorite human's legs.

"Wow, somebody missed you," I say. Finan sets the pot down long enough to give Humboldt a scratch and then stops on the bottom stair so we're eye level.

"Anyone else miss me?"

I clamp his head in my hands and kiss him until he groans.

"Tell me there's more of whatever I taste on your tongue," he says.

"Come in, said the spider to the fly," I purr. I reach down and grab the pot, and now that he has a free hand, he wraps an arm around my middle and bites at my ear as we walk into the cabin.

"I hope you like crab," he says, following me into the kitchen. He sets the cloth bag in the sink and I dare peek in. Six Dungeness crabs, still alive, sit at the bottom.

"You're going to bonk them on the head before you boil them, right?" I ask.

Finan chuckles and settles the Dutch oven under the tap to fill with water. "Have you not cooked fresh crab before?"

I shake my head. "I don't know if I can eat them. They look scared."

"They're crab, Lara. They don't look scared. Wine, please." Finan hoists the full pot onto the cooktop and adds sea salt to the water.

"Easy for you to say. You're not about to be boiled alive."

The burner clicks on and he turns his attention to me, his hands on my nape, his lips against mine, our bodies sliding toward one another like they were meant to do just that. Finan kisses me hungrily before pulling back and resting his forehead against mine. "Do you want me to set the crabs free?"

"Maybe."

He kisses me again, but then the playfulness leaves his eyes as he studies my face. "Are you OK?"

I bury myself in his chest, hugging him tight so he can't see my fear. "Today has been very, very hard."

He kisses into my hair, refills our wineglasses, and leans against the counter as we wait for the water to boil. But he reaches over and takes my hand in his, our fingers intertwined, our arms stretched across the short distance. "Tell me everything."

I regale him with the adventures of my very weird day—spreadsheet of settler files, how Kelly got in my face after I hammered my way into her precious office, oh, and the confrontation with Connor—

"Is he still on the island?" Finan's jaw clenches.

"No idea. Humboldt chased him out of my office."

Finan smiles through a sip of wine.

"Not even kidding. Big Dog didn't like the way that dickhead talked to his mom, so he went after him. It was actually kind of awesome."

"Bonus points for Humboldt the Badass."

"I thanked him in dog treats." I look over at the overgrown puppy sprawled in front of the quiet hearth. "Before I left Vancouver, Rupert told me about my mom. About her ... entanglements."

Finan lifts a brow but doesn't let go of my fingers.

"I don't know how much of what Kelly said last night is true. But Rupert gave me a thumb drive, along with a note from my mom. I finally looked at the files."

He closes the distance between us, his hands gentle on my shoulders as he searches my face. I've never had anyone look at me with such kindness. It weakens my knees.

"I need to spend more time going through it—there are a ton of letters and notes from her. I didn't have the strength to read them all today. Plus my priority was to get through the settler files, looking for anything we can give to Wes."

"Anything suspicious?"

"Not yet." I drink to give my tense throat a second to relax so I can talk again. "The drive, though—it has photos of me from my entire life. Like, photos my mom took, but then photos taken after her disappearance. I don't quite understand it."

"And you haven't had a chance to talk to Rupert."

"He's been a little preoccupied, ya know, with cancer," I say through a sad smile. Finan pulls me close, arms locking me to him.

"Let's take this one step at a time. Read through your mother's correspondence when you're feeling strong. Right now, there is a lot going on." Finan maneuvers so we're face-to-face again. "First, we're going to figure out who the hell is trying to sabotage Thalia Island. We will handle the situation with Kelly through legal channels."

"You mean, I can't kidnap and feed her to the wood chipper?"

Finan chuckles. "That just got really dark."

"Really? I thought the wood chipper would be a kindness to humanity. I might get a prize for my service to the planet."

"Remind me not to get on your bad side," Finan says, kissing my forehead.

"Darling, I don't *have* a bad side." I strike a pose as if I'm walking a carpet just as the pot boils.

"Speaking of dark, I need to call Rupert while you commit crabicide."

"Aw, now you're making me feel bad."

"Oh! Shit! I almost forgot! You have to see this!" I hustle around to the other side of the kitchen bar to my bag. From the zippered pocket, I extract the abandoned bracelet I found in the council chambers and hand it over, watching Finan's expression as he inspects it.

"*Tiamat Mea Fortitudinem.* Latin. Meaning what?"

"Haven't looked it up yet—afraid to after Rupert warned us to stay off Lutris and our phones. I found it right before I left town hall, wedged in one of the gallery benches." I grab the satchel Catrina brought and pull out its contents: yet another cell phone, this one small and plain, like the 7-Eleven burner I bought after everything fell apart, and a chunky laptop that looks like it belongs in a war zone.

As if Rupert knew I had my hand on it, the new phone rings. Finan and I lock eyes as I reach to answer it. "Hello?"

"Oh, wonderful. I'm glad to see the package reached its target."

"Rupert, how are you feeling?"

"Fine, fine, I'm fine. I'm home and I have too many carers flitting about monitoring my pee and how many times a minute my heart beats."

"I'm so relieved to hear it."

"Yes, well, I don't want every conversation to be about my health, so let's talk business, shall we?" he says. I smile. "Is Finan within shouting distance?"

"Yesss ... he's right here."

"Hi, Rupert," Finan says.

"Excellent. Put me on speaker, Lara."

It takes a second to figure out how to do that as this alleged smartphone leaves much to be desired.

"Tell me what happened last night and then today with Wes. Start at the beginning and talk slowly. I want to take notes before Wes's arrival within the hour."

I talk, recounting the town hall meeting in the detail I could remember, Finan adding commentary and a different perspective. I repeat Kelly's threats of earlier today, the harsh things she said about me and my mother. I have to stop for a minute to take a deep breath and wipe my nose. I was mad earlier; now I'm just hurt.

"Rupert, she said the residents took a vote after I left. Apparently most of the settlers want me to leave."

He snorts on the other end. "Nonsense. Some informal call to vote from Kelly Lockhart is not how Thalia Island's democracy works. Plus, it's your name on the deed. Or it will be in eleven months, if you successfully complete your year of service."

"We should probably not let Kelly in on that little caveat."

"Right now, I need you two to focus on issues more pressing than Kelly's hyperbolized discontent. Wes is with his forensics contact as we speak. I don't live under the illusion that we're in an episode of some network-television police procedural, but I am hopeful we will find an answer to who those bones belong to in relatively short order. It will determine our next steps."

"And what about Thalia? What do I do until we have news from Wes?"

"You do your job. The island still requires a steady hand on the wheel. Finan will need to meet with the fire inspector—"

"Yeah, two guys are here—my private hire plus the insurance company has sent their inspector over."

"Excellent."

"They're on the island overnight. I had two of my managers take them to the site today. We'll have a sit-down first thing tomorrow," Finan says. I did not know this. Then again, as soon as he showed up with crabs in hand, I blathered on about my own Very Bad and Yucky Day.

"Finan, meet with them at your cabin. Let's keep them out of downtown for now." Rupert pauses for a moment, poking at my nerves. "Sorry. Text from Wes. He's here. Now, Lara, the new laptop and phone are on a private, encrypted VPN. You may use your Thalia-issued phone for day-to-day business, but if you have sensitive developments or information, use this secure burner only. The same protocol shall be followed with the laptop."

"No drone yet?" I ask.

"Ha. The drone laws in British Columbia are very strict, and you don't have the credentials to avoid trouble. And I simply do not have enough red blood cells for any more dramatics."

"Yes, sir," I say. "Have Wes tell you everything he knows about Dea Vitae while he's there. I think we might need a forensic accountant to dig deeper into the settler accounts to see if there's anything hiding in plain sight." *And maybe into the spreadsheets on my mother's thumb drive …*

"Duly noted."

"Update as soon as you can?"

"Indeed. Good night. And please don't burn anything else down." Rupert ends the call before I can ask him about my mother's files. Probably for the best. It's not a conversation I'm wholly comfortable having in front of Finan yet. Sure, I may have offered him every inch of my skin last night, but this level of emotional nakedness … I don't think I'm ready to open myself up like that so early on in whatever *this* is.

Finan kisses my temple and moves back around to deal with the crabs and prepare an ice bath in the sink. I unpack the computer, top up my wineglass, and settle onto the couch. Boxy laptop open, I navigate to the incognito search engine and type in *Tiamat Mea Fortitudinem.*

It takes less than a second: *"Tiamat is my strength*, or *my strength Tiamat*. Tiamat is the sea goddess they're allegedly obsessed with."

Finan's eyebrows stretch toward his hairline. "Not freaky at all."

I then look up Dea Vitae, confident the secure connection Rupert promised will keep my inquiry concealed. I've never been particularly paranoid, but the earlier feeling in council chambers, that I was being watched, is slow to recede.

The search engine returns with a number of hits, most related to the American DEA, or Drug Enforcement Administration, and professional résumé services (*curriculum vitae*). Nothing related to a vengeful goddess. I'm guessing whoever started this cult didn't do a lot of research about who they'd share the name with. I keep scrolling until I find one tiny article deep in the search history, dated just two months ago, with a jarring headline: "Dea Vitae Is Here and They Are Coming for Us All."

I click through. It doesn't look like a legitimate news source—more like a blog if anything—so I'm immediately skeptical. Except as I scan the article, everything Wes told me about Dea Vitae and their practices is detailed within. The article goes and goes, and the writer has hyperlinked footnotes included to back up their claims. Clicking on a few takes me to other sites that mostly offer 404 errors, though there are two articles from legit news sites, including CBC and a *Vancouver Sun* article, both dated within the last twelve months.

I shudder.

"This is real," I murmur. I scroll up and click on the author's bio—allegedly his name is Hale Watts—and search for him separately. He's a journalist with a master's degree from Ryerson, a well-respected Canadian university in Toronto. Bylines that come up include coverage of mostly politics, but then there's a very thin article about his firing from his newspaper job in Victoria due to some inappropriate interaction with a Parliamentary staffer. Nothing else notable after that. He doesn't even appear to have a social media footprint, at least not under his byline name.

I navigate back to the article on Dea Vitae, reading further. Watts is clearly a little off his nut, ranting about Dea Vitae and what they're doing right under the noses of government officials and how he was fired not because he patted some intern on the ass but because he went to Victoria to talk to Members of Parliament about what's going on with this cult and they refused to hear him, "because a number of MPs, particularly from the Fraser Valley, have a financial stake in Dea Vitae interests."

"Whoa," I say. "Finan, you have to read this."

"Read it to me."

I move the laptop to the breakfast bar so I can keep my voice low, just in case someone is in fact listening. I scan Watts's article and share the juicier bits, looking up between breaths to see Finan's concerned scowl. Once I've gotten to the bottom, I click through to the other articles on Watts's website, trying not to let his more out-there pieces diminish what I've just read about Dea Vitae.

"Why isn't there more online about these people?" I ask. "Clarke Innovations has to jump through major legal hoops and petition courts to get Google to take stuff down about us. Or the SEO team buries the articles with positive spin, but there's, like, *nothing* here about Dea Vitae. Makes me skeptical."

"You heard what Wes said—they have smart people in their ranks. Smart people who know tech."

"Sure, but hacking Google? Come on."

Finan shrugs. I try to pretend I don't hear the squeaks coming from the huge pot as he drops in the last live crab.

I retrieve the found bracelet, grasping it with a tissue instead of my bare fingers. "There is nothing here that would make me look twice if I didn't know any better," I say.

BAM!

I shriek at the same time Humboldt jumps to his feet and barks aggressively; even Finan bites off a curse.

"What the hell was that?" I ask. The inside of the cabin is deathly quiet, other than Humboldt's anxious breaths and the susurration of frothy boiling water. Finan and I exchange looks; Humboldt bounds toward the front door, sniffing with zeal at the crack between door and floor. He growls and woofs deep and loud again, hackles up.

"Probably just an animal," Finan says. "Humboldt, come." He snaps, and the dog looks back at him, quieting but not moving from his spot. "I'll look."

I reach over and grab a knife from the butcher block on the counter as Finan rounds the island and moves toward the cabin's front. He peeks between the closed curtains.

"Anything?"

He shakes his head no. "Humboldt, sit." The dog obliges, though reluctantly. "If it's a bear, I don't want you to get hurt, man."

"You said there were no bears here!" I whisper-yell.

Finan cracks the front door, his body behind it in case something is waiting for him outside. He widens it a few more inches and when he's certain there's nothing and no one there, he opens the door all the way, barely able to hang on to it as Humboldt races past, his bark on full blast.

I tiptoe toward the open door, my hand on the back of the couch in case I have to hurl myself over it. Finan is crouched on the dimly lit porch, head down, like he's looking at something. I move behind him just as he stands again, his back to me.

He turns, and in his palm is a huge rock. "Uh, what were you going to do with that?" he asks, nodding at the narrow blade tucked against my leg.

"Cut the bad guy into fillets?"

He smirks. "Next time, grab the big one." He then surveys our uncultivated front yards. "Someone threw this." He gives me the hefty stone and then steps off the porch, Humboldt all too happy to join him as they inspect the property.

I don't want to be out here for a second longer, so I retreat back into the warmth and safety of the cabin, struggling to grip the heavy rock in my left hand. I slide the knife onto the counter and drop the stone beside it, noticing that my palm has come away blackened. "What the ..."

I spin the rock by its edge under the pendant lamps hanging over the bar counter. "Finan!" I yell.

He comes bolting back, pausing at the front-door threshold. "Just turn the heat down—"

"It's not the crabs. Come here."

He does. "Is that *writing*?"

I read the rock's cryptic message out loud: "Cordelia Beach. Now."

FORTY-SEVEN

ESCALATION

"Should we tell someone where we're going? In case something happens?"

Finan drained and potted the cooked crabs on an ice bed and stuffed them in my empty fridge while I changed into warm, all-black clothing. He pauses, thinking. "No. We don't know who did this. Probably best we don't tell anyone anything."

"Even Rupert? I could text him on the burner—"

Finan shakes his head no. "Write a note. Leave it on the counter. If we go missing, they can start there."

"This is really freaking me out."

He dries his hands on a kitchen towel and then pours Humboldt's dinner. "We need to leave him here."

Once we have my cabin secured—and Rupert's military-grade laptop hidden in my armoire—we jog over to Finan's and I wait for him to change. When he emerges from his room, also in head-to-toe black, he has a dark camo backpack in one hand, binoculars in the other, and a huge camera hanging from his neck.

"You're a photographer?"

"I dabble," he says, grinning.

"You know my mom was a photographer."

His smile softens. "Archibald gave me my first camera."

"I'd love to see your work sometime."

His cheeks flush as he leans over to tie his hiking boot. "I take pictures of boring stuff—buildings and dirt and solar panel arrays."

"Finan Rowleigh, nothing you do is boring."

He throws on a heavy black jacket, hoists the stuffed backpack over his shoulder, and stops to kiss me, his soft lips lingering. "You ready for an adventure?"

"I hope we don't die. I was really looking forward to dessert."

"Oh, there will be no dying tonight. And I *promise* you will get dessert, my lady." He kisses me again.

We take Rupert's navy-blue Tesla because it is absolutely silent, and it disappears into the shadows far better than Finan's huge silver truck. The only place on the island to see Cordelia Beach, other than by boat, is Mt. Magnus. Navigating the twisty, gravel road in the blanketing dark will be an interesting feat, which is why Finan is behind the wheel—I've had at least two glasses of wine, and I don't want to drive us into a ditch on an island with no tow truck.

"Are you nervous?" I ask, mostly because I can't stand the quiet of the car's interior.

"A little rattled."

I nod. My head itches from the black wool cap he shimmied over my head when we climbed into the car. "Who could've left the rock?"

"No clue."

"It couldn't have been Catrina or Tommy. They would've just knocked. Why the cunning?"

Finan gnaws at his lip. "I'm trying to think of anyone on the crew who would know that any activity at that beach would be of interest to you."

"Because we haven't told anyone *anything*, other than Number Two."

"And Wes."

"Wes the cop who is currently at Rupert's townhouse in Kits and therefore not on Thalia and who wouldn't be a weirdo and throw a rock at my house." I swallow hard. "Jesus, Finan ... this is beyond eerie."

He reaches across the console between us and offers his open hand. I gratefully take it. "Pretty far from those fundraising galas in False Creek ..."

I wrap my other hand around our entwined fingers. "Actually, those things can be terrifying. You never know who has a poisoned tip on their stiletto or a spring-activated blade in their brogue."

"Real tradecraft stuff in society circles?"

"Where do you think Q gets all his ideas for 007?"

He lifts our conjoined hands to his lips for a soft, reassuring kiss. "I'm fresh out of dart-firing fountain pens tonight, but I *do* have your back, Princess Lara."

"I shall promote you to the head of the knights' league without haste."

"It is my honor to serve." He bobs his head quickly but then pulls his hand free to manage the steering on the bumpy forest road. "At the top, we'll park in the tree line and sneak to the overlook so no one sees us."

"This would be so much easier if we just had *surveillance* on the island."

"But not nearly as fun."

"You just don't want to hear *I told you so.*"

"There *is* that." He winks.

～

We're so quiet with parking and exiting, a doe and her baby hardly notice when we tiptoe past them dining on tall grasses. Mom looks up, stiffens for a moment, and then resumes her snack.

About ten feet from the ridge's edge, we drop onto all fours, crawling and then scooting to get the best vantage point without being seen ourselves, which, in all honesty, would only be possible if the people on the other end had binoculars or high-powered lenses aimed at us.

A single glance over the edge reveals that Cordelia Beach is alive with a roaring bonfire—and people. Lots of people.

Finan pushes the binoculars to his eyes. "Uhh …"

"What? What do you see? Can you tell who it is?"

He pulls the cups from his eyes and hands them over. "Prepare yourself."

My stomach tilts. "Is there blood? Am I going to see something terrible—"

"It depends on your definition of terrible."

I gulp and summon whatever courage I can find to push the lenses against my eyes. "Ohhhhh my god … are they—they're having an orgy!" I drop the binocs and look at Finan, barely registering the whites of his eyes in the pitch-dark. "Is that what I'm seeing?"

A cutting wind blows past, carrying noise from the beach to our ears. "Drumming. You hear that, right?" I ask. Finan nods and takes the binocs again.

"Do you recognize anyone?"

"I recognize everyone," he says, his voice icy. "Kelly, Hunter, Stanley, Ainsley, half my crew, new residents—oh dear, I think your ex is down there. They're all naked and dancing around that fire. Well, the people who aren't screwing, at least." He hands over the binocs again and then scoots back to pull his camera from the backpack.

"Are you kidding me? *Connor* is down there?"

"Pretty sure that's him."

"I feel sick."

"Feel less sick and have another look. We're going to need as much eyewitness evidence as possible, and right now, *we* are the only eyewitnesses not engaged in … that." He combat-crawls forward again, his camera affixed with a 180-400 mm telephoto lens. With the viewfinder against his right eye, he clicks shot after shot.

"Is it clear enough? Will we be able to see their faces?"

"Mm-hmm."

I keep watching, even though I know I will never unsee Kelly and Hunter naked and dancing and pausing to do unholy things to one another and whoever else passes by. Even Connor and Suze. "I swear that Connor wasn't into any of this weird crap when we were together."

"What, he never invited his acting buddies over to dance naked around your loft?"

"It's not funny. I am going to need to get tested for absolutely everything under the sun now."

"Don't panic. Maybe he's a new recruit."

"Oh god." I drop the binoculars when I see Suze kneel before Connor, her hands on his ass cheeks. In front of EVERYONE! "I can't watch this."

"Do I want to know?"

I rest my forehead on my wrist for a second. "I cannot believe sweet little Ainsley is down there."

Finan snorts. "Yeaaaaah, 'sweet' is not the adjective I would use here." His shutter clicks a series. "Makes you question whether you can ever really know a person."

I look over at Finan. "Please, *please* tell me you're not part of this. You're not some alpha predator who's dragged me up here under a ruse, and now you're going to knock me out and take me down there for their next sacrifice."

Finan's grin is so wide, it wobbles the camera pushed against his face. "I'm not saying I wouldn't gladly do some of those things to your naked body."

I nudge him with my shoulder and resume spying. "So now I know that if you ask to light a bonfire, you're going to want to dance in our birthday suits and have outdoor sex?"

"Maybe we can have s'mores first."

"Ugh, I will never unsee Hunter's floppy, bouncing little wiener now. Or Stanley! God, gross! And ewww—they're doing all this on the beach named after my mother!"

Finan chuckles but presses a finger against his lips.

He pauses on the trigger for a sec, his smile melting as he switches to video mode. "They've stopped screwing and are gathering ... they're drawing something in the sand. Are you seeing this?"

Reluctantly, I hold up the binoculars again. "It's dark away from the fire. What are they doing—" A large naked man with a very white, protuberant belly, who I recognize as one of our new settlers, has a flailing animal, a raccoon, by the scruff. Kelly is next to him. Her lips are moving, her throat strained as if she's yelling, but we cannot hear what she's saying from this far away.

"Oh shit, Lara, don't look. *Don't look.*" Finan reaches with his right hand to push the binoculars down, but I shrug away and keep them pressed against my eyes.

Lips still moving, Kelly thrusts her right arm into the air. The firelight reflects in whatever's in her grasp, pointed toward the sky.

"Is that a knife—"

Before Finan can answer, Kelly slashes down and cuts the raccoon wide open, blood and innards pouring onto the sand. People launch toward the crimson flow with cupped hands and then wash it over their faces and bodies.

I shriek and drop the binocs, the burn of tears in my eyes and bile in my throat. I scoot backward and launch myself toward the car, stopping to lean one hand on the hood so I can throw up.

I cough and spit and then open the car to retrieve my water bottle from the console to rinse my mouth. Finan remains fixed, taking photos and video. What they just did crossed the line from being some crazy sex-cult bullshit to something far beyond evil.

I sit sideways in the open front seat, my booted feet on the cold, dark, stony ground, just in case I get sick again as the image of that poor raccoon rushes through my head in an endless loop. I can't stop crying ... who would do such a horrible thing?

By the time Finan returns to the car, I'm shivering so hard, my jaw aches from clenching. "Memory cards are full." He tucks his pack and camera into the back seat. "I think we have plenty."

He quietly closes the rear door and kneels before me, his warm hands cupped around my cold ones. "You OK?"

"No."

"Let's get you home and into a tub." He kisses my head. "Don't worry, Lara. We're going to fix this."

I nod, but a fresh wave of tears washes over me as soon as my door clicks shut.

I cry all the way home.

FORTY-EIGHT

INJUSTICE

Though I fell asleep last night sobbing in Finan's arms, I'm awake this morning already exhausted—but with a renewed sense of rage.

I will rid Thalia Island of the vermin that have infested her.

Starting with Kelly Lockhart.

I apply collagen under-eye strips to combat the purple pillows that sprouted overnight—honestly, I still have a shred of pride—and then Finan and I call a weary Rupert, who then adds Wes to a second call. Finan recounts everything we witnessed from Mt. Magnus, and I try to power through the part about them sacrificing that poor raccoon. A few tears slip out, especially when Humboldt whimpers and drops his head in my lap, and the fury of what I would do to anyone who hurt him sears my chest.

"I'm waiting for a call from my forensics guy about the bones," Wes explains.

"So fast?" I ask.

"Depends. If it's a missing persons' case, we should have a quicker answer. We're holding on sending to the provincial crime lab at this point, which is usually what slows things down. Backlogs and all that. If we can get an ID, I'll put the bones in the system then."

"Rupert, what the hell am I supposed to do today? I can't just go into town hall and work. How? *How* can I see her there—or Hunter or Stanley or *Ainsley*—oh my god, and here I thought she was just this nice Scottish grad student growing carrots!"

"Now is not the time for hysterics, Lara," Rupert says, his voice curt. I try not to be offended because I know he's feeling like absolute shit right now, but I don't like being scolded, especially not in front of Finan and Wes. As if he senses this, Finan reaches from his adjacent stool and wraps his hand around mine, settling them both in his lap.

"This has clearly evolved into a criminal investigation," Wes says. "I need you to stand down and behave in a business-as-usual manner until I can get your photos and videos to the investigators. Last thing we need is a misstep that could result in dismissal of evidence. I'll also need recorded and written statements, everything you just told me, from both of you, as soon as possible."

"Will that be enough to get them off the island?" I ask.

"Based on these images, the only thing we have certain evidence of is Causing an Animal to Suffer. Still a big charge, but we want the whole picture."

"Having an orgy on a private beach isn't illegal?"

Wes smirks. "Not technically. We could try to get them for mischief under section 430 given the damage in the cave, and maybe under the Trespass Act, but since the participants presumably live on the island, they're not technically there illegally."

"What about drugs?"

Wes shakes his head. "You'd have to find direct evidence on the beach, plus testing people is complicated, especially after the fact when the drugs might be out of their system and it's doubtful they would willingly comply with testing. Where we're really going to get these people is by establishing their direct ties to Dea Vitae through financial records, bank and wire fraud, things like that. White-collar misdeeds are what will eventually take these people down. That cult leader back in Albany, New York, was convicted of human trafficking too. Who knows what else these people are involved in."

"But animal sacrifice and having group sex on a private beach isn't enough," I say, anger suffusing my face.

"It will be part of the bigger case. We just have to be patient and collect all the crumbs." Wes sighs.

A tremble buffets through me as I think of the bones Humboldt found. "I want them *gone*. My grandfather will roll over in his grave if Kelly and her depraved nitwits are allowed to stay here."

Rupert leans closer to the camera. "Every single one of these people signed conduct agreements when taking residence on Thalia Island. They can be removed for their offenses based on that alone, outside of any criminal involvement."

"When? When can they be removed?"

"As soon as we can activate our private security team," Rupert says.

"Of which we have none on the island," I remind him. "No security, no surveillance. Which is why this is the perfect spot for Dea Vitae to plant seeds."

"Clarke Innovations has private security. Who do you think kept you from being kidnapped all these years?"

"Wait—what?"

Rupert rolls right over me. "We haven't needed private security on Thalia, Lara. Not with fewer than fifty residents up until our first wave of settlers," Rupert says. "We trusted that our selected population would be able to self-manage. These people were *thoroughly* vetted."

"Darling Number Two, hate to tell you, but your vetting system is broken," I bite back. Finan flattens his hand atop my thigh, as if to calm me. I take a deep breath, remembering that Rupert is sick, and he is not the enemy here.

"Bottom line, we're confident these people are involved in Dea Vitae," Wes interjects. "With the cave photos, the bracelet you found, the footage and images from last night—"

"Don't forget the salmonella and the burned-down vertical farm—and the bones! We don't even know who the bones belong to yet!"

"All those pieces will find their place, if they're related."

"They're *totally* related," I mutter.

"But we have to follow the *law*. And what we have in terms of visual evidence, plus statements from you two, should be enough for search warrants. That's where we start," Wes says. "Dea Vitae is definitely on your island. It's just a matter of who, and how many."

Finan squeezes my hand again. "How long will it take for them to move on this?" he asks. "Someone else is on the island—someone who warned us about last night. And we don't know if they're friend or foe."

"We can assume they're friend, if they warned you," Wes says.

"Maybe, unless they're somehow involved. Maybe someone who was with the group but got scared that things were going too far?" Finan rubs a nervous hand over his beard. "It's disturbing. Way above my pay grade, Rupert."

"I will call my head of security at CI as soon as we hang up."

"And what? They will zoom over on hovercrafts and pull Kelly out by her bad blond highlights?"

"We will work in cooperation with what the police would like us to do. This isn't an action film, Lara."

"Get her *off* my island," I growl.

Number Two opens his mouth to speak but is then overcome by a coughing spasm, hard enough that he has to cover his face with a handkerchief and excuse himself for a moment.

"Wes, is he OK?" I ask while Rupert is off camera.

"He thinks he picked up a bug at the hospital."

"Perfect. Just what he needs. Doesn't treatment start tomorrow?"

"I'll stick close," Wes says. "You guys keep your phones with you, just in case."

I make sure he has the number for the new burner. Finan and I then say goodbye with a quick message in the chat to Rupert that he is to GO TO BED. Wes promises again to text or call the second he hears anything and/or if Rupert needs me. I remind him that we can be over to the Lower Mainland by boat within a couple hours if needed.

"You any good at poker?" Finan asks, concealing the rugged laptop in one of my kitchen cupboards.

"I've been known to hide a straight flush when I need to."

"Good. Because today, you're gonna need to."

FORTY-NINE

BAD OPTICS

For the remainder of the week, Finan and I carry on as if nothing is out of the ordinary. We go to work, we manage our unending to-do lists, we juggle Humboldt responsibilities and answer residents' questions and field media inquiries and handle shipments of food and cargo arriving via the marina and manage the agritechs and maintenance crews and ignore Kelly Lockhart and her stupid sex toy Hunter as much as possible. We forgo Friday after-work beers at the Salamander so as not to put ourselves in view of crews or other residents. I text Eugenia and Benny regular pictures and video of Humboldt being goofy and adorable and of Andromache being lush and green. I post on Instagram so that everything on Thalia Island looks idyllic and peaceful to the rest of the world, quickly deleting trolls who spew their noxious waste in the comments.

We don't revisit Cordelia Beach in search of more evidence, per Wes's very explicit instructions that we stay off that side of the island to avoid messing with search warrants and what they will find once on Thalia. The last thing Finan and I want to do is undermine any forthcoming investigation—and I don't want to stumble over whatever became of that murdered raccoon.

Rupert sends an email over our secure network to put me in direct contact with the Clarke Innovations head of security, some guy named Len Emmerich whose bio pic in the private CI corporate directory looks like Dolph Lundgren—square-jawed, blond, and mean. Emmerich and his team will be waiting for word from the RCMP about next steps, but within ten to fourteen days either way, we will have evictions from the island.

I just have to keep my poker face polished and bright a little longer. And my email response to Rupert is thankful and subdued instead of what I *really* want to say: *Why the hell weren't Len and his team here before?* Because Rupert already explained this—there was no need. Or so we thought.

How will I trust anyone ever again?

At night, behind drawn curtains and locked doors, Finan and I pretend that none of this is happening, finding solace and connection in one another until we're so tired and sore, we can't move. We stay up far too late talking about our pasts—I learn that his sister is expecting twins and the pregnancy has been rough, how his mom is already pestering him about bringing me home for their annual Canada Day barbecue. Finan walks me through the scars on his body, besides the one I gave him with the Waterford Crystal—others from hockey, skateboarding, appendicitis, a fight with a racist punk at his high school. He asks questions about my mom, about what it was like growing up under a microscope, about the craziest adventures I had before Thalia Island turned me into a nine-to-fiver, about the meaning behind my grandfather's ring and why I never take it off. Small talk, basically, only more than that. Especially since we're naked.

We timidly approach any talk of the future, as if the impending investigation has the power to change everything.

Because it does.

What if Thalia Island doesn't survive this, once the police do whatever they need to pick Dea Vitae out with their lice combs? Who will be left to safeguard my grandfather's beautiful dream? Will there even *be* a dream to call home? Will I end up back in a downtown loft or at our house in Copenhagen, back to my old life? But what then? What does it mean for my inheritance if Thalia Island goes up in legal smoke?

Finan has plenty of education—he'll easily find fulfilling work somewhere else. But this—whatever *this* is between us—is too new for me to tag along wherever he might land. And I've spent enough wasted years chasing men around the globe.

And what about everything with my mother? The mysterious files on her thumb drive? And Rupert's cancer? What if he doesn't survive the treatment? Will I bury him next to my grandfather in his mushroom suit, beside my mother's commemorative plaque since her body was never recovered?

Sometimes it is so hard for me to believe where I was only four weeks ago. I never would've imagined a life like this, a life without my every whim just a pushy command or bossy phone call away, a life removed from a bustling metropolis surrounded by all the modern luxuries where I felt like the queen bee, untouchable by pretty much anyone—and apparently protected by a security team I didn't even know existed.

I had no idea how complicated things could get—or how quickly. It wouldn't be a lie to admit that I sometimes wish I could close the curtain again, maybe not see how the Wizard works in Oz.

By the time I get to the end of this overwhelming thought load, my tears again drip onto Finan's broad chest, the reality of our situation near unbearable. He wraps his arm tighter around me and caresses my forehead, kneading my knotted brow until I eventually fall into a deep sleep, only to wake for the wave to rush back in.

One small piece of the puzzle slots into place when the fire inspector phones Finan midday on Saturday with the unanimous conclusion between himself and the insurance company's fire guy. Vertical farm B burned with the help of an accelerant that should not have otherwise been in the building. Additionally, unusual holes were discovered, likely drilled in floors and walls to aid in the fire's oxygenation and thorough spread.

Verdict: arson.

Something we are to keep close to the chest, sharing with Rupert and Wes only who will in turn share with the appropriate authorities.

The salmonella. The ruptured irrigation pipe. The torched farm. The orgy-indulging, raccoon-murdering, blood-bathing, coup-staging cultists.

Last I checked, *none* of this was listed in Schedule A.

And upon arrival at the Monday morning council-only meeting, it's clear Kelly Lockhart's arrogance and bluster is intensifying. She clearly has *no idea* we're circling around nailing her as the leader of the Dea Vitae faction that has infiltrated my grandfather's precious island. She's as obnoxious and condescending as ever, reiterating that she has a call in to Rupert and the board of the Clarke Foundation about my mother's unsavory past and the propriety of me remaining as project administrator. Catrina and Finan act as buffers, reminding her that her contract is not forged in iron and that the Foundation doesn't take orders from individual council members.

The room is so combustible I swear I smell sulfur as they go at each other. The remaining councillors abstain from joining in, though it's clear where lines have been drawn, even if I hadn't witnessed the horrors of Cordelia Beach. I avoid eye contact as much as possible, afraid they will read the disgust on my face.

While Finan redirects the meeting to things that actually matter, beyond Kelly's egomaniacal posturing, an idea takes root.

We have all those photos and videos, and sure, we've uploaded and sent them, encrypted, over to Wes and his RCMP colleagues. With my limited understanding of evidentiary procedure based on Wes's quick explanation, the photos and videos were taken by witnesses—us—in public, in view of anyone who happened to be near Cordelia Beach that night.

And the more Kelly drones on, the more I think I'm in the mood for a little vengeance of my own.

I take a long sip of my cooled orange pekoe and sit straighter in my chair, waiting for Kelly to finish whatever she's currently harping about.

"I'd like to say something, if I may." I fold my hands on the table, shoulders back, chin high. Finan raises a brow across the way, his face questioning what's about to come out of my mouth. "In light of Kelly's allegations last week regarding my mother, I think it's important that I be allowed to address our residents, to answer for whatever wrongs they might perceive, to reassure them that I will do whatever is in the best interests of Thalia Island and her new families ..." I take a measured breath. "Even if that means I have to abandon my post for someone better suited."

All heads turn in my direction. I don't miss the shit-eating grin stretching across Kelly's and Hunter's faces, nor do I miss the shift in posture or bent finger resting against the puckered lips of my current bed buddy. "I just want to do what's right for Thalia. I don't know much about Cordelia's past, but if it makes people uncomfortable, I want to be open to their questions."

Kelly stands from her high-backed chair at the table head. "We could easily put out the call for another town hall meeting. When would you be prepared to do this, Lara?"

It's the nicest she's spoken to me since my first day; she's not even trying to conceal her glee.

"This week sometime? I'd like to get my thoughts straight. Maybe we could send out an email via Lutris to see if anyone has questions or concerns for me to address directly?"

"That sounds like a terrific idea." Kelly sits again. "In the meantime, I will check in with the board to see how they're coming along in their search for your replacement."

"She hasn't agreed to step down," Catrina argues. "She's merely offering to address any questions from the settlers."

"Mm-hmm," Kelly says. "But it's common sense that we cannot have the daughter of a known member of a dangerous criminal organization at the helm of this operation. The optics are not good. Not good at all."

It takes everything I have to bite my tongue. I'm afraid I will punch a hole through the top of this table if I don't get out of here.

"Does anyone else have anything for the agenda?" Hunter butts in.

Blue ink has smeared over the corner of his mouth and up his cheek from the pen actively leaking all over his fingers.

I stand. "I think I'm done for this morning," and before Kelly has a chance to rap her dollar-store gavel, I see myself out.

Upon walking past her office, I note that her lockset has been replaced.

Which is good. She should get used to being behind locked doors.

As I'm walking into my own office, the burner phone rings in my front pocket. I can't answer it in here, so I hurry out of town hall, extracting the phone and answering just as I slide into the garden courtyard.

"Lara, it's Wes. You got a second?"

"Yes, just got out of a meeting. Everything OK? Is Rupert OK?"

"He's at an appointment, so I'm calling you first. I just got off the phone with my forensics guy. You somewhere secure?"

I look around, making sure no one is in proximity. "I'm outside. Alone."

"We have an ID on the bones. Came back quick since we had good DNA, and the victim was reported missing by his family. They thought he was away at work this whole time."

"Seriously?"

"He worked in private security. Does the name Derek Irving ring a bell?"

FIFTY

TIT FOR TAT AND ALL THAT

"Are you sure?"

"As sure as DNA gets, which is pretty damn sure."

"Oh my god … what does this mean?"

"It means things just got a whole lot weirder. Can you send me everything you have on this guy? I don't want to bother Rupert today. He's going to feel like a train hit him by tonight."

"Yes. Sure …" I'm stunned. "Derek Irving was supposed to be the on-island security guy. Our own cop."

"Did you ever meet him?"

"No. Finan did once. But apparently he went back to Abbotsford to deal with family or something and then never returned. Rupert said he just stopped responding to emails and calls. Figured he maybe got another job and didn't bother telling us."

"This is a wild guess, but I don't think he ever left the island. His family in Abbotsford hasn't heard from him in a couple months."

"And they didn't think that was strange?"

"Not every family keeps in close touch, I suppose."

A chill pours over me. *This means someone on the island is an actual murderer.* "Wes, where is the rest of him?"

"Don't know. But we're going to look."

"I am now officially one hundred percent spooked," I say, looking around me to double-check no one is close.

"Talk to Finan only. I'll get back to you tonight." He disconnects. I stare at the quiet phone in my palm, cold in my bones despite the warmth of the midday sun on my back.

"Lara? You OK?" A shadow falls over me. I look up and exhale a relieved breath.

"Care for a walk?" I ask Finan.

We end up at Tommy's Diner, glad that Tommy and Catrina are still at town hall while we pick up our lunches (and actual espresso from the machine I quietly ordered and had installed) from the two young staff working the grill and tables. It's difficult to know who among the residents was on that beach the other night, but I'm pretty sure the two diner employees weren't part of the throng. Still, I don't breathe a word about Wes's call until we're outside again, lunches in hand.

When I tell Finan about Derek Irving, the color spills out of his face, and he stops. "You're shitting me." I shake my head. "That's why he's not been here," he says.

"Well, he was *here* ..." I lower my voice as a mom pushes past with a stroller. "Just not like we expected."

"Dear god, this is bad." We move down the block and across the street. When Finan nods at the picnic table in the town hall garden courtyard, I follow him over. We sit and pull out our sandwiches, but other than sipping our coffees, neither of us moves to eat.

I scan our immediate area to make sure we are indeed alone. "They ID'd him so quickly because his family reported him missing."

"Why didn't they call Rupert or Clarke Innovations to ask after him?"

"I don't know. I haven't talked to Rupert yet—he's got treatment today. Maybe they didn't know where he was supposed to be working?"

"This is so unbelievably bizarre," he says. He rewraps his untouched sandwich and slides it back into the brown paper lunch sack.

"Does it make you second-guess your job here?" I ask, worried he might decide this is too much for him.

"It makes me second-guess the *people* we have living here—"

"Ohhhh, hey, there you are," a voice says from the sidewalk. Ainsley—a fat, eggplant-colored backpack thrown over her shoulder—bounces under the trellis and along the flagstones until she's next to our wooden table. She directs her conversation to Finan, hardly acknowledging my presence. "Just wanted to let you know I'm going into Vancouver on the afternoon ferry to deal with my student visa at the consulate. If you could pop in and check on my agritechs out in the lower fields, that would be great."

"On my list," Finan says.

"Need me to bring anything back for you?"

Seeing her tiny frame and that flaming red hair and those innocent, wide green eyes set in a freckled face that looks barely old enough to drive—and then transposing what we saw the other night on Cordelia Beach—I'm glad she's doing her best to ignore me. My poker face is exhausted.

"No, I think we're good, Ainsley. Thanks, though," Finan says. "Good luck at the consulate."

"Beautiful day for a picnic," she says, winking at Finan as she turns on the heel of her muddied work boot.

I wait until she's out of earshot. "Yes, Finan, beautiful day for a picnic."

"It's hard to look her in the eye now."

"Right? Thank you." I also wrap my untouched sandwich, my stomach not interested in food. "Where's Big Dog?"

"Your office. He was napping when I walked past."

"Everything feels different, you know, after …," I say. "I'm kinda scared."

"Don't be. You have a really nice filleting knife." He grins.

"Har har … I'm serious, Finan."

335

He reaches over and covers my hand with his. We've been careful not to show any public affection, but at this point, half the people here will be gone within a fortnight, so who gives a shit. "Are you serious about wanting to do a Q&A with the residents?"

I school my expression, careful not to blink as I look up. I don't want to lie to him, but if I tell him the truth behind what I'm planning, he'll try to talk me out of it.

"Seems fair. And it'll distract people from what's really going on behind the scenes. If everyone is looking at me, they won't be looking at what we're doing to ensnare Kelly and her merry band of perverts."

Finan chuckles, but then he's serious again. "You don't have to explain *or* defend yourself. You don't owe anyone that."

"I know. But I'm also not ready for the residents—those who will be staying once the shit hits the fan—to think I'm a useless, selfish leader or that my mom was a bad person. Because she wasn't. She maybe just made some not-great choices."

"Again, Lara … we've talked about this. You are not your mom."

"No, but I am a Clarke. And I have to keep this island running. My grandfather's good name must remain untarnished. I want to stay committed to the *mission*."

Finan smiles. "Archibald would be really proud of you right now."

I look down at Grandfather's ring, my smile tight, hoping Finan doesn't see my unease. I'm not sure Archibald would be proud of what's coming, but he's dead—and Kelly Lockhart is not going to get away with bullying me any longer.

Who was it who said, "Turnabout is fair play"?

FIFTY-ONE

UNDERWAY

Humboldt is all too happy to eat my sandwich, once I pick out the yucky tomato and pickles, of course. My canine calamity has a discerning palate. And I have to tear it into small pieces or else he'll swallow the whole thing in one bite, choke, and vomit it all over my floor (and then, yes, re-eat it—dogs are so gross).

I spend too long with my hands under the hot tap, scrubbing away organic mayonnaise and dog slobber (also organic), staring at the sudsy water disappearing down the drain, thinking about what the hell is going on—part of Derek Irving's body was found on this island, by the very beast who now has a belly full of artisanal brioche, smoked turkey, and vegan Gouda.

But where is the *rest* of Derek Irving? Was he buried on Cordelia Beach? Was he tossed into the strait and what didn't feed the local sea life washed back in, like those random feet in floating tennis shoes?

Most worryingly of all, *how did he die?*

Without the rest of his body, can they even figure out what happened to him? Maybe he was surveying the island and had an accident. But then, wouldn't they have found a boat or seen an oil slick if it capsized? Reportedly he was only on the island for a short time in the early days. Was he exploring his new territory when he happened upon a visiting cougar who then had a bit of dinner, and the arm was all that was left? Can the forensics people figure out if the bones have been chewed on by scavengers? I didn't look too closely—because, *oh my god, human bones*—but they seemed pretty intact. Smooth and unbroken, other than a little dried meat and the repaired part at the top held together by the metal thingie.

The burner phone again buzzes against my hip.

I dry my hands and hustle down the hall, past Kelly and Hunter in her office and into my own. Phone out, I answer but don't say a word until my own office door is closed.

"Finan tells me you want to have a meeting with the residents to address their concerns about Cordelia?"

Thanks, Finan. "How are you feeling, Rupert?"

"Like hot garbage. Answer me, Lara."

My armpits dampen with cold sweat. "I offered to field any questions about what Kelly told everyone last week. I think it's only fair. The settlers voted—half of them don't want me here any longer."

"Yes, and *that half* will be evicted soon, in light of recent criminal developments. It no longer matters what they want."

"Maybe, but *they* don't know that. I think we should carry on as if everything is perfectly normal. Let them think they have some control here, that Kelly is the queen they should all bow to."

Rupert is quiet except for a terse exhale. "Keep the meeting short. Do not answer questions that could get us into legal trouble. Do you want to have a briefing with PR beforehand?"

"No … I think I got this," I say, opening PowerPoint on my computer. "You've talked to Wes today?"

"Jesus … yes. Derek Irving."

"What the hell, Rupert?"

"Thank god all this happened after Archibald passed. I think it would've killed him."

"Didn't Derek's family call you to find out if he'd reported for work?"

"Not to my knowledge. We're looking into it."

"His family is going to sue us, aren't they."

"Very likely." Rupert coughs. It sounds wet.

"Are you sure you're OK?"

"You worry about yourself and our island."

Reluctantly, I sigh. "All right … but go rest. You're going to need your strength for what's coming."

"Don't do anything stupid, Lara. Please. You know the dance," Rupert says.

And by dance, he means avoid saying or doing things that could get me splashed across a tabloid's coveted front page.

Yeah, not sure I brought my dancing shoes with me, Number Two.

F inan pokes his head into my office just after five. "If you keep pinching your brow like that, it's gonna be permanent."

"That's what Botox is for," I say, hurrying to switch the screen before he walks all the way in. "What's up?"

Humboldt stands, stretches, and happily greets his buddy.

Finan scrubs the dog's huge head, looks at the boxy watch on his wrist, and then saunters into the room. "Quitting time? You hungry?"

I push my keyboard back as Finan sinks into my couch. "Yes, since I fed Humboldt my sandwich. What joy did your day bring?"

"Working on the demolition at farm B. The new construction is set to begin next week."

"Already?"

"These insurance guys don't mess around." He leans forward, still petting Humboldt, and lowers his voice. "With the arson confirmed, they paid out already. We have to get the new building in. We need the yield that farm was producing."

I match his lowered tone, near whispering. "But do we? With the coming adjustments to our population?"

Finan bobs his head once. "It'll take six months before she's even ready to plant," he says. Fatigue, and maybe a hint of sadness, flashes across his face before he squints at my screen. "Is—is that a count-down clock?"

"Uhhh, yes." Sheepish smile.

"Only 338 days to go. And then you'll run back to your old life?"

I'd flip the screen, but I don't want him to see what's on the other tab. "It's been a rocky start. I thought the clock would help keep me grounded."

He stands and leans on the armrests of my chair, his face hovering above mine. "Is life so unbearable that you need a clock to remind you when you can escape?"

"Life has gotten much more bearable lately."

He grins. "Has it?"

"I made a friend."

"You *did* make a friend." He brushes his lips over mine. "A very *good* friend." Humboldt insinuates himself between us, grumbling as he squeaks his ball in his jaw.

"I think he's jealous," I say, trying to push the dog back so I can kiss the beautiful man arched over me. "He wants you all to himself."

"I understand the feeling," Finan whispers. "Can we go now before I tear off your clothes here?"

I push him back. "Ha! No tearing. This is Stella McCartney. Hands off, you brute."

Finan snorts and backs up as Humboldt nudges him to play.

"Give me, like, five more minutes. I just want to wrap up what I'm working on."

"Meet you at my truck in ten?"

I nod. He stretches, his shirt lifting just enough to show a hint of abs, and then picks up the sloppy ball from where Humboldt dropped it. It's not safe, within these walls, for me to share Wes's text message from an hour ago, that the RCMP is readying search warrants and will arrive on the island *tomorrow*, and how it would be really convenient if we could somehow surreptitiously gather residents so the Clarke Innovations security detail could work in conjunction with the police to manage suspects at a single central location.

Like, in a town hall meeting, say, five on Tuesday afternoon? I typed to Wes.

That would do it, he responded. *See you then.*

It's clear my deodorant gave up trying hours ago, but even more so now as I open a new message in Lutris:

Fellow council members and Thalia Island residents,

Please accept my invitation to an informal town hall meeting Tuesday at 5 p.m. in council chambers wherein I will address any questions you might have about the allegations leveled last week by fellow councillor Kelly Lockhart. I know many residents have made inquiries about my fitness to continue as project administrator for Thalia Island, as well as questions about the validity of the sensational claims made regarding my mother, Cordelia Clarke.

Though this meeting is not mandatory, your attendance would be appreciated. Remember our joint mission here on TI, and rest assured, I am absolutely committed to seeing it through, not only for my beloved grandfather but for all of you and your families.

Thank you,

Lara J. Clarke

My heart in my throat, I hit Send. I then password protect my PowerPoint project and save it in the cloud so I can open it at home and add the finishing touches. I want it to be *perfect*.

Before I move my hand to click my Mac into sleep mode, my Lutris inbox pings with the first RSVP.

By the time I buckle myself into Finan's truck, it's obvious most of the island will be in attendance tomorrow.

Finan clutches his phone, balanced against the steering wheel. My message is open on his screen. "You just do this?"

"Yup."

"Are you sure?"

I pull the burner from the inside pocket of my blazer, navigate to Wes's message of an hour ago, and share it. Finan's eyes widen as he reads. "No shit? Tomorrow? That was fast."

"Identifying the bones of a missing person who was supposed to be working here seems to have inspired haste on the part of our law enforcement brethren."

He returns the phone. "I guess so." His hand is on the gear shift, but he remains in park, the almost-silent truck whirring around us.

"What are you going to say? If you're planning to answer questions about your mom ..."

"I'll tell them as little as possible and that most of what Kelly said was untrue. The stuff about me, I can't exactly walk back—she brought pictures and Connor Mayson to spill those beans—but I can explain myself, explain how Thalia has changed me, how the last six months have been very hard for my family."

"Appeal to their compassion." He nods. "That could work."

"I'm appealing to their *humanity*. I've made a lot of mistakes, but that doesn't mean I can't learn, that I can't do a good job here, finishing what Archibald started."

"At least until your year is up ..."

The look I throw his way is harsh, but so is his comment. "My first day on Thalia, I wasn't sure I'd last until dinner. But I did. And then I lasted until the end of the week. Then I saw what people were doing, how they all seemed to be working together to make everything work—"

"Stop. Exactly everything you're saying right now? Say it to them." He points out the window at a few residents walking the sidewalks and heading in and out of the handful of open Main Street businesses. "*I* already know the truth about you. You don't have to convince me," he says, reaching to squeeze my shoulder. "Convince *them*. Show them who the *real* Lara is, the one I get to see, not the one everyone else in the world thinks they know."

His words, however sweet, make me uncomfortable given my actual plan. "Does it matter so much, though? Half of these people will either be arrested or evicted tomorrow."

"Maybe it won't matter to them—they're already lost to Thalia. They were never here for her anyway," he says, resuming his hold on the inert steering wheel. "But the rest of us, the true settlers who will, we hope, remain on the island and help us fulfill Archibald's mission, *they* are the ones we need on our side. From here on out."

I nod. He's not wrong.

Maybe I should just try appealing to the empathy of my fellow Thalia residents.

But what Kelly did cannot go unpunished. She brought CONNOR over! He humiliated you in front of everyone, Lara! And what about Cordelia? Are you going to let the lies about her spread like a noxious weed? When has taking the high road ever truly resulted in comeuppance for people like Kelly Lockhart?

"If you think any harder, your hair will catch fire," Finan says, tucking a few wayward strands behind my ear. "Shall we?"

"Yes. I'm tired … probably should have an early night."

"Tomorrow's a big day."

I sigh, exhausted. "I miss the days that started with gin."

Finan chuckles and eases down the street. I'm glad he thinks I'm kidding.

FIFTY-TWO

NO ONE SAYS NO TO DESSERT

Finan works his kitchen magic—arguably the best chicken fettuccini I've had in North America—and we share a beer. I need a clear head to prepare for tomorrow. When I kiss him good night, he offers to follow me home, to stay over "for safety," but I promise I will scream super loud if any bad guys show up. Plus, I have Humboldt, and he's the biggest, baddest guy on the island.

"I'm heading directly to farm B in the morning, so I'll text you to check in," Finan says, his hands around my head as he kisses me on his front porch. "Keep your phone close."

"I'll be fine. Thank you for dinner." I kiss him again, though my heart's not in it—I'm too distracted by what I have yet to accomplish tonight.

Once Big Dog and I are secure in our cabin, I flash the porch light twice so Finan can go back inside. Even though I have the dead bolt thrown, I scoot a heavy upholstered chair in front of the door. "Just in case," I say to Humboldt, who watches me, head tilted.

I get ready for bed—quick shower, fresh jammies, a cup of peppermint tea, some fresh water for Andromache and my daily reminder of how pretty she is with all her new growth—and climb under the covers with both laptops and both phones, checking email and Lutris and text messages for any new fires that have started since I unplugged to eat.

Nothing new from Wes or Rupert. My Lutris inbox is full of responses—tomorrow is going to be a repeat of last week. Another full house.

Excellent.

I sip my tea, exhaling slowly to ease my prickled nerves.

For the subsequent three hours, I put the finishing touches on my PowerPoint presentation, as well as tweak and retweak my talking points for the meeting, making sure not to give away too much about my mother—especially since I don't *know* very much, and Rupert isn't in any state to have a lengthy heart-to-heart. They will get what I give them, and that's plenty.

As for me, I'm going to follow Finan's advice and appeal to my fellow Thalia Islanders, to reinforce that everyone deserves an opportunity to prove themselves and that living in the very wide Clarke spotlight has been more difficult than one might imagine. I will reiterate my grandfather's mission statement, what he believed in, for Thalia Island and the planet at large—appeal to their sense of duty as members of this unique, curated community.

And like any good hostess, I will finish with dessert, because no one says no to dessert.

When the computers are tucked away and Humboldt is snoring on the side of the bed that has been taken up by other male company recently, I close my eyes ... and imagine Cordelia Clarke's wide, white smile, her toned, tanned arm waving to me from the side of her open Cessna.

FIFTY-THREE

FULL DISCLOSURE

Upon arrival at town hall, I have to remind myself to not hold my breath when I see how many people are here. Looks like pretty much everyone. A spike of pain blows through my chest when I see a guy who, from the back, looks like Connor, but then he turns around and it's not him.

It doesn't matter. Once news gets out of his involvement with Dea Vitae, his career is over.

Finan texted earlier from farm B and asked if I wanted to drive in together, but I told him I'd meet him here. I don't want to lose my nerve—and being around Finan's reasonable, calm nature might cause me to do just that.

I try not to look obvious as I scan the area outside town hall for evidence that the police and security teams have arrived—it's just after four o'clock, and I don't know how precise they will be with their appearance. Wes didn't offer details in his brief text this morning other than *Today is the day.*

Head held high, society smile on, I walk through the crowd and inside, as if I own the place—since technically, I do. I don't allow the indifferent smirks or dirty looks get to me. *I am a Clarke. Protect Thalia.*

I've already been here once today, early this morning before everyone else so I could figure out the AV system in the closet-size booth that overlooks the council chambers. I wasn't even aware it existed, though I knew Kelly's fun little slideshow of last week had to have originated from *somewhere* in the building. And since I don't have anyone to help with the theatrics—to slide the screen down behind me while I talk or dim the lights—I've got a system jury-rigged that *should* work. Fingers crossed.

At 4:40 p.m., the council chambers are almost at capacity. It's going to be standing-room only again.

I'm seated up on the dais, in my seat from the other night, my laptop open in front of me. I mostly keep my eyes on my screen, pretending to read the notes for what I've dubbed the Compassion and Empathy speech, but the reality is, I don't want to look at the faces of these people yet. No matter how many times my drunken, stumbling self was splattered across the internet or how many former friends shared sensationalized details about my private life, this thing today—everything that has gone sideways on Thalia—feels far more personal.

These people were allegedly chosen because they represented my grandfather's best hope for a prosperous future. I still don't under-stand how Dea Vitae found its way here—and I'm sure there is much left to discover—but these people were supposed to be allies. Friends. Cooperative living partners. And this is how they repay Archibald Clarke's generosity of spirit? His kindness? His vision? With orgies and sacrificial offerings and *murder*?

The devil who lives on my shoulder smiles and whispers in my ear: *For Archibald. For Cordelia.*

When Kelly and nearly the rest of council take their spots, Catrina and Tommy are the only ones who acknowledge me. Kelly cackles and flutters energetic hellos to her sycophants already seated in the gallery; she blows a kiss to Hunter, sitting front and center. He pretends to catch it and pop it into his mouth.

These people have *got* to go.

The nerves in my gut shed their apprehension and form a shield wall.

At 4:55 p.m., I stand, laptop in hand, passing a freshly showered and handsomely dressed Finan as he moves toward the council chair next to mine. "Break a leg," he whispers. I offer a tight smile, take the three steps down, and assume my battle station at the podium in the half-round before the gallery. The huge screen is already in position behind me; the remote for my slideshow is tucked in the front pocket of my eggshell linen power blazer. The little icon for the screencast tech flashes green on my laptop, indicating it's ready to go.

No sign of anyone other than residents in the gallery yet.

I tap the mic. "Hello, and welcome, fellow settlers and friends of Thalia Island. Please take your seats. We will begin in one minute."

Stragglers squeeze into the benches. Those who don't fit line up along the back wall. Again, I don't think these chambers are big enough. Something to address with Rupert once he's on the mend—*if* there's still a Thalia Island to worry about.

My phone alarm silently blinks when it rolls over to 5:00 p.m.

I adjust the mic before me and straighten my spine.

"Good afternoon, and again, thank you for your quick agreement to attend this meeting on such short notice. As you know, I am Lara J. Clarke, the granddaughter of our beloved benefactor, Archibald Magnus Clarke. We miss you, Grandpa." I pause for a beat in case anyone wants to applaud. A few do. One of Finan's crew, a tall kid with dreadlocked hair, hollers from the back, "Yeah, Archie! We love you, man!"

The crowd titters, and an inch of tension eases.

I launch into my prepared speech, reminding residents of Archibald's vision, why we're all here, what our mandate is, how we are tasked with "protecting the mission" so we can be of benefit to our planet and fellow humankind. I'm careful to not drag on too long—the PR tips gleaned from years of Rupert's nagging about public behavior remind me to keep it short and sweet.

"Next, I want to move on to address some questions fielded from residents after Councilwoman Lockhart's allegations during our last meeting." I answer their emailed questions about my past problems with alcohol, the few run-ins I've had with the law, and my qualifications to participate in the governance of Thalia Island. I report what Rupert has approved regarding his condition, confirming the rumor that he is indeed fighting cancer and will be physically absent from the island as necessitated by his treatment plan, though he will "continue with the day-to-day administrative oversight of our operations as he is able."

I am heartened when I see real worry on the faces of some residents. I know he is well liked, even if they think I'm an ass.

"With regard to my personal history, I'm not trying to hide anything from you. In the spirit of open and honest discourse, I will admit this is the first big-girl job I've ever had. I've made some dumb choices throughout my life—who among us hasn't? And while privilege and immaturity are not in any way excuses for my behavior, my grandfather's death left me alone in the world. He was the last of my family, and I don't want to let him down." I take a moment, sniff as if my emotions are getting away from me, and then, after a count of three, I look back up at the crowd.

"I've lived a unique, incredible, weird life. And I want to let you in on a little of what it's like to live under a microscope where every move is recorded, catalogued, and dissected." I detail how I've been tracked from birth until now, how, as I grew older, the gossip got meaner, more spiteful, how everyone in the world has an opinion about how my family lives, from what we eat to the cars we drive to the clothes we wear and the politicians and charities we endorse and support.

"It makes sense—we stand on a platform of sustainability and environmental symbiosis that my grandfather founded back in the days when people were still smoking in hospitals and installing lead pipes in their homes." A few people chuckle. I pick up my phone. "Have you ever looked up what's in a smartphone? And yet, every single person in this room has one." I set the phone back down. "We are *all* a work in progress—just like Thalia Island.

"With regard to my mother, that is a little more complicated. She died when I was ten. Councilwoman Lockhart's hurtful assertions regarding my mother's activities are based on rumor and hearsay. I don't have anything concrete to offer you in that regard, simply because *I do not know* what is true and what is myth.

"My mother was a vibrant, talented, hyperintelligent, wild woman. My memories of her are few, and precious. She, in fact, did a lot of good during her short lifetime—the Clarke Foundation website has an entire page devoted to Cordelia's deeds and accomplishments, the charities she started and the causes she championed to save rainforests and threatened and endangered species and promote education and deliver healthcare for women and babies in rural and impoverished villages throughout the world. There's a lot to dig through, and I'd ask that you spend some time doing so.

"However, scurrilous remarks about her criminal affiliations will not be tolerated, not unless you are able to bring actual evidence. Canada is a country that embraces proof, innocence, and the rule of law. And slandering my dead mother in an effort to further one's own agenda is reprehensible."

I turn and look directly at Kelly Lockhart. The smug smirk is still there, though diminished.

"To finish my presentation tonight—and before I open the floor to any relevant concerns relating to life here on Thalia, I wanted to share a little something I put together." I point up to the corner where the lights are. "If someone could dim those, that would be great."

The dreadlocked guy from earlier obliges and the gallery goes dark. It's then I notice that Wes Singh is here, just inside the door. My heart skitters.

Holy shit, this is about to happen.

The slideshow starts, and I narrate alongside the images as they pop onto the screen. Shots of our gorgeous island, of the residents as they settle in, smiling people at Tommy's Diner, their glasses and mugs aloft for the photo, of smiling, waving folks stocking up on essentials at the Tipping Point, of crews and agritechs holding up young chickens or handfuls of newly harvested fruit from the vertical farms, of Finan and a very muddy Humboldt, of the crews fighting the fire at vertical farm B—bona fide, heartfelt snapshots of life on Thalia Island.

I sense the pride and camaraderie in the room. It feels like the tide has turned, almost enough that, for a second, I consider stopping the slideshow before it gets to the good part.

Naaaaahhhh.

When the next image pops on the screen, the warm chatter stops, replaced instead by gasps and then ... dead silence. With each subsequent image, the emotional temperature plunges—faces are aghast, some are beet red, hands fly over the eyes of the few children present, and everyone adjusts in their seats, as if they cannot believe what they're seeing.

"This, fellow residents, is Cordelia Beach, on the west side of the island. It is not accessible by land, only by sea, and we have asked residents to stay off the beach due to the protected status of seabirds and other animals with whom we share this island.

"The people *on* the beach are some of your fellow council members as well as prominent members of our new community." The next photo flashes onto the screen. "Oh, this one—this is where they sliced open this poor raccoon and bathed in its blood."

"That's *enough*, Lara!" Kelly yells into her desk mic. "Someone turn on the lights!"

"But wait—I haven't even gotten to the best one yet." I click to the next photo, a close-up of a completely naked Kelly slathering the dead raccoon's blood over her ecstatic face as Hunter, also smeared with raccoon blood, gropes at her from behind.

I turn and look up at Kelly, careful to keep my lips from showing my teeth.

"Lies! This is all lies! This isn't what it looks like! Are you going to believe the bastard of a drug smuggler?" she shrieks, the latter part of her rantings overwhelmed by the growing cacophony.

As I face forward, Hunter leaps from his front-row seat and lunges at my laptop on the podium, but the side of my flattened hand slapped against his Adam's apple stops him, and he falls to his knees, gasping. The gallery erupts in chaos just as the lights go on—

And as many RCMP and private security as we have residents file into the room.

FIFTY-FOUR

BEST SERVED COLD

Chaos. That's the best way to describe it.

Wes and two other constables move quickly to the left stairs off the elevated council seats, toward Kelly who has stopped yelling and now has her bag thrown over her shoulder and is obviously preparing to make a quick exit.

She is instead stopped, questioned about her identity, to which she starts shrieking again about "rights" and "this is all lies" and "I need my phone call," even though no one has yet wrapped her in a pair of the zip-ties all the officers have dangling from their belts. It's not until she lashes out with a long-nailed hand that she is introduced to our eco-friendly merlot carpet.

As one constable restrains Kelly's wrists, another helps her to her knees. Wes crouches before her and I can see his lips moving, but I can't hear what he's saying. Obviously something Kelly doesn't like—she spits on him.

Delightful.

A clamor at the main door pulls my attention. I'm still standing at the podium, not sure what I'm supposed to do. The men dressed in black cargos and black, long-sleeved shirts must be our guys, judging by the subtle Clarke Innovations logo embroidered in the fabric at the shoulder. There are enough muscles in this room to hold a competitive Mr. Universe pageant. But the yelling is coming from the fact that the CI guys won't let *anyone* leave, not even the people with kids.

Wes approaches from my left, wiping Kelly's spit from his face with a cloth handkerchief. He points at the podium mic. I step back. Another huge guy pushes through the main stairs and stomps toward us—I immediately recognize him as Len Emmerich. He is *ginormous* in real life.

He nods at Wes and then offers me a hand that would be more suited to a silverback. "Len Emmerich. Wes and I can handle things from here."

"Thank you."

Wes taps the mic. "Attention, please. Quiet down," he says, his booming voice freezing everyone where they stand. "This will go much faster if you cooperate. I am Sergeant Wes Singh, here working in conjunction with the Serious Crimes Team of the RCMP, as well as Les Emmerich"—he gestures to the Drago lookalike—"the director of security for Clarke Innovations. Everyone here will be asked to identify themselves. If you refuse, you will be escorted to the North Vancouver RCMP detachment, where you will be appropriately processed in accordance with the Trespass Act."

"Who's trespassing? We're legal residents here. You can't do this!" Kelly screams from her kneeled position.

Wes ignores her. "Those of you who have been identified as participants in the activities of Cordelia Beach on the evening of May 25 will be detained as we execute our bevy of search warrants." Wes points at a corporal to my right who holds aloft a thick manila file folder. "Those of you named in these search warrants will be departing Thalia Island tonight to participate in the next phase of our investigation. Even in the absence of criminal wrongdoing, all of you who violated the Code of Conduct signed as part of your residence agreement on Thalia Island will be evicted within forty-eight hours.

"It would behoove you to cooperate. Form two lines, people. Once your identity is confirmed, you will either be allowed to leave or required to remain. Get to it."

The noise kicks up again as people protest what's unfolding. Other than the one outburst, Kelly sits quiet, mascara streaming down her face. Hunter has moved in beside her, his hands still uncuffed, though his tone with the surrounding officers suggests he might yet feel the burn of serrated plastic against skin tonight.

I turn to see who is still in their seats behind me. Catrina and Tommy look like they're watching a bad horror movie; Stanley is somewhere in the throng yelling about his rights in the face of a constable who is about to help him find a seat; Ainsley was a no-show, which is not ideal and could be problematic if Kelly somehow tips her off.

Finan. He's still here, standing against the dais wall, arms crossed over his chest, jaw clenched, his eyes on me.

And they are not kind.

I offer a sheepish smile, hoping he'll see my shaking hands, how freaked out I am now that this is all *actually* happening, and move down next to me. To be the one who has my back, like he promised.

He doesn't.

Instead, he pushes off the wall, pulls his wallet from his back pocket, and moves down the short steps to the gallery. He approaches the fast-forming line and nudges in front of the residents already there who look too stunned to whine about him cutting in. Two constables are at the front of this line, one holding a clipboard, the other an iPad stretched over his beefy forearm. Finan hands over his ID, waits a few seconds for them to confirm who he is and that he is most assuredly not on the list, and then he eases through the crowd, up the stairs, and exits the chambers without looking back.

My heart falls into my feet.

"Wes, Wes"—I tug on his sleeve—"do you need me for any of this?"

"Not at the moment. Don't go too far, though."

I nod and then scan the gallery seating to find the fastest way to the exit, opting to take the glass door at the northeastern corner that opens into the rear courtyard still in need of landscaping. I'm in four-inch, red-and-black suede Miu Miu ankle boots, which are not great for running—especially through dirt—but I can't let Finan leave without finding out what's going on.

I round the front of the building, hoisting myself over the rough-hewn, thigh-high fencing. "Finan!" He's stomping toward his truck. "Finan, wait!"

Once I'm out of the flower beds and across the strip of grass and onto solid ground, I pick up the pace. Huge transport vehicles line Main Street, as well as two RCMP supervisor rigs and a boxy black truck-van thing that looks like it belongs on the set of a SWAT drama. More police are out here, a few of them taking note of the shrill woman running on tiptoes down the block.

"God, will you wait a second?" I'm out of breath when I finally grab his arm and stop him. I lean in half, hands on knees. Definitely need to get some gym equipment on the island.

"Where are you going? Are you not staying to help, after everything?" I straighten and balance with one hand against a car-charging station so I can adjust the straps on my right heel.

The softness has left Finan's face. "They don't need my help. Plenty of guys here to do the work."

"You're on council. You should stay and make sure everything goes smoothly. I need you tonight—Tommy and Catrina and I are all who are left."

Finan exhales, his jaw still clenched.

"*What* is going on? This is what we wanted! This is *necessary* for—"

"What you did in there tonight?" He stabs a finger at the town hall building. "That was total shit."

"I was showing the truth! The residents deserve to know who Kelly really is!"

"No, Lara," Finan says, his voice rising. "What you did tonight was revenge. Nothing else. No one needed to see those pictures—there were LITTLE KIDS in there! Little kids who saw the photos of that raccoon being sliced open, of naked adults having sex and rubbing blood on their bodies. What you did in there was the sleaziest thing I have ever seen in my life."

Traitorous, hot tears stream down my face with the fervor of his anger. I knew he probably wouldn't approve of me showing those photos—maybe worried they'd risk the pending criminal case—but I didn't think he'd stand on Main Street and yell at me. "Do you have any idea how *humiliating* it was after her little slideshow? The garbage she said about my mother? Jesus, Finan, she brought Connor here! Do you know what it's like to have every second of your life paraded around for the whole world to tear apart and make fun of?"

"Yes, poor rich little Lara. I know the story."

That one feels like a slap to the face. "Wow ... so that's what you think of me?"

Finan scrubs a hand through his hair. "No one knows what it's been like to live your life. None of us know what it's like to have gossips and paparazzi lurking behind corners. But most of us DO know what it's like to have crap friends and terrible things happen. And the things that happen to us define who we are—they define our CHARACTER," he says, jabbing his chest with his fingers. "They define who we are inside."

Finan lowers his voice. "That little stunt showed me a side of you I didn't know existed, a side I never thought I'd see. You were raised by geniuses, and tonight, you acted like a jackass."

"Ha! A jackass? Are you even *serious* right now? Oh, so, what, I don't live up to your exceedingly high expectations of interpersonal behavior, Mr. Advanced Degrees Big-Brain Engineer?"

I hate that I can't come up with anything pithier—or meaner. My game is off, thoughts racing, cheeks blazing.

Finan chuckles under his breath and rubs his beard, head shaking as he looks down at his boots. "Revenge isn't going to make you feel any better, Lara. Lashing out at Kelly tonight, that's not going to help you feel better after all the rotten things people have said, the things they've done to you. Being this version of yourself will never bring back your grandfather, or your mother. I would never be so bold as to say your life has been easy, but you've had a lot of opportunities most of us have not. And instead of using tonight to build community, to build solidarity, to bring these people back to your side, you waded into the raw sewage right alongside Kelly Lockhart."

It's my turn to shake my head in disgust, even as I curse the tears cracking my stony exterior. "You spend a few weeks with me, in my bed, and you think you know me?"

Hurt flashes across Finan's face, but only for a second before it's replaced by the hardness. "I guess I should've known who you were when you hit me in the head with that plate."

He digs into his front pocket for his keys.

"Don't forget, Finan Rowleigh," I say, crossing my arms and looking him square in the eye. "This is Planet Lara. This is my realm, and I will not be made to look like a pariah on my own turf."

He laughs sadly under his breath. "Funny. I thought it was called Thalia Island." He then moves away without another glance, climbs into his truck, screeches out of his spot, and races in the opposite direction until I can no longer see the silver of his tailgate.

FIFTY-FIVE

SURPRISE!

Once I get my heaving sobs under control—and mostly because I really, *really* need some tissue—I thrust my shoulders back, spin on my stiletto heel, and march back into town hall, ignoring the curious glances of the constables and security contractors waiting for orders outside the front entrance.

The lobby is filled with residents talking to paired RCMP and CI security officers with clipboards and iPads in hand. One at a time, residents are cleared while others, people I recognize from Cordelia Beach last week, are asked to remain. They will all be leaving the island, just as Rupert promised, which means I will have a lot of work in the coming weeks to replace the people we're evicting.

How will I avoid more Dea Vitae nonsense with future applicants to Thalia Island?

I slide into my office and grab the tissue box, soaking up the damage. A quick look in my compact reveals that I am indeed a red-faced, puffy-eyed mess—again. But there is much to be done before I'm allowed to leave tonight, and worries about the future population of my grandfather's island will have to wait.

Fresh lipstick reinvigorates my confidence, though I bump my cell

358

phone on my desk and the lock-screen photo makes my heart hurt. It's a picture of Finan and me with Humboldt—I took it the other night while we stretched out on my bed, a perfect, quiet moment—Finan reading some book on best practices for vertical farms, me curled into his left side trying to concentrate on a steamy romance novel, and Big Dog squished into Finan's other side, dead to the world, a long string of drool drizzling from his spoiled, happy mouth.

I slide open the screen and change the photo. I don't have time for drive-by sentimentality.

Yelling has restarted in the hall and in council chambers, so I tuck my purse away, grab my giant key chain and both phones, and rejoin the fray. Stanley is now seated in an office chair in the hallway with his hands zipped behind his back, his thinning hair mussed, his face scrunched with fury. He glares at me as I pass and mumbles something that does not bear repeating.

The lockset on Kelly's office door has again been broken off. The investigators within, gloves on, are filling boxes with pretty much everything from her filing cabinets and desk drawers. Even her computer has been disconnected and put into an evidence bag. I pop my head in.

"Does your search warrant include the files for the residents?"

One of the RCMP guys nods.

"Those are in my office—in my closet." I wrangle the appropriate key off my bulky ring. "Kelly wouldn't let me see them, so I helped myself. You'll need boxes."

The constable takes the key and asks a few questions about the Lutris database. I explain that I don't have access to a lot of the Thalia-specific files in the cloud—password protected by Kelly Lockhart—but that I would have Rupert touch base with Wes about this. He thanks me and drops my key into a sandwich-size evidence bag that he then writes on with a Sharpie and tucks into his pocket.

In chambers, the crowd has dispersed, only the people from the beach left. Seems I was right about Hunter's attitude. He, too, is now sitting against the far wall with his hands behind his back. About six feet separates him from Kelly, though his mouth is still moving as he assures her, "We'll be fine, baby, everything will be fine. We're not going to jail, I promise." The constable standing between them smirks.

"Lara." Wes is behind the council members' seats on the dais alongside Len Emmerich and other muscled dudes I haven't yet met. He signals me to join them.

"Did Finan leave?" he asks as I approach.

"Yes. Did you need him?" My stomach tightens. *Don't ask me to call him.*

"No, not for now." Wes flips through the pages of a very fat three-ring binder filled with photographs and printouts in clear slipcovers, the faces and bios of every single person on Thalia Island.

"Wow ..." I lean closer. "You guys do your homework."

"The law is funny that way," Wes says with a tight smile. "So, we think we've ID'd pretty much everyone from the beach. They're about to start executing warrants on the residences now, and that could take a few hours. Once that's finished, we'll load everyone onto the transports and head over to North Van."

"OK. What do you need from me?"

"Forgive me for sounding sexist, but some coffee would be great," Len Emmerich says. Honestly, if he'd arrived in boxing gloves and a bathrobe made from the Russian flag, I'd believe he was about to kick Rocky Balboa's ass.

"I'll find Catrina and Tommy. They own the diner."

Wes checks the iPad sitting on the desktop next to his binder, scrolling through their spreadsheet that lists our residents. He pauses on one line and leans closer to read it before returning to the notebook and flipping through. When he lays the page flat, he looks at me, fingertip resting on the person's face.

"Ainsley Kerr," I say. "A student on loan from the University of Edinburgh, here finishing her PhD in carrots or something. She went into Vancouver yesterday to deal with her visa—I didn't see her here tonight. Figured she probably got held up."

Wes turns the page, and instead of a new resident, it's another photo of Ainsley, although she looks very different in this eight-by-ten. Longer hair, chocolate-brown and bouncy, versus the red pixie cut I'm familiar with. "Her name is actually Iona MacChruim, and she's the suspected head of the North American branch of Dea Vitae."

FIFTY-SIX

REALIZATION

"Nuh-uh." Probably not the smartest thing to ever come out of my mouth, but I am very tired. "How is that possible? *How* did we not see this?"

Wes smiles and glances briefly at the zip-tied detainees slumped in the gallery seats. "How did any of these people squeak through?"

Len Emmerich leans against the desk. The intimidating service weapon holstered on his belt is a solemn reminder that what's going down here is no joke, even as Hunter wails cartoonishly at Kelly about his undying love. "That's the thing with Dea Vitae. These fuckers are smart. If Iona wanted you to think she was Ainsley, then that's who she was."

"But she's, like, in charge of growing food. She seems really good at her job. *How* is this even possible?"

"She's very good at growing all sorts of things, Lara," Emmerich offers. "Including salmonella."

I'm woozy. "I'm sorry—what did you say?"

"And not just your standard garden-variety strain, either. Hers is particularly effective. Works faster, though not usually lethal. The BC CDC folks were both horrified and delighted with what they found during their investigation of your recent event," Emmerich explains. Wes nods in agreement as he scrolls through the spreadsheet.

"How long have you known this? No one told me. I didn't even know the report had come back," I say, annoyed to be blindsided with this information.

Wes stops scrolling and looks up. "Rupert has the report. Len and I, and appropriate parties, have been briefed."

"But I wasn't briefed. Why did none of you share this development? You know I got really sick that night, right?"

"The final findings just came through the other day. I'm sure Rupert has his reasons. Don't stress about it. We're telling you now," Wes says, resting a hand on my upper arm. "It's been a crazy week, hey?"

I nod. It has been. Rupert probably just forgot to tell me.

Ainsley—or Iona—she poisoned us. *On purpose.* I can't wait to call Émile and tell him the food poisoning wasn't his fault. That is, if he's willing to go against counsel's advice and talk to me, now that his company is suing Thalia Island, and specifically Clarke Innovations, for the damage caused to his reputation from that evening's fallout.

"What about the bones?" I ask.

Wes looks up quickly and shakes his head. "We're not talking about that in here tonight. Investigation still ongoing."

Right. Makes sense. Lots of people still present, some looking dejected and scared, others looking like they want to set me on fire. I turn my back to them.

"I'm going to see about that coffee, if you don't need me for anything else at the moment."

"That would be terrific. Thanks, Lara," Wes says and then pivots in a clear indication he'd like to talk to Emmerich—alone.

I'm halfway up the carpeted stairs when Wes calls out from behind me. "Lara, milk and sugar, too, if you can."

I've never felt more useless. Here I thought I'd be involved in this big dramatic sweep, saving my grandfather's island from deviants and evildoers, and instead I'm nothing more than the coffee bitch.

By the time everything is wrapped—involved and arrested parties loaded onto the buses, search warrants executed, evidence squared away into the trucks, the Clarke Innovations contractors tucked back into their SWAT-like buggy of doom—it's two in the morning. Tommy and Catrina were able to put together meals to feed everyone, officers and detainees alike. I promised I would e-transfer money first thing to replenish their larder.

Although, with Stanley booted out, looks like it will be me handling the replenishment of larders for everyone who remains. A crash course in how to run a general store, starring Lara J. Clarke.

Catrina, exhausted after spending the whole day in clinic prepping for Dr. Stillson's arrival Thursday, hugged me tight and offered for Tommy to drive me home so I don't end up in a ditch. I politely declined, promising I'd get home safe. I also promised I'd sit down with them tomorrow and explain *everything*. They were as taken aback as everyone else when the RCMP and Clarke Innovations security team appeared. I'm so frayed, I forgot they weren't in on the whole scheme.

I bid Tommy good night, and Catrina follows me out of the diner, walking me to my car. "You don't look OK," she says.

"I'm not," I admit, new tears falling. "I messed up. Tonight. The slideshow. What I did ... What if he never speaks to me again?"

Catrina takes my hand in hers. "Finan is a good man. Give him a moment to process everything."

I shake my head. "I've never cared if I hurt people. They never seemed to care if they hurt me. All I could think about was getting back at Kelly for what she did, what she said about my mom." I'm crying hard enough now that talking is difficult.

"We often think a little vengeance will make us feel better," Catrina says, her thumb stroking the top of my hand, "but the reality is, it leaves us feeling emptier than before." She laughs a little. "Well, most of the time."

My cheek pulls with the hint of a sad smile. "Sometimes it feels good. But not tonight. Not if it means Finan will never speak to me again."

Catrina then releases my hand and pulls me into another of her famous hugs. I'm hunched over her marathoner's frame, especially since in heels, I'm near six feet tall. Power heels for a powerful night.

What I'd give for those ugly hiking boots right now.

She pushes back and cups my cheeks in her soft hands. "He will forgive you. I've known Finan Rowleigh since he was a kid. He's a thinker. And he feels things very deeply, including how he feels about you." She boops my nose with her fingertip. "Go home. Get some sleep. Talk to him tomorrow when the light of a new day offers fresh opportunities for forgiveness."

I hug her again. "Can you adopt me, please?" I ask through a renewed sob.

"Gladly." She rubs my back and then waits until I'm in my car before stepping back. Catrina watches me drive down the block, waving until I round the bend in the street and can no longer see her small shape under the triangle of light from the streetlamp.

FIFTY-SEVEN

HOW DO YOU LIKE THESE PICKLES?

I park and before the door is open, I can hear Humboldt's deep barks and whines. Worry buffets me when I realize that he hasn't had dinner, nor has he been out to pee or poop in … hours.

"I'm coming, Big Dog!" I holler, hurrying across the gravel toward the porch stairs. At the top sits a shoe-size, gift-wrapped box tied with a big craft-paper bow, a square envelope tucked under its edge. The porch light activates when I step into the sensor's path, and when I see the handwriting is Finan's, I'm emboldened by a flurry of emotions, not the least of which is relief that it's not from whoever warned us about the horror show at Cordelia Beach. If it's in Finan's casual script, it's less likely the package will detonate when I untie the bow.

I unlock the cabin's front door, package tucked under my arm. Humboldt races past, whimpering as he flies into the field and sniffs for the perfect spot. With the front door wide open, I walk into my darkened cabin to the sole source of light from a very cute shabby chic lamp near the kitchen sink. I slide the box onto the counter and tear open the envelope:

Lara,

Taking the boat over to Vancouver to be with my mom. My sister's in prema-

366

ture labor and there are complications. About tonight ... I'm sorry I don't under-stand what you've been through. I need a minute to think. Will get in touch with my agritechs about covering for me.

I was going to save this for another occasion, but it felt appropriate now.

Don't forget to water Andromache. She's a good girl. And tell Big Dog I'll bring him some soup bones.

Take care of yourself.

xo

Finan

I drop the letter on the counter and swipe at my cheek. I'm so tired of crying.

After he promised he'd always have my back, he's leaving. He's *left*. Past tense.

I unwrap the package, my own angry laugh bouncing off the kitchen walls as I set aside the box lid.

Inside is a Waterford Crystal pickle plate and a fresh jar of dill pickles.

The lamp in the darkened corner of the front room clicks on. I scream at the shape sitting there, my chest on fire and hands instantly cold.

A woman, her thick, black ponytail draped over her shoulder. Army-green cargo pants. Black, combat-style boots. A pair of aviator sunglasses tucked in the neckline of her long-sleeved, off-white shirt.

And the heavy rock with the warning about Cordelia Beach balanced in her open palm.

She looks familiar.

"Who the fuck are you and how did you get in here?" I reach over to the butcher block—and it's not the filleting knife I pull free this time.

The woman stands, holding the rock out to me. "Hi, Lara. My name is Jacinta Ramirez. I knew your mother. And I think we should talk."

END BOOK ONE

THIS PARTY IS JUST GETTING STARTED.

Planet Lara

TEMPEST

BOOK TWO, SEPTEMBER 14, 2021!

S·G·A
BOOKS

**COVER REVEAL
THIS SUMMER!**

JOIN THE RAFT!

If you want to be the first to hear about the **PREORDER** for the sequel, *Planet Lara: Tempest*, which picks up right where we've left off, join the Raft*! Publication date for Book 2 is September 14, 2021, with Book 3 publishing in December 2021.

Two ways to join the Raft: Join my private readers' group on Facebook, or sign up for my newsletter!

Welcome aboard!

(*In the wild, sea otters hold hands so they aren't separated in the tides. These groups of floating otters are called "rafts.")

ACKNOWLEDGMENTS

Years ago, frustrated with whatever I was frustrated with at the time (this changes pretty much every day), I declared: **"I want my own planet."**

I thus set to compiling early notes for how this planet would come to be, e.g., who would be invited to live there, how we would spend our days, and how many cats each person would be allowed to have (answer: as many as they want). The sun would shine at my command, and we'd have plenty of those perfect rainy afternoons where we could keep the windows open to enjoy the petrichor but not drench our book collections or fluffed pillows along the window seats. Tea and coffee would pour from steaming fountains, as would chocolate. Bad guys would be punished via mandatory scrubbing of toilets and completing of tax returns while listening to improvisational jazz.

In a word, my planet would **ROCK**.

Except when I *really* thought about it, I realized running a planet would be a *lot* of responsibility. Every time someone's tea or coffee or chocolate tap went kaput, I'd have to send a shirtless, hard-bodied plumber to fix it. Every time the library ran out of books, I'd have to stir up drama so our authors would have things to write about. Every time someone did something terrible, I'd have to decide if we had enough toilets in need of scrubbing or if we should just feed the evil-doer to the dragons in the public square where everyone would have access to the taps from which our wines, handcrafted from our exquisite planetary grapes, would flow without end.

Also not being good at math—and with Elon Musk not returning my calls about borrowing one of his fancy rockets—I came to the sad conclusion that galactic travel and thus claiming of a new planet would be impossible. We *could* find a perfect plot of land on *this* planet to start a planet-like compound, but all the good spots are already taken, and I don't think people are super excited about the idea of staging a coup just so we can have chocolate fountains in our kitchens. (If I'm wrong about this, email me.)

Alas, I decided I would foist all these tough decisions and hulking responsibilities onto the well-adorned shoulders of our young heiress, Lara J. Clarke—she needed something to whip her into shape, and I think Thalia Island is just the ticket to straighten our wayward socialite.

In concocting her world and story, I had help from a select group I would *definitely* invite to live on my planet—I may even invite them to my own Thalia Island, once I can find that vein of gold with which to complete the transaction.

Thanks, therefore, go to the following future settlers of my new planet:

Brandee Bublé for incredible insight into what it's really like behind the curtain of fame and celebrity. I've known Brandee since our kids started elementary school in the same class, and she is one of the funniest, most down-to-earth humans I've ever met, even in light of her brother being some big-time singer dude. (I did hear him sing *Rudolph the Red-Nosed Reindeer* at our school concert once—it was pretty good, I guess.) The real star of the family to me, though, is Miss Brandee, who has been a huge fan of the Eliza Gordon books since the first one dropped in 2013. And her enthusiasm for Lara has kept me going. She read an earlier draft and messaged me along the way, offered tips and pointers, as well as answered my litany of questions. Brandee's support is a balm to my raw, charred ego. She is a devoted bibliophile, a true-blue human, an author in her own right, an incredible mom and advocate, and a cherished friend. Thank you, Brandee, for making Lara shine.

Stephania Schwartz, my editorial partner in crime, who fixed errors I never would've picked up on. Thanks to your sharp eye, your keen wit, your intensely interesting life, and your superb taste, Lara J. Clarke is a real person and not a caricature of a rich girl written by a poor kid from Portland, Oregon.

Ann Moffitt Whitson, my cousin, who has been fighting COVID on the front lines this entire time as a respiratory therapist, who only very recently kicked breast cancer's ass after it had the audacity to come for her mid-pandemic. She is a badass, someone you want on your side in the after-school brawl when all the teachers have cleared out.

Dr. Arvin Gee, an assistant professor of surgery and trauma/critical care surgeon at Oregon Health Sciences University—a friend of my cousin Ann—who generously provided great help with the medical situations forthcoming in *Planet Lara: Tempest*. Ohhhhh, it's gonna get juicy, guys! Thanks, Dr. Gee, for taking time out of your busy schedule to help me. And I still wish I'd been smart enough to be a doctor. Thank you for saving lives, both in real life and in my books.

Staff Sergeant Tyner Gillies of the Royal Canadian Mounted Police, my whisky-appreciating friend and fellow scribe, who patiently explained to this expat how the RCMP works and how it is, in fact, different from the American police agency hierarchies. Thanks for your time and for understanding that when I ask questions about DNA, body decomposition, forensics, and bioweapons, there is absolutely no cause for concern.

Michael Slade, author and lawyer extraordinaire, for answering even more questions about law and its enforcement in this big, beautiful country. Slade is a regular feature at the Surrey International Writers Conference every year, and he's hilarious. Check out his many books, which are not actually hilarious but chilling and scary and perfectly shaped to keep you guessing until the last page. Start here for all that is Slade: http://specialx.net/

And with all the expert advice collected for this story, it goes without saying that any screw-ups are 100 percent mine.

Bailey of Bailey Designs Books who was my FIRST reader for *Planet Lara* and offered excellent feedback to help strengthen Lara's story. I've never had a cover designer actually read my projects, so I'm very grateful—and her immersion in and understanding of *Welcome to Planet Lara* is obvious in the GORGEOUS cover art. Cannot wait to design future books with you—I'm so glad our paths crossed.

Samantha Young, my darling friend and longest-running editorial client. I've been with you since almost the beginning, and I am so, so, *so* proud of and impressed by you. Thank you for reading *Planet Lara*, and for your continued camaraderie. You are a glittering example of class and diligence in this weird, weird business.

Suzy Krause, Lake Union sister and provincial neighbo(u)r, author and mom of two littles, I salute you and your remarkable talent. Thank you for spending your time, a nonrenewable resource, on my book. Your opinion means so much to me—and I'm *so happy* you picked up what I was hoping to achieve. Zhampagne toasts for David, Alexis, Patrick, Stevie, Moira, and Johnny!

Katrin and Deb, my little sisters, our friendship is a harbor. Katrin, thank you for reading the early draft and messaging me as you did so. It's that kind of supportive nudge that keeps me typing toward the next page. And Deb, thank you for cheering me along all these years. I'm so glad *Must Love Otters* made us friends! (P.S. No for-fun reading for you until that degree is finished. We are counting on you, missy!)

My ARC team and Raftmates—London Sarah, Kristen, Katie, Stephanie, Miranda, Susan, Mariel, Valérie, Sandy, Jackie, Francesca, Nati, Bernadette, LJ, Leslie, Melena, Amber, Andrea M., Andrea B., Ashley, Lena, Jane Oh, Toni, Dr. Marsha, Tammy, Annette, Shannon, Corinne, Louise, DeeJay, Saira, Jeanine, Jen A., Sarah R., Anima-Christi, Christina, Dena, Nebula, Kat T., Vicki, and Dr. Kira—I know I'm forgetting someone and *I'm sorry*—thank you for your enthusiasm for *Welcome to Planet Lara*. Your feedback is so appreciated—it helps make for better books when the team behind it cares about the product!

Carmen Jones, my longtime friend and owner of the fantastic Tomes & Tales Books (https://www.tomesandtales.com/), for selling my wares to the world and for always being ready with a smile, even when it's been an eternity since we've seen each other.

Kelly Kazakoff at the delightfully perfect Quarrystone Bed and Breakfast on Salt Spring Island (http://quarrystone.com/), thank you for our quiet weekend away. It was the perfect research trip that really helped round out what BC island living feels like. (Also: I am so sorry that my bad guy is named Kelly. That happened before I met you. Dear readers, Kelly the innkeeper is LOVELY, not yucky like the other Kelly.) Please also give my regards to Rosie and Bourbon and the cats.

Lisa Fear, who helped with the tiniest details about local Vancouver hospitals. It's crazy the things that come up that, if I don't get them right, readers will let me know. Thank you, Lisa, for your help!

Frontline and healthcare workers around the world … *thank you* doesn't begin to cover it. What a year, what a year.

And …

GareBear for listening to me rant about needing my own planet and then making me one in our backyard where I am able to escape to write without a cat snagging my sweater for cookies or kids asking me existential questions I am ill-prepared to answer. And as far as kids go, my babies, my little ducklings, Yaunna (and Rosie), Brennie, KennyG, and CheeChee, thank you for always supporting your crazy-ass momma. My love for you is boundless.

ABOUT THE AUTHOR

A native of Portland, Oregon, Eliza Gordon (a.k.a. Jennifer Sommersby) has always lived along the West Coast. Since 2002, home has been a suburb of Vancouver, British Columbia. When not lost in a writing project, Eliza is a copy/line editor, mom, wife, bibliophile, Superman freak, and the humble servant to two very spoiled tuxedo cats.

Eliza writes women's fiction and romantic comedies; Jennifer Sommersby writes young adult fiction. Her debut YA title, *Sleight*, was published in 2018 by HarperCollins Canada, Sky Pony (US), and Prószynski i S-ka (Poland). *Fish Out of Water*, a riff on *The Little Mermaid*, in conjunction with the wildly popular YouTube film production company, the Young Actors Project, released in 2019. The sequel to *Sleight*, titled *Scheme* in the US (Sky Pony) and *The Undoing* in Canada (HarperCollins), released spring 2020. Eliza/Jenn are represented by Stacey Kondla at The Rights Factory.

FROM THE AUTHOR OF **DEAR DWAYNE, WITH LOVE**

ELIZA GORDON

Hollie Porter is the chairwoman of Generation Disillusioned. At twenty-five, she's saddled with a job she hates, a boyfriend who's all wrong for her, and a vexing inability to say no. She's already near her breaking point, so when one caller too many kicks the bucket during Hollie's 911 shift, she cashes in the Sweetheart's Spa & Stay gift certificate from her dad and heads to Revelation Cove, British Columbia.

One caveat: she's going solo.

Hollie hopes to find her beloved otters in the wilds of the Great White North, but instead she's providing comic relief for staff and guests alike. Even Concierge Ryan, a former NHL star with bad knees and broken dreams, can't stop her from stumbling from one (mis)adventure to another. Just when Hollie starts to think that a change of venue doesn't mean a change of circumstances, the island works its charm and she dares to believe rejuvenation is just around the bend.

But then an uninvited guest crashes the party, forcing her to step out of the discomfort zone where she dwells and save the day ... and maybe even herself in the process.

Available now for your choice of e-reader or in paperback. Audio available from Dreamscape Media!

SEQUEL TO **MUST LOVE OTTERS**

ELIZA GORDON

raft (noun): when two or more otters rest together, often holding hands, so they don't drift apart

Hollie Porter has put her old gig as a 911 operator and sad single girl in an attic-bound box, right where it belongs. She's rebounded nicely from her run-in with Chloe the Cougar in the wilds of British Columbia, and this new life alongside concierge-in-shining-armor Ryan Fielding? Way more fun. After relocating to Ryan's posh resort at Revelation Cove, Hollie embarks on an all-new adventure as the Cove's wildlife experience educator, teaching guests and their kids about otters and orca and cougars, oh my!

When darling Ryan gets down on one NHL-damaged knee and pops the question of a lifetime, Hollie realizes this is where the real adventure begins. It's all cake tasting, flower choosing, and dress fittings until a long-lost family member shows up at the Cove and threatens to hijack her shiny new life, forcing Hollie to redefine what family means to her. What is she willing to sacrifice to have one of her very own?

As Ryan's words echo in her head—"Our raft, our rules"—Hollie has to face facts: a raft isn't always tied together with blood and genetics. Sometimes it's secured by love and loyalty … with occasional help from the clever creatures that call Revelation Cove home.

Available now for your choice of e-reader or in paperback.
Audiobook available from Dreamscape Media!

Frankie Hawes is happy to shrink into the background and play personal assistant to her superstar-photographer father and prodigy older brother. But when bad luck and bad timing collide, Frankie has to dust off her photography skills and head north to shoot the Meyer-Nelson wedding at the picturesque Revelation Cove in British Columbia.

It's one thing to take Instagram pics of neighborhood dogs, but unless an Alaskan malamute wanders into the bridal portraits, Frankie fears the worst. Enter wedding guest Sam McKenzie, childhood friend turned handsome bachelor, who brings with him the tricks he learned hanging around the Hawes family, including how to manage the abrasive bridezilla who happens to be an old bully from their shared past.

Reuniting with Sam helps Frankie see that her black-and-white existence on the sidelines has the potential to snap into high resolution—if only she'd allow it. As feelings grow between the pair and Frankie juggles the business during a family emergency, she realizes that maybe it's time for her to pull focus in her own life.

Love Just Clicks is a standalone romantic comedy, set in the Revelation Cove universe and featuring a few of your favorite characters from *Must Love Otters* and *Hollie Porter Builds a Raft*.

Available now for your choice of e-reader or in paperback. Audiobook available from Dreamscape Media!

DEAR DWAYNE, WITH LOVE
FROM LAKE UNION PUBLISHING

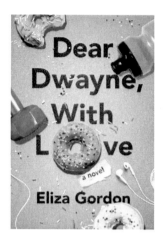

Dream big. Movie-star big.

Wannabe actress Dani Steele's résumé resembles a cautionary tale on how *not* to be famous. She's pushing thirty and stuck in a dead-end insurance job, and her relationship status is holding at uncommitted. With unbearably perfect sisters and a mother who won't let her forget it, Dani has two go-tos for consolation: maple scones and a blog in which she pours her heart out to her celebrity idol. He's the man her father never was, no boyfriend will ever be —and not so impossible a dream as one might think.

When Dani learns that he's planning a fund-raising event where the winning amateur athlete gets a walk-on in his new film, she decides to trade pastries and self-doubt for running shoes and a sexy British trainer with adorable knees.

But when Dani's plot takes an unexpected twist, she realizes that her happy ending might have to be improvised—and that proving herself to her idol isn't half as important as proving something to herself.

Available for Kindle and in paperback, as well as via Kindle Unlimited, Audible, and audio CD.

If you find yourself talking to Jayne Dandy, limit the conversation to ducky collectibles and *Star Wars*. Best not to mention men, dating, or S-E-X. Jayne's fine with the way things are—writer of obituaries and garage sale ads by day, secret scribe of adventures in distant galaxies by night. But a crippling fear of intimacy has kept her love life on ice, and hiding behind her laptop isn't going to melt it anytime soon.

When her therapist recommends she write erotica as a form of exposure therapy, Jayne is hesitant—until she's unexpectedly downsized at work. Since rent and cat food won't pay for themselves, Jayne adopts an intergalactic pseudonym and secretly publishes her sexy stories to make ends meet. To help out, her adorable, longtime friend Luke, co-owner of the popular Portland food truck Luke Piewalker's, hires her to sling turnovers at his side.

Right on schedule, sparks ignite.

As Jayne's secret career soars, she has to juggle the unforeseen demands of her alter ego alongside her newfound feelings for Luke, threatening a tailspin that will either make her face down her neuroses or trigger a meltdown of Death Star proportions.

Formerly called *Neurotica*—same fun story with an updated look!

Available now for your choice of e-reader or in paperback.
Audiobook available from Blackstone Audio!

Piracy hurts authors.

Pretty please, with sugar on top, don't steal our work.

Figures from 2018 report that $315 million USD is lost annually to piracy. Very few authors are wealthy; most have day jobs because the arts are notoriously difficult for purveyors to earn a living wage.

And yet, we all turn to books, music, TV, and movies to get us through.

Support authors.
Buy our books.
Tell your friends to buy our books.
Give yourself a high five for being awesome.

Thank you.

Find the Eliza Gordon library at the following retailers, available in e-book, print, and audiobook*.

Links via elizagordon.com!

Amazon globally

Angus & Robertson

Apple Books

Barnes & Noble

Biblioteca

Bol.de

Chapters/Indigo

Google Play

Ingram

Kobo

Mondadori

Overdrive

Scribd

Thalia.de

24 Symbols

and more!

S·G·A
BOOKS

*Audio from Dreamscape Media, Blackstone Audio, and Lake Union/Amazon Publishing, *Planet Lara* audiobook to be announced.

Made in United States
North Haven, CT
07 February 2022